The Night

The Night

RODRIGO BLANCO CALDERÓN

translated from Spanish by
Noel Hernández González
and Daniel Hahn

Seven Stories Press
New York • Oakland

Support for the translation of this book was provided by Acción Cultural Española, AC/E.

 AC/E
ACCIÓN CULTURAL
ESPAÑOLA

Seven Stories Press
140 Watts Street
New York, NY 10013
sevenstories.com

College professors and high school and middle school teachers
may order free examination copies of Seven Stories Press titles.
Visit https://www.sevenstories.com/pg/resources-academics
or email academics@sevenstories.com.

Library of Congress Cataloging-in-Publication Data

Names: Blanco Calderón, Rodrigo, 1981- author. | Hernández González,
    Noel, translator. | Hahn, Daniel, translator.
Title: The night / Rodrigo Blanco Calderón ; translated by Noel Hernández
    González and Daniel Hahn.
Other titles: Night. English
Description: New York, NY : Seven Stories Press, [2021] | Originally
    published in Spanish as The Night.
Identifiers: LCCN 2021003142 (print) | LCCN 2021003143 (ebook) | ISBN
    9781644210406 (trade paperback) | ISBN 9781644210413 (ebook)
Classification: LCC PQ8550.412.L36 N5413 2021 (print) | LCC PQ8550.412.L36
    (ebook) | DDC 863/.7--dc23
LC record available at https://lccn.loc.gov/2021003142
LC ebook record available at https://lccn.loc.gov/2021003143

Printed in the United States of America

9 8 7 6 5 4 3 2 1

For Luisa Fontiveros

in girum imus nocte et
consumimur igni

(we spin about in the night and are
consumed by fire)

~~~~~~

I. Theory of Anagrams

the devil, madness, political irresponsibility: these are the only possible explanations for the practice of wordplay, or for the slightest interest one could take in it.

—TZVETAN TODOROV

1
Blackouts

In the beginning was a long, unexpected five-hour blackout. Caracas looked like an exposed anthill. Despite the canceled meetings, the uncashed checks, the decomposing food and the collapse of the subway system, Miguel Ardiles remembers that day with an almost fatherly affection: the city felt the shock of finding itself both cave and labyrinth.

In the months that followed, as the blackouts recurred, the city's inhabitants began to paint their first bison, using stones to mark out familiar bends. Then the government announced its plan for power rationing. Opposition spokespeople were quick to draw comparisons with Cuba during the nineties, claiming that its energy-saving policy during the Special Period was identical to the one soon to be enforced in Venezuela.

The announcement was made at midnight on Wednesday, January 13, 2010.

Two days later Miguel Ardiles met up with Matías Rye at Chef Woo's. As he did every Friday evening after his last patient of the day, Miguel waited for Matías at this Chinese restaurant in the Los Palos Grandes neighborhood. Matías Rye ran creative-writing workshops at a local high school and was about to start his most ambitious project yet, *The Night*: a crime novel that would restore the genre to its Gothic origins. He had borrowed its English-language title from a Morphine song, and hoped to translate the nuances of the band into his writing:

entering the horror like a person slowly falling asleep, turning their back on life.

Rye claimed that the classic crime novel was dead.

"Things go full circle from 'The Murders in the Rue Morgue,' in 1841, to 'Death and the Compass,' in 1942. With that one short story, Borges effectively finished off the genre. Lönnrot is a detective who reads crime stories and novels. A moron who's killed for mistaking literature for reality. He's the Don Quixote of detective fiction."

Gothic realism, he believed, was the only alternative.

"Writing crime novels in this country is an act of disingenuity, doomed to fail," he added. "Miguel, of all the cases you see every day, how many actually get solved? Who's really going to believe that the police in this city is ever going to put a criminal away?"

Rye seemed to remember something.

"When do they take you to the Monster?" He was speaking more quietly now.

"I don't know yet. The president himself rang the Office of Forensic Medicine to get the details of the case. You know he's pals with Camejo Salas, right?"

"The president called Johnny Campos?"

"Uh huh. I don't think my report will be much use anyway, whichever way it goes."

"Campos is a rat."

"Apparently the president's heard about the organ trafficking thing. That's enough to have Campos by the balls."

"No shit."

"Yeah."

The lights flickered and went out. There was a wave of shouting and laughter, and then, as if muffled by the blackout, the conversations resumed in quiet conspiratorial tones. One of the waiters pulled down the shutters while Marcos, the owner, added up the checks armed with a small flashlight. Within minutes Chef Woo's was almost empty, its dense blackness studded only by the cigarettes of the final customers, the regulars, the dependable ones.

"You're not nervous?" asked Rye.

"Why?"

"I'd be shitting myself if I were in your shoes."

"This stuff with the Monster in Los Palos Grandes isn't new. It's not even the worst thing going on now."

"The guy kidnapped that girl, raped her and tortured her for four months. He hit her so hard it tore off her upper lip and part of an ear. You don't think that's a big deal?"

"What happened to Lila Hernández is horrible, we all know that. But the thing that's really got everyone's attention is that it was done by Camejo Salas's boy. The son of an award-winning poet. How is that even possible? Salas won the National Prize for Literature, for Christ's sake. And he's the father of that freak?"

"I took classes with that asshole when I was in grad school."

"But as for it not being the worst thing happening, how's this for an example: One morning a guy sees two girls walking down the street. He likes what he sees and decides there and then to take them to his apartment. At gunpoint. They're not even fifteen. He locks one in his bedroom while he rapes the second girl in the living room. The girl in the bedroom can hear the other one screaming. After a while, things go quiet— half an hour, an hour, two hours: she's not sure. At last, hearing only silence, she manages to force open the door. But what do you think she finds in the living room? Her friend's torso. The guy chopped her into pieces, he raped her, killed her. He's gone out to get rid of the head and limbs. The one who's survived goes into a panic, screaming from the window until the neighbors come rescue her."

"Are you talking about the Casalta case?"

"San Martín."

"Have you seen her yet?"

"Yeah."

"And?"

"Totally lost it."

"Maybe you won't even get to see the guy."

"Probably not."

"Well, that's something."

"Is it? And then what, Matías? They catch the asshole, and most likely he gets finished off in prison. And then what?"

"What else do you want?"

"That's the problem. I don't know what you can do after that. Because there's always something left behind. Every murder leaves a lingering trace. And that's got to be toxic."

"What's the time?"

They looked around and realized they were the last customers in the restaurant. It was just them and the waiters, who were leaning on the bar, smoking, their eyes barely outlined by the glow from the cigarettes. When Matías and Miguel stood up, the four Chinese men interrupted their conversation and, for a moment, stared at the shapes they could barely discern in the darkness. Matías went to pay at the cash register while Miguel waited for somebody to open the shutters.

Once in the street, Miguel felt more relaxed. For that brief moment, he had felt an inexplicable fear. He'd suddenly pictured himself and Matías being chopped up by those same waiters who served them every week.

The street was dark and empty. There was no activity except down at the end, near the crossing. Miguel wanted to quicken their pace toward the Centro Plaza mall where he'd left his car, but Matías was in his element.

"Deprivation has its beauty. And I'm not talking about magical realism. García Márquez and the rest of them think they glimpsed it, but they didn't. Magical realism put some blush on poverty, dressed it up, gave it wings. Gothic realism, on the other hand, finds truth and beauty in undressing, in digging things up," said Matías.

A shape was moving among the bags of garbage piled up around a lamppost.

"See?" he said.

The tramp followed them with his vacant gaze, then carried on with his business.

"Does that look beautiful to you?" asked Miguel.

"Of course."

"Give me García Márquez any day."

"What's the best entry ever to win *El Nacional*'s short-story prize?"

Matías Rye entered the competition every year, and every year he lost. Over time he had developed a thorough yet resentful knowledge of the prize's history. He would name award-winning short stories and authors as metaphors for the fairness or unfairness of life.

"'The Hand by the Wall,' I guess."

"No. That story was only successful because of its timing. Meneses has the dubious honor of having created a useless genre: lyrical crime fiction. The only story worth reading from that competition is 'Anchovy.' Humberto Mata was the first among us to understand that crime fiction is a genre with more of a past than a future."

"I haven't read it."

"Read it. Once you have, every time you see a tramp, you'll

picture him living on the banks of the Guaire, waking up among herons every morning. And that's beautiful."

"If you say so."

"Now, tell me. What's the worst story to have won the prize?"

"The one by Algimiro Triana."

"You're only saying that because of that thing with Arlindo Falcão. Sure, Algimiro is scum, but that's not the worst story. The title of the one I'm thinking of is impossible to pronounce. I can never remember it; I just know it's by Pedro Álamo. It won in 1982, the prize's most controversial year to date. The story is incomprehensible from start to finish. I've always taken it for the text of a madman, but some critics were determined to see a masterpiece. I think I may finally get a chance to confirm my hypothesis."

"What hypothesis?"

"You're going to help me. I've got Pedro Álamo as a student in my writing workshop."

"What's that got to do with me?"

"We've become almost friends. I gave him the number of your private practice. Can you squeeze him in next Monday? Álamo's been having panic attacks."

2

Origins of Symmetry

I like symmetries and detest motorbikes. Actually, I love them, and I think it's down to some kind of fear. Symmetries, I mean. And motorbikes. I know what I'm saying. And because I know what I'm saying, I don't need to go on about it. I don't have to tell anyone either. If I'm talking to you, doctor, it's only as a courtesy to Matías. He was so insistent I should come see you, especially given what happened after class, I had to promise I would. He convinced me with the fact that you're a psychiatrist—that is, a physician, not a psychologist, a psychotherapist or a charlatan. I mean, I presume you treat your patients with medication, and I'm an advocate for the prescription and use of medication. Take depression, for instance. They say it's the illness of the century. Depression, leaving its causes aside, is a biochemical process. Serotonin levels drop and antidepressants restore them. That's why I say, when it comes to health matters, it's medicine first and words after. And if words can be avoided altogether, so much the better. Since I'm convinced that all the evil in this world originates in them. In words.

That's why I came. So you could prescribe me tranquilizers or whatever to help me erase the anxiety when it suddenly overwhelms me. Or, at least, build some kind of firewall to buy enough time to maneuver before the *instant* strikes, so that when I sense the motorbike approaching, I can be braced for the impact. Or run away from that damn chainsaw sound all the faster. Ever seen those *Friday the 13th* movies? Remember Jason? That's what I feel like whenever I hear a motorbike coming. In fact, I don't need to hear them anymore. Just imagining the damn sound—like a saw drawing near to cut my head off—that's enough to make disaster unravel.

I'd like to point out, Dr. Ardiles, that *Friday the 13th* is only an example. I'm not traumatized by it. Freddy Krueger and Jason have always left me cold. Here in Caracas, Jason would just be a tree surgeon and Freddy some emo kid with long nails. Freddy and Jason are brats compared with the plague of motorized thugs who've taken over the city. Wipe them all out: that'd be the first step to truly rebuild this city. Hit them with their own helmets until they die. One by one. Margarita, a friend of mine from the workshop, told me something unbelievable the other day. She took a motorcycle taxi in Altamira to go to Paseo Las Mercedes. It was six in the afternoon, the subway system had collapsed and the buses were packed. When they were about to pull out of Chacaíto to take the main road to Las Mercedes, just opposite the McDonald's in El Rosal, the taxi driver took advantage of a red traffic light to pull out a gun and steal a BlackBerry from the woman in the car alongside them. He didn't wait for the light to go green. He left the cars behind and continued on his way. When they arrived at Paseo, Margarita was shaking all over. Even though she can defend herself better than your average guy, she could barely take the cash out of her purse. The driver received the fare and, seeing her so rattled, said:

"Don't be scared, honey. I would never rob my customers."

See what I mean, doctor? What are you supposed to do with a piece of shit like that? Huh? Excuse my language. The thing is . . . you know what I'm saying. But don't go making assumptions either. It's not PTSD. Despite everything, I haven't been robbed for a while—touch wood. The thing about the motorbikes comes from before, from when I was married to Margarita. No, not the one from the story about the motorcycle taxi. Another one—my wife.

I could tell you about one particular experience that might explain it all. But I'm not going to, because I didn't come here to talk. Let's look at this, if you will, as a mere formality, so you can prescribe me the drugs. Because if I start talking about what happened to me back then, you'll forget about the present, about what's happening to me now. It'd be unfair to blame that one biker—just check out my ability for synderesis: I'm talking about being *fair* to such a scumbag—for all the excesses of today's bikers. Also, it'd be impossible for them to be one and the same. It'd be too much of a coincidence. And for me, coincidences don't exist.

Last week? Where should I start. . . . From the beginning, Aristotle would say. But where are the origins of symmetry? The thing could have started more than twenty-five years ago, or a month ago. It doesn't matter, whatever suits you, the only thing that'd change is the direction you're going in. You're right, it was me who said I didn't want to talk about the past, about the causes. Let's start with the present then, and with the consequences, and hopefully, we'll leave it there.

It all started, or started again, or started to take shape, when Margarita stared at me. Yes, the one in the workshop, not the one who was my wife. It was Matías's fault. I'd sort of hoped Matías wouldn't recognize me, that my name wouldn't make him go back to 1982. But the morning after the first lesson, I read an email from Matías where he asked whether I was the author of "Neercseht." I answered a simple "yes," as if to suggest I didn't want to talk about it. Doctor, if you want to know more, you should ask Matías. I wouldn't recommend that you read my short story under any circumstances. I wouldn't put anyone through that. Though there is a version of the story you might find interesting. It's the same story but from back to front. Its title is "The Screen," and it's by a young writer called Rodrigo Blanco. I've been racking my brains but can't think of anyone who could have shared the information with that young man. Anyhow, his story is totally misleading when it comes to my affair with Sara Calcaño. It's true I slept with her, but it's also true that Sara Calcaño slept with each and every one of the writers there at the time, male and female, young and old. A fact that is as true as it is useless, since Sarita ended up crazy and must be dead by now.

After the last class of December, Margarita, Matías and I stayed behind to discuss some details from "Theses on the Short Story" by Ricardo Piglia. Now I think of it, the whole thing was an ambush, with Matías playing a dirty trick on me.

"So, you *are* Pedro Álamo," said Matías.

Margarita looked at him and then at me as if waiting for an explanation.

"Pedro caused one of the biggest scandals in Venezuelan literature," he told her. "Of course, you weren't even born yet."

He went on to tell her all about my short story, the *El Nacional* award, the angry reaction of most critics, the incredible reaction of the few who championed my work, my stubborn silence in the following months and subsequent retreat from public life.

"Pedro Álamo was what people call—with sincere admiration but somehow bitterly—a *rising star* in our literature. Then he vanished. What were you up to, Pedro?"

I'd have liked to explain that all it takes to vanish from our literature, as he put it, is to avoid book launches and stop taking calls from the press. Instead, I said I'd been doing something else.

"I'm an advertising executive."

I must confess, doctor, I enjoyed seeing the disappointment on his face. But it's the truth: I'm an advertising executive.

"Do you still write?" Matías wouldn't give up.

"No," I said. "That's why I'm here. I want to try to start afresh."

Matías seemed unconvinced. I'm not sure myself whether what I said was true. Is it *writing*, this thing I've been doing ever since? As in, what *writers* usually understand by *writing*? I don't know. I don't care either. All my life I've been trying to play down the high hopes that, despite myself, I raise in those around me. Matías didn't bring the subject up again, but that time, when we said goodbye, Margarita stared at me.

That night I dreamed about a noise. It sounded like a motor-bike, and in the dream I didn't know whether it was moving closer, moving away, or doing both things at once. I live in the annex of a house in the Santa Inés development. Not sure if you know the place. I'd guess not. Most Caraqueños haven't a clue where it is, as they get it mixed up with Santa Paula, Santa Marta, Santa Fe and every other eastern *santa*. Meaning only the people who live there know for sure where Santa Inés is, as if Santa Inés was more than a development, it was a bond. This only happens because the place is just a handful of houses scattered in a sort of canyon that lies between the old road to Baruta and Los Samanes on one side, and the hills of Santa Rosa de Lima and San Román on the other. Santa Inés is, how can I put it, it's a weird echo chamber. Sounds bounce around, cutting off their source on their way back, as well as the notion of what's far away or close, like errant atoms tuning the universe.

The truth is that midway through my dream, in the dead of the night, I heard a motorbike. A humming that was gaining ground on the silence of the hour, eroding the night. That noise, the dream of the noise, seemed to go on forever. I woke at last, anxious, rolling out of bed and falling onto the floor of my room like a dead tree.

I knocked over the glass of water I always leave on the bedside table. Even though I could've cut myself with the shards I didn't turn the light on. I remained on the floor like that, sitting there with a wet ass. Margarita used to hate that habit of mine. Leaving an overflowing glass on the bedside table, only to toss the water in the sink in the morning, almost untouched. I'd hardly take a sip after brushing my teeth and before turning out the light. My marriage with Margarita was a short and miserable obstacle course. Our financial situation would force us to move from one apartment to the next, from one side of the city to the other and, in every place we lived, the glass of water on the bedside table was the subject of our conversation. In the beginning, that habit of mine used to provoke a kind of affectionate confusion. But as time went by, her reaction became pure hostility. Toward the end, it was just indifference. I was very young and focused on my job in advertising after failing as a writer, and palindromes had already become an obsession. I failed to see what was evident, that things were coming to an end. Margarita would look at the glass of water on the bedside table and accept I wasn't going to change, that I wasn't going to give up this absurd routine or any other. That's what Margarita would see every morning: how the fluids of our first intimacy were slowly drying, even within that glass still filled with water.

I was still on the floor, mind wandering, but one last feeling finally woke me up. The distant sound of the dream reverberated in my ears. The motorbike could easily now be a small plane disappearing into the horizon. And the slow fading of the sound was so subtle it became indistinguishable from the collapse of the night. I looked around before getting up. The small puddle of water and the bits of glass made me think about global warming and melting ice caps. I couldn't help but notice that the puddle was pulsating, and I kept thinking about it for the rest of the day.

Time flies.

Sorry to have taken up your time, and thank you. I really appreciate the prescription and the Xanax.

Yeah, sure, anything you like.

Don't worry, honestly, go ahead.

Margarita? My wife?

Oh, she died years ago. Killed, poor thing.

3

Gothic City

Matías had been avoiding me all week. He didn't answer
my emails—although he did forward me a few threads with
updates on the blackouts and the state of the power stations.
He also sent me, in an email without a subject or a signature
or any comment, an article about the bodies of women found
in the wastelands of Parque Caiza. He behaved similarly on the
phone. He was always just about to go into a movie theater
or attend a meeting. He didn't want me to let on until Friday.
He didn't say as much, but it's obvious, I know what he's like.
Pointless, as I wouldn't have told him anything anyway. Not
only because Pedro Álamo never talked about his famous short
story, but because it wouldn't be right for me to gossip about
the private lives of my patients.

"That's nonsense." Matías seemed annoyed. "You always tell
me about the cases you see in Forensic Medicine."

"That's different. A lot of those stories end up in the papers
anyway."

"But that's even worse. You're breaking a gagging order."

"You're right. I won't tell you about those cases anymore."

"You know what I mean."

"Álamo hasn't even mentioned his short story. Trust me, the
story is the last thing he wants to talk about. And if he'd said
something, I still wouldn't tell you. It wouldn't be ethical."

Then I thought about the voice recorder. My habit of

recording and transcribing the sessions with some of my patients. "Atoms," "Universe," "The collapse of the night," "Global warming," "Icecaps." What would I call what I was doing? Definitely not ethical, that's for sure.

I felt more relaxed after the first beer.

"At first sight, he seems the obsessive-compulsive type."

"Why would you say that?" said Matías, his face hardening.

"And with paranoid tendencies. And some idées fixes. Especially about motorbikes, but also about his wife, this Margarita who was killed years ago."

"There's a girl in the workshop called Margarita. Apart from me, she's the only one he talks to."

"There you go."

I changed the subject. I asked him about the book.

"*The Night.*" He liked saying the book's title aloud before talking about it. Maybe because it's a great title. Maybe because it's been a while since Matías wrote anything but titles. "I'm still taking notes and working on a rough draft. I think I've figured out the main character. A psychiatrist who rapes and kills his patients. Only women. It's based on Dr. Montesinos, obviously: *the* national psychiatrist, go-to intellectual, president of the Central University, former national presidential candidate."

I thought about Camejo Salas. I tried, without much luck, to remember some of the verses I'd been made to memorize in school.

The lights flickered at Chef Woo's.

"We've been raised by murderers."

I hadn't meant to say that. I was just thinking about it and said it without realizing.

"What if one day we found out our parents were murderers. Can you imagine, Matías?"

"At this rate, we'll wake up one day to discover we're murderers ourselves," said Matías. "And lighten up. You can be such a bore sometimes. You should retire. How long have you got left?"

"Five years."

Now it was Matías who changed the subject. He wanted me to go over the case of Dr. Montesinos again, giving him *chapter and verse*. He took out his Moleskine notepad, as he did whenever he wanted me to tell a story.

I told him what I knew about the Montesinos case.

"I need to know everything about psychiatrists."

"Go on."

"Facts, habits, routine, jargon. That kind of thing."

"Let's see. Forty percent of male psychiatrists in Venezuela are homosexual."

"And what do you expect me to do with that?"

"I don't know."

"Why are you telling me, then?"

"You asked for facts. That's a fact."

"Forty percent?"

"Maybe fifty, I don't know."

"How do you know?"

"I can work it out from the cases I know. A few are quite open about it. But most of them are married men with children."

Matías went quiet. I thought he was finally going to ask me what he had always wanted to ask me. Instead, he said:

"So?"

"What?"

"You are telling me that forty or fifty percent of male psychiatrists in Venezuela conceal their homosexuality?"

"Uh huh."

"What do you think that means?"

"Nothing."

"Nothing? Don't you think that's *unethical*?" He was getting his own back.

"Not at all."

"On what moral grounds can a closet homosexual tell another closet homosexual to come out?"

"It's got nothing to do with morals."

"Yes, it has. It's just talking the talk but not walking the walk. It's like a doctor prescribing a drug he wouldn't take himself."

"That's exactly the point. Look at priests, for example. The less they know about life, the holier and wiser they are. I'm convinced one doesn't learn anything from experience. Ideas aren't much use either, but if you stick to them you might at least survive."

Our conversation came to a dead end. We argued for a while but couldn't convince each other. I would build an argument that was logical, albeit deplorable, while Matías would take the opposite end of the moral spectrum. My view on the matter is simple: morals have nothing to do with a profession that has fiction at its core. Yes, with the exception of the brief, and sometimes pernicious, islands of objectivity reached with the help of medication, the whole psychiatric discourse is fiction. The patient's words seek to convey something that cannot be conveyed by words. In return, the psychiatrist comes up with his own words, words that would never stand a chance of leaping over the fence erected around the original words and that, as a result, branch off toward other words, like those of his own knowledge, of the concepts he's familiar with, of categorized behaviors, of previous cases he is reminded of by this new one. With luck, the patient will come out protected by that elaborate cloak of words woven during the therapy sessions, feeling safe from the chill of his own helplessness.

"I don't believe a word of what you just said."

"On the contrary, words are the only things we do need to

believe in. The words I say to my patients every day help them deal with sadness and familiarize themselves with horror. It's an endless, ongoing negotiation, like everything in life. What's more, life itself might consist of this tacit negotiation, which doesn't mean you've got to pay it much attention either."

I sensed some unease in Matías, and changed the subject one more time. That's how it goes: we protect each other from falling.

We talked about his novel again. He said the most stimulating stage was drafting and plotting.

"Everything is possible at that moment; the connections blossom and you become Don Quixote."

"That's the problem, Matías. I told you so in our very first session: you get carried away with your projects, you become whatever it is you want to write about, and end up almost the way you were when you started. Without a novel, but destroyed."

"Foucault called him a *pilgrim of similitude*," said Matías with a wink.

"Called who?"

"Don Quixote."

"His lectures on psychiatry are outstanding."

"Did you get my email?"

"I did. Not sure why you sent it."

"How many women did it say have been found?"

"Eight."

"It's nine."

"The article said eight."

"But it's nine."

"Why did you send it then?"

"The article is accurate."

"So?"

"The article enumerates the corpses discovered this year in the wasteland behind Parque Caiza. And it's eight, true. But it doesn't mention the fact that the first body that was thrown in there was Rosalinda Villegas. Do you get it?"

"What?"

"The first body discovered in Parque Caiza was Rosalinda Villegas. A few months later more bodies started to emerge around the same place. Can you see it now?"

"Don't forget they caught Dr. Montesinos straight away. Everything pointed at him: traces of blood at his practice, their affair, the young woman's blog."

"I read online that he's in Miami."

"Not true. Because of his age, he got house arrest instead of prison. And he's still there. That's all there is to it. The thing about Montesinos is he has a lot of friends, and they managed to keep things quiet."

"It doesn't matter. That's not going to happen in *The Night*. Or it may happen some other way. Montesinos will be behind all nine murdered women. And, like you, he's going to live in Parque Caiza."

Matías was euphoric.

"You shouldn't pay too much attention to that detail," I said. "It's just a coincidence."

"For a writer, the only coincidences that exist are the ones he creates."

Claims like these made me uncomfortably sad. Matías was one of those writers who were bankrupted by the invention of the printing press. He is, first and foremost, an oral narrator. Someone who produces seductive and volatile arguments that are easy to forget, like cigarette smoke after you've left the bar. He began to unpick signs, symbols and connections from the fact that Parque Caiza, on the outskirts of Caracas, was the place the killers chose to dump the dead women. He talked again about the story "Anchovy," about the corpses of beggars that would appear in the tunnel that connects Caracas with the port of La Guaira, about the banks of the Guaire River—that rotten artery that passes through the city where the beggars live—and about the importance of these coordinates for understanding the story and our own reality.

"Gothic is a genre that relies on space. As soon as you leave the centers of urban life, you go back a couple of centuries. You can find the fascinating side of horror by moving outward, but also inward, toward La Guaira or the Guaire, that's what Mata's saying with this story."

He then talked about Israel Centeno, who according to Matías was Humberto Mata's successor in the Gothic crime-fiction genre. From him, from his book *Night Creatures*, Matías was going to borrow the outline of a detective story that becomes a classic horror tale.

I know the book well. I read some of its short stories when I first joined the workshop myself and heard Matías talk about that stuff.

That night at Chef Woo's, he mentioned a Centeno story in which the character is attracted to the pale complexion of a woman at a party. The man and woman decide to leave and head for La Guaira. They're going to chase their shadows against the complicit background of the sea. The woman asks the man to pull off the highway and take the old road instead. They drive the longer route beside a parade of hungry apparitions, the halls of almost ghostly poverty, the dreadful show of all the squalor that had solidified, as if in a rancid time capsule, when they built the new highway.

"The viaduct, for instance, collapsed in 2005," said Matías.

"March 19th, 2006," I replied.

"Fucking hell."

"I know because that very same day, at five in the morning, I arrived back from a psychiatry congress in Buenos Aires. Half-asleep, half-awake, I saw, as I drove up to Caracas, the immense backbone of the viaduct. I felt like an ant at a museum. I got home to sleep, woke up at midday and only then found out the bridge had collapsed that morning."

"Like in a dream."

"Right."

They brought us the check. It was almost midnight.

"Your turn," said Matías as he passed me the check. "The viaduct of the Caracas-La Guaira highway was one of the greatest engineering feats of the time. And for all the decades it was there, we forgot there'd been an old road in its place, and amid this forgetfulness, several slums sprung up, whole shantytowns. And then the viaduct falls and the government has no choice but to restore the old road, and there we are, crawling like cockroaches among the endless bends, praying we won't fall over a cliff and die."

They brought us our change. I left a small bill and we departed.

The street was a tunnel. Looking up, the few illuminated windows resembled shining torches. The crossing where the avenue met the street remained dark too.

"Mata's short story is from 1992, and Centeno's book from 2000. They bookend a decade in which you had to travel to find the ancestral ways of horror. And look at what we have now." Matías extended his arms like a priest, as if all that darkness was a divine gift and he its mediator.

We were about to reach the junction that leads to the Centro Plaza mall.

"Don't be surprised if certain things start happening during the blackouts," said Matías. "This year, Caracas is on its way to becoming the true Gothic City."

"Holy power stations!"

"You can laugh now, but what's coming is ugly, Miguel. And you and I have got be ready for the stories that we've got to tell and to hear. Let's hurry."

There were a couple of shadows following us from halfway down the street. They started to run.

So did we.

4

Two Purple Marks

I had to run away. I did it to save my life. That's how it felt at the time. Afterward, when I read Matías's email and realized it was only a motorcyclist from Domino's Pizza, I began to laugh. I laughed out loud, nonstop, I don't know for how long, until the tears of laughter and crying became one and the same. "I think you need to get some help," wrote Matías. When I saw him in class, he told me about you, Miguel. I can call you Miguel, can't I?

The Xanax? Yeah, it's working. Too well, if you ask me. I don't feel anxious anymore. The fear is still there, but I can look at it now, like in slow motion. Things are happening, you know? Things are always happening, but people mostly ignore them. I've never ignored them, that's been my fate. Reading the signs left on the words. I've asked myself over the years if there are other signs, if there are other people like me, collecting signals, reading those things that are moving in the dark. But now (thanks to Xanax, I don't mind saying), I can see that *other* things are happening.

Why did I run away? I want to make it absolutely clear that I love pizza. In fact, I'd arranged with Margarita to go to Il Botticello that night after the workshop. The time Matías talked about my story, Margarita stared at me. Not sure if I've told you this already, but she stared at me in a way I recognized. She looked at me, tilting her head ever so slightly, a sideways movement, like a weighing scale, revealing the moment a decision has been taken. She looked at me the way Margarita, my wife, looked at me some decades earlier, the day she first noticed me.

On December 24, she sent me an email. She said she had gotten hold of my short story and read it. *I didn't understand a thing. I found it really annoying. One day, if you want, we can talk about it over a drink. Merry Christmas. Marga.* That's what she wrote. I was moved by her common sense and frankness. And also by that strange mix of disappointment and curiosity I had filled her with. I didn't want to seem desperate, and told her we could meet up after class in January. *There's a cool little Italian near the school, Il Botticello.* She thought it was a good idea.

But Margarita didn't come. She didn't send a text or email either. After the workshop Matías and I stayed behind, standing on the sidewalk. He kept talking about literature—about anything, really. I started to feel ill. It was then that I heard a humming, the same humming from the dream, the maddeningly corrosive noise of a motorbike approaching at full speed. My heart started racing, my throat went dry in a matter of seconds, and a sudden wave of sweat left me drenched. When I came to, I'd already left Avenida San Juan Bosco behind, and Plaza Altamira, and I'd even gone through Francisco de Miranda without remembering. I was near the Torre Británica. If I had run a bit longer, I'd have reached the highway.

The next morning I received an email from Matías. He'd been very worried. I told him about my fear of motorbikes, especially the big ones, with thundering engines that can engulf a whole street. He told me the only thing he saw was a Domino's Pizza delivery scooter.

Yeah, I get it. A scooter becomes a Suzuki. The motorbike noise, a chainsaw. Don Quixote? Ages ago, why? OK. The motorbikes would be my windmills, for tilting at. Didn't know that's what it was called. In any case, I'd be a pilgrim, one of those ones who flagellate themselves, a martyr of similes. But I'm not crazy. Similes and symmetries *happen* to me. That's how I know I'm not crazy.

Margarita, my daisy, skipped that class and the next. With every absence, I'd pull a petal off her name. I had lost all hope, but she came back on Friday. She had a purple mark on one of her cheekbones. It surprised no one. If anything, we were kind of proud. Margarita studies literature and psychology. She also does kickboxing.

And, to top it off, as if validating all this, or rather, as if it was the reason for all this, Margarita is beautiful.

"Shall we go?" she said.

"Go where?"

"For dinner, where else?"

She didn't feel like Italian food. She would rather have Mexican or Middle Eastern. We walked down the whole of Avenida San Juan Bosco until we reached the corner. They sold shawarmas at one place. Margarita stopped to look, thought about it for a few seconds and then carried on walking. We crossed Francisco de Miranda and continued down the road. We came to a little street stall that sold tacos and burritos. From where we were, we could see the dark lump of the Torre Británica.

I remembered the panic and the running. Margarita had been a bit late, I thought. That was all.

After that, we went to a bar called Greenwich, where I think I remember going in the nineties. There weren't any customers now, so we could grab a seat by the bar. The first thing Margarita wanted to know was what I'd been smoking when I wrote "Neercseht." I told her I hadn't smoked anything, which makes it all even worse.

"You should ask the jury about that too," I said.

"Who were they?"

"Oswaldo Trejo, Antonieta Madrid and Gustavo Díaz Solís."

"Trejo died. And the other guy?"

"I'd guess he's died too. It'd be just Madrid left."

"Have you ever spoken to her?"

"No, never."

I fell silent, waiting for the conversation to change. Talking is dangerous, it accelerates intimacy, and at any time, with any word, we might step on a land mine that would explode and destroy the other person's heart.

"I read 'The Screen.' I suppose you're familiar with it?"

"I am."

"Is it all true?"

Margarita was excited. Then I understood why, even though she had read my short story, she still liked me.

"Mostly."

"That's amazing. And to think Sara Calcaño is still around."

"I thought she'd died."

"No. She hasn't been to the university for a while. Nowadays she hangs out in Plaza de los Museos."

"No way."

"You haven't seen her?"

"It's been almost thirty years. I haven't heard from these people since leaving literature."

The thought of bumping into Sara Calcaño terrified me. Seeing what she'd become is something I wouldn't be able to erase from my memory, or my body. I'd been inside her, and that's a bond you cannot break. Sex is the invisible thread that keeps far-apart beings connected. The thread that carries misfortunes, that triggers dark thoughts: those stray bullets we can never dodge.

"What made you disappear?"

"Was it a rat I saw?" I said.

"You like Lancini?" Margarita said.

And then I fell in love.

We talked all night about Darío Lancini and palindromes. It was just a couple of hours, really, which for me haven't completely ended yet.

By midnight the bar had gotten too busy, so we left. Stepping out into the street was bursting a bubble. It was a bit cold and our words lost momentum. I didn't know what to do, what she expected me to say. Or whether she expected me to do or say anything at all.

In any case, there wasn't much time for awkward silences. We started walking toward the square when a brand new black sports car pulled up to the sidewalk. Margarita took hold of my arm. The tinted window from the passenger seat rolled down, and she let go of me.

"Can I give you a ride somewhere?" said a voice from inside the car.

Margarita looked shaken.

"Let me talk," she said to me. "What do you want, Gonzalo?" asked Margarita, now addressing the man in the car. Leaning through the open window, she looked like a prostitute.

"To know if I can give you a ride anywhere."

"Why are you doing this to me?"

"Who's your friend?" asked Gonzalo, looking past Margarita to check me out. He switched on the inside lights. "Hi. You want a ride too?"

"Gonzalo . . ." said Margarita, reproachfully.

"Hi," I said.

"Let your friend answer. I'm just asking."

"Hi," said a voice as if in stereo. Then I heard some laughter.

The rear seat window had been rolled down. Two more men, indiscernible under the dim light, waved at me.

"Hi," I said.

Margarita kept talking in a quiet, almost inaudible, voice that irritated and grated. Then she stepped away from the car, like someone who's negotiated a price, and told me she was going with them.

"Are you sure?" I whispered.

"Yeah, it's fine."

Margarita got into the car. Gonzalo waved goodbye, switched off the inside light and revved the engine.

He was a handsome man. I thought I saw a purple mark on one of his cheekbones.

5

Ana and Mia

"You're a filthy, fat ass," said Ana.

Rosalinda pretended she hadn't heard and went on checking herself out in the mirror.

"You're disgusting," said Marcos. Or rather, that's what she remembers him saying when he found out.

She couldn't pretend any longer.

"You listen to him, huh? You're a pig. A whore and a pig."

Rosalinda pulled down her T-shirt. She looked for her purse, took out a few bills and left them on the bedside table. She took some sugar-free gum from the table and put it in her bag. She looked in the mirror one more time. She thought for a moment but, in the end, decided to put on a thick hoodie. Once in front of the computer, she moved the mouse to reactivate it and reread the text. She clicked *publish*, turned off the computer and went out.

The class, as always, moved as slow as honey. Her knee under the desk, restless, would mark the seconds out. Rosalinda didn't like honey. Energy content: 300 kcal. Nor did she like milk, eggs or cheese. She didn't like being vegan either. Such a specific term, so lacking in ambition.

Ambition: A kind of hunger known only to humans. To some of them.

Hunger.

She fished out the last piece of gum from the packet. Her

subway train was delayed so she had chewed five while waiting
and on her way there. She would have to buy more after class.
Then she remembered she had only the exact change for two
subway rides and the bus.

Chewing gum.

She thought about the heat, the crowded subway cars, the
long minutes when the trains are trapped inside the tunnels.
Would she faint? She might do, without chewing gum in her
bag. Then the alarm, the call to her sister, the call from her
sister to her mother, hell starting all over again. Under the circumstances, Dr. Montesinos would lend her the money for a
cab. But she'd look like a whore. And though she was fat, she
was not a whore.

Rosalinda decided to ration the chewing gum.

It's hard to believe, but the blog is still online. You need only
search *doctor montesinos case + rosalinda villegas*. It comes up in
the third or fourth spot. Searching for *princess ana and mia* is
more tedious. The number of blogs by Anas and Mias increases
daily. Also, they are all similar.

Rosalinda Villegas's blog has a pink background and fonts in
loud colors. On the right-hand side, standing proud like a flag,
is the picture of an emaciated girl: *Fight to be perfect*, says the
caption.

The blogger's profile is under this image. Rosalinda with
costume glasses, those ones that have a frame, a nose and mustache. She's sticking out her tongue. The picture, like all the
portraits of those who have been killed, is macabre. Rosalinda
is making fun of life, her own death, us.

She is nineteen and studying social communication. *Read
more* links to her profile, where one can find the same brief
information. Under favorite books, movies and music there

is nothing. Almost nothing. Just one reference that will prove quite significant to anyone who does a bit of investigating. Her favorite book, the only one she reads and rereads is *Abzurdah*, by an Argentine called Cielo Latini.

She was born on September 11, 1989. I know it, I can work it out, from the post published on September 12, 2008:

> *Hello!!! My little princesses!!! It's been my worst birthday ever. I'm a fat cow, nobody loves me. Ana and Mia are my only friends, the only ones who help me keep going, to find my dreams. I'm tired of being a failure. Yesterday wasn't a good day. Marcos forgot all about my feelings. And on top of that, he blames me for everything. I need help, I'm lonely. I'm desperate . . . sometimes I want to die.*

The blog has a dictionary that gets you up to speed with the subject. The first two entries of what is really a glossary are fundamental:

> *Ana: someone with anorexia.*
> *Mia: someone with bulimia.*

For the anorexics and bulimics of the Internet, these two hyphaereses are real advisory beings. Split personality is a key concept for understanding an illness that, even when described and narrated in detail by one of its victims, can still be incomprehensible. Ana and Mia are people—women, I'd venture to specify—who suffer from anorexia and bulimia. But they are also two major forces, disorders transformed into totems that enslave their subjects. Two despotic queens who treat their little princesses mercilessly.

Some other terms in the glossary, which also compose the

second post on the blog, give a taste of the emotional roller coaster the reader is going to experience, since the days of Rosalinda Villegas's life go by in what I'm tempted to call a *live broadcast*, but a chilling fact prevails: nearly all the comments on her blog, hundreds of them, were posted after her death. There is only one comment from somebody writing to Rosalinda while she was still alive. Judging by her use of the *vos* form of Spanish, this was an Ana from the South, a would-be anorexic asking for advice.

But I was talking about the other terms. I've picked the most interesting ones:

> *ED: eating disorder. (Sometimes also "DA" for the Spanish.)*
> *Self-injury: self-mutilation.*
> *Thinspiration: inspiration for someone thin or anorexic.*
> (I must confess it took me a moment to spot the wordplay here. Pedro Álamo would have got it straight away.)
> *Bipolarity: mood that fluctuates between two phases, one of great happiness and another of deep depression.*
> *Manic phase: this is characterized by an excessive good mood, hyperactivity, less need for sleep, etc.*
> *Depressive phase: crying, indifference, depression, suicidal thoughts, changes in diet, etc.*
> *Obsessive-compulsive disorder: an anxiety disorder characterized by obsessions (unwanted impulses or images) and compulsions (repetitive rituals to alleviate anxiety). E.g., excessive fear of germs, washing hands every half hour.*
> *Panic attack: repeated periods of fear and instability together with a racing heart, with no apparent cause.*

Rosalinda left a written trace of all these disorders between August 2008, the approximate date the blog was created, and July 15, 2009, when she published her last, revelatory post.

Her case is textbook OCD. Just browsing her third post and some of the other lists with tips, it's obvious there was an invisible monster tormenting her.

In fact, the third post is the dictionary that the second post promises but doesn't deliver. It's called *Calories* and is a catalog of foodstuffs listed alphabetically alongside their energy value. A total of 320 entries or words with their respective calories. Rosalinda boasted of knowing the list by heart, and she used to recite it from beginning to end on the street, at university, in the subway, at home, when hunger made her cry from the pain.

She also gives detailed techniques for vomiting without the family finding out. There are several lists of this kind. However, it's the so-called *Ana Tips* that reveal more about her personality. I'll quote those related to behavior. This post is undated, it just has this headline:

> *Ana Tips that work. They helped me; they may help you.*
> *Go for it, princesses!*

She follows this with the following recommendations:

> *Eat in front of the mirror naked.*
> *Use polish on your nails, so they don't look so pale.*
> *Every calorie counts: Don't stop moving while sitting*
>   *down. Move a pencil. Move your leg.*
> *Sitting down with your back straight burns ten percent*
>   *more calories than sitting down with a bad posture.*
> *If you are cold, don't put more clothes on. Your body burns*
>   *calories to try to keep warm.*

Use smaller plates.
Clench your butt cheeks all the time: it burns calories and
  keeps you fit.
Use your mind, that's very powerful: imagine what the
  food looks like in your stomach once you've digested it.
Remember to eat in the same place every day. Never in front
  of the TV or the computer, since your brain won't reg-
  ister the warnings your body sends to say it's satisfied.

"You don't have an appointment," the receptionist said.

"I know. But when you have a moment, let him know I'm here anyway."

Rosalinda sat down. She didn't find it hard to disconnect from the miserable surroundings of the waiting room. She was a fat girl, and fat girls are invisible. They're also disgusting and filthy, but above all invisible.

She put on her headphones but didn't switch on her iPod. The urgency of music, like every other living thing, hurt her. She put on her sunglasses, folded her arms, and pretended to fall asleep. Other people would see her as a typical dysfunctional teenager. She still had the face of a child. She imagined that Cielo would see herself like this: pretty, thin, too thin for other people and, for that very reason, unyielding.

"He's asking you to come back another day because he's fully booked until tonight," the receptionist said.

"I'll wait for him anyway," Rosalinda said.

The receptionist gave her a dirty look.

"It's still only three," she said, looking at her watch. "Don't you want to at least go to the café?"

The café. Bitch.

Thankfully, she had only the exact amount for the train fare. It was obvious Dr. Montesinos had told her something, something about her case. Was he also sleeping with her? She had dark, silky hair, and she'd had work done on her breasts. Now, with more determination, she was going to sit waiting in that room the whole afternoon. She would make the receptionist uncomfortable with her adipose presence. That would be just the warm-up. Then it'd be the doctor's turn. It'd all blow up then. That would be the prescription, the authorization her life would give her once again to fuck it all up. Throwing up, fasting, cutting her veins until she fainted.

But she still had the whole afternoon ahead. Patience. To escape, with her inner sense of movement, yet nailed to the same chair for hours. To travel with her mind whenever hunger struck.

Going over the list of calories. Choose one category and start. Fish, shellfish and crustaceans:

> *Albacore, 225; Anchovies (in olive oil), 175; Anchovies (in sunflower oil), 252; Bass, 115; Bream (grilled), 98; Bream (steamed), 138; Cod (cured), 322; Cod (fresh), 74; Cod (salted), 108.*

Cod.

That's what they'd call girls like her at school. Cod, sometimes trout. Different ways of digging the same dagger into one's soul, over and over.

Marcos was different.

One day he came to her house with his sister and right from the start behaved like a gentleman. Or rather, he simply paid attention to her, listened, treated her with respect, without pity. She fell in love from that day. Marcos seemed to see through her, through the layers of fat, to talk to her real self. Soul, heart? None of that. The real Rosalinda was a thinner version of herself lying in the depths of her body. If people had souls, their souls would be buried in their bones: the last, unswallowable wholeness where willpower lies.

In the first week of September 2008, Rosalinda shows symptoms of going through a manic phase, as she termed it. All the posts published in those days have the same goal: to encourage herself and others to carry on fasting. I quote three examples:

September 1, 2008
Abzurdah
Hello, my princesses. I've got a great book to recommend you—I think we princesses have heard of it. If you haven't, let me know and I'll send you a copy. It's called Abzurdah, by Cielo Latini. She was anorexic and bulimic. Reading the book gives you the strength to carry on with Ana or Mia. If you want it, leave a comment with your email and I'll send it. Love you, princesses, good luck!

September 2, 2008
Go for it, princesses!!!
Princesses, we can't get upset, we've got to gather all our strength and be the princesses we want to be. You can count on me, and I hope I can count on you too. Helping each other is the best way to reach our goal, we got to stay united. Here's my email so you can write to me or chat online, whatever's best. We can cheer one another on, help each other or even compete among ourselves. Not to beat each other, but to support each other, so we can be what we want. That's what Cielo Latini was like, she's totally my thinspiration, and that's how we can be too. Go princesses! Go us! You go girls.

September 3, 2008.

Today I've decided I won't hide Ana anymore. She's my friend, my only friend, and it's not fair to hide her. No one can force me to do what I don't want to do, that's what my sister taught me, and she's right. If I can't force anyone to love me, then nobody can force me to do something I don't want to do: that is, I WON'T EAT!!! I don't care what people who don't agree with me say. Food destroys me, just like love. Love and food are my worst enemies, they hurt me. One destroys my heart, the other destroys my body.

The first confident stage, a period of certainty about achieving self-destruction, is soon followed by a depressive phase. A decay that worsens after her nineteenth birthday, seemingly motivated by a romantic impasse with that Marcos guy.

Personally, I find these posts tedious—maybe it's professional bias. For psychiatrists—contravening Tolstoy's rightly celebrated quote—misfortune, not happiness, is the most monotonous experience. Misfortune always seeks to look like itself.

The depressive phase is interrupted by several months of silence. It is around that time that Rosalinda Villegas is referred to Dr. Montesinos and her fate is sealed. Wounded by her unrequited love for Marcos, she will fall prey to the first wolf that wants to devour her. "You disgust me," Marcos will tell her when he hears about her affair with the psychiatrist, and any possibility of becoming more than friends, as Marcos had apparently once promised her, now disappears.

Dr. Montesinos will seduce her from the outset, before taking her virginity and, in the subsequent appointments, introducing her to the pleasure pill (negative calories). She falls in love and he starts to distance himself from her. He recommends that she go to see another psychiatrist. However, they keep seeing each other now and again. They make love at his practice. Hastily between appointments, or for hours at night, when the hospital wing is deserted. There, in that cage of sin and sorrow, within a whirlwind about which we will never know all the details, Rosalinda will die.

Her corpse was found on July 17, 2009, in some wastelands around the Parque Caiza development. A contusion on her head, perhaps provoked by a blow from a heavy object, was the cause of death.

The evidence against Dr. Montesinos is irrefutable. The luminol tests showed that the traces of blood and hair found in Dr. Montesinos's car and practice matched the samples taken from Rosalinda Villegas's corpse.

Dr. Montesinos didn't run away. Instead he ran straight ahead, presenting himself to the authorities as soon as he read rumors in the press pointing to him as the culprit, even though no charges had yet been filed. Not long after, he gave a statement on TV that finally convinced the whole country that he had indeed been involved. His performance in front of the cameras was so bad, his willpower so weak before the temptations of vanity and cynicism, that Montesinos ended up giving himself away. The best-regarded psychiatrist in Venezuela, former vice-chancellor of the most prestigious university in the country, founder of that university's Schools of Psychology and Arts, a former candidate for the presidency of the Republic and confidant to three national leaders, was lost.

What trail did the police follow to link the names of Rosalinda Villegas and Dr. Montesinos? The easiest, the most obvious. The trail Rosalinda had opened up, plowed and harvested in plain sight for months, and whose only possible final destination was death. The trail that was available to everyone, but which nobody followed, or understood, in time.

The final post on Rosalinda's blog reveals her affair with Dr. Montesinos. It was published the same day she went out onto the street with the feeling, the absolute conviction, that this time, yet again, everything was going to be fucked, for good.

6

Onomancy

I got here, home, and started shuffling her name. Anagrams, for me, are a kind of tarot. Or like the *I Ching*. Each letter is a card or a rune that creates a different meaning, though still close to the original, when it switches places. Of course, the resulting words are largely just flukes, which might distract but which might, in fact, emphasize hidden meanings, the interpretations that are buried in the letters.

Margarita, for example, that night provided a grim rat, a trim raga, a rat mag, tar grit, taiga ram, arm a git, ram a tiara. Just to name the few combinations I happen to recall.

I'm comparing it to tarot or the *I Ching* so you understand, because onomancy was a known practice in the seventeenth century. Even then, some would dismiss the belief that all names are divine registers that contain the keys to interpreting a particular fate as no more than typical French bamboozling.

I always think about that Lily Tomlin line: "Why is it that when we talk to God we're said to be praying, but when God talks to us we're schizophrenic?"

Something similar happened to me with language. Contrary to the norm, it's the language that uses me: I was born to listen to what language has to say by itself. Very few people understand this, and for this reason, I have preferred to keep quiet, in every sense of the word, for most of my life.

It's this, and nothing else, that underlies my ridiculously

famous short story. Letting the sounds flow with no interest whatsoever in finding out where those sounds would lead me. I can only barely remember starting off with a random accumulation of words, and then there was this numbing feeling, like when you hear quiet music you can't identify. Then I woke up with the text in my hands, and that was it.

Entering the award was meant as an unseen prank, like drawing a mustache on a newspaper photo of a politician. At least that's what I had in mind when I submitted the text. I had been annoyed with my linguistics lecturer over what I considered an unfair grade, which became a public argument in the classroom. Submitting that text to the *El Nacional* award was my revenge: stick one to the literary system (since in my head, the university, lecturers and the media were all part of a dark alliance with indiscernible objectives). A dose of nonsense, delirium even, to remind them that, as the patron saints of Russian formalism rightly said, in the beginning was the Word.

In the final exam for Linguistics 1, in the question about the dichotomy between language and speech, I defended Saussure's notion of seeing the abstract system of language as the only possible source of linguistic knowledge. "Speech is just a flutter in the air, it never leaves a trace, really," I concluded. The lecturer limited herself to highlighting this sentence and crossing out my answer. After class, I asked her about the meaning of that X over my lengthy spiel.

"It means it's wrong," she said.

"And what's your argument?" I asked. That was enough to convince the ten or fifteen people who were about to leave the room to stay and see what would happen. The teacher looked me up and down and delivered a lecture on the irrefutable findings of structuralist approaches and social anthropology. She also summarized, forensically, the course bibliography, which, naturally, I hadn't read, busy as I was drawing *little pictures* while in class.

I remember pressing the notebook against my chest, the very same one containing the little pictures I'd been drawing in class, and remaining silent.

Much later, however, I confirmed I was right. Language pre-dates speech. It's an organ, or a tissue, or one cell of the many that make up the human body. What I mean is language exists at a biological level. Like blood flow, like neural electricity, however its miracle might happen in every word we say, think or draw. Because that's what I did: I drew words.

In 1996, when I traveled to Barcelona, I found the missing piece in a bookshop. The title instantly caught my eye. *Words Upon Words.* That was the hook. The subtitle then grabbed me by the larynx and yanked me out of the depths where I had been submerged for many years, leaving me gasping for air over the store's New Titles display. The subtitle read, or reads: *The Anagrams of Ferdinand de Saussure.*

It's a collection of unpublished notes on the investigations Saussure carried out between 1906 and 1909, transcribed, and with commentary, by Jean Starobinski. The original French edition is from 1971, and the Spanish one, 1996. The delay in the publication (which was also incomplete) of these texts is outrageous, but somehow reflects something I hadn't truly grasped at the end of that humiliating linguistics lecture in the year 1982: we pretend to have in-depth knowledge of certain things so as to forget that we know nothing about so many others. Among them, perhaps, the very same things we think we know well.

Saussure's theory of anagrams is not only his most brilliant and ambitious project. It is also, above all, the most fascinating and complex attempt to decipher the enigma of literature.

The worst part is that Starobinski himself didn't discover a thing. Saussure's investigation of anagrams is collected in the 117 notebooks in which he recorded all his findings, including the elation and paralyzing self-doubt that overwhelmed him during just three years of frenetic work. In 1958 the notebooks were donated to the Geneva University and Public Library by Saussure's children, and have been there ever since. Both Bally and Sechehaye were aware of this project but failed to appreciate its scope. Even Robert Godel, who classified the notebooks in 1960, didn't realize the magnitude of the work. Godel just dismissed them, saying they were the result of a *longue et sterile* search.

Saussure's thesis was so radical: all ancient poetry in Indo-European literature, particularly Latin poetry of any era, used to revolve around a proper name, generally that of a thematically relevant hero or god, which the poet would impose on himself and take as a phonic motif, insofar as this name, broken down into syllables, would resonate through the verses of the poem, determining elements from word choice to syntactic structure.

Now you understand the impact this discovery had on me. No, that's right. You can't. For you to understand you'd have to know the story of my life. Maybe from now on, since you have agreed to come to my house, I'll have time to tell you everything. Well, almost everything.

I remember that the first and only precaution I took to avoid sullying the total independence of my short story was choosing a random title beforehand. I looked for my Scrabble set, put my hand in the little felt bag and took out several letters. That's how I ended up with "NEERCSEHT," whose strangeness fitted my purpose. For the rest, as I said a while back, *I went with the flow.*

When I read the text the following day, I felt a chill running down my spine: I didn't understand a word. Was I really saying anything? Was there anything there apart from totally wild language?

A few days later the incident with the linguistics lecturer happened. Around that time, I also saw the call for the *El Nacional* annual story competition. I reread my story, ending up even more confused than I was the first time, and that's why I decided to submit it. At the last minute, just to mess around, I added a quotation about narrative space by Bachelard. A symbolic straitjacket that would open up to unleash madness.

I submitted the thing and forgot about it. I'm telling you, it wasn't my intention to get anything out of it. But then it happened. One afternoon I get home and my mother tells me I've won the award.

My reaction was to lock myself away and get sick. The insomnia and lack of appetite of the first few days laid the ground for a stubborn tonsillitis. Thanks to that, I avoided having to go and collect the prize. Then, when the story got published and the whole thing blew up, I simply didn't answer the phone.

I didn't leave the house for more than a year.

What did I do that whole time? Everything and nothing. After my illness I spent my time thinking, trying to understand what had happened. I remembered that Trejo had been the chair of the jury and that his own experimental body of work, which was so prone to wordplay, had an obvious affinity with my text. But what about the other members of the jury? I'd read some things by Madrid and Díaz Solís, but nothing that could justify their verdict.

Then I toyed with the idea of the jury having awarded the prize to my story as a prank. But a prank on whom? Not on me—I was, and still am, a nobody. Perhaps on some of the *committed* writers who abounded in our literature at the time.

Indeed, the statement issued by the jury to justify their deci-sion against the many attacks from both renowned intellectuals and anonymous readers did support this reasoning.

A prank on a prankster, I thought. This was the most con-vincing hypothesis, but also the one that most irritated me. Which was why I rejected it.

In any case, I said to myself, despite our intentions, despite ourselves, despite whatever we may have wanted to write or read in that text, there was something *there*.

With that in mind, I tried to decode the story. The first read-ings threw out some common shadow patterns I transferred to a notepad. As the days went by, the shadows began to spread and clear, like clouds after a storm.

Then I worked on processing those clouds as the cotton from which the plot is made, spinning it into the missing narrative thread that would connect the words and give them meaning. I had the impression my story was like a dream dreamed by another text that lay within those same pages and which I needed to wake.

I managed to compile around three hundred pages, between notes, roughly drafted scenes, characters who would suddenly pass through a paragraph like ghosts, and narrative sequences that would rise up and then vanish like swirling dust the moment they began to gain consistency.

Happy days of writing were followed by others of excruci-ating reading. Whenever I retraced the path that would lead to the best passages of my *novel* (my text had outgrown the "short story" label by then), I would get lost in some corner and lose the link between the initial shadow-cloud and the final passage.

I was split over the transposition of two misplaced feelings: sometimes I'd write with the ease and joy brought only by reading, then I'd read with the discomfort, uncertainty and fra-gility that characterize true writing.

I wish I'd been able to read Saussure's notes and letters on his theory of anagrams in those months of 1982. My loneliness would have been less severe, the anguish more manageable.

Saussure would dive into his books and notes as if entering a labyrinth or stepping onto a battlefield. On a few occasions, he referred to his investigations as *the Monster*, and when he'd confirmed, or thought he had confirmed, a real discovery, he felt like a heavily armed soldier breaking through the enemy's lines. But those moments of euphoria would be followed by bursts of sadness, of paralyzing self-doubt. Saussure feared that his theory might be a mirage. That the hypothesis of one key word being behind the structure of every work belonging to humankind's most ancient and important literary tradi-tions was a mere ghost produced by rhyme. A hallucination provoked by that strange tendency of language to follow a musical pattern. The sort of sidetracking that words do when we are distracted, which makes them end up alongside others that sound the same.

Saussure knew how to negotiate the path that connects bril-liance with madness. He knew that some truths may burn and that some men are destined to carry these truths, while others are to be burnt by them, and others still just meant to gaze at them. Saussure belonged to this last group, as did Wittgenstein and I. At twenty-four he published his thesis on the use of the genitive absolute in Sanskrit, and then, with the exception of some brief essays, he no longer published anything at all.

These men had gazed into the great mysteries of the human mind. Me, I gazed into those of my own insignificant existence. The difference between them and me is minimal, as you can see, just a touch, but one as dense as a universe.

There are some sausages, but I'm not sure if there are any hot dog rolls left. Let me check. I can do a stir-fry you wouldn't believe. I've got a bottle of whiskey somewhere. I don't drink much. I don't get many visitors either. So I'm sorry I haven't much to offer. Thank you so much for coming. Just let me know when you need to leave. But I promise I'll make it worth your while. As you can see, I'm desperate to talk, I can't stop. And I think you might be interested in hearing what I have to say. Intuition, let's say. Intuition and Matías. He's told me some things about you. That's why I don't trust him. Matías is obsessed with the idea of being a writer. You can tell he's always alert, jumpy, salivating at the thought of absorbing someone else's experiences. You're different. A psychiatrist, and a forensic one too. Being a vampire is your duty. Your need for writing is, firstly, therapeutic. It's as if you want to write to forget or understand, and maybe you do. You will come to understand it's pointless, and then you'll forget about writing altogether.

Just like Saussure in mid-1906, I in 1983 was up to my neck. It was a time when I wasn't sure about anything anymore, and I got carried away by the desperation. The anxiety that was part of reading infected the writing. My brain was a ravaged anthill. Every idea, a Minotaur.

Enter Sarita Calcaño.

That night at the Greenwich bar, when Margarita asked me if everything in "The Screen" was true, I didn't want to disappoint her. Let's just say that in terms of sequences, or actions, nearly all the sections match. But they're in totally the wrong order. And that alone is enough to change the story.

To start with, Sarita and I knew each other before I won the award. We were good friends. Before the award, I wasn't as much of a dark horse as they say. Despite her beauty, Sarita wasn't a femme fatale either. We were even happy.

Sarita walked into my room one morning, without notice, like slanting sunlight.

"This room smells of shit" was her way of saying hello.

I was bent over my desk, lost among the lines of my own calligraphy. It took me a few seconds to register she was actually there.

Sarita walked past, drew the curtains and opened the windows. Then she told me to go eat my breakfast.

"I brought *cachitos* and Riko Malt," she said, gesturing toward the kitchen.

I obeyed.

When I came back, she had started cleaning the room.

"Go bathe," she said.

I obeyed again.

I stood under the shower for a long time.

I got back to the room. It was gleaming. The last traces of water on the floor were evaporating.

Sarita was lying on the bed reading. She had changed the sheets. She looked up from her book and gestured for me to join her. I lay by her side, my hair still wet and a towel around my waist.

She had on one of her hippie dresses, a floral print, almost see-through.

"Listen to this: 'Dogma—I Am God?'"

She looked at me waiting for an answer.

"Isn't it brilliant?" she said.

"What's brilliant?"

"It's a palindrome. It reads the same forward and backward. 'Dogma—I Am God?' You see?" she said, showing me the page.

The book was square and thick, with a white cover. Its title was *OIRADARIO*, by Darío Lancini.

"I've just bought it from Suma. It's called 'Hear Darío'—and the title itself makes a perfect palindrome in Spanish: 'Oír a Darío.' Isn't that amazing?"

Sarita was glowing.

She went on reading palindromes. She would read them and I would go over the sentence in my mind, from left to right and right to left.

Was it a rat I saw?

Some men interpret nine memos

So many dynamos!

Too far afoot

No, Sir. A war is on!

Do geese see God?

Reading each sentence back and forth would take us down a path from which Sarita and I would always return with a smile.

"You know what?" she said. "When I first read your story, I thought it was about us. Because of the title, you know?"

"I don't understand."

"The title. I thought the wordplay had to do with us. But then I understood it wasn't about us, or about anything really."

It was then that I realized. Through her reflected confession, Sarita was letting me see the folding screen.

Sara Calcaño was the only one of us who owned an apartment. She had been a contestant for Miss Venezuela in 1978, and finished as first runner-up. After becoming famous in the beauty pageant, she worked as a model for a couple of years. Then, one day, she decided to leave the fashion world and study literature, and that's how we met her.

Sarita was beautiful, smart and fun. We were all in love with her, one way or another. We were so in love that nobody, man or woman, was possessive about her. Sarita was a wonder, like a nature reserve that sustained us, so we worshiped her and looked after her.

With the money she had made as a model she'd bought a car and an apartment. As soon as she began her studies, she shared everything with her friends. She was the one who would fill up the tank of her van and drive us around. It was she who would organize marathon meetings of three or even four days in her house that were literary salon, party and orgy in that order.

Sarita was the first woman I slept with. Margarita was the second. Margarita will be the third. I'll come full circle, as it was meant to be, and I'll stop regretting the humiliated beauty or the impossible love story.

Sara's apartment had a large living room with big windows framing the greenery of the city. In one corner, there was a folding screen. Sarita would unfold it when she sat down to paint. Hiding there she would paint words. Not the way I'd draw the letters in linguistics classes, instead she painted what words suggested to her: images that grew in her inner world and often contradicted the usual meaning of the word in question. Or not exactly contradicting it, it was more that Sarita's paintings were sculptural representations that overshadowed conventional functions.

Late at night, once we had finished with movies, literature and clothes, Sarita would choose a boy or girl and take them to her corner. She would take their hand, open out the folding screen, put on the little lamp and start making love. The first time I was lucky enough to be chosen I saw Sarita's *work*. It was she who showed me how to see words in a different way, or simply to *see* them.

Each of us had our experience behind the folding screen. No one was left out; nobody was the same afterward, and we never fought over it. We were a utopian society. Since then I've been convinced real equality comes with the equitable sharing of love. And I'd venture to specify, sexual love.

Neercseht, the screen.

Some might say it's a coincidence. That would be logically

correct, but spiritually wrong. Life tends to be either horrible or plain boring, but that's because people aren't usually worthy of its miracles.

Among the many possibilities inside that little felt bag, what came out was what, until then, had been my most intimate word. And it came out in the most suggestive way. If the letters had come out in their normal direction, in their quotidian order, let's say, I would probably have written a story about my life as a literature student. I would have written about my loneliness, my readings, my thoughts. A bland landscape that would later be shaken up by Sarita. I would have written a love story, as simple as that. "The Screen" is no more than a love story.

"Neercseht," on the other hand, is infinite.

At the time I was accused of being a formalist, as if that were an insult. The wordplay, the neologisms and the unhinged syntax in my text were interpreted as a late and poor understanding of the experiments carried out by the avant-garde and the surrealists. They didn't know, I wouldn't have known myself, that my short story (the only thing I've ever published) is a sin of realism, of autobiography, since my whole life is encapsulated within it. My past, my present and my future. This conversation we were having and the hours yet to come.

The morning Sarita put an end to my seclusion, I glimpsed part of the solution, and it came to me naturally: I must surface from the water to breathe. Following Saussure's theory of anagrams, I understood I should focus on the signifiers, on the roulette of assemblage, and not so much on the content.

Sarita read on:

"*Dali Lad*"

Madam, I'm Adam.

Sir, I'm Iris.
Sex of foxes.
Dr. Awkward.
"That's us," I said.
We laughed.

I felt a low-range trembling, the turning-up of some long-subdued earth, and I couldn't help myself: a tent had been raised up in the middle of the towel.

I laughed again. Sarita didn't. She undid the loose knot in the fabric and revealed (credit where it's due) a formidable erection. Sarita sat up, put the book down beside the bed and started blowing me.

I remember the way she took off her dress, that last watery glimmer evaporating to give way to new humidities.

I passed out. When I awoke, Sarita was gone. Lancini's book was on the bedside table.

That was how my physical seclusion ended. Using palindromes, I began with scrupulous detail to build a prison for my soul. Incarceration and sanctity aren't experiences you forget in a hurry. And reality shows the wildness at its heart with the fact that, deep down, both prisoner and saint long to return to the hell that is jail or desert.

Palindromes were my last frontier, the perfect gallows for dreaming.

I made my first attempts the day after Sarita visited. I spent almost five hours trying to construct a palindrome. The result was pathetic, but I didn't feel bad.

The first *findings* were chromatic: *Red art trader, no gray argon, a pink nipa.*

Some to do with animals: *Bird rib, lion oil, star rats.*

A violent one: *Red rum? Murder!*

A festive-deadly one: *Party booby-trap.*

An absurd one: *Nate bit a Tibetan.*

In the afternoon, after lunch, I went for a walk around Caracas.

Beyond this fumbling start, I didn't have much luck with palindromes. Soon afterward, I settled for reading and collecting them. I came upon the works of Miguel González Avelar, Enrique Alatorre and Rubén Bonifaz Nuño, and though I enjoyed them, it felt nothing like reading Lancini. *Oír a Darío* is one of a kind in the Spanish language. When our civilization dies, this book will prevail. And in 3,500 years it'll be an enigma as extraordinary and baffling as the Nazca lines.

It'll be like the paperback version of the Nazca lines.

From palindromes, I moved on to anagrams and then to acrostics and all kinds of wordplay.

It didn't take me long to find a job where my particular sensibility could be an asset.

My mother came to an arrangement with a distant cousin for an office-boy job at an advertising agency. Lenin (that's what my mother's cousin was called) was a manager, and from day one he tried to show me the ropes. The main thing was to sell the product at any price, literally and figuratively speaking. "Advertising is the modern rhetoric," he would say. "Its aim is to convince, even at the risk of falsifying or altering facts." Lenin had studied philosophy when he was young, and even though he never graduated, he's the only person I know who's able to marry Aristotle and Plato convincingly.

My promotion from gofer to copywriter came about thanks to a palindrome. The client was a consumer electronics company that wanted to promote their new Elysion synthesizers. When Lenin told me about it, I said:

"Noisy Lenin in Elysion."

"Come again?"

"What?"

"Repeat what you just said."

"*Noisy Lenin in Elysion.* It's a palindrome."

Lenin took a pen and wrote the sentence in his diary. When he'd finished, he was elated.

"This will be the slogan for the advert."

Developing the idea was easy. Comrade Lenin himself coming from 1920s Russia to 1980s Venezuela just to have a go on the new, top-of-the-range Elysion keyboards. Vladimir Ulyanov doing the return journey from one side of the world to the other over that bridge of words that's a palindrome.

Though I feared I might disappoint him, I confessed this particular palindrome was not of my own invention.

"There are no original ideas in advertising," he said. "Everything we use is taken from the public's psyche. And that's the key: we sell them something they already have."

Over time, I've learned this can be applied to palindromes too. To literature in general, but especially to palindromes. Note that Lancini ends his book with two exemplary texts. One is a palindrome of over 1,200 words, which is also a parody of the play *Ubu Roi*. The other is an appendix comprising the vocabulary used to form the palindromes in the book. All the words he uses, in alphabetic order. *Oír a Darío* is a puzzle that works backward: the final picture is only complete when you take out all the pieces, by showing in these separate words, these simple and common individual words, the raw material from which that immortal work was created. A work that's a result not so much of imagination but of attentiveness.

Attentiveness to the murmur of the words.

I showed a natural talent for advertising. Soon I was coining amusing, catchy slogans and puns that captured the product's essence and the customer's attention. I would win all the assignments given to the copywriting team. It was around that time I also caught the attention of a young girl who'd joined us as an intern.

Her name was Margarita.

From the moment we started to go out, I felt overwhelmed by a kind of inebriation, just from being together, and I'd recite a poem by Darío (the other Darío), that goes: "See, Margarita, How Beautiful the Sea." Borges said that universal history was nothing but different intonations of the same few metaphors. Rubén Darío, around the same time as Saussure, seemed to be stating that poetry was nothing but the different intonations of a name. No one has ever done so much with just a name. The sea in the poem is, from the first verse, a departure and arrival gate: the perfect symmetry between a name and its destiny.

I couldn't say for sure when or how things started to go awry. The shift into a higher gear happened fast: going out, engagement, moving to a new house, buying a place. I think both of us could already hear the same background noise: a murmur telling you some piece isn't working, that the mechanism is out of sync.

In my case, it was a matter of oppressive shyness.

Living as a couple doesn't just mean sharing a home. You are sharing your body: its routines, its moods, its space, the movements that reveal a shamelessly liberated consciousness.

I could never do any of the intimate actions that cement life as a couple in Margarita's presence: peeing with the bathroom door open, sharing the sink while brushing our teeth, reading in bed together, let alone falling asleep before her.

When it came to sex, I wasn't prudish or boring, I like to think. I'd perform all the perversities of a healthy relationship, but then I'd get ashamed afterward and feel the need to say sorry. I still remember Margarita's face in those moments: an expression that would go from humiliation to resentment.

What intimidated me, though, was the glimmer of hope I'd find, despite everything, buried in the back of her eyes. Margarita thought I was one of these men with *something to say*. She had fallen in love with my intelligence, my sense of humor, the determination that had helped me advance in the company. That sense of ambition all women need to smell on a man before they'll notice him. A sense that in my case—working as the perfect repellent for other women—was muffled by my modesty, by the way I'd turned my back on a promising literary career to focus on something none of us could truly identify but that she believed was my secret vigor.

We would move house to distract ourselves from drifting apart. But as soon as we'd gotten used to a place, we'd start finding things wrong with it. Often it had to do with the neighborhood: the insecurity and the unbearable thundering of the traffic. La Pastora, La Campiña, Los Chaguaramos and south of Bello Monte, in that order, were places where we lived over just three years.

Becoming a partner in the advertising agency helped make lots of decisions. I proposed to Margarita and bought a house. We moved to San António de los Altos, half an hour from Caracas, the perfect place to escape the violence and noise of the city.

Living in that duplex, breathing the Mirandean mountain air, we renewed the air in our lungs. Serenity, we both thought, would arrive as punctual as an arranged delivery. In fact, things did seem to go well for the first few months. Margarita finished her studies in social communications and would soon be starting work for a TV channel. We bought a secondhand car for her to use, as I have always been afraid of driving. She would leave at seven in the morning and I, making the most of my new position as a partner, would take the bus to town a couple of hours later.

One morning I woke up with a cold and didn't go to work. I spent all day in a house that, with its pristine, freshly painted white walls and almost complete lack of pictures, was still in the process of unfolding its secrets.

I felt irremediably alone.

Suddenly, I forgot the reasons that gave my life meaning: Margarita, that house, myself. I don't know how many hours that investigation lasted, but it served only to make me aware of the silence that had accumulated until then. An absolute silence, as if an invisible gauze were muffling every space. A silence that gave off a murmur as it gained momentum: that murmur I had always seen as a metaphor for my relationship with Margarita and that now I could clearly make out between the folds of that unbearable stillness.

A silence like this, Miguel. Can you hear it? As if made by termites. A late-night silence in the middle of the day, over-shadowing the day, devouring it in the maggots' nest of its spent seconds.

That night, I heard it. I heard the motorbike moving around in the night. Its echo resonating like applause from the lonely mountainous curves, and my open eyes, imagining the motor-bike's trajectory, both far away and close by, muddling the line between fear and desire, not knowing whether the bike was announcing its arrival or bidding farewell.

In the following months, I would always wake in anguish, with desert-like thirst, feverishly relying on the glass of water on my bedside table, seeing its overflowing edge and the possibility of its emptiness as a sign, the confirmation of a phase coming to an end.

Up until 1996, I didn't have the tools for deciphering my life. Saussure's theory of anagrams opened up the possibility of a fresh attack on my old text. That massive trunk you see over there contains all the results I've recorded to date.

This time around, it was way easier. Of course, to start with, it was hard to see the logic behind it. I would sit down and just wait for the text to adopt its new configuration, as if by osmosis. What was the image, what was the tale behind it? I didn't know. That's why during my first attempts, the old and feared shadows reappeared.

I was about to give up, to fall into that old forest I'd lost myself in years earlier. I was saved by my own impatient whisper:

"What the fuck d'you want?"

I said it out of desperation.

I said it to myself and also to the text.

Then I felt the old notes trembling. It was an undulation, as if the pages were yawning, like the quivering of the water in the glass on my bedside table.

This time I understood that my text was an oracle. I thought about Margarita, my wife, and the letters began to vibrate.

Following the rhythmic pattern drafted by Saussure, I classified the words by the resemblance of their sounds. Then I counted consonants and vowels and they started to add up. It was amazing how symmetrical the text was on every level. Vowels or consonants that didn't have their match within the same phrase would match up with loose vowels or consonants in the preceding or the following phrases. In the end, all that was left were these consonants: *m, r, g, t.*

I don't need to tell you what name is enfolded within these letters.

Using different starting questions or thoughts, previously defined, as a compass, I would decode the text, opening the folding screen that was obscuring the words. That's how I saw, with mild horror, the outline of Margarita's death, the parabolic course that, between the folds of our lives, long before she and I had met, had been plotted by the biker who'd killed her. I saw the loneliness that had been part of me ever since, and that will still be with me until Margarita's awaited return. Because the text said Margarita would come back. It didn't specify how. It never said whether it would be resuscitation or reincarnation, or my finally falling into the world of dreams or memories. But she would come back, one way or the other.

I signed up for Matías's workshop with the puerile idea of meeting women. I regretted it even before the first class. You know Matías lays out the chairs in a circle, as if to reinforce a horizontal relationship between teacher and students, as well as among students themselves. As soon as I sat down, it felt like an AA meeting: I said my name and why I was there. I was the first to speak and then I suffered when I heard how elaborate the other people's reasons were. I felt ashamed that I'd lied (I gave the typical explanation of always having felt the need to write but having had to settle for a more economically sustainable job), but in the following weeks, I discovered that, except for a few marked exceptions, everyone had the same *extradiegetic* expectations that I had.

The last person to introduce herself, completing the circle, was a young woman. She was heavily built, but pretty. She said she studied psychology and literature. That she practiced kickboxing. She was called, still is called, Margarita.

I'm not that into theater. I think its prevalence is just a way of opposing the advance of technology. However, I've always thought that covering and uncovering the stage with a curtain is an unbeatable innovation. It's the trembling of the cloth from the light touch of the air and nervous last-minute adjustments. I used to go to the theater often, just to feel the rush when the curtain reveals its secrets. But lately, plays haven't offered even that trepidation. They merely switch the lights on and off, which has nothing to do with that unhurried premonition that art requires.

Margarita, just by saying her name aloud, drew back the dark curtain that had covered my life in recent years. With a single word she erased the lethargy and brought back the pain.

I've finished all the assignments set by Matías. I do my literary exercises imagining I'm listening to Margarita. I must confess, the exercises have helped me. They've sent me back to the roller coaster of writing, although I can't say for sure whether these peaks and valleys I go through aren't linked to the times I'm close to Margarita or apart from her.

The night we went out for dinner and drinks was almost perfect, like a delicate glass. Love equals love plus the fear of losing what you love. That's why the first thing I did when I got home, after the bizarre episode with that guy Gonzalo, was to shuffle the letters of her name: MARGARITA LAMBERT.

According to my notes, one must discard those combinations that have nothing to do with us, at least for the moment. I mean constructions without sense, that are almost primitive. For example: *Grab material mart*, *Bar Magritte alarm*, *I am tart-barrel Mag*, *A marram bilge tart*, or *Marriagable Marta T*. Also, the several, likewise irrelevant, that relate to animals—*A grim lab-rat tamer* and *a rat-ram-tiger-lamb*—and to eating them, in the form of *a grim lamb tartare* and *Gibraltar ram meat*.

So that only a few remarkable cards are left. If you pay attention, you'll find that the remaining elements can be gathered into semantic groups according to the law of similarity, sometimes by metaphoric dynamic and others by metonymic dynamic.

R a Big Mama Rattler and *A Mamba Aglitter* complement each other, a pair of snakes, a deadly threat, but with the clear erotic suggestion that the image of the snake always contains. (And while I'm talking of suggestive snakes: *Marital Garter . . . Bam!*)

AAA Grim Battler M. R. and *Great Martial Bram* show the clear presence of two of the fathers of the Gothic, M. R. James and Bram Stoker. And the presence, too, of their dark under-world is also here reinforced with drugs (*a bitter gram alarm*) and whores (*a bar tart aglimmer*), no less than you would expect.

But for what I really want to tell you (and that's the only reason I've invited you this evening, or late into tonight, and also the reason for my long rant), the remaining three are decisive.

Marital Barrage MT is an almost offensive allusion to the violent death of a lover, like the death of Margarita caused by that biker. Here we could narrow it down, it's not a case of metonymy or metaphor: just the hard and irrevocable blow of reality. But the two that remain are the most specific, the most conclusive. For this Margarita aspires to be a writer—*I, a Grammar Battler*—and to be a kickboxer—*Martial Arts Grab Me*. And this time the threatened *marital barrage* might be no more than an empty threat (an *MT* threat?), since Margarita's life somehow depends on me. And this time around, I'm willing to do anything to save her.

From what? What am I going to save her from? From death, of course. We always are, in every circumstance, fighting off death. The problem is not from what, but how and when, and that's precisely what I haven't yet deciphered. On paper, Margarita's name is very clear, and so is the threat, but there aren't any major clues.

Here's the piece of paper the biker gave me on that night of onomatomania. There you have it, the piece of paper that confirms I'm not mad, that I'm telling the truth.

7

Lecter & Co.

The next time I saw Matías, I knew it was hopeless. In under two weeks, a crevice that muddled his features had taken hold of his face. Pedro Álamo's surprising call inviting me to his place on a Friday night had had unforeseen effects.

As soon as he set foot in Chef Woo's I recognized the streaking twitches, like magnetic field lines, of the addict. Matías knew I'd notice his relapse, but the fact that I had missed our last meet-up had somehow given him license to go back to using drugs.

"How's *La Noche* going?" The novel, like an old friend, had a nickname. "I need an update."

My words sounded too enthusiastic. I'd broken the homeopathic rule of helping the defeated: let them sink till they can't take it any longer, and offer a hand only when they feel that it's time to come back to the surface.

"It's not," he said.

"Well, some weeks are worse than others. I've got some material you may find useful."

Matías didn't seem too impressed.

"It's a long article that came out when the news of the case first broke. It's by Alejandro Peralti, have you heard of him?"

Matías drank some beer and gently set the bottle down on the table.

"No," he said.

"He became famous for *Sane as a Hatter*. The book, among other things, is a collection of short biographies of psychiatrists, both real and fictional, who ended up mad or in prison or accused of multiple perversions or terrible crimes. Its publication caused a real stir in medical circles because Peralti was a psychiatrist himself."

"That's crazy," said Matías. He seemed to be listening now.

"I know. He was expelled from the Argentine Medical Association and they took away his license. It wasn't even because of the book, or not only because of it, but because they found out the therapy methods he had used on his patients were, how can I put it, too *alternative*. The guy had been combining neurolinguistic programming, yoga and marijuana."

"A visionary. If I'd known, I never would have started therapy with you."

"What you do with your life is up to you. Last time this happened, we agreed I wouldn't interfere again."

"It's only temporary."

"That's what you always say."

Matías is one of the few writers who can truly say writing is a terrible habit. His literary projects have been unfailingly associated with the consumption of some drugs and certain bits of reading.

At first, as one might expect, it was alcohol. Via Poe-Hemingway-Bukowski. Then it was marijuana, hash and opium (although I don't believe he dared to smoke opium). Via De Quincey-Baudelaire. And only recently, cocaine, LSD and amphetamines. Via Ramos Sucre-Hunter S. Thompson-Philip K. Dick. All of them terrific writers, all addicts and all dead (in Ramos Sucre's case, Matías came up with a syllogism linking cocaine, insomnia and this Cumaná writer's work).

We revisited this journey during therapy. For Matías it was a map of his life that had been unconsciously drawn.

When we first met, he was already in the Phildickian phase of his turmoil. He lent me *The Three Stigmata of Palmer Eldritch*. It was his way of going straight to the point. I didn't fully get that book, apart from the obvious: Philip K. Dick was an addict and a paranoiac. Plus: Philip K. Dick readers are also addicts and paranoiacs. Matías had joined an online PKD fan club (they used this acronym to refer to him), where they would debate the high points of his life.

Not long after, Matías would insist I had saved him. I don't remember doing all that much. I merely reframed his moral compass before showing it back to him. His was a damaged instrument, missing some pieces, but still pointing north.

Matías had a son he used to consider a constant source of guilt and hope. He had conceived him in Santa Elena de Uairén, a town on the Brazilian border, with a woman who'd been, in his own words, the love of his life. I never knew the woman's name, or why he had gone to live so far away, nor did I know the reasons he'd had to leave that place for good, to set out on one of those typical back-packing journeys across Latin America from which most young Latin American backpackers return silent and feverish.

His son's name was, or still is, Santiago. That much I knew. I also knew he had him at twenty. At the time of our first sessions, Santiago was the same age Matías had been when he moved to Santa Elena de Uairén. This symmetry merely served to emphasize Matías's hopelessness. In the depths of his drug-induced comedowns, and at the heights of his hallucina-tions, the abandoned, fading image of Santiago would appear to him. It was a coin that, depending on his mood, would urge him either to sink completely or to try to save himself.

Uncharacteristically, I got carried away with Freudian theory and suggested that this painful image of his son, accentuated by the intervening twenty years, was a clear case of projection: Santiago, during these appearances, symbolized Matías himself, his youth and dreams, the despair at seeing what his existence had come to, but also his still strong determination to recover.

"You're telling me Santiago is not Santiago," he said.

"Santiago is Santiago, but he's not your son anymore."

"You mean in the images, or in life?"

"In neither. How long since you last saw him, since you last heard from him?"

"I haven't seen him in fourteen years. But I know he moved to the US two years ago."

"What's he doing there?"

"I don't know."

"What's his girlfriend's name? Is it a girlfriend he's got or a boyfriend? Does he drink coffee? What baseball team does he support? Does he even like baseball?"

"I don't know."

"You see what I mean? The heart, Matías, like any other organ, grows, but there's a point when it settles into a fixed structure. Some emotions come too late in life, when it's almost biologically impossible to develop certain feelings, or even to contemplate them. Not even resentment, since the passing years remove us from the pain we've suffered and, especially, from the pain we've inflicted. That's when, getting beyond the various images we use to kid ourselves, we begin, and never stop, mourning for ourselves."

That's all I did. I helped Matías desacralize the image, or the story, of his son. That and talked about Philip K. Dick. Talking about PKD would relax him more than the tranquilizers I pre-scribed ever would. Therapy sessions gradually turned into a book club. I'm not sure whether we went as far as discussing these terms, perhaps it was just an unspoken agreement, but all I needed to do, for him to stay clean, was meet his weekly reading assignments.

I agreed to exchange emails during the week, something I don't normally do with my patients, so as to share any *burning issues*. That's how Matías put it, and it was an excuse for him to send me articles, interviews, links to websites that specialized in PKD, science fiction, electronic music, cinema and designer drugs.

I would be lying if I said those conversations about literature had an exclusively therapeutic goal. Or that they helped only Matías. I'm the sort of person who would choose a science degree while secretly wanting to be an artist, or to admire art, or to feel its touch. The sort of person who would approach writers with the nostalgic urgency of an exile. As if literature were the homeland one had been forced to leave behind after some dramatic turn of events.

I have never actually done what I've just written. I am too shy or too proud to even think about approaching a writer. I have never asked for an autograph. Let alone shown a writer my texts, those questionable trophies made of intentions that one accumulates over time. I have never done it, but I have seen strangers do it, and friends and colleagues too. I have seen them, and I have been a bit embarrassed, for them and for myself, because I can understand perfectly why they do it.

My long-standing stoicism crumbled when I met Matías. First, I dared to articulate laconic and accurate comments during our literary sessions. Then, I loosened up and wrote long and disjointed emails with bookish opinions I had previously kept to myself, gathering dust, for many years.

Three months passed in which I not only talked about literature but was paid to do it. And just when the pleasure of talking started to be tainted by guilt, Matías asked me the question I secretly hoped someone would ask:

"Do you write?" he wrote in one of his emails.

"Yes," I replied. "But I wouldn't classify what I do as literary practice. Literary *rehearsal*, maybe. I'm sending you something anyway." Two finished stories of medium length and a good number of short texts and miscellanea under a page long.

"You have vision," was all Matías said. I never knew what he meant by that. I didn't ask either. He invited me to join his creative-writing workshop. I understood this was a way of continuing our conversations in a different environment.

"Have you taken anything the last few months?" I asked him one day.

"Only a few joints."

"How many?"

"A few. Only some nights, when I can't sleep."

"You have to cut it out."

"OK."

That's how we ended therapy and I began to attend his workshop.

"Has something happened?" I said. Matías had been quiet for several minutes.

"Why do you ask?"

"You know why. A few weeks ago, things were going well, you seemed really excited about the novel. And now this."

"It's all fucked up."

"Uh huh, but why?"

"Because of Anthony Hopkins."

"Are you fucking kidding me?"

"It's true."

"Look, if you don't want to talk, just say so."

"I don't, but I'm telling you the truth."

"OK. Can you tell me what Anthony Hopkins has done to you?"

"He made me realize it's all fucked up. Or rather, that it's always gonna be fucked up, and you can never really know why. You never know, but at the same time you can't help asking. For instance, what happened to Rosalinda Villegas in the end? What happened in that consulting room?"

"They quarreled and it all ended unfortunately badly."

"Just like that."

"Yes, just like that. Boring and absurd, if you will, but it's pretty likely that's how it was."

"So why throw the body in Parque Caiza?"

"Cowardice, despair. Same old, Matías."

He didn't seem convinced.

"I don't really get why it's so hard for you to see it," I said.

"Did you watch Dr. Montesinos's first statement to the press?"

"I did, at the time."

"You need to watch it again. Look it up online, it's priceless. When he's asked about the traces of Rosalinda's blood they found in his consulting room, he says they could have found similar traces from many patients. He applied electroconvulsive therapy to his patients, so they'd often bleed. That's what he says. Are you with me? That line is amazing. Then the journalist asks him about his alleged relationship with Rosalinda, to which she confessed in the last post on her blog. And Montesinos, with chilling modesty, goes and dismisses the claim saying that many patients used to fall in love with him through the mechanism of transference. 'Female patients,' he clarifies, and laughs. But the best is yet to come, because toward the end of the interview, something unbelievable happens, when Dr. Montesinos, in his own smug and twisted way, confesses. Being over seventy, he'd be placed under house arrest if found guilty.

'And what do you think you'd be doing if that happened?' asks the journalist. Montesinos answers, with a big grin filled with confidence, or feigned confidence, that he has a vast library at home. 'I could reread the classics at last. Perhaps I could fulfill my most secret vocation: writing.'"

"Writing," repeated Matías. "Do you get it now?"

I don't know whether I was having a bad night or if whatever Matías was taking gave him an impenetrable lucidity, but I didn't fully get what he was saying.

"And the bit about Anthony Hopkins?" I asked.

Matías made a show of pausing here, making me wait for his answer. He ordered two more beers.

"That same night, when I got bored of watching videos and poring over statements, I turned on the TV. Jodie Foster appeared, running in an FBI training camp. I caught it from the start and watched it until the end. *The Silence of the Lambs*—or *The Silence of the Innocents* as the terrible Spanish translation would have it. The dialogues between Foster and Hopkins, between special agent Starling and Dr. Lecter, really got to me. Hannibal Lecter. Now that's what I call a character. I bet not one of the psychiatrists Peralti mentions is fit to tie Lecter's shoelaces."

"Peralti mentions him, of course. He says the character created by Harris is like a mythical figure that sets the boundary. Only Radovan Karadzic comes close. But not quite."

Radovan Karadzic's story is the most interesting in the book. Radovan Karadzic, a psychiatrist, was one of the people responsible for the ethnic massacres in the Balkans during the first half of the nineties. A nationalist who became president of Serbia, the Serbian Republic in Bosnian territory, who longed for, in an ultimate redundancy and obsession with the identical, a Serbia only for the Serbs.

In 1996, when the political situation turned against him, Karadzic disappeared. The United States offered a multimillion-dollar reward for his capture. Twelve years on, he was detained to face charges for war crimes and genocide. Where had Karadzic been hiding during those twelve years? Like Poe's purloined letter, Karadzic had been hiding in plain sight: in the city of Belgrade itself.

Karadzic had lived there under an assumed name, Dragan Dabic, selling multi-vitamins and promoting the advantages of alternative medicine with discretion and success. How did that happen?, Peralti asks himself. What kind of society protects a mass murderer, masquerading as a new-age guru, whose long white beard made him look like Santa Claus? "People claim he was nice and well loved. He wrote children's stories," Peralti concludes ironically.

"A mass murderer dressed up as Santa Claus is quite good," said Matías. "A mass murderer psychiatrist is even better. But a cannibal psychiatrist is unbeatable. While watching the movie I couldn't help comparing Lecter to Dr. Montesinos. When they confirmed Montesinos was involved and they searched his apartment, they found a DVD. It contained footage of women in a bathroom, checking themselves in the mirror, touching up their makeup, peeing and sometimes taking a shit. The footage was taken with a hidden camera. A camera hidden in the bathroom of one of Dr. Montesinos's consulting rooms. I also heard the story of a medical inspector whose car brakes were apparently cut, or ordered to be cut, by Montesinos, causing the man to crash and nearly die. And similarly, many other stories, or rumors about stories. All of them reprehensible, it's true, but of a wickedness that's so vulgar, a viciousness that's so crude, that they are pathetic. Or funny, or repulsive. But never scary, never terrifying."

"Would you have preferred it if Montesinos had won the presidential election and become a mass murderer? Would that be better for your story?"

"Yeah. I think so."

I thought Matías was winding me up. Then I remembered Pedro Álamo's words, and for the first time, I questioned the benefits of having Matías as a friend.

"There's no experience without tangible and exemplary fear," he said. "So yeah, I think having Montesinos as president and mass murderer would have been the better option for the story. Not so much, or not only, for *my* story, the one I wanted to tell, but for the story we're living out. Just think about the dead. Almost two hundred thousand killed in the last ten years by what the journalists so cynically call *common delinquency*. Two hundred thousand murders that weren't committed in the name of any ideology, or by decree, or to follow any particular political or ethnic objective.

"You always hear about a lack of leadership. And when people talk about it they're always referring to positive leadership. Nobody in this country has realized as yet that evil needs worthy representatives too. Men and women up to the task of representing our hatred and resentment. Our president is a clown—a clown out of a Stephen King novel, but a clown just the same. That kind of power, which makes you laugh but kills you, corrodes more than serious power does, where the very presence of its leaders or symbols is a cause of fear. It's a power that, instead of stabbing you, lets someone else do it and merely watches as you bleed to death. And sometimes not even that, because often that same power decides it's best to turn around and walk away.

"Miguel, this is a dictatorship. Everybody here knows it with more or less certainty, all of us can feel it. But there's no way of saying it without sounding silly, like those kids who cry when they see clowns."

"What are you going to do, then?" I said.

"For now, keep listening to Morphine. Seriously, listening to their albums is an anesthetic. I fall asleep listening to them. Mark Sandman's story is fascinating. And exemplary too, following on what we've been talking about. He was lucky enough to fulfill every artist's dream: to die onstage."

Beacons

The piece of paper that the biker gave Pedro Álamo *said*:

TEXT COMPRESSED FOR CENSORSHIP
ΠAQRES.Ppppp
UβλYZLNEOOOφ
4Aπ4θBEɪ0@TLNE
O2ηπ@TINVU
YNINVUU²AET
2BA*2AV8A†AC
2CA♥Eπ4LNEFXU72LE
NEELⅼⅼⅼⅼ
OL ½Aπ4A√2C
4WρμDəNμ2UBɘ2
(QTLNEɪ@π)

Álamo let Miguel Ardiles take the piece of paper away with him. It was a transcription of the *original* the biker had given him that night.

"We can meet again next Friday if you want. Or do you need more than a week?"

Miguel thought about Matías Rye. Missing one of their meet-ups was considered high treason. Missing two in a row would be sheer neglect.

"I can't do next Friday," said Ardiles.

Álamo seemed flattered by the answer.

"Very good. I'll give you two weeks to solve it, then."

Miguel didn't solve the riddle in those two weeks, instead he just added two more people's problems to his life.

He devoted about forty-five minutes to the piece of paper from the supposed biker. He didn't decipher a thing or find any clue that might reveal a secret message. He just got dizzy from banging his head against that wall of letters and symbols. He started to think Pedro Álamo might be a paranoid-schizophrenic.

The Friday after his long conversation with Álamo, Miguel met Matías Rye. That night, he left Chef Woo's feeling worried. Matías had given up the novel, he'd started using again and, worst of all, he had shifted the focus of his attention. Or rather, he had prioritized a new focus, a spotlight brighter than the previous one. White light on black light. The brightness of an idea in the middle of the night, moving away infinitely until it was indistinguishable from the pale, disorientating fabric of the morning.

Mark Sandman was, officially, the new *beacon* of his existence. Sandman's life and work were what seemed exemplary to him now. Under this influence, amid the cigarette haze usually associated with blues, rock and jazz, Matías decided to give up *conscious* writing and instead follow a rigorous improvisational technique.

"And what happened to the night, the death of classic crime fiction, the return of the Gothic genre? Where is all that?"

"It's out."

"You mean you're done with it."

"No. I've only left it out. On the periphery, if you see what I mean. Before, that was the content of my writing. Now, darkness, fear and intuition have become the atmosphere around it. It's a tunnel where my words walk in line and then get lost. And my words are like drunken detectives that follow other words that are more intelligent and faster."

Miguel didn't insist. He thought about Sherlock Holmes, bored in his house on Baker Street, with no cases to solve, injecting morphine. He thought all madmen, drug addicts and saints were drunken detectives, savage and deluded.

"How did you say Sandman died?" asked Miguel.

"On stage. In '99, during a concert on the outskirts of Rome."

"Yes, but how did he die?"

"Heart attack."

"Natural causes?"

"All heart-attack deaths are by natural causes, Miguel."

"Yes, if you suffer from a heart condition or you're eighty. Not if you've sniffed a bag of blow or get carried away injecting shit."

"Don't be so sure. It's especially natural in these cases. According to the logic followed by the body, it's natural."

"I see what you're saying. If it's natural, in the sense you are implying, it's even a good thing."

"It isn't good or bad. It just is."

Miguel Ardiles had to wait until he got home to go online and research at his leisure. Sandman had indeed died on July 3, 1999, in the middle of a performance. And, as he suspected, a heroin overdose circulated as an unconfirmed cause of death.

Heroin.

Apart from unrefined distillations such as crack or coca base, and the many permutations of synthetic drugs, heroin was the last artificial paradise Rye had yet to visit.

Only then, completely out of sync, did Miguel Ardiles notice the comment Matías Rye had made when they said goodbye.

"We should camp out around your place," said Rye.

"I've got a two-bedroom apartment. You can come and stay for a few days if you need to. But, honestly, I don't think it'd be a good idea."

Matías began laughing on the inside. Like an idiot, thought Miguel.

"I said we should camp *around* your place. Around the mountains of Parque Caiza. One night, that's all."

Miguel smiled.

"What will we do? Read Lovecraft?" he said.

"Yes. Or kill a bird and eat it. Or listen to Morphine. Or watch the night," said Matías.

"I'll pass," said Miguel. And, almost without realizing, he hugged Matías for the first time.

Matías had had similar ideas in the past. Reading *Night Creatures* by Centeno deep in the Ávila National Park, using the Silla de Caracas mountains as a green velvet sofa. Taking a tab of LSD, dropping ecstasy and writing a two-hundred-page novel, no shorter, no longer, guided by the *I Ching*, all in a single night. And some other plans Miguel didn't remember. He carried out some of them. Or at least he tried. The results weren't too praiseworthy, nor were they too disastrous: hangovers, one page of writing here and there, flu, some minor theft.

After some tossing and turning in bed, Miguel Ardiles got up and went over to the window. The highway allowed itself to be sensed from afar through a dirty murmur, like a turbine. Only the lower buildings of the development were visible, and the poorly lit communal areas. And, in the background, the night. Total darkness. The thick scrub, almost liquid in its malleability, where they'd dumped the corpses. Women murdered and left behind. The killers hadn't even bothered to bury them. He wasn't sure why, but this detail made him angry. It was a final discourtesy, he thought, looking out the window. As if you could snub a woman even after her death. Walk out on her, instead of burying her. Leave her waiting for the neighbors to smell her dead scent, that divine moisture, now disregarded, which they didn't want to distill, or didn't know how.

Ardiles walked over to the bookshelf, picked out Peralti's book and got back into bed. He read random passages. Between its pages, there was a photocopy of the article Peralti had written about Dr. Montesinos's case. Ardiles read it from beginning to end. He underlined two sentences he hadn't noticed before and looked for the notebook where he kept quotes from the things he'd read, as well as handwritten comments about those readings.

Ardiles had the strange habit of collecting arguments against himself. He gathered other people's skeptical or contradicting quotes, things that criticized the practice of medicine and psychiatry. It was his anchor.

A psychiatrist is a doctor who always arrives late, he had noted down once. *He is like an ambulance driver doing the midnight shift, who, on his sordid rounds, tries to salvage the battered fragments that still throb in the middle of the street. Cold slices of heart that can be crushed over and over again, no matter how small or battered they are.*

That's how Ardiles sees himself: somebody who draws little bits of life toward the shore.

Ardiles felt this kind of moral jetlag in the case of the adolescent from the Plan de Manzano neighborhood. He was accused of drug trafficking. When they caught him, he had a sports bag packed full of drugs. His mother claimed some local thugs had tricked him, they'd set him up, her boy had never set foot outside Plan de Manzano, her son was suffering from mental retardation. Apparently, having been tipped off about a police raid, some guys asked the boy to hang on to the bag, knowing that Ramiro always helped everyone. (Was that his name, Miguel wondered?)

Ramiro had trouble speaking. He hardly understood the questions Miguel asked him. And it was clear he didn't grasp the seriousness of the situation. Ramiro's mother was desperate. The kid was locked up at La Planta prison, with rapists, murderers and *common* delinquents. Miguel Ardiles confirmed that Ramiro was suffering from a mental retardation, that he hardly understood what had happened, that there was no way he could be involved knowingly in any illegal activity, and that it was a matter of urgency, considering his disability and the fact his life was at risk, that he be moved to a medical institution until the hearing took place.

Since his report was to be sent as soon as possible, and in terms that left no room for doubt, Miguel Ardiles dared to go beyond his strictly clinical responsibilities and tried to influence the case.

A couple of weeks later, Miguel received a call from the judge assigned to the case. She told him, sobbing, that they'd killed Ramiro. The usual clash among inmates over control of the drug business. Ardiles pictured the edge of the blade piercing Ramiro's entrails while his now useless report doubtless lay among the many papers in the office of the prison warden's secretary.

It was the first time Miguel heard a judge—male or female—crying. He hadn't cried yet himself, but he'd learn soon enough.

The boy was six. His body was covered in scars, long and short. That was, in broad strokes, the story of his life. His mother had hated him since he was born. When he was three years old, she'd started methodically abusing him. At first, she would tie him to the sink in the evening and leave him there until morning. Then, when she got hold of the cage, she turned him into an even more domesticated animal. The boy was the youngest of a scattered bunch of children. Some had died, others had moved to the provinces and still others had crossed the border to Colombia. One of them discovered what was going on during an unexpected visit. He was terrified by what he saw. Even though his mother had never been a loving person, the other children couldn't say she used to make a habit of beating them, let alone torturing them. At most, she gave them the occasional thrashing, just enough to prevent them from becoming hoodlums themselves.

The mother claimed she did it because the boy was crazy and liked pinching himself, cutting himself and banging himself against the wall. That, according to her, explained the bruises and scars. Later, it was discovered the boy was born out of rape.

Both the psychologist and the neurologist came out of their cubicles in tears. First one and then the other. Miguel watched them with some disdain. The antipathy he already felt toward the two of them was aggravated by their lack of composure.

After eating a cookie and drinking some water, the boy went into Miguel's office for his last interview of the day. Miguel Ardiles came out of his office half an hour after they had taken the boy away. Once in the corridor, he ran into the psychologist and the neurologist, who were still discussing the details of the case. Miguel couldn't hide the red in his eyes or the wet rim of his blocked nose.

Miguel Ardiles never complained. No one had forced him to do this job. He only wondered, with almost sportsmanlike curiosity, how much further he could push himself.

After all the things he'd seen over the last few years, it would have been indecent to reflect on who he was, or why he was a forensic psychiatrist and not a writer. Other people's pain made him take his own story out of his life. Like the large foundation blocks used when building great structures, which then are removed, leaving a necessary void that is invisible in the final result. Or like a third-person narrator, a piece of glass only justifiable by its transparency. Since glass, when broken, distorts things. Or, even worse, it cuts.

The night of insomnia was over, and now it was Tuesday. He had had the worrying encounter with Matías last Friday. This Friday he'd go back to Pedro Álamo's. Looking at his diary and the consultations he had booked for the day at his private practice, Miguel Ardiles mused that, rather than being a day, Tuesday is a hinge. A hinge in an old door, like the ones that open just a crack in horror movies.

He just read the patient's first name and knew at once that it was her: on this Tuesday he was going to meet Margarita Lambert.

9

Revelations at Mr. Morrison's

On Friday, on the second and final evening Miguel Ardiles would spend at Pedro Álamo's, Álamo seemed to have forgotten the task he had set his former psychiatrist. He didn't mention the text the biker had given him that night, or show him the decoded message. Ardiles understood that, after two weeks of trying to find Margarita, Álamo had decided to face up to his destiny.

"She doesn't answer my emails, her cell-phone number won't connect, she hasn't been back to the workshop," said Álamo.

His expression was friendly. He brought a tray from the kitchen with a couple of coasters, a bottle of whiskey, two glasses with ice and a jug of water.

"Help yourself," he said, heading into his room.

He came back with two Macs. He put them on the dinner table, plugged them in and switched them on. The computers started up, and Álamo invited Ardiles to take a seat in front of one of them.

"Tetris," he announced cheerfully after a few suspenseful seconds.

Álamo had the manners of a mystic. He smelled tragedies and transcendental configurations amid normality, or else showed total calmness in critical situations. And this was a critical situation.

Ardiles wanted to tell him that Margarita had come to his

office, that she was very beautiful, and that she was in danger. But he didn't dare alter the order of events Álamo had planned for their evening. Not only because it isn't advisable to wake a madman from his delirium, an obsessive from his routines, a somnambulist from his nocturnal incursions. But because it seemed that ignoring the abyss was part of their script for the night.

They went to a games website and started playing. Ardiles needed to sign up first. The words *El Gaucho Rubio vs. Darío Mancini* appeared at the top of the screen on both computers. Álamo didn't ask Ardiles about his username. Ardiles, on the other hand, couldn't help himself from asking Álamo about his.

"It came to me in a dream, a long time ago. I haven't told you about my dreams. Not because I'm shy, it's not that. It's just that dreams are the most important part of my life, so one mustn't talk about them. Also, what's going on at surface level is more than enough. The surface tells you how things could have been."

Álamo paused the game to give him a tip: by pressing the shift key, he could put a tricky piece on hold and use it whenever he needed it.

"Dreaming about the life of some guy called Darío *Mancini*, which is almost *Lancini*, but not quite, tells you a lot about my own life. It let me see the unique chord in each letter. Or a different stage in the migration of our souls, if you prefer. Lancini, Mancini, Nancini, etc.—do you follow? There are certain names under which certain patterns of existence are grouped, which other people, with different names but identical souls, spend their whole lives searching for. Almost always, these lightweight beings never get to identify the model they are instinctively following. They're the ones who feel the absurdity of life most brutally. Moreover, there is an infinitesimal percentage of equally lost beings who, faced with a lack of guidance figures, forge themselves into role models. These will be the heavier beings, the heroes. And lastly, there is a substantial percentage made up of what I call the middleweights, with whom I identify, who are the middle class of the spiritual spectrum. They are the ones who recognize which life path to follow and go down that route, but leave no trace. Their existences are the necessary little voids needed for the great truths to reverberate, like a constant murmur that resonates over time."

Only once, three years earlier, had Álamo been able to verify the authenticity of part of his dreams. He was at the El Buscón bookstore, killing time before going to watch a movie, when his hand and somebody else's met on the cover of a book. It was *Birds of Latin America* by Augusto Monterroso.

"Excuse me," said the woman.

She was a beautiful lady, very elegant, with brown hair.

"Don't worry, go ahead," said Álamo.

"No, you take it, I was only looking."

"Thank you. I just need to check something."

Álamo quickly looked for the index of names, went to page forty-three and pressed on a line several times, as if hastily calling for an elevator.

"It's in here, I'd better take it."

"It's good. They're Monterroso's views on other authors. Although he repeats many pieces found in his earlier books."

"I understand. But there's hardly any information around on what I'm looking for, so I'd still rather have it."

"What are you looking for?"

"References to Lancini. Darío Lancini, I don't know whether you know him."

The woman laughed.

"The terrible thing is, I can't actually say I know him that well," she said after a while.

She laughed again.

"I'm sorry, I find these things amusing. I'm Darío's wife. Antonieta Madrid, pleased to meet you."

Pedro Álamo was petrified. He had to spur himself to react and extend his hand.

"Pedro Álamo," he said.

A shadow passed over her eyes.

"Writer?" she asked.

"No," said Álamo. "I work in advertising. But I love your husband's work."

"Come and meet him. Darío!" cried the woman.

They went over to where an older man, thin and with a long mustache, stood. That is how Pedro Álamo met Darío Lancini.

"I was shaking, Miguel," Álamo said. "I started sweating. I was blushing."

"Darío, this gentleman happened to be looking for information about you."

"I'm your biggest fan," said Álamo.

Those were his first words to Lancini.

"Can you believe it?" said Álamo to Ardiles. "Can you believe I made such an ass of myself?"

Álamo was pleased to discover Lancini was as shy as he was. On hearing those words, he'd gone just as red as Álamo.

"I'll leave you two alone," said Antonieta, and she carried on browsing books.

"There was an awkward silence," said Álamo to Ardiles. "Or rather, I was the only one who found the silence awkward. Lancini looked at me and the green transparency of his eyes told me he found that silence amusing; that, in fact, he could remain in that situation, silent, forever."

"I was looking for a text in which Monterroso talks about you and other Mexican palindromists," said Álamo. "You lived in Mexico, didn't you?"

"I did," said Lancini.

Another silence. Álamo was about to say goodbye, defeated as he was, but forced himself to say something.

"What are you working on now?" he said, just to say something.

"*Now?*" repeated Lancini. The word seemed to amuse him particularly. "*Now* I'm working on double-texts."

"What's that?" said Álamo.

Lancini's eyes brightened. He explained what they were by using a familiar example:

"*Alone, too, by myself, but noble, no regrets.* You know the line, I suppose? But it can also be read as *A loan to buy mice, elf, but no bell nor egrets.*"

From that point on, the conversation flowed. He then tested him.

"Here's one," said Lancini. "*Fighters sold war for fun.* So go on, how else can you read it, other than as a headline about mercenaries?"

"*Fighters sold war for fun,*" Álamo repeated to himself. "*Fight a* something?" he began.

"Uh huh," said Lancini, with an approving nod, like a Latin grammar teacher.

"*Fight a . . . a sole dwarf. A sole dwarf.* What else?"

"What kind of dwarf?"

"*A sole dwarf. . . . A sole dwarf orphan? Fight a sole dwarf orphan!*" exclaimed Álamo.

"Very good. A powerful transformation," said Lancini stifling a laugh. "A story about a great betrayal in war transmuted into a fight with a solo dwarf."

Álamo could hardly hide his excitement.

"Another one," said Lancini. "*Two real eyes watered—I, alone.*"

This time Álamo couldn't come up with an answer, make the right cuts to create a new sentence.

"*To realize war, to die alone,*" said Lancini.

They spent half an hour like that, sharing word games.

"Have you played for long enough?" said Antonieta suddenly. She seemed like a mother coming to fetch her children.

They said goodbye to each other with a firm handshake. It was then that Álamo put his foot in it.

"I wanted to talk to him again," Álamo explained to Ardiles, "I wanted to find out whether everything I'd dreamed about for years was real. But I didn't think Lancini wanted to waste more time with me because I was a nobody after all. So I made up something about how, apart from being in advertising, I was a journalist and wanted to interview him, to write a profile on his work and life."

"No," said Lancini resoundingly. "I am Nobody."

Antonieta and Darío left. Álamo watched through the glass walls of the bookstore, as they walked away, back into the storyline of one of his dreams.

Despite the unfortunate ending, Álamo was exultant. He could confirm that Lancini had indeed lived in Mexico.

Miguel couldn't understand Álamo's excitement about a fact that could surely be found by googling, or by looking in some library or just by asking around.

"There's hardly any information about Lancini," said Álamo. "In 1975 he published *OIRADARIO*. Twenty-one years on, Monte Ávila published a second edition, this time with a title in the double style: *Oír a Darío.* That later edition is important as it includes the picture by Vasco Szinetar and the letter from Julio Cortázar. Apart from that, from Monterroso's references and some other scattered articles, there isn't much about him. And I discovered that day that a part of my dreams coincides, temporally and geographically, with Lancini's life. If that's the case, there is nothing to stop me thinking that other parts of my dreams may also coincide."

"Just because Lancini was in Mexico," said Ardiles.

"Because of that and Antonieta. Don't forget about Antonieta. Don't you think the fact Antonieta is Lancini's wife is a strong enough sign?"

"I'm tired. My fingers hurt."

"I could go on playing all night. But don't worry, let's move onto the sofa."

Ardiles lay down on the sofa next to the window. Álamo occupied a black recliner.

"A sign of what?" said Ardiles.

"Antonieta Madrid was one of the three judges who gave my short story the award," said Álamo.

That coincidence, symbolized by those two hands randomly coming to rest on the same book, confirmed once again the real foundation of the system of signs and intuitions that constituted his life. The award wasn't just a prank by Oswaldo Trejo. Evidently, there was something about the text that had attracted Antonieta from the outset. Something undefined, not even comprehensible, to which she wanted to remain forever connected by awarding it the prize.

"Ever since I was a boy, I've always believed that literature is an act of unrequited love, deliberately constructed *not* to be requited. For example, I've always felt uncomfortable about the expectations created by novels. The promise of passion and adventure that from the start is set to fail. I think it's unfair the way feelings are encouraged into existence just for the pleasure of seeing them fall. The same with writers: they leave us a sentence or an image that may change our lives, and then when we realize this and want to search for its origin, they turn out to have died many years ago, as they say happens with long-dead stars and the traces of their glow.

"But writers suffer too. Most of them have lived and written without ever finding an answer, a light on the far shore that might confirm there's someone there, somewhere. I may be an anonymous and failed writer, but at least I did once find my ideal reader. Someone whose soul synced perfectly with my text, even if the circumstances surrounding the production, and especially the reception, of that text weren't a totally perfect match. In 1982, according to my sources, Antonieta and Darío were back in Venezuela after their stay in Athens, their lives now welded together. Around this same time, I began to consciously recognize the path my life might take. I wrote the short story; I sank into my own hell and was partially rescued by Sarita Calcaño. But, as you can see, life had something in store for us both: for me, an absurd persistence with an aimless existence, and for Sarita, the street and madness."

Miguel Ardiles looked at his watch and decided that was enough for one night. This time they said goodbye without ceremony. Álamo's unchanging, puerile smile annoyed Ardiles.

In his car, pulling out of Santa Inés to take the highway, Miguel Ardiles kept thinking about Álamo's words. He had created a character out of a jumble of air and had designated it the role of a shadow, of a symbiotic existence that looked only for the leftovers of greater entities. And what about himself? he wondered. What character and role had been designed by his will or his unconscious to govern his life? For so long had he been the threshold across which other stories traveled that the image he had of himself had faded. Every three or four months he would undergo this sense of unease. He needed the sensation of being touched.

He pulled off the highway, took the Altamira road and headed for Mr. Morrison's.

When he walked in, the speakers were blasting the Christian rock that Magdalena liked so much. Miguel Ardiles followed her twists and contortions with familiarity and, as always, the cumulative effect (the name, the music, her beauty) made him feel he was experiencing something quasi-mystical.

It was still quite a while till Gioconda's routine. He sat at the bar and focused on the flow of women. If he wanted to be with her, he needed to hunt her down early.

"What's going on, doctor?" said a woman. She was wearing a very slight, yellow bikini and black-rimmed glasses. A lethal combination, thought Ardiles the first time he saw her.

"Where have you been?" asked Ardiles.

"Around."

"Will you stay with me tonight?"

"I don't know. It's still too early."

"Get yourself a drink."

"Nice. Now you're top of my list."

"Stay with me, just the two of us."

"You'll still leave, in the end. Save your money."

She kissed him on the corner of his mouth and proceeded on her fishlike way through that current of perfumed and oily air.

After a while, a woman's voice from the speakers announced Gioconda. "Nothing Else Matters" by Metallica started playing. It was the romantic part of the song. These sequences were all the same. Gioconda, however, with those dark-rimmed glasses on, suggested a more complex inner life than the rest of the girls. After a few encounters, having talked beyond the stereotypical porn-like dialogues, he had been able to glimpse Gioconda's personality. And apart from the rimmed glasses, she was like every other prostitute.

Metallica gave way to Rammstein. The walk in the woods had ended and Gioconda was falling into a hell without hope.

Two dominatrices came on stage and the hardcore routine began.

When the song ended, the three girls left the stage laughing like cashiers at the end of their shift.

Three whiskeys later, Ardiles looked into his wallet. He had two of his credit cards. He made up his mind and called Gioconda over.

"Let's go," he said. "We're having therapy today."

"Whatever the doctor says," replied Gioconda.

Ardiles first went to the cash register and paid, then headed off toward the cubicles. He was leading Gioconda by the arm.

Once inside the little room, Gioconda put her glasses on the bedside table and undressed in two quick movements, two magnetic passes that hypnotized him.

"Mesmer was an asshole," said Miguel.

"Who's that?" asked Gioconda.

"An asshole."

Gioconda undressed Miguel, took his penis and started sucking him. When he was ready, she put a condom on him and mounted him. After a while, Miguel pulled out, turned her around and penetrated her from behind.

"Harder, doctor. Harder," moaned Gioconda.

He knew Gioconda was faking it but, strangely, that aroused him even more. He finished in a few seconds. He stood up and went over to the bathroom. He took off the condom and looked at it against the backlight. His own semen, seen through the latex, seemed fake. He tied a knot and tossed the condom in the bin. He felt as though God had strangled him in a million parallel dimensions.

"Put the belt on," he told Gioconda when he came out of the bathroom.

Gioconda was surprised by the request but jumped out of

bed excitedly. She looked for it in the chest of drawers until she found it.

"Is it clean?" asked Miguel.

"Totally. But let me wash it anyway," said Gioconda, and this time she was the one who went to the bathroom.

When she came back to the room, she was already wearing it. What Miguel called a belt was really a kind of jockstrap, only the band was wide and black, like the belts used by weight lifters. It had an enormous green rubber penis sticking out.

As if it had been cut off García Lorca's *duende*.

Gioconda came toward the bed and Miguel turned around. He focused his attention on the rimmed glasses, which were re-creating shrunk-down versions of the scene. They looked like two TV sets in the window of an appliance store late at night. The movement and the slight thickness of the lenses seemed to draw the image even further in.

If I could just grab the frame and blow, thought Miguel, I bet the lenses would pop out like bubbles.

10

A Paper Stem

As Gioconda had predicted, Miguel Ardiles was gone before daybreak. The letters on the Mr. Morrison's sign were barely readable amid the colors of that early hour. He checked inside his pockets (cell phone, keys, wallet, audio recorder), paid the valet and got into his car. He took Avenida Blandín, skirted Plaza La Castellana and drove down a street that took him to Avenida San Juan Bosco. It was a few minutes to five in the morning.

He stopped at the red light on the corner of Avenida Francisco de Miranda. Before the light turned green, he connected his iPod and searched for the Morphine album Matías had recommended. In a way, he found Matías's almost daily emails comforting. He wasn't angry at him anymore and accepted that breaking a routine was also a form of adventure. He remained on guard, nevertheless.

M > Morphine > The Night > Play

The first chords rang out. The combination of sax, drum kit and two-string bass made him close his eyes. A stream of slowness straight into his veins. And he would have fallen asleep behind the wheel, in front of that traffic light, and slept all morning, or until a policeman asked for his documentation or a loud horn woke him up, if it wasn't for the engine roaring in his ear. He opened his eyes suddenly, the way you do when you groggily fall asleep for a few seconds, and saw the biker.

He was a white man, immense, his head covered by a red helmet that revealed a beard that was also red. He was wearing very short pants from which two robust and pale legs stuck out. He gave Ardiles a slip of paper, limp as the stem of a flower, revved his motorbike and, when the light turned green, disappeared at full speed toward the highway.

For an unspecified time, Miguel Ardiles remained in the same position: his right hand on the wheel, his gaze locked on the windscreen and in his left hand, hanging out of the window, the piece of paper.

"Move, cocksucker!"

Ardiles jumped.

A car with four drunken men blasting reggaeton at full volume had stopped beside him. They all laughed out loud and then turned onto Francisco de Miranda, headed for Petare. He finally roused himself and set off toward Parque Caiza.

By the time he opened the front door of his house, he had come up with a plan. It was an easy and logical plan: he would lie down to sleep and dream about everything that had happened, and when he woke up, the paper would be nowhere to be found.

But what if when he awoke, he thought, as proof of his passage through the night, he still had the paper stem in his hand, well, and what then?

Miguel Ardiles couldn't sleep under such a threat. Nor did he have the strength to stay awake. He brought his hand to his pocket and patted the audio recorder. It was time to take a shower, make a liter of coffee and, in the light of the new day, make an incursion into the night: to enter the dream with eyes wide open:

Insecurity. Hunger. Unemployment. Chaos and violence. Injustice. Inflation. Militarization. Power cuts. Castro-

*Communism has taken over. That's the sign that we have
entered the Year of Mercy. Forgiveness for all sins is nigh,
but God's revenge will come first. Don't get used to living
in darkness. The Fire must be started. We Soldiers of Christ
will bring back the kingdom of Light.*

The signature on the text was childish but effective: The
Dream Thief.

The text itself was nothing remarkable. Miguel Ardiles
was used to listening to the paranoid ravings of some of his
patients. He remembered the case of one woman who feared
her husband might die crushed by any light fixture breaking off
a ceiling. The woman had transformed her husband's life, the
most precious thing she had, into a hell of adoration and care.
Along with cases like these, there were others that were more
mundane, although equally dramatic: depression, stress-in-
duced breakdowns, panic attacks. One way or another, the
cause of the anguish was the same: the situation of the country.
A country that, like the woman's ceiling lights, always seemed
about to break off and smash into pieces.

There weren't many options: anxiolytics, antidepressants,
therapy. Share their decision to walk away or stay and put up
with it. And to those who chose to put up with it, instruct
them in the whining business of victimhood.

Like the message, the biker himself didn't seem all that
unusual at first sight. The anonymous avenger, both in movies
and real life, with Charles Bronson's face or someone else's,
is a symptomatic character of wild cities where the state has
lost control. But this *avenger*, Ardiles had to admit, was different from the others. He didn't seem the type to go out and
kill people in order to single-handedly restore some notion
of justice. He was someone, Miguel thought, who would go

out at night to deliver messages to strangers. Words that travel through darkness to land in the mouths of those who do the last circuit, with the conviction that those who know how to listen would be united, like isolated limbs from the same body, a spiteful golem eager to wake.

Beyond condemning the lack of basic necessities and issuing biblical warnings against a *Castro-Communist* invasion, the text led to a concrete question with metaphysical implications: When did we get used to living in darkness? Major cities such as Caracas, Maracaibo or Mérida, the day after the announcement of the power cuts, had risen up. It was just a taste of anger, enough to make the government back off and suspend the plan shortly afterward. In practice, three-hour-long daily cuts continued to be enforced in all the states, cities and towns of the country.

In Caracas, street lighting was switched off and never turned back on. Something in the city and its inhabitants was damaged by that return to the night.

How had people adapted? What kind of process had taken place?, Miguel wondered. It's not as if people developed night vision. It was more like a sixth sense for disaster, which made us follow violent and seemingly irregular trajectories, bat-like, if we happened to be surprised by nightfall when out on the street.

Miguel Ardiles switched on his computer, connected the voice recorder to the USB port and downloaded the audio file. He saved it with the other files in the folder for the last month. He had several conversations stored. The latest to be transcribed was Pedro Álamo's first visit. Matías had said Álamo would be a patient with interesting things to tell him. This promising start, which led Ardiles to consider him a possible *case*, was interrupted in the following weeks when he, uncharacteristically, had stepped into the plot himself.

He spent that Saturday listening to the recordings. The voices of Matías, Álamo, Margarita and himself emerged from a muddy turbulence to contribute to a story that had already started, and which needed to be understood. And understanding, for Miguel Ardiles, meant accepting that, for the first time, he was part of a story. Perhaps this explained the strange late-night scene: the biker was inviting him to accept his part in the script.

The files were full of *source errors*: noisy interferences, long segments in which it wasn't possible to identify what had been said or by whom, or sudden interruptions caused by the voice recorder's memory being full. A whole ecosystem of obstacles that made the conversation hostile territory, averse to a final transcription. However, he found these difficulties stimu-lating. In fact, Miguel Ardiles believed that psychiatrists were the script doctors of intimacy. Childhood traumas, person-ality traits, critical experiences: whatever could have caused the problem the patient brings to his practice, this is precisely the element he's trying to conceal from his story. And when they aren't concealing these elements, they have no idea how to articulate them. A patient, thought Miguel Ardiles, is someone who cannot tell his own story, or does not know how.

And what about Miguel Ardiles's story? When is this novel going to broach Miguel Ardiles's true story? He'd solved that problem in some professional manner a long time ago. Being a psychiatrist instead of a psychoanalyst had allowed him to avoid the hurdle of making a confession. The cult founded by Freud established that psychoanalysts also had to attend therapy themselves. Such a provision, so like the Jesuits' enigmatic vow of obedience to the pope, seemed demagogic to him. Under the cloak of democracy there hid a fact that, to use the biker's biblical jargon, constituted a true mystery of injustice: Freud himself never submitted to an analysis with another therapist.

Nonetheless, Miguel Ardiles had allowed himself a friendship with Matías Rye and Pedro Álamo. Like any of his own patients, he needed to talk. That had been the initial motivation, established years ago, behind writing about the cases. He had Freud's texts on hysteria as a reference point, and Oliver Sacks's books too.

Secretly recording his patients, both those he saw at his private practice and some of the cases he attended at Forensics, was reprehensible from anybody's perspective. But the experience of transcribing the conversations led him to believe there was something lost during the sessions, another meaning that emerged only by sieving the same words time after time. Even Marilyn Monroe sensed the particular magnetism produced when a person talked to somebody else but did so while in solitude. The cassettes she recorded for Ralph Greenson, her last psychiatrist, who also happened to be the person who found her dead, are proof that truth is a performance for just one person.

The problem wasn't finding this truth so much as keeping it alive and recognizable outside oneself, thought Miguel.

The first person to sabotage this enterprise was Miguel Ardiles himself. He would add fictitious situations and details to his drafts. It wasn't a conscious decision. It happened as soon as he tried to incorporate certain arguments and feelings that were hard to express in words. Along the way, between one word and the next, between the ideas that in his head marked out a dense geometry like that of the trees in a forest, what one wanted to say would get obscured by what one actually said. Doubt, that feeling of having taken the wrong path at a crossroad, was enough to alter everything that had been written.

By nine p.m., Miguel Ardiles was exhausted. He had spent the whole of Saturday in a fervent vigil listening to the audio files, over and over. He had taken notes about some of the things said by Matías Rye, Pedro Álamo and Margarita Lambert. He had googled the available information on the country's electricity crisis, followed by an overview of the history of electricity in Venezuela, and encountered basic concepts in physics that he hadn't seen since high school. It hadn't been a stimulating experience. He could see the different parts, guessed at the big picture, but couldn't piece it together. Miguel Ardiles saw his own brain, barren of ideas and sleep-deprived, like one of those collapsed hydroelectric power stations.

Language is like electricity, thought Ardiles, light-headed with exhaustion. Only there isn't a Nikola Tesla of linguistics. By substituting direct current with alternating current, Tesla made it possible for electricity to travel inconceivable distances from the big power stations. Mikhail Dolivo-Dobrovolsky also presented his discoveries at the 1891 International Electro-Technical Exhibition. An event covered by a scientific magazine that was read by Ricardo Zuloaga in the same year, leading him to build the first hydroelectric power station in Hispanic America on the banks of the Guaire River, and to develop a system of power lines for the city of Caracas.

Something similar to Dolivo-Dobrovolsky's and Tesla's systems but applied to language, Ardiles said to himself. Maybe the pronouns *I*, *you* and *he* were the closest thing to a three-phase alternating current. Except that the degree of separation of the electric waves between them tends to narrow until subjects and points of view are completely muddled. Language was an electric pulse that, while passing through the cables that represented words, abandoned its power source and erupted into the open space with the indifference and expansiveness of dust.

I'm raving, thought Ardiles.

He saved his notes in a Word document, moved the audio files out of their original folder and put the whole lot away into a new folder.

When the moment came to name the folder, he didn't hesitate. Transgression and a warped sense of duty dictated the letters under which he would collect everything related to that imperfect system that was drawing him in with the same intensity with which it was refusing to reveal its secret laws to him: *The Night.*

II. Theory of Palindromes

According to the dictionary, the extra-grammatical meaning of the term palindrome is 'running back again.' Therefore, it is not about turning one's back on the horizon and backtracking, which in its apparent simplicity is totally impossible, but about continuing the movement in the opposite direction, making the tangible move away, while the unknown, the lethal and unspeakable abyss, approaches interminably.

—SALVADOR GARMENDIA

11

A Nearly Perfect Eight

The life of a smoker is condensed between two critical moments: the first cigarette and the last. What happens before the first clumsy drag, which hardly manages to carburize the tobacco, is pure unconsciousness. What happens after the last drag, when all you can think about is the next, which will never happen, is endless anxiety.

Darío Mancini Villalaz* smoked his first cigarette on July 5, 1943, in Santiago de Chile, when he turned eleven. In 1941, Silvia and Anita had decided to put an end to the successful American tour of the Villalaz Sisters Theater with a European vacation. After visiting several cities in Third Reich Germany they arrived in Cologne, and from there traveled to Italy, to the city of Brindisi, where some distant cousins lived. From that harbor in the Adriatic, they boarded a ship that took them straight to Venezuela, where their sister Matilde lived.

Shortly after starting to tell their sister about their trip, Silvia and Anita had to stop. Matilde looked haggard.

"And Aldo?" asked Anita.

"Gone away."

"Where?"

---

* This is the first example of a strange habit of Álamo's: altering the real name of people he mentions, sometimes by just one letter. The night we played Tetris, he explained the supposed oneiric origin of everything he narrates in this section. According to him, he dreamed in episodes, and in the third person, about the life (which only he and I know about) of Darío Lancini.

"I don't know. His last business didn't go well. He's gone off to see whether he can make up for it."

"When did he leave?" asked Silvia.

"Two months ago."

"And when will he be back?"

"I don't know."

Matilde's eyes, so clear and wet, seemed about to evaporate.

Anita and Silvia decided to take Darío with them. Ramón was too young. Aixa, Luis and Matildita, on the other hand, would be able to start working soon.

In Panama, the Villalaz sisters were received with honors for "having brought fame to their fatherland." President Arnulfo Arias Madrid offered for them to take charge of the Recitation Department in the recently created National Conservatory of Music and Recitation. Anita Villalaz accepted the offer, but Silvia declined it. She needed to go back to Chile, where she lived with her husband and children. Darío went with her.

On the morning of July 5, 1943, during recess, Darío was rubbing his hands together because of the cold. Sebastián, the class bully, saw him and secretly offered him a cigarette. Darío took it, and in doing so he tacitly accepted a protection agreement that lasted until the penultimate week of the school year. During those months he put into practice what would be his principle for living: go unnoticed. He managed for a long time. In part, due to his physiognomy. Darío came from Venezuela, but there was nothing in his features to give it away. He had very white skin, prone to flushing, brown hair that was straight with yellow ends, and eyes that were blue, green or gray, depending on the weather.

In the last week of school, Sebastián and some other classmates invited Darío to fly kites. Until then, Darío had resigned himself to going to the same faraway corner to smoke a cigarette every recess, returning only when his teacher called the students back inside. Sometimes, Sebastián would keep him company, and they would talk. In a way, this was a sacrifice. During those minutes of conversation, Sebastián would stop being the center of attention, the indisputable champion in kite-flying or whatever game or sport he always used to win. He would stop feeding the admiration that Marcela, his girlfriend, felt toward him. But, on the other hand, there was something in Darío, in the words they'd exchange, that comforted him. A sort of satisfaction he couldn't identify at that age. Sebastián was experiencing, without knowing it, his first (perhaps his only) intellectual infatuation. The particular moment, which is off limits to more resentful souls, in which another person's genius becomes the main enigma in one's own existence.

The Chilean kids made fun of Darío's kite. Starting with the fact he called his a *papagayo*, like the colorful bird. Instead of the single spar the others used, Darío made a cross-shaped one, gluing two small blades to the tail. They told him it wouldn't fly with that weight. Darío didn't answer and reinforced the joint with an extra loop of tape.

The whole class was there. They had finished their last exams the previous week and were in extra time, those golden days when one goes to school only to play. They were the eldest in their school. Next year they would go into high school, many of them would go to different ones, and in any case, they would be the youngest in the next stage. Without words, but with the self-awareness of rituals, they were saying goodbye to each other.

When they were all ready, they stood behind a line drawn in chalk at the entry of the schoolyard. Sebastián gave the order, they all started running and the kites took off. All but Darío's, which flopped instantly back to the ground. The girls studied in a separate building, connected to the boys' through the schoolyard. They could only watch, and seeing what happened to Darío's kite, they laughed. Darío picked up his *papagayo*, went back to the starting line and started running again. The kite glided drunkenly, zigzagging like a butterfly. It looked as if it was going to go down again, but a quick movement of the line by Darío, like a boatman starting up a motor, allowed it to catch an air current and take off.

The initial movements resembled those of a dance and a parade. Sebastián's kite glided at a height that was both inaccessible to the boys and a distant delight to the girls. Darío, as if having boarded his own vessel, flew in a different orbit, tracing figures only he could make out. When he was about to complete a number eight, another kite drew near, almost skimming his. The lines barely passed over each other, but the message was clear. The other boys, like vultures smelling carrion, reeled in their gliders to circle the battlefield. Darío saw another threatening kite coming, but this time he was prepared. With two magic tricks, he avoided the attack, then slashed his adversary's cellophane sheet from top to bottom.

His schoolmates' kites went down one by one, fatally scalped by Darío's holy blade. Sebastián, like a capo waiting for his thugs to do the job, watched the massacre from a distance. Once the sky had been cleared out, the two birds, kite and *papagayo*, came closer. The other boys, with their colorful bits of scrap, and the girls, holding hands, proceeded to witness the duel.

Darío triumphed.

The problem with Sebastián wasn't the defeat. Or, at least, not the defeat in itself. Darío picked up his kite like a lunar anchor and gave it away to his friends, who rushed to pore over the tail.

The girls welcomed him by chanting his name.

"Da-rí-o! Da-rí-o! Da-rí-o!"

Darío went beetroot red. He came over and said:

"Enough. Stop." But he said this while having a laughing fit, while dying of embarrassment, so they carried on even louder.

The next day Sebastián asked him to go with him.

"A cigarette?", Darío said.

"Last one. Tomorrow I'm going on vacation with my mom and dad."

They walked to the usual corner.

This time it was Sebastián who was quiet. Darío asked him something about the city where he was going to spend the summer with his family, but Sebastián didn't answer. Only later did he say:

"Marcela dumped me."

"Why?"

Sebastián went silent for a few seconds. He had his hands in his pockets, as he painstakingly kicked at the tiny stones in the gravel.

"Why?" insisted Darío.

"Marcela says she's in love with you."

Sebastián tried to smile, but he grimaced instead.

"With me?"

"Yeah, with you, asshole."

Though he kept quiet, Darío was still asking the question, pondering the words, trying to solve the riddle. When he had recovered his composure, he noticed that Sebastián was holding his shoulders. It was time for a farewell hug.

Being punched in the belly, getting his breath knocked out of him and dropping to his knees all happened in a matter of seconds. He just saw Sebastián's legs walking away.

He wasn't angry at Sebastián, or Marcela. Just annoyed with himself for having given in, for not having measured up to that near-perfect eight, the only thing that could have justified that foreign sky.

12

Psychological Autopsy

"A psychological autopsy?" asked Oswaldo Barreto. "And what on earth is that?"

"It's one of the methods used in modern psychiatry to investigate completed suicides," said Miguel Ardiles. "It consists of creating a psychological profile of the deceased from testimonies collected from people in their inner circle."

"A completed suicide? What do you understand by completed suicide?"

"A successful suicide, that can be verified."

"Successful? Are there unsuccessful suicides? A half-finished suicide?"

"Well, you know how confusing criminal jargon can be."

The old man seemed to calm down.

"How can I help you?"

"I'm investigating the case of Pedro Álamo, an economist who committed suicide a couple of weeks ago."

"How did he die?"

"He hanged himself. In India. He went to a place called Maharashtra to investigate a wave of suicides among the local peasants and ended up committing suicide himself."

Barreto just raised his eyebrows and stroked his beard. He was a lean, wiry old man. His body a chain of knots, as strong as wire. He reminded Miguel of Baron Munchausen. At least the one in Terry Gilliam's version, in the opening scenes when, defeated but vigorous, he bursts into a theater where they are staging a misleading version of his own life. But Ardiles wasn't kidding himself. Although he didn't know much about the man, he had learned enough to know he should tread carefully: a superfluous word or a discourteous gesture and the old man could ruin him.

"I don't know any Pedro Álamo," said Barreto.

"That's what I thought. Not many people knew him, really. I've had to play detective to find his trail. I told his son it'd be better to give up, but the boy insists on finding the truth. Poor kid came all the way from Santa Elena de Uairén, quit his job, sold his car and moved to Caracas to follow his father's case closely—a father who, by the way, he only ever got to see a few times."

Barreto raised his eyebrows again.

"So?" he said after a while.

"Álamo had only one son. No known wife, lover or friends. The old people who rented him the annex where he lived haven't given me much information either. I need to cling to anything I can get hold of. And when I was digging around in the papers he left behind, I found some notebooks. Some notebooks where he mentions your name."

Oswaldo Barreto, who had been leaning back on his chair, sat up. He frowned, crossed his legs the other way and asked:

"Señor?"

"Your second family name is Miliani, right?"

"Yes."

"And you were a representative for the Communist Party, weren't you?"

"I was."

"And you participated in the hijack and assault of an Aeropostal DC-9 aircraft in December 1980?"

"Who the fuck are you?"

The old man stood up. At no point did he raise his voice, but there was a tense silence that gave away his mood. A couple of cats, which until now had been walking around the kitchen, came closer and watched him. On one of the walls hung a pair of portraits, of Jean-Paul Sartre and Simone de Beauvoir, who seemed to be watching too.

"I've already told you. My name is Miguel Ardiles, I'm a forensic psychiatrist and occasionally work as an adviser for individuals in criminal cases. Here's my ID if you want to check," and he held out the card.

Barreto looked at the ID card for a few seconds without taking it. He sat down again.

"I'll explain. Pedro Álamo left a sort of biography he'd written on Darío Lancini."

"On Darío?" he interrupted.

"Yes."

"What could that man know about Darío Lancini? What could anybody know about Darío?"

"I'm only trying to find out about Lancini's life, to see if that way I can get close to Álamo. To tell you the truth, all I want is to create a nice story for Álamo's son. A story to allow him to return home peacefully."

"What does the text say about me?"

"It talks about someone called Oswaldo Miliani. A member of the Communist Party, a law graduate from the Sorbonne, a professor at the Central University of Venezuela, an ex-guerrilla."

"I was the first Venezuelan to do it."

"Do what?"

"Graduate in law from the Sorbonne."

"I didn't know that."

"Doesn't he say in the biography?"

"He doesn't. But he does say you and Lancini shared an apartment in 1962 in Vista Alegre."

"How do you know that?"

"Apartment number seven, in the Residencias Venezuela building."

"Who told you that?"

"It's in the notebook."

"Do you have it with you?"

"No. That notebook and the others are with Álamo's son. I only have access to photocopies. I can bring you those if you're interested."

"I am interested."

"I didn't realize you were Oswaldo Miliani till I read an article about Lancini's death. Then I looked you up and came across a news story from 2000, about the capture of some people who'd robbed an armored truck."

"I never robbed an armored truck."

"The article mostly talks about your namesake Oswaldo Ojeda Negretti, who up until that year had led the most powerful gang that robbed banks and armored trucks. The police began to track them down after the one-and-a-half-billion-bolívar robbery they carried out in July 2000 in a neighborhood in Barcelona, in Anzoátegui state. They realized Ojeda Negretti had been involved in the well-known robbery of the Transvalcar armored truck, and from there they went back to the first of the hits, a really famous one: the mid-flight hijacking of an Aeropostal DC-9 in December 1980. Among the detainees were the brothers Jorge and Oswaldo Ojeda Negretti, the brothers Mauricio and José Rivas Campos, and Oswaldo Barreto Miliani."

Miguel Ardiles read the list of detainees from a printed copy of the news story, then handed it to Barreto. The man took the piece of paper and put it down gently on the table at which they were seated, without looking at it.

"That's how I came to you. I need to know more about Darío Lancini to write my report. So I can give Álamo's son a mirror to allow him to see some of his father's features."

"What do you know about Darío?"

"I know he wrote *Oír a Darío*. Álamo considered him the greatest palindromist in the Spanish language."

"What else? Draw me a timeline."

Ardiles took out his notebook and started to enumerate chronologically, and with big gaps in between, all the things he knew about Darío Lancini: the part of his childhood he spent in Santiago de Chile; the five years in prison during the Pérez Jiménez dictatorship; his tour around Mexico City, Paris and Warsaw; the writing of palindromes; his decisive encounter with Antonieta Madrid; the start of his travels and his life as a diplomat; the long, sustained and unwavering silence into which Lancini decided to encode his life toward the end.

"Is that all?" asked Barreto.

"That's all I could gather from what was in the notebook."

"That's not enough for a biography."

"Perhaps the notes were for a novel."

"And why would anyone want to write a novel about Darío Lancini? At the end of the day, the only thing Darío published was one short book."

Barreto stood up and partly disappeared, engulfed in the darkness of the kitchen.

"I think," said Ardiles, "that to Álamo, Darío was a true artist. A genius who wanted only to be left alone with the secret he had discovered in the words."

From the kitchen, Barreto's eyes sparkled, in the play of light and shadow. He returned with a bottle of whiskey and some olives.

"You're sure you want to write about Lancini? Are you aware of the trouble you're getting yourself into? I'm only saying this because Darío Lancini is the most complex person, ethically and aesthetically speaking, I have ever met."

13

Jail

Private Aldo Lancini had survived the Great War untainted: he wasn't wounded, he didn't kill (or, which comes to the same thing, he never saw anyone he killed), and he wasn't taken prisoner. War was a gigantic piano that crashed to the ground by his side. He was merely coated in fine dust, the dust of death. He decided that, when he went back to Calabria, he would pick up his backpack and head off to see the world. The only possession he took with him, apart from backpack and clothes, was his chess set.

While he was at the front, he had more than once forgotten about the bombings or the rain all around him by playing imaginary chess games against himself. There was no way of winning without losing. That, to him, was the law of fear. He would forget that law once he left the camp and would be able to find it again only when either fear or boredom cornered him in his mind. He would emerge from these games as if from an even deeper trench, straight onto the battlefield.

In the first year, he survived by playing chess for money. After this, he began to be recognized at the different ports in America and Europe, so no one wanted to play against him anymore. He became a familiar face. That's how the first orders came about. A businessman in Buenos Aires liked the style of his chess set: the design of the board, the finish of the pieces.

"They were made by old Bonanno," said Aldo. "I'd need to

see if he's still alive."

"Very good. If he is, bring me fifty sets."

Old Bonanno was alive. And lived several years more. Since
he was a hardened smoker, Aldo began to trade in tobacco. For
some years, his job was to supply smoking houses in the main
coastal cities of South and North America.

In 1925, he settled in Caracas, in an area that, following the
widening of Avenida Sucre, was called Nueva Caracas. Two
years later, on a boat trip from Panama to the United States, he
met Matilde Villalaz. They both felt struck by a prolonged gaze
that seemed to slow the hustle and bustle of the deck. They
never confessed, and perhaps they weren't even aware of it, but
what they liked about each other the most, what captivated
them from the start, were each other's eyes, which were identical to their own. More than one person thought, on seeing
them walking together, that they were father and daughter.
That Matilde, twenty-one years his junior, had inherited Aldo's
eyes. Only those who knew Aldo could confirm that it was he
who had inherited something from Matilde, a twinkle in the
eye that deposited him, feverish, in the port of New Orleans.

Anita never liked that whole business. She would come to
be proven right. But at the time, she was opposed to it simply
because it made her uneasy. The Villalaz sisters had been edu-
cated by the nuns at the Our Lady of Sion school, in Costa
Rica, and then by Franciscan nuns at a boarding school in New
Orleans. In fact, Anita's first childhood dream had been to
become a nun. That trip to attend the funeral of Sister Prisca,
her beloved singing and acting teacher, was a return to the
chastity of past times and those yearnings.

"I'd like to see you try explaining to papá that you went to
a funeral and came back married to an old man," Anita told
Matilde.

The couple got married in Panama and moved to Venezuela immediately afterward. The marriage didn't last. Just long enough to give birth to five children, who kept showing up to bear witness to a bond being gradually dissolved by repeated contact. Apart from love, Aldo Lancini gave his children something that was impossible to erase. He gave them not only a surname but also a first name and a middle name. He called them Alda Aixa, Aldo Luis, Alda Matilde, Aldo Darío and Abdem Ramón. No one knows what led Aldo Lancini to finally break that chain of declensions composed of his children. And as the children grew older, his presence would become a distant port, and their first name just a denomination of origin, the small print on a label that no one reads.

Before that first cigarette smoked in Santiago de Chile when he was eleven, a lot of things happened in the life of Darío Mancini.* Except that Darío himself didn't remember them. Two moments remained standing after the gale of childhood, fluttering like shreds of a flag stuck in a dream. His Siamese twin, Arnaldo Acosta Bello, used to make fun of the first, asking Darío to tell the story of the Milky Way, as they sat at the round table in the basement of the Cervecería Alemana.

It was a rather brief story. It was, in fact, his first memory. Darío would say he remembered being breastfed. He remembered having detached from his mother's breast and receiving a jet of milk in the face.

The other memory was more likely but also more confusing. Darío is five or six. His brother Ramón, three or four. They are

* When I wrote to Álamo to ask him why he kept *Mancini* only for Darío, but not for the father, he answered as follows: "That's how I dreamed it, my dear Miguel. Writing is already a foolish pretension. Correcting a dream would be positively insolent. Although I know that, deep down, you don't believe me, so best not to talk about these things." I didn't yet know what Pedro Álamo understood by *dreaming*. I still hadn't read about the Dreamachine in the notebooks.

both in a bedroom with lots of bunk beds, in the middle of a room with tiled floors, in a house long as a tunnel, dark and unknown. The other children made a point of scaring them during the day. The shadows of the trees would do likewise at night. How long did they live in that house? Was it days, weeks, months? Did that house really exist or was it merely a nightmare? He never asked his mother. It didn't occur to him to talk to Ramón about it either.

After their time living in Chile, once they were back in Venezuela, his adolescence and adventures with his brother Ramón and with Jacobo Borges in Catia began. Divided between his first reading and his dabbles in drawing, he was searching for a ridge to grip hold of, just to hang on to this world. Sometimes, the shape would get stuck and threaten to become petrified. On those occasions, it was the world that was wrong and needed to be transformed. On one of those distressing days, Darío accepted Juana Iro de Matos's invitation for him and his two brothers to attend a clandestine meeting organized by Democratic Action at Plan de Manzano.

When they arrived, Darío and his brothers realized that the party meeting was, in fact, an excuse to plot the assassination of Marcos Pérez Jiménez. On that occasion, he barely got to see some plans that had been laid on the table with pistols as paperweights. He decided to leave after a few minutes. What had happened in '49 was still fresh in his memory, the nearly identical meeting Manuel Muñoz Palencia had taken him to, also seemingly at random. That was his first visit to The Office, which is what they called the headquarters of the NS—National Security—in El Paraíso. Thanks to Manuel's skillfulness, they had managed to escape the same night. But it was 1952 now and things had changed forever.

The first to fall were his brothers Luis and Ramón on April

7, when the government ordered a surprise raid on the house of Comrade Flor Maíz, where they were plotting. The NS found twenty-one pipe bombs ready to be taken to the Plan de Manzano house. Just one month and eleven days later, on May 18, they detained Darío at his own home. They knew he had visited the house in Plan de Manzano and that he was aware of the plot. They also seized over two hundred sheets of subversive propaganda that incited workers to join a big demonstration in support of university students; books and texts of communist literature; a pamphlet; a roll of thin white canvas; ink; crayons and tubes of paint; letters, photographs and a portrait of Lenin signed by Darío himself.

They weren't too cruel to begin with. Pretty soon they had sent them to the Modelo prison. José Vicente Abreu would join them a week later, after receiving his share of beatings, after spending nights and days without eating, not even a piece of bread, without drinking a drop of water, hours standing on the cylinder, receiving electric shocks to his testicles. All of it to the rhythm of a single repeated question:

"Where's Ruiz Pineda?"

And a single repeated insult (at least, what the NS, who were no fans of those leftist parties, considered a single insult):

"*Adecos*! Communists!"

Ever since Delgado Chalbaud's assassination, in November 1950, protests had been taking place like ripples that barely disturb the surface of the sea but hint at its depth. The government junta, now in Pérez Jiménez's hands, had dismissed the authorities at the Central University, creating a Council of Reform, finally deciding in October 1951 to shut the place down entirely.

Opposite the old San Francisco church, students would meet up, creating a whirlwind of slogans and pamphlets that would dissolve as soon as the antiriot squad showed up. One afternoon in February 1952, the NS turned up earlier than usual and crushed a shoal of unruly students. They processed them through the system, through their headquarters at El Paraíso and El Obispo and then on to the Modelo. Jesús Sanoja Hernández, Manuel Caballero and Rafael Cadenas, along with some others, were taken to cell number three. In the months that followed, they would be joined by Darío Mancini, Arnaldo Acosta Bello and Pepe Fernández Doris. It was the first meeting of the Knights of the Round Table. They couldn't have known it at the time: that they, who thought they had been called upon to perform the subtlest of gestures, must first endure pain.

They learned to conjugate mutism. A word that silenced others became quotidian: *informer*, rugged and thick, like the stony silence they were ordered to maintain. The group of students were displaced soon after. Caballero and Sanoja departed for Mexico and from there to Paris, where a group of Venezuelan exiles, mainly communists and supporters of Democratic Action, survived in a *maison meublée* at 23 Rue de Constantinople. From there they joined in with the writing and publishing of gazettes, pamphlets and newspapers condemning the dictatorship. There were already mentions of a terrible place called Guasina, a word related to *informer*, that inherited its silence and transformed it into a swamp.

Cadenas made a stopover in Trinidad, a stay that was a sensual confinement in the open air.

In exile, they heard about the successive tragedies that marked the year 1952: the situation at the university, prisoners constantly being sent to Guasina, and especially, the assassination of Leonardo Ruiz Pineda, gunned down by an NS patrol on October 21.

For those locked away, jail became a game of Russian roulette. Each day was like an endless cigarette standing opposite the firing squad. On November 3, 1951, the first contingent for Guasina departed from the Caracas, Tucupita, Barcelona, Cumaná and Carúpano prisons. From that day on, everything became simply a question of who was sent to Guasina and who was not.

On July 25, 1952, the steamboat *Guayana* departed from La Guaira en route to the Orinoco Delta. The third group of prisoners to be sent to the Guasina and Sacupana concentration camps were piled up like cargo. Among many other convicts were José Vicente Abreu, Arnaldo Acosta Bello, and Luis and Ramón Lancini.

Darío had been left behind at the Modelo, gripped by sadness and fearing the worst.

Things got so bad in December that, in one sense, they started to improve. On the second, the day of the elections to the Constitutional Assembly, Pérez Jiménez decided to stage a coup and make himself interim president. Then he made himself constitutional president. One of his first rulings was to shut down Guasina and Sacupana. On December 21, 1952, their prisoners, along with those who were in the Modelo prison, were moved to the Nueva Cárcel in Ciudad Bolívar, where they were reunited.

In that new prison, Darío listened to some horrific testimonies. But there weren't many. Guasina made sure it would leave an impossible knot in the throats of its survivors. Those who spoke, spoke little, and that was plenty.

Darío stopped sleeping. He began to stare at the prison walls, the corridors, the courtyards, the rooms he didn't know, like a night watchman. Deep in the night, he would smoke imaginary cigarettes and would pass through the walls with the imaginary smoke, always as far as the main gate and then back. Sometimes, from his mat, he watched himself gliding over his fellow prisoners, returning to his own place and remaining awake until sleep erased the dream.

One morning he started drawing. He sketched portraits of his closest inmates: Catalá, Consalvi, Velásquez, Abreu, Acosta Bello.

"What are you doing?" asked Erasto. "Are these your drawings?"

"Yes," answered Darío.

He was never very keen on Erasto. Too much talk for his liking. He always asked too many questions.

"They're a really good likeness," he went on. "That one's Simón Alberto. This one must be José Agustín. And this other one, that's José Vicente. Who's this one without eyes?"

"That's me," said Darío.

"And who's Sebastián? Why do you sign like that?"

Darío didn't reply. He went over some lines in the background of one of the portraits, and Erasto returned to his corner of the cell.

There was one drawing that grabbed everyone's attention. It showed the face of Cabrera the guard, not with his usual cruelty, but helpless. He was surrounded by a forest of eyeless prisoners. Anyone who saw the drawing would think Cabrera was about to scream.

"Yes," said Arnaldo.

Now a similar forest had formed around the drawing itself.

"A sleepless landscape that talks to him," he added.

Darío turned around and saw Erasto, who was one step behind the group. His expression was fearful, similar to that of the character in the drawing.

In April 1956, the dictatorship gave visas to seventy exiled students to allow them to return home. Sanoja and Cadenas came back. Along with other members of Democratic Action and the Communist Party, they sent a letter to the United Nations Human Rights Council asking for the release of comrades who already had years of punishment under their belts.

Darío Mancini, who had been locked away for four years, listened to the news of his friends' return as well as the ongoing negotiations. He didn't pay much attention. Thinking had stopped being a distraction or mental exercise and had become an almost physical act, a way of breathing. He would spend several hours a day lying down, like a fakir, untangling threads of air. Sometimes he would play long chess games with his father, at other times, he'd recall passages of *The Human Condition*, by Malraux, which he knew by heart, and at others still he would see himself locked in a house or painting, or duplicated in a mirror, reading the cards and foretelling the future of his own image.

He wasn't talkative, but he liked listening to others. He particularly enjoyed, during the walks in the courtyard, the rantings of Luis Ordaz, a young *adeco*, claiming that one day he would be the president of the Republic. The first time Ordaz confessed his aspirations, he received a sign: some bird-shit on his forehead. Darío thought it was a nice image: a perfect metaphor for life. With a gesture, Ordaz thanked him for not laughing. He wiped the shit off his forehead and carried on talking about his project to take power.

In mid-1957, Ernesto de la Guardia Navarro, the president of Panama, made an official visit to Venezuela. Among the subjects discussed was the question of political prisoners. De la Guardia Navarro was especially interested in the case of the brothers Lancini Villalaz, in prison for five years, sons of a Panamanian woman resident in Venezuela, who belonged to a family that was very important in Panama.

"Good Lord, Dr. de la Guardia, you're putting me in a tight spot," said General Pérez Jiménez. "What would you do if you'd found a group of armed men plotting your assassination?"

"Same as you, General. I'd send them to jail. But these boys' aunt is a renowned artist in Panama. Their great-uncle is Nicanor Villalaz, creator of our national coat of arms. Can you imagine? This small favor the family's asked me is the least I can do. But I understand, General. Let's drop it."

The negotiation worked nevertheless. In September 1957, after five years, Luis, Ramón and Darío were released.

"Is it true the president of Panama himself interceded?" Ordaz was euphoric.

"I don't know," said Darío. "That's what they say. But it's true that tomorrow we are getting out."

"I will remember that man's name. I will honor him, come the day. What are you going to do?"

"We need to leave the country. I think I'll go to Mexico. Sanoja has talked to some friends from there."

They sat down on the last bench, near the mango trees.

"But what are you going to do with your life?"

Ordaz was looking carefully at the interweaving of leaves and branches.

"I have no clue. Painting, I guess."

"Painting? Fuck off. With everything that's happened, and you're going to paint?"

"What's wrong with that?"

"Soon we'll get the whole country going, get this shit moving. We're going to take hold of this shit and get it moving."

A sound like the crack of a whip echoed from among the trees.

"Yes!" cried Ordaz, jumping up from his seat.

Some blood-drenched feathers dropped to the stool, between his feet.

"Did you set that trap?" asked Darío.

"Got it at last, motherfucker."

Darío couldn't believe it.

"But that was four years ago, Luis. How on earth could it be the same pigeon?"

"It doesn't matter. Some pigeon or other was going to have to pay for it."

14

Rhythm and Syntax

Do you know Aragon? Yes, Louis Aragon. But have you read him? Of course, you haven't. A forensic psychiatrist who reads Aragon would be very suspicious. *Les médecins-chefs des asiles de fous.* That's what Aragon called psychiatrists, using those words of Artaud's. André Breton said that by age twenty-two, Aragon had read everything. Aragon is one of the greatest poets, and the most marvelous writer ever to join the French Communist Party.

In August 1965 I was in Prague as a representative for the party. One night Pierre Hentgès invited Roque Dalton and me to his house.

"I want you to meet Aragon," said Pierre.

As it happened, Roque and I had for months been discussing the possibility of doing a Spanish translation of *Elsa*, one of Aragon's best poetry collections, published a few months earlier. We met him at that dinner party, and we talked about a lot of things, the translation of his book among them. Those crazy times meant we grew apart and ended up not publishing anything. But I'll never forget the impression made on me by meeting not only Aragon but also Elsa Triolet, who naturally came with him that evening.

Elsa Triolet was Louis Aragon's woman (his companion, as we used to say back then). The love of his life and his muse, a constant theme in his best poetry: *Les yeux d'Elsa, Elsa, Le fou d'Elsa, Il ne m'est Paris que d'Elsa.* Those are the titles of Aragon's books.

You can understand why, after reading those poems over the years, I believed Elsa Triolet the incarnation of truth and beauty.

I didn't understand it at first. Elsa Triolet appeared to be an ordinary woman. It's true they were very old by then (she would die just five years later), but I couldn't see anything special in Elsa, apart from her legendary eyes, that might have justified that exquisite poetry. No magnetism or hidden dimension.

I'm telling you this because it surprises me that someone would have wanted to write or know about Darío Lancini's life just from reading *Oír a Darío*. As if literature had anything to do with life. Life has to do with literature, but that's something else.

In those years I was reintroduced to Vida Javeyid, my first wife. It was her who started a very interesting conversation at the end of that dinner party, which, years later, made me understand what I hadn't understood the one time I met Elsa Triolet.

Someone brought up Breton's words on his renowned friend, about his extensive knowledge of literature, art and languages. Aragon played it down by saying that the only language he really knew was French.

"That can't be true," said Vida.

"Why not?" answered Aragon.

"If that's the case, you're a fake."

"Why do you say that?"

Vida made reference to some poem, I don't remember which, where Aragon quoted some verses in Persian.

"That's right," said Aragon, "but I haven't a clue what they mean."

"Then how do you dare to use them?" asked Vida.

"Because of their sound and rhythm. Do you remember them? Could you recite them?"

Then Pierre got Aragon's books from his library and, together with Vida, looked for the poem. When they found it, Vida read it aloud. We all circled them, paying attention to her voice and to Aragon's reaction. Next to them were Pierre and his wife, Elsa Triolet and Roque. Behind them were Lily Brik and her husband, and a little further back, Eduardo Gallegos Mancera and me.

When Vida had finished reading, Aragon asked her to recite only the verses in Persian. It was then that he started to perform his magic, deciphering the sense of those words in his own way just by their sound, by the interplay between vowels and consonants, by where the accent should fall, by the universal laws of poetry that only a few beings in the history of the world knew as exactly and mysteriously as Louis Aragon did.

Thanks to Vida's impertinence, that night we learned an unforgettable lesson. But now that I think about it, it was really Lily Brik who should have assimilated Aragon's words more deeply.

Lily Brik was Elsa's older sister. Her name won't ring a bell, probably. Lily Brik was Vladimir Mayakovsky's lover, his real widow. Elsa and Mayakovsky met in 1915, and through her, he met Lily. Mayakovsky and Lily fell in love. The betrayal destroyed Elsa, who decided to escape from the pain by marrying a boring officer called Triolet, who would take her out of Russia, launching her life's journey.

The whole thing was a scandal, not only because Lily stole her own sister's man, but because Lily was married to one of Mayakovsky's best friends, the Russian formalist Osip Brik.

Osip Brik was a man of few words. Compared with Roman Jakobson or Viktor Shklovsky, he hardly published anything. However, Osip Brik has an essay that proved decisive for the formalist method. It's called "Rhythm and Syntax." Let me just go fetch it so I can read you a few things.

"Rhythm," says Brik, "is the name we give to all regular alternation, independent of the nature of what is alternated." He then adds: "Rhythmic movement precedes verse. Rhythm cannot be understood through the line of verse; on the contrary, verse can be understood through the movement of rhythm." Ironic, don't you think? That Lily Brik had had to hear her sister's husband, the same sister she'd betrayed by stealing her lover, who in turn was her first husband's best friend, speak a confirmation of her first husband's words, words she probably witnessed in their first formulation and which reappeared at the end of her life, revealing in their intermittency the meandering *de-dum de-dum* that always guides our steps.

But this is the sentence I wanted to read you: "Verse is merely the result of the conflict between nonsense and everyday semantics, it is a particular semantics that exists independently and is developed according to its own laws." That's the conundrum of literature within life itself. This also used to be said in regard to motivation, although very robotically: the world is a pretext for activating the literary work. We know all this and still insist on establishing links, on trying to foresee, on looking for secret doors that connect both realities. The truth burns. It's a blinding, burning light. We search for it, it's our fate to search for it, but we pray never to see it head on. That's why we prefer its multiple reflections, and sometimes the trail of that chained brightness is enough for us.

You, for example, want to search for this Álamo through Lancini, and in order to do that you must search first for Lancini through Álamo. Without your realizing it, your autopsy has become a palindrome. I'm not just playing with words. What I'm telling you is not a game. Seen up close, a palindrome is a labyrinth. From afar, it's more like a cell of a prison or a monastery. In the perfection of the identical sections of its return journey, palindromes can withhold great truths, as well as tremendous nonsenses or wise hallucinations. The thing is, whoever discovers a palindrome, sentences themselves to perpetual slavery. Darío's case is highly singular. He was so obsessed that he was distracted and reckless, and that's why he always was under threat.

"We need to talk," Gallegos Mancera said to me at the end of our evening with Aragon.

"What's happened?"

"Darío fucked things up. I'll tell you on the way back."

15

Master and Slave

Between 1953 and 1958, Oswaldo Miliani studied law at the Sorbonne. As if synchronizing with the title he earned, Venezuela itself also graduated to being a nation of *formidable national unity*. Marcos Pérez Jiménez had managed to leave the Dominican Republic, where he had been received by Rafael Leónidas Trujillo. The return of the exiles began. Miliani arrived back in April 1959 and, without even waiting to see whether the promises made by the emerging democracy would be kept, he committed himself to union work and plotting. So arduous had been Rómulo Betancourt's effort to leave his communist past behind, since the years of the October Revolution, that they were no longer able to retain any favorable expectations of him.

He arrived at University of the Andes, together with his wife Vida, and they moved to Caracas two years later. Vida decided to leave him toward the end of 1961. Oswaldo started teaching at the Journalism School of the Central University. In those days, the offices for humanities lecturers were in what are now the reading rooms at the central library. Ever since Vida left him, Oswaldo had lived there. He slept on a mat surrounded by books, students' exams and also shotguns and explosives he would hand out to guerrillas.

Next door to Oswaldo's workspace was that of the lecturer and writer Humberto Camejo Salas, a much-garlanded poet, founding member of the Literature Department, advocate of realism and *criollismo* as the defining tendencies of Venezuelan literature. Camejo Salas would become the main opponent to the so-called University Renewal, which started at the Escuela de Letras but was to expand to the rest of the university in 1969, with the cry of *Cervantes, my friend, your death shall be avenged!*

Everything that happened outside the university campus was replicated inside, like a shock whose effect was often to return to its clandestine point of origin. In the sixties, the Central University of Venezuela was the meeting place between the mountains and the city. It was a laboratory for testing the limits of the new system. The free expression of ideas was allowed here, as was the brazen sharing-out in No Man's Land of the loot from the latest bank robbery.

It was quite normal, then, that Camejo Salas should be aware of Miliani's activities. Miliani, on the other hand, never knew what his workplace neighbor was up to. Planning a strike, taking a border post from the army, printing a pamphlet calling for revolution—all these activities seemed less dark than the lightbulb that always remained switched on in Camejo Salas's office.

Oswaldo got a call from Vida in early 1962. She said that, after giving it a lot of thought, she had decided to come back. She just needed him to buy her the plane ticket.

Oswaldo didn't have any money. He went to the teachers' savings bank and asked for a loan. After several weeks of paperwork and long chats with Vida, they informed him he could pick up the check from the office at the School of Humanities. The loan amounted to twelve thousand bolívars, a fortune at the time. He went to a nearby bank, cashed the check and, before going to a travel agency, stopped by a post office. He needed to send Vida a telegram with the good news. Back at his desk he found Vida's reply. He told himself it was impossible;

it had been only a matter of minutes since he had sent his telegram. He read hers (*"Trip canceled. Maybe later. Or not."*), and
he told himself anything was possible.

Defeated and immensely rich, Oswaldo left university with
no idea what to do. He stepped out of the gate at Plaza Venezuela and walked to Sabana Grande. He thought about visiting
a brothel at Avenida Casanova, finding the most beautiful prostitute and asking her to marry him. He thought about going
into the Suma bookstore, spending half the amount on books
and using the other half to pay rent and locking himself away
until he had finished reading. He thought about depositing the
money in a bank and then robbing it. He was thinking about
many other things when he bumped into a thin man with a
long mustache and a gaze like an enchanted pond.

"What's up, Darío?"

"All good, real good," the man replied with a grin.

He didn't know Darío all that well. He knew he'd been
imprisoned during the dictatorship, and that, just like him, but
coming from Mexico, he'd been one of the many Venezuelans
who had returned in '58.

Oswaldo got carried away and, suddenly confiding, admitted
he was in a bad place. He told him about the disagreement with
Vida. About her promise to come back to him, about the telegram.

"I'm more or less in the same situation, but the other way
around," said Darío. Since Oswaldo didn't understand, he
added: "Magdalena has left, you know."

Magdalena Salma and Darío Mancini were lovers. Magdalena had been a psychiatrist but had quit her medical practice
to become an actor. In 1961 she reached a career high with her
performance in Peter Ustinov's play *The Love of Four Colonels*.
During the four months the play was staged at the Mini Teatro
del Este, Darío sat in the first row for every performance. The

fact that friends and acquaintances would bump into Darío on different nights led to speculation. Soon people were saying that the apartment Darío had in Vista Alegre, which he used as a workshop and a home, was paid for by Magdalena.

Everyone knew about their relationship, but no one could state anything categorically. Not only because nobody could boast of being Darío's friend, but simply out of discretion: at the time, Magdalena was still married to Humberto Camejo Salas.

After *The Love of Four Colonels* and a minor role in a soap opera that turned out to be crucial to the plot, Magdalena felt too constrained by the Venezuelan arts scene. She had also received a job offer in Mexico. The only thing stopping her was Darío. She asked him to go with her, but he didn't want to. His exile had taken place in that country, a period he refused to talk about. Now he just wanted to live in peace in Caracas and paint. It was Darío himself, his heart pierced by the cold that comes from making the right decisions, who helped Magdalena Salma to board a ship departing for Mexico.

Darío spent the first months painting, working with an energetic stroke over canvases that in the end registered a stream of blood that was turbulent and useless. He spent what little money he had on materials that fed this chromatic revenge, which had little, or nothing, to do with art. By the time he met Oswaldo Miliani, Darío owed three months' rent. Manuel Caballero had promised to move in with him and cover expenses.

"But Manuel won't be coming for another two months," said Darío, smiling but worried.

"How much do you owe?" asked Oswaldo.

"Seven hundred fifty bolívars."

Darío watched Oswaldo take the biggest roll of money he had ever seen from his jacket. Without checking from side to side, with the gesture of a bandit who shows his money but conceals it at the same time, Oswaldo counted out the notes and gave him seven hundred fifty bolívars.

"Oswaldo, I can't accept this," said Darío.

"Take it, I'm telling you."

"Let's do this: I'll take the money, but you come to the apartment with me. There's plenty of room for the two of us."

"What about Manuel?"

"We'll tell him there's been a change of plan."

Oswaldo thought it over for a few seconds. At last, he said:

"Darío, you know I got some troubles."

"Doesn't bother me at all."

That same night, Oswaldo Miliani moved in with Darío Mancini, into the apartment he was occupying on the seventh floor of Residencias Venezuela, in Vista Alegre, which hitherto had been paid for by the not-yet-very-famous actor Magdalena Salma.

First he stopped by the university to pick up some of his few belongings. As always, the lightbulb at the next cubicle was switched on. He worried about how little the light seemed to illuminate, how blind Camejo Salas seemed to be over the circumstances of his own life. Or maybe, he thought, that lightbulb reached other things beyond the man and the desk beneath it. Oswaldo Miliani tried to imagine the focal point of that light that rose up in that corridor of shadows like a lighthouse in the middle of the night, but he could see nothing.

That evening they celebrated with a bottle of wine. The date, April 23, 1962, was the anniversary of Comrade Cervantes's death, which seemed like a good omen. As the evening progressed, Oswaldo asked about Camejo Salas.

"Did he know?"

"I guess he did. In any case, I never wanted to ask Magdalena."

"That Camejo is so weird. He spends all day locked away as if he were building a nuclear bomb. And then you read the shitty verses he publishes, so simple, so stupid. I don't like him."

"He's a writer. Good or bad, all artists have a double life. They're essentially hypocritical."

"You can say that about anyone."

"What I'm saying is, for an artist, especially a writer, the world is just an excuse to let them live that second life. And that second life tends to be a room they lock themselves in to laugh at everybody else."

"What about you?"

"I'm not a writer, or an artist."

Oswaldo didn't know how to interpret those words, but he understood that Darío was one of the few people who had learned to truly know themselves.

Women tended to be the first to identify his sense of harmony, like a smell. During the time they shared the apartment, between April 23, 1962, and August 1963, Oswaldo was able to see the effect Darío had on women. Darío was a sort of shy prophet who, with just his gaze, or with the gentleness of his movements, or with the peace his silence irradiated, offered an invitation to go on a pilgrimage across symmetries and deserts.

Darío's mysticism was accentuated by the fact that he didn't take advantage of his power. He would see a mutual attraction, unconscious and unavoidable between beings, as an unobjectionable moral fact. Yet he distrusted seduction, believing it always had deceit and violence at its heart. That creed, which Oswaldo could only sense, must have been taken very seriously by Darío, since the only time Oswaldo saw him angry was because of it.

The elevator doors had not yet opened and already Oswaldo could hear Darío screaming. He rushed to open the door and found John Navarro and his wife protecting each other from the storm.

"That's not love! That's not love!" screamed an upset Darío. "Get out of here. I don't want to see you again!"

Oswaldo stepped aside to make way for the departing couple of friends, who tried to show him everything with a single gesture: shame, perplexity, regret.

After his third cigarette, Darío stopped shaking and managed to explain what had happened with a few words.

Navarro and his wife had visited Darío to tell him they had a problem. A conjugal problem. Darío didn't have a clue how to help them but said he would do anything. It was then that Navarro confessed that his wife was in love with him.

"With whom?" asked Darío.

"With you, Darío," said John.

Darío couldn't believe it. He couldn't believe what was happening to him for the fourth, fifth or sixth time in his life.

"Is that true?" he asked the woman.

Not daring to look at him, she nodded, crying.

"And can I ask why you are here?"

"After thinking it through, and considering our friendship, we decided that the sincerest thing to do would be to come here and talk to you, Darío."

"The sincerest thing to do, John? Are you utterly fucking insane? Do you really have no clue what love is, after all this time being married?"

That's how the rant Oswaldo witnessed in its final moments began.

This mental clarity would be translated into a chaotic relationship with objects and space. Darío would leave a trail of dirty socks, paintbrushes, notebooks, shirts, books and cigarette butts around the house, like the bread crumbs we leave to know our way back home. When sitting down, instead of moving his chair closer to the table, he would drag the table toward him, creating domestic earthquakes that exasperated Oswaldo.

Often, Oswaldo would interrupt Darío to ask him to clear the plates from the table where he was working, or to ask him to return a pair of scissors that, of course, he had no memory of borrowing in the first place.

One of these times he interrupted him to ask for help.

"What have I done now?" asked Darío, his hands black with paint.

"Nothing, man. It's just I need to talk about some university stuff, about my classes."

For some months Oswaldo had buried himself in *The Phenomenology of Spirit*, and there was one passage he found increasingly difficult. No matter how many times he thought about it, read and reread it, he couldn't completely understand the parable about master and slave as different approximations of order and thought. Freedom and purpose, desire and submission, were categories that he muddled in the card trick with which Hegel practiced his dialectics.

Darío asked him to read the passage, which, by the way, was short, and listened carefully. Then he effortlessly started to formulate an interpretation that left content aside and was instead centered on the structure of the thought. When he finished, he reversed what he had said, demonstrating that each affirmation negated its counterpart, in a way that wasn't from above or below, but simply dynamically, after which it was understandable that, in that Babylonian lottery that was pure reason, one could sometimes adopt the position of master and at others the position of slave.

"I didn't know you were a Hegelian" was all Oswaldo managed to say.

"Me neither. That bit you read is the only thing I know about Hegel."

"You are a genius," said Oswaldo, only half-jokingly.

"Believe me, not even Hegel had as much time for thinking as I did. I spent five years thinking nonstop."

That Hegelian anecdote happened in April 1963, when Oswaldo was about to complete a year of living at Darío's apartment. A month earlier, Teodoro Petkoff had been detained during a street action. They were holding him at San Carlos barracks, where, as Darío himself would put it, he'd have plenty of time for thinking. However, Oswaldo started planning the escape straight away.

Once the plan was all confirmed, each person learned their role and function. Through his wife, Beatriz, they would send Teodoro some medical articles that explained the symptoms of a gastric ulcer about to burst. Antonieta would be behind the wheel of her Vauxhall together with Beatriz and Marina, Oswaldo's sister, waiting for Teodoro outside the Military Hospital. Oswaldo needed to find the rope and get some capsules with blood to Teodoro just a few days before the operation.

Everything was ready on the morning of August 23, 1963. Before going out, Oswaldo stopped to look, amazed, at Darío's face—his friend could sense that they were up to something.

"Lend me your ID," said Oswaldo.

Darío gave it to him without asking what for. He wanted to know only when he would get it back.

"Tonight, if everything goes to plan," said Oswaldo.

On the preceding days, after the other prisoners had gone to bed, Teodoro had taken the capsules out the fridge he had in his cell and held them up against the lights that filtered from the lamps in the courtyard. He was preparing himself for what he thought would be an immediate reaction.

The first mishap that morning was that the blood didn't taste bad or make him sick. He drank it all up and nothing happened.

He needed to go ahead regardless, so even though he felt fine, he fell to the floor and started to shout and squirm. His cellmates raised the alarm and called the doctors. They took him to San Carlos's infirmary straight away. The doctor recommended that he be sent to the Military Hospital, but he had no conclusive evidence of the prisoner's being really ill. Colonel Pulido Tamayo, the head of the barracks, came and went all morning to monitor the progress of Teodoro's case firsthand. Each time, he would approach the stretcher and whisper things in his ear:

"You're a fucking liar, Teodoro. The moment your stomach-ache's gone, I'm going to fuck you up."

Every time, Teodoro would give a childish wave to shoo him away, as if he were another of the many nightmares conjured by the pain.

After two hours of that horse trading, with grimaces and insults, Pulido Tamayo made a decision:

"Send him back to his cell."

The doctor helped him to stand up, and Teodoro knew it was his last chance. He called upon all the strength he could, visualizing this energy like a mass of worms at the bottom of his stomach fighting to get out. When he passed Pulido Tamayo he screamed, and he felt a jet of blood bursting out like a miraculous fountain and straight onto the colonel's chest.

Once he was at the Military Hospital, the second phase took place. At reception, Beatriz confirmed that Teodoro had been admitted for a burst gastric ulcer. She came back to Antonieta's car and took the passenger seat. Marina Miliani, wearing a floral maternity dress and a cotton jumper, came out from the backseat. Her belly and the way she walked belonged to a woman who was seven or eight months pregnant. Hanging on her arm was a basket with bread, jam, cold cuts and a thermos of still-hot coffee.

At reception, they told her Teodoro Petkoff was in room 717, on the seventh floor. She caressed her belly in the elevator, praying that the number of months in her pregnancy was equivalent to the number of floors. When the elevator doors opened, she saw a guard post occupied by a very young corporal with a shotgun. Behind him, she could see a long, clean, unguarded corridor. If she could get past the control post, the plan would succeed. The corporal even checked her hair but didn't touch her belly out of respect. Then he opened the basket, opened the jam jar, cut the bread loaf into several pieces, opened the flask. He smelled the contents and Marina could tell, just by looking at his face, that his shift had been a long one.

"Just save at least a small cup for me," said Marina. "I'll be back for it in a minute."

The corporal poured himself a cupful in the flask lid, took a sip and let her through.

Outside room 717, Marina knocked on the door six times, waited for ten seconds and went in. Teodoro was standing, waiting for her. They hugged and exchanged a few rushed words of love and strategy.

"We need to hurry," said Marina. Then she put her hand inside her dress and took out several meters of rope. Teodoro took the rope from her, lifted up the false ceiling and hid it. Marina grabbed one of the pillows and put it where the rope had been. She spent the next few minutes patting down the pillow to make it resemble the shape of the belly she had come in with. Before leaving the room, she handed him the ID.

"What's this?" asked Teodoro.

"It's from Oswaldo. In case they ask on your way out."

Once he was alone again, Teodoro went back to bed and felt the hours passing at an excruciatingly slow pace. At six o'clock, once it had started to get dark, he looked out the window. He waited half an hour, then began. He took the rope from the ceiling, tied it to one leg of the bed and threw the rest out the window. The rope didn't seem to cover the whole distance. From where he stood, he couldn't tell whether, from where the rope ended, he would need to jump down one floor or three. It was then that he started to feel the nausea he hadn't felt when he drank the blood. The plan, up till that point, had gone well. Now it would all be down to him whether it succeeded, for the risks taken by his comrades not to have been in vain and for the escape, the first out of the three he's predestined to go through in his life as a guerrilla, to be complete, so that Teodoro Petkoff's legend might be born.

He checked the knot on the bed leg one more time and started climbing out the window. On his way down, Teodoro recalled a passage from *The Magic Mountain*. There weren't many similarities between Caracas and Davos, or between the Military Hospital and the sanatorium where Hans Castorp arrives. But anything to distract him from the vertigo was good, so Teodoro immersed himself in going back over his memory of the novel. He did this so well that he reached the ground with almost no trouble. He straightened his clothes, tried to comb his hair, smoothed his mustache and walked over to the exit. In his pocket he was carrying an ID with a photo of his, though he didn't know when it was taken or how Oswaldo had gotten hold of it. Then he paused at the name Darío Mancini, recalling the face of that painter who did time at the Modelo prison, and was amazed at how similar they looked. The man guarding the entrance didn't ask him for ID, and let him pass without paying him the slightest attention.

Teodoro Petkoff's first escape became one of the most talked-about episodes in the history of Latin American armed struggle in the 1960s. To this action he added another, in 1969, which was no less risky: the writing of the book *Czechoslovakia, Socialism as a Problem*, one of the earliest and most lucid critiques by a communist of the 1968 invasion of Prague. The book caused such a stir that Leonid Brezhnev himself declared Petkoff a defector at the Twenty-Fourth Congress of the Soviet Union Communist Party. That defection led him to establish his own political party in 1971, Movement Toward Socialism, to which Gabriel García Márquez, in 1972, donated the twenty-five-thousand-dollar prize money when his *One Hundred Years of Solitude* won the Rómulo Gallegos Prize. García Márquez would be an admirer of Petkoff's from then on, even supporting his 1983 presidential candidacy with a text called *Teodoro*, in which, albeit with a few inaccuracies, he summarized the famous escape from the Military Hospital.

García Márquez's inaccuracies are minor. For example, he talks about cow blood, when what Teodoro drank was actually human blood. The omission of two decisive details could be considered serious were it not for the fact that nobody but Teodoro himself would have noticed. How could he have remembered, chapter by chapter, and word by word, a novel as extensive as *The Magic Mountain*, let alone under such circumstances? In addition, Teodoro couldn't explain, either, the fact that as his feet touched the floor, the rope had stretched, growing like an uncoiled snake.

A telephone call interrupted Darío's reading. He set the thick gray book down on the nightstand and went to the kitchen to pick up the phone.

"Come down in five minutes and open the door for Teo. Don't stand around talking at the door," said Oswaldo.

Once he was downstairs, and despite his orders, Darío got distracted for a few seconds. Teodoro was already calling the

152 de Rodrigo Blanco Calderón

elevator, but Darío stayed by the door, watching Antonieta driving away with Beatriz and Marina.

In the elevator, they shook hands and said nothing. Their eyes met in the mirror, and seeing their reflections multiplied, they burst out laughing.

"Before I forget," said Teodoro, taking the ID from his shirt pocket and giving it to Darío.

"Did you use it?" asked Darío.

"I didn't, luckily."

Once in the flat, Teodoro headed straight for the bathroom to take a shower.

"Are you hungry?" shouted Darío from the other side of the door.

"No," replied Teodoro. "A coffee would be great, though."

When he saw him coming out, freshly showered and dressed, Darío thought about how Teodoro was a more battle-hardened version of himself.

"What's up?" asked Teodoro, drinking the boiling coffee in one gulp.

"Nothing. I was just thinking what my life would have been like if I'd tried to escape prison."

"They would have killed you. Remember, despite everything, those *adecos* need to save face. At the end of the day, that's what democracy comes down to."

The telephone rang again, and this time Teodoro answered it.

"OK," he said, "I'm coming down."

They said goodbye downstairs at the front door.

"Thanks for the coffee."

"You're welcome," said Darío.

Back in the kitchen, he poured himself the dregs left in the cafetière.

Such a great guy, that Teodoro, thought Darío, not knowing this would be the last time he would ever see him.

Darío returned to his room, lay down on his bed, took up the book from his bedside table and went on reading *The Magic Mountain*.

16

Painting, a Weapon

"'Those to whom evil is done, do evil in return,' wrote Auden," said Oswaldo Barreto. "Guasina, for instance, started as a concentration camp for Nazis. Can you believe it? For Nazis and also for escapees from Cayenne, like that Papillon. Also there, you have those people who never caused any trouble and are nevertheless pursued by evil. It's even worse for them, if you ask me," he added.

Darío was nearly imprisoned again after Teodoro's escape, even though he hadn't done anything. They took Oswaldo away immediately. The first interrogations were predictable: Where is Teodoro, where are the weapons, and how about the Puerto Ricans, who are your contacts in the FALN? Typical. But he began to worry when they started getting the questions right.

"You live in Residencias Venezuela, in Vista Alegre, don't you? That's your bolt-hole," said one of the policemen.

"That's where they meet up and organize everything," said another.

Oswaldo would deny the accusations without much conviction, wrapping himself in a thick fog of learned stupidity.

After the questions and the first round of beatings, a policeman came in whom Oswaldo didn't remember having seen before. He was the replacement. Time for a change of routine.

He was a strong, elegant, bearded man. He watched Oswaldo for several minutes in silence, hands in his pockets.

"How's Darío?" he said suddenly.

Oswaldo had to fight hard to remain still.

"I don't know any Darío," he said after a while.

"Are you sure? You've been living with him for a year. You must know him."

"I don't know who you're talking about."

"Sure you do. Tell me something, kid. Does Darío still have a mustache? Is he still painting?"

Some movement or other gave Oswaldo away. It was enough for the policeman to consider his job done. He headed for the door.

"Who should I tell Darío was asking after him?" said Oswaldo.

The policeman stopped and turned around. He smiled like a farmer.

"A friend. Tell Darío his pal Erasto Fernández sends his best."

That same night Oswaldo passed the message on to one of his sisters, Graciela. She met up with Gallegos Mancera, who talked to Darío immediately.

"We need to provide you with a grant and get you out the country," said Gallegos Mancera.

"Eduardo, I'm thirty-one," said Darío.

"No matter. The grant is really a monthly allowance. Nothing extraordinary, but at least you won't starve."

"A grant to do what?"

"Whatever the party needs."

"I don't know which is worse."

"Prison, Darío. Prison is worse. Knowing you, you're going to be shitting yourself, but go out and take a stroll around Paris and it'll pass, right?"

"Paris?"

"Now you understand the advantages of belonging to the party. Leave the apartment in Vista Alegre and try to stay away from trouble."

"Thank you, Eduardo."

"Don't thank me. Thank the party. If it weren't for the party, you'd be in jail again. Or else checking chicken assholes at the Guaicaipuro market."

In February 1958, Darío and Arnaldo had returned to Venezuela from Mexico, via Panama. Arnaldo had found them jobs as poultry inspectors at the Guaicaipuro and Coche markets.

"It was hard. It's a role in demand among poets," said Arnaldo. "Sanoja, Pepe and Rafael also applied, but we beat the fuckers."

Darío nodded, not really listening to Arnaldo and not asking what a poultry inspector actually did.

They'd worked at the markets for a year. The words, images and smells from those heavily spiced corridors would hang around his neck, choking him with their sweetness. Darío painted canvases with ethnic motifs and fruit. Strong black women, with breasts like cocoa fruit and *bachaco* asses. Workers and peasants looking powerful, always powerful, holding a fainting world in their arms as if about to carry it away.

Early in 1959, Darío and Arnaldo became Knights of the Round Table and left the poultry inspectors' job. The group's name wasn't because of Manuel Caballero's Francophile influences, as someone insinuated, nor was it linked to his knightly surname, as suggested by someone else. It was all down to the shape of the table they had occupied at the Cervecería Alemana, on Sabana Grande Boulevard.

In May, they printed the first issue of the group's magazine. There Darío published "On Painting as a Weapon," an article in which he stated that painting "fundamentally means defining one's position, taking sides, becoming an activist on the side of life. . . . Creation is never compatible with indifference. It may be a constant struggle, which is nothing but a validation of life itself, but it can never be tranquility in stagnant waters. Art has roots that are social, collective!"

These outbursts of social realism were followed by periods of isolation. Months in which his comrades didn't know where he was, what he was up to, or what he was living off.

He would reappear, thinner and with bigger bags under his eyes, around the Sabana Grande, at the Cervecería Alemana, at the Chicken Bar or the Paprika. He would emerge from these periods with new contributions to the magazine. Aestheticist and melancholic texts that would demand the right to solitude for artists such as Van Gogh or Reverón.

Erasto Fernández collected issues of the magazine. He would read every article carefully, no matter whether these were by Jesús Sanoja Hernández, Manuel Caballero, Joaquín González, Darío Mancini or anyone else. He would read them all, between one torture session and another, one police raid and the next.

He kept a close eye on the controversy between the Round Table group and Juan Liscano. Juan Liscano was a real poet, useful to society with his unforgettable folkloric poetry. Even Uslar himself, for that matter, was a better writer than all those communists put together. He also tried to find some way of using these poems, articles, drawings, and reviews to decode future conspiracies. Issue number nine, published in April, had especially annoyed him. It was clearly the most anti-governmental and subversive issue so far. The silence they had maintained during the previous year, 1962, made him toy with the idea of the magazine having shut down. Along with the PCV—the Communist Party—and the Revolutionary Left

Movement, he thought that RT, as he called them, may also have been deactivated.

With the little drawings Darío had made for that issue, along with the fact he had just confirmed in Oswaldo's interrogation, Erasto had enough to send him to jail for another five years. It wouldn't hurt to pay a visit to the Vista Alegre apartment. He was almost certain it would be deserted by then. In reality, the message he had radioed to Darío through Oswaldo was a favor for the sake of old times at Ciudad Bolívar.

On the evening of September 1, 1963, not only had Darío not moved out of the apartment, but he had organized a small goodbye party. He hadn't yet set a definite date, but after talking to Gallegos Mancera, he could already see himself at the big city gates. Some people thought that it was going to be one of those strange pranks Darío would pull from time to time and that he wouldn't show. The three or four who did attend thought the Paris trip was code for Teodoro's incredible escape, which everybody was talking about.

Antonieta was the last to arrive. Erasto was unable to react. His mouth had dropped open at the sight of that thin, beautiful, feline woman coming through the door holding a bottle of wine.

"Who are you? Show me your papers," said Erasto at last.

"She's my model," Darío cut in, grabbing the first painting he found, one of the many scattered around the apartment.

Erasto moved closer to the painting that Darío was holding as if around the waist. The canvas showed a naked woman, who had dark brown hair like Antonieta's, but was fat. Certainly with much more flesh on her than *La Maja desnuda*.

Erasto looked closely at it for a few minutes and then looked at the thin, gazelle-like figure of Antonieta from the top of her head to the tip of her toes. He scratched his head, and spent a few more seconds comparing the painting with the supposed model before he noticed Darío's expression.

"What are you laughing at?"

"Nothing, Erasto."

"Superintendent Fernández to you, asshole. Everybody, pick up your things and get moving."

Antonieta got off the hook quickly. When they arrived at the headquarters of the DIGEPOL police directorate, she called her dad, who in turn called Uncle Pedro, who was friends with Minister Montilla, who managed to get her out without any major issues. Nothing to worry about, except for the pandemonium with which she was going to be received at home.

The others underwent the usual interrogation.

"Leave the artist to me," asked Erasto.

Fernández waited until they had taken details from Darío, who with his usual good manners spoke softly but clearly in answer to every question.

When Darío stood up, handcuffed, Erasto took him by the arm and pushed him into one of the cubicles.

Ramón had spent two hours in the DIGEPOL waiting room with no news on his brother. He walked to a public phone on the street corner and made a couple of calls, and when he returned he saw Darío. He was coming down the corridor, peacefully, smiling, as if nothing unusual had happened. At the end of the corridor, behind the reception desk, Ramón saw the silhouette of Erasto Fernández. They recognized each other.

"What's up, Abdem?" said Darío.

"Are you all right?" said Ramón.

At that moment, Erasto came over.

"Remember what I told you," he said, his voice trembling.

"Don't worry," said Darío.

Erasto was pale. He returned to the far end of the corridor, dragging his feet.

"Are you all right?" asked Ramón again, once they were out on the street.

"I am, Ramón. Honestly, I'm fine."

"What did he say to you?"

"I need to go."

"What else did he ask you? Old Soto has already said some terrible things. He's gone out of his mind, what with Teodoro's escape."

"We didn't talk about that."

"What did you talk about, then?"

"Painting, art. That kind of shit."

Ramón started laughing. Typical Darío comment. He stopped feeling that anchor-like oppression in the pit of his stomach. Then he remembered Erasto's face, the breeze of fear that for a moment had rustled his movements, and he thought maybe Darío was being serious. Perhaps that really was all they talked about. He thought both impressions were real, although he couldn't find the link between them. In any case, there was no time to waste. If he wanted to save his brother from prison, he needed to help him get out of the country.

He knew this, and he also knew it would be a long time before he saw him again.

17

The Princess and the Circus

Princesses are women who hurt other people unintentionally. They do so much harm with their beauty that in time they become shy. They turn their grace inward, as if it were possible to hide it. Their personality is transparent and docile, like cellophane that barely protects a rose.

Aged five, María Antonieta knew only that she was a princess and she was happy, and that was enough for her. She lived in a palace among many people who loved and looked after her. Her parents lived there, and they loved her more than anyone else did, and Catalina—who wasn't her sister, or even a relative, as they tried so often to explain to her, but was always a step behind her, ready to help in any way—lived there too.

The palace had a vast garden with jasmine plants that whispered their perfume to her. At the end of the garden, as in a fairy tale, there was a sinister kingdom: the horses' cemetery. No one could go to that place, since the cemetery was guarded by a dragon who, if woken, would spread panic through the whole palace.

For a while, María Antonieta was the undisputable queen of that Versailles (in those golden years, being a queen or a princess was a matter of will rather than hierarchy). Later, other princesses would come, and a prince, and the palace would be transformed into a very busy house, the meeting place for two Andean families, who had come to Valera from Boconó and Trujillo.

Her father taught them to read when they were very little, and he let them into his library: "The safest place on earth." Even though from that moment, and for the rest of their lives, all seven siblings were avid readers, only María Antonieta understood that message in all its depth. Her father seemed to be telling them that this was the safest way to be alone.

From then on, reading was the safe passage that allowed her to lock herself in the library for hours and avoid the visits, or at least some of them, of the dozens of uncles and aunts, cousins, and great-uncles and great-aunts she had. The older people would always ask the same question: "How old are you?" Followed by a comment, always in just the same words: "Euricia, the girl is so pretty."

How she wished someone could ask her, for example, "Why is a raven like a writing desk?" But the adults didn't ask those questions. They didn't answer her questions either. "If Catalina isn't my sister, who are her parents and why doesn't she live with them? If she's my cousin's age, why can't she play with her?"

Every time they heard that "if," Euricia and Eduardo would ready themselves.

"Where is Catalina?" asked María Antonieta once. "Is it true she ran away with the circus?"

"Who told you that?" answered her mother.

"Josefina did. And Ramiro is saying the same thing."

"I'll have a word with them, so they stop making up stories."

"When the circus comes back, can I go with them?"

Euricia widened her eyes, and shot Eduardo a terrified look.

"Keep asking silly questions, María Antonieta, and the next time the circus comes you won't even see it from afar. You won't set foot outside this house till you're married."

Her mom left the room, upset, bringing things to an end. Her dad winked at her.

Adolescence was like a winter barracks. Calm in nature, María Antonieta and her sisters committed only one fault every three months: becoming even prettier. Grandad Alfonso followed his granddaughters' developments with concern. Starting with María Antonieta, who was no longer very skinny and was starting to grow some curves.

Alfonso Granada Urrieta was an old soldier from the Andes. After Juan Vicente Gómez betrayed Cipriano Castro, he occupied himself with his farms, raising horses and burying them. Many people thought the Urrieta family's horse cemetery was a myth. Whenever some horse broke its leg, it was General Granada himself who, regretfully, would deliver the coup de grace. He would use his own spade to dig the animal's grave and bury it. Scenes like these made Grandad Alfonso a figure of terror in the house.

However, life never gave him an opportunity to train his gun on any of his granddaughters' suitors. He died one day, sometime between one and five in the afternoon, on the sofa in the living room next door to the dining room where he used to sit after lunch. Grandad Alfonso's postprandial sleep was never longer than three quarters of an hour, but the fear of waking him up and making him angry was stronger than the strange fact of his being on the sofa for over four hours in the same position, his features dappled by the room's chiaroscuro, his face frozen in the same grimace, somewhere between asleep and awake.

María Antonieta, after thinking about it for a long time, finally came closer to the sofa, touched her grandad's shoulder and realized that her childhood dragon was dead.

With the door to the rose garden finally breached by destiny, the first suitors appeared. From the moment she met him, María Antonieta didn't hesitate to choose Mauricio Caminos. Her family approved of the young man's attentions, and before she could get used to walking accompanied or holding the gaze of a man ten years her senior, the marriage was decided. María Antonieta didn't remember being asked by her parents, or by Mauricio, but the families were so happy with the idea that she thought she ought to be happy too.

Their honeymoon consisted of a trip across Central America, Mexico, and the United States. A couple of months after returning, she got pregnant. María Antonieta and Mauricio were married for seven years, and during that time had four children.

On drowsy afternoons when extreme tiredness and a sort of tranquility became the same thing, María Antonieta would do the sums: seven years, four children, three years pregnant, two and a half days giving birth, four years and nine months raising babies, never knowing a full night's sleep.

She never would have imagined that this expending of energy that so exhausted her was happiness. That what she was given in the blink of an eye was what many other women searched for, sometimes for years, and did not always find. Life could be inconsiderate, dropping those bundles of happiness onto only a few men and women.

Then the anguish came. It happened one day when Mauricio had taken the children to visit their grandparents and she had the house to herself. She finally had that haven of peace that had eluded her for so many years, and now she didn't know how to handle it. All she could do was bury herself in the silence of that empty space, with no music, without the murmuring turmoil that any living soul feels when they are alone.

The next day she gave the order to build her own version of the safest place on earth. A partition wall was added to an entrance hall that was never used, a door was fitted and a library installed.

Her father allowed her to take many of the books she had read in her childhood and adolescence. The Russian masters and classic French and English writers from the nineteenth century took up the first bookcase. Rómulo Gallegos, Teresa de la Parra, Andrés Bello and other Venezuelan authors shyly occupied two shelves of the second. The other two bookcases were filled in over the following months with the work of Jean-Paul Sartre, Virginia Woolf, Marcel Proust, Sigmund Freud, Franz Kafka, Henry Miller and James Joyce, among others.

Reading those authors, she understood that it is possible to be happy and love some people and, at the same time, to want to be happy in other ways and love other people. To love an idea, for example, with the same passion with which one could love someone in particular. She understood that this contradictory knot where so many different desires fluttered about was called *plexus* and was located, like a shadowy fold, between the stomach and the heart.

Mauricio watched. He would see her go into her library with renewed anticipation, only to see her come out a few hours later with her gaze inflamed by some distant intuition. It was apparent to him that there was a lot going on. More and more families from Valera, Trujillo, Boconó, Mérida or San Cristóbal were moving to Caracas. The way business was going, he had to travel to the capital often. The fall of Pérez Jiménez had been the starting shot of a race everyone knew they had to run, even though the finishing line and itinerary had not yet been defined. Two years later, when María Antonieta told him she wanted to separate and move to Caracas with her family, Mauricio wasn't surprised, and he resigned himself to the course things were taking. He would always have the memories, and the children. He could always say he'd had beauty sitting on his knee, with its guarantee of enchantment, pain and eventual escape, and that he had been brave and had never disrespected her.

Locked in her library, María Antonieta didn't just read. She could stare at an indefinite point, piercing the air with her gaze. During those trances, she would come up with the most absurd scenes. Versions of herself that were both comforting and melancholic. She would imagine, for example, that the library was her father's and she was still sixteen. Mauricio would come in and they would make love behind the folding screen. Her father would open the door unannounced and catch them by surprise. He would get so angry he would become her grandfather, taking out a shotgun and firing at Mauricio. At night, she would suddenly grasp her husband's chest to cast out these images that she didn't yet understand.

At other times she would read and reread the letters from Oswaldo, a friend of hers and of her family's, who had been living in Paris for a while. She was fascinated by the news from a world she found as attractive as the one in *Alice's Adventures in Wonderland* had been when she was little. Oswaldo would tell her about authors and books he had recently discovered, sometimes he would send her some of these books by post. She would surprise him with references and readings that were unheard of for someone who had barely traveled outside a city like Valera, a place that was enveloped in an eternal aura from another time.

In April 1959, Oswaldo returned to his country. He studied in Caracas for a month and then found a teaching position at the University of the Andes. From Mérida, he could travel frequently to Valera to visit family and friends. In 1961 he found a job as a lecturer in the Journalism School of the Central University, so he moved back to Caracas.

The night before his departure, Oswaldo and María Antonieta had a conversation.

"What do you think you're going to do, Antonieta?" That's what Oswaldo called her. "I spoke to Doña Euricia and she said they're also going to be moving to Caracas by the end of the year."

"Yes, my parents are finding it harder and harder to sell the land."

"You have to come too, then."

"I can't. And anyway, go to Caracas to do what?"

"Whatever you want, Antonieta."

"To study."

"There you are."

"I like studying. But I can't leave."

"If you stay, you'll end up being just another one of those ladies who don't do anything apart from playing bridge and canasta."

María Antonieta didn't know how to play bridge or canasta, but she figured she would be an expert by the time the children were married and had left home. She could imagine herself, during one of her digressions at the library, like an Andean Miss Marple. A nice little grandma by day and a clever crime-solving detective by night. But what crimes could she solve in Valera? Some livestock theft, a peasant who'd gotten shot in the face, a treacherous stabbing under a bridge. Crimes explained by jealousy, greed and rowdiness. Depending on her mood, those fantasies could make her cry or have her in stitches.

In October 1961 she received a letter from Oswaldo. He had talked to Beatriz Rivera, a fellow lecturer at the School of Education of the Central University, who had enrolled her as a student there. She needed only to formalize the enrollment in person. Classes would start in March the following year.

Oswaldo talked about his "plan" in the same mysterious tone with which he talked about revolution. She didn't remember telling Oswaldo what studies she wanted to pursue. She didn't know herself.

Even though it was sheer madness, she was secretly glad, once again, not to have to make any decisions. She simply needed to follow the path indicated to her by the distant fireworks of someone else's interests.

"Peace has ended in this house," Doña Euricia would now say every so often, although, between the move and the new life in the capital, the house had never experienced a quiet moment yet.

Jorgito, who had become a communist in high school, especially because of Uncle Alejandro's influence, contacted the city "cells" as soon as he arrived in Caracas. That's how they grouped together, and that's what they were called, as if they were spores. And, to tell the truth, they were indeed a bit like spores, the way they met.

"Bad company has always stuck to Jorgito, like burs to clothes," Doña Euricia complained.

"Always," added Grandmother Estela.

Jorge spent the day at university and would come back home at night, have dinner and then disappear into his room. Sometimes he would arrive with other boys whom Jorge would introduce as comrades-in-arms, and Doña Euricia and Doña Estela crossed themselves whenever they heard the term. *In arms, struggle, comrade, cell, committee*—these were words that could only mean bad news.

María Antonieta wasn't worried about Jorge's militancy. In his room, he and his comrades would just talk about Cuba, the USSR and revolution, while smoking joints. She knew because from the moment she caught them, she wanted to try it too, and from then on she never missed a chance to smoke with them. María Antonieta wouldn't give her opinion about politics, revolutions or guerrillas. It was enough for her to be a silent attendee at the meetings organized by Oswaldo, who really was, as they say, in the thick of it. A common expression among Jorgito and his friends, who, while very pleased with themselves, were in fact themselves far removed from anything more substantial than the marijuana smoke they inhaled.

Even though they couldn't recognize the smell coming out of that room, Doña Euricia and Doña Estela knew there was something going on, since even María Antonieta, always so obedient and cautious, was now hanging out with bad-looking people, possibly even worse than Jorgito's friends.

"The circus is coming to town," the grandmother would say when she saw Oswaldo's car arriving at the parking lot of Residencias Valencia.

"It looks like a bandwagon full of clowns," added Doña Euricia when she saw them getting out the car. And she would go to knock at María Antonieta's door.

The members of the circus were Verónica Dennis, The Giant; Josué González, The Dwarf; Oswaldo Miliani, The Consumptive; and Darío Mancini, The Mustachioed One. Nicknames and their assignation were an invention shared between Doña Euricia and Doña Estela. A joke that didn't always conceal the mistrust with which they received them whenever they came to bother María Antonieta.

The family moved again in early 1963. From Residencias Valencia, in Las Mercedes, they went to Residencias Manchego, in Chuao. The distance between the apartment complexes was quite short, yet Doña Euricia believed she had managed to baffle her children's friends with that ingenuous castling move.

The circus took note of the change of address and started frequenting the apartment in Chuao. If there was one positive thing to say about those guys it was that they had good manners. Not like Jorge's friends, who would just honk the horn to call him, like fugitives. María's, meanwhile, would get out of the car to say hello. Sometimes they wouldn't go anywhere and would stay chatting in the living room until midnight. On occasion, they would still be in the same room at daybreak, waiting frankly for the older women to make them breakfast. It was better that way, even if they left the apartment stinking of nicotine. Eduardo would be cheered up by having his morning coffee with the youngsters, and at least María Antonieta wasn't out all night on the streets.

Then there was that other man's escape, in which they'd managed to involve María Antonieta. How scandalous, dear God, at least no one outside those closest to the family found out. Only Pedro, who spoke to that man with the surname Montilla, the minister, to get the girl released straight away. Beyond the anguish and the shame, there was a silver lining to that fright: now Jorgito and María Antonieta would understand how dangerous it was to be hanging with such companions.

At last, Doña Estela and Doña Euricia had a couple of months' peace. They read stories in the papers with the details about Teodoro Petkoff's spectacular escape from the Military Hospital. Who would have imagined, even knowing her just a little, that María Antonieta could have had anything to do with that? That's the problem with living in a city like Caracas, where families stay apart, and no one knows their neighbor's surname.

The circus had dispersed. Darío had escaped to Paris. Because of her husband's activities, Verónica had had to leave for Mexico in a hurry, taking her young children with her.

Once he was free, Oswaldo went back into hiding. Although she was concerned about all their fates, Doña Euricia was above all worried about that of María Antonieta, who now, at last, would be left alone and could devote herself entirely to her studies, which were the reason she had come to Caracas in the first place.

That's why Doña Euricia got the shock of her life when her daughter, her eldest child, informed her about her decision to move to Paris by the end of the year.

"To Paris? What for?" asked Euricia.

"Just for six months. I've enrolled in some courses with Beatriz."

"What about your studies?"

"I'm going to skip next semester. I'll re-enroll the one after."

"I forbid it, María Antonieta. You're being reckless, you're not thinking things through. You have studies to finish and a family to look after."

"Mamá, it's only six months."

"You just want to follow that guy. Don't think I haven't noticed what's going on between you. I bet the rest of the circus is going too. That's all you do: you follow the circus."

That scolding was an eye-opener. She had enjoyed knowing that within her group, between the tangle of projects, actions and plots, there was an intimate conspiracy only he and she took part in, which until now had been so subtle she thought it was a mirage.

But at that moment, the most important discovery was made by her mother, who knew her better than anyone else did and had figured out her true intentions for the trip. In a second María Antonieta understood what she had been trying to understand since her childhood, what Ramiro and Josefina used to whisper in the kitchen or in a corner of the garden.

172   Rodrigo Blanco Calderón

What she had hidden from herself since then, because the mere thought of it was an acceptance of something painful and shameful, and which wasn't her fault, but of which she wasn't completely innocent either. She understood who Catalina had really been, and why she had run away as she did. And then she decided, just like Catalina twenty years earlier, to follow the only possible path, which was also the most dangerous one, the one with the fewest assurances, the one that frightened her the most.

"Yes, mamá. I'm going to follow the circus, too," said Antonieta.

That "too" reverberated in Doña Euricia's ears like the slam of a door, bringing a whole era to an end.

18

Paris

Darío found the name of the magazine, *Peace and Other Socialist Problems*, so funny that he never managed to take his job seriously the whole year and a half he was living in Paris. He was the proofreader of the magazine's Spanish edition. He was good at proofreading. One needed only to know the language and pay attention.

Altogether, it took him two weeks to get used to the new routine and one more week to get bored.

Routine then began to take its toll, and he started to introduce mistakes into the articles. He was amazed at the way a "not" could completely change the sense of a text, transforming its author from a consistent revolutionary into a reactionary and a traitor.

Initially, he thought he would end up in prison or deported or expelled from the party. But nothing happened, and little by little, by altering the spelling of a word, or changing the syntax of a phrase, or introducing codes by modifying the first letter of each paragraph ("Stalin, suck my dick" was his most reckless acrostic), he confirmed what he already suspected: that nobody, not anyone from the CIA or the KGB, nor a single comrade from the party, actually read those articles. Or, alternatively, they read them without paying attention, which is the same as not reading them at all.

Otherwise, he spent his time enjoying the city, enveloped in an air of drunkenness, of indolence, that kept him apart from real life. He would spend his free time discovering cafés, bookstores, hidden passages among busy streets. The Louvre and the Rodin became his ever-changing labyrinths. In Paris, he gorged on art and gave up painting. He had never felt so free. His friends, in turn, completed the aporia when they started referring to him as a true artist, a genius.

Belén was the first to fall under his influence as an artist without a body of artworks. She was also an artist but thought her work would always be inferior to anything Darío had decided not to create. Shortly after they met, she moved in with him, without asking, into the apartment he had been allocated at 51 Rue Mazarine. The apartment was rented under the name of Antón Parra, who was the Latin America coordinator of the communist youths who lived in Paris or were passing through on their way to the countries of the Eastern Bloc.

Darío couldn't explain how Comrade Larralde had managed to get into the apartment with all her belongings and art materials. It didn't seem to bother him.

"Please don't make too much of a mess," Antón told him.

Darío looked at him puzzled, pretending he didn't know what he was talking about.

Later, when Edmond visited, it became clear to Parra that Belén was a silly and dangerous woman. When Edmond got out of the car and she recognized him, the first thing she said was:

"I'm gonna fuck that guy today."

She said it in front of Antón, and Darío himself. With no shame whatsoever, behaving like a male on the prowl the way the most idiotic women in the party did when a Cuban, with his beard, beret, and cigar, turned up at a meeting. The thing Antón most disliked was Darío's answer: he snorted as if hearing a bad joke, neutralizing the venom of Belén's comment.

That night, as she had promised, Belén went to bed with Edmond in the spare room Antón Parra had prepared for his friend in the apartment on Rue Daguerre, where he had moved after lending Darío the one on Rue Mazarine.

Edmond was doing a doctorate in Marseille, but he would spend weekends in Paris, staying with the group of Venezuelans. It was he who told Antón about the state of the apartment. Belén had taken him there one Saturday afternoon. He saw paint pots spilling over the floor, cigarette butts making paths of ashes, empty bottles of wine lined up like skirting boards along the hall, the backpacks of other comrades who would spend the night there, the concierge's long face, suggesting arguments with the tenants for one reason or another.

"And Darío?" asked Edmond the second time she took him to the filthy apartment.

"At the magazine, I guess. Or at some museum. Or walking around. Who knows?" said Belén.

Edmond caught a glimpse of resentment and understood that the apartment was an altar to despair, an angry attempt to grab Darío's attention.

"Can I see his room?" asked Edmond.

"Sure," said Belén. And he was surprised she had replied so willingly, without suspicion, as if it were the most normal thing in the world that someone like him would want to take in every detail, with impunity, of the space where someone like Darío slept, woke up and killed time.

It was a clean, austere room, a monk's room. Or maybe he saw it that way because of the contrast with the neglect of the living room, the kitchen and, in particular, Belén's room. The mattress was laid on the parquet. On the mattress there was a pillow, and a folded set of sheets and duvet. In a corner, a record player next to a pile of classical music records and a freshly emptied ashtray. At the foot of the mattress, there was a paperback edition of Alfred Jarry's *Ubu enchaîné*, published by Le Livre Club du Libraire. He registered this detail because of a curiosity. There was a mistake in the colophon, as it said that the book had been published in 1965, and it was still only 1963. There was a nearly new copy of *Finnegans Wake*. There was also a copy in Spanish, without a jacket, of Malraux's *The Human Condition*. He looked at the colophon and was surprised again. The publication date was 1950, but the worn-out pages, smeared with an oily yellow color, would have led him to believe it was actually a much older book.

What were the chances of finding two different books in the same room with mistakes in the colophon? Was Darío into collecting books with imperfections? Why?

He felt like opening the closet and rummaging around his clothes, but thought that would be excessive. Belén didn't miss any of his movements and probably wouldn't understand any of it. Did he understand it, though? He hesitated for a few more seconds before a nauseating smell made him react. He felt it in his clothes, someplace very close. He raised his hands and brought them to his nose. Then the fetidness hit him and he had to run to the bathroom to wash.

On that visit, he didn't want to stay much longer. At night, lying in the spare room, he smelled his hands again to make sure there was none of that smell still on his fingers, but at the same time he was scared of finding the tiniest trace. Yes, there it was, hidden among the disinfectant and the lavender fragrance. The same smell he'd become familiar with during his years as a medical student, when he'd carried out his first autopsies. The smell that had adhered to the bone-colored pages of that copy of Malraux's book was the unmistakable reek of the dead.

Edmond told Antón only part of what he had seen, and

especially sensed, when visiting the Rue Mazarine apartment. When his friend asked him about Darío, he just said:

"Darío is a greater spirit—I'm not sure that I'm making myself clear."

"No, you aren't. Please, explain yourself."

"Just be patient with him."

Beatriz and Antonieta arrived in late 1963. They stayed at the Four Nations Hotel and took the winter semester classes in a school on Rue Mouffetard. Whenever he left the magazine early or managed to sneak out of the office, Darío would wait for them at the table of some café on that street, always with his copy of *Ubu enchaîné* and his notebook, in which he drew pictures and completed crosswords, as far as the friends who ran into him could see.

Sometimes, a sort of Venezuelan delegation in Paris would assemble by chance, hopping between the city cafés and ending up in the apartment of some party representative who had enough space to accommodate them all. On such occasions, Darío would say goodbye early, or, if he stayed, he would assemble a *petit comité* from the groups at the big tables or in the living rooms of whichever apartment they were at. Those councils were like an oasis of irony in a desert of unshakable vocations and mission statements.

"Be careful, Darío, and hold your tongue," a comrade told him one night when he heard him laugh, mockingly, at the guerrillas' chances of winning in Venezuela.

Edmond, who had been listening to the conversation, had no difficulty in understanding what his comrade was trying to say. There was something Socratic about Darío's ways. He was like a dormant volcano that diminished any overexcitement with its silence and its ashes. And in a sense, Socrates was a metaphor for out-of-control intelligence, like a scorpion that stings itself when it is bored with the world.

However, thought Edmond, Darío could save himself. Deep down, he's like a child. And then there's Antonieta, of course. Edmond had noticed that Darío's sarcasm disappeared only when he was with her. How long until they realized? And once they were together, how long until they realized they had not in fact changed despite their meeting, and that everything had been doomed from the start? Once, drinking a coffee with Antonieta at Le Dôme, while waiting for some comrades, he told her as much:

"I can tell you're looking for something, but the search is dizzying."

Antonieta didn't like Edmond. Nor did Darío. They talked about this once, the time they walked through Père Lachaise Cemetery. They had stopped in front of a tomb that had grabbed Antonieta's attention. The inscription said it was the tomb of a painter. His most important picture, apparently, was reproduced in a large bronze plaque with relief.

"*Le Radeau de la Méduse*," said Darío. "By Géricault. Do you know the story of the shipwreck?"

On July 5, 1816, the passengers and crew of the French frigate *La Méduse*, after three days of futile struggle, realized that their vessel had run aground irreversibly. Only a few crew members (ultimately, the more experienced ones) remained on board for several more days until they were rescued. Many others saved themselves by securing places on the auxiliary boats, and the rest, around 150 people, were left to their own devices on a sort of shoddily made raft. Of these post-Napoleonic boat people, only about fifteen survived. As the days went by, many killed themselves, some others were thrown to the sea while fighting for a sliver of wood, while still others prompted the acts of cannibalism and madness that characterized the last leg of that tragic drift.

"On July 5th, 1816," repeated Darío. "And one hundred sixteen years later, I was born."

Darío smiled. He found the coincidence amusing, as if his own life were a piece of the frigate that, borne along by a century of water, had survived the shipwreck. Antonieta sank into those eyes that had always called to her, and grabbed hold of that piece of wood in the middle of the storm. At that moment she knew she was in love, and that she had loved him ever since they'd met.

"How do you know all that?" was the only thing Antonieta managed to say.

"By chance. The first time I noticed the painting was thanks to Edmond. I bumped into him one morning at the Louvre, when he was studying it, absorbed. I found it weird that when I left, at nearly five o'clock, he was still sitting on the same bench opposite the painting. In fact, every time he goes to the Louvre, at least all the times I've seen him, he's always sitting there."

After that first encounter, Darío found some time during the week when he could visit the Louvre and study the painting too, at his leisure, making sure he wouldn't run into Edmond.

"I don't like him," said Darío.

"Me neither," said Antonieta. "It's like he's always spying on us. You talk to him and it's like he's psychoanalyzing you."

"Occupational hazard."

"I guess."

Then they walked to the top of the hill from which, according to Victor Hugo in *Les Misérables*, one can see an incredible view of Paris. They couldn't see a thing. Barely an outline of the city, between the trees, covered by fog.

The sky was overcast. In the distance, a lightning bolt scratched the gray sky and then they heard the thunder.

"There's a storm coming," said Darío, the same happy expression on his face.

"Yes, let's go," said Antonieta, who, without knowing why, felt the weather was reproaching her for something.

Antón Parra managed to get Belén to leave the apartment on Rue Mazarine. It was then, in the spring of 1964, that Víctor Teixeira showed up in the city and took Belén's room. This time around it was Darío himself who asked Víctor to move in with him. He told Antón, pointing out how different it was this time, without realizing that yet another stranger had moved into the apartment and that Antón, who was the actual tenant, had been ignored once again.

Darío introduced Víctor in cafés and meetings as an old friend. Nobody knew him, neither from Paris nor from Caracas. Someone said he came from the GDR, but Siddhartha Arrecho, who had been studying cinema in Leipzig, denied having seen him in that neck of the woods. When it became known that he had actually lived for almost twenty years in different cities and towns in the United States, they mistrusted him even more.

Víctor Teixeira was a poet. The greatest Venezuelan poet since Salustio González Rincones, Darío would claim, but no one in the group knew whether he was being serious or teasing them. Just like Darío, Víctor seemed to be a poet without poems, a condition that similarly gave him an aura of possibility.

Later on, rumors began to multiply in so many exotic directions that Víctor Teixeira became almost a madman or a freak. They said he was close friends with the Beat writers; they said Jack Kerouac himself had mentioned him in *On the Road*; they said he'd had to flee the United States after killing his wife; they said he carried around a jar of formaldehyde, with his dead wife's brain inside it.

Someone bothered to search through Kerouac's novel and

did indeed find, toward the end, a reference to a Venezuelan poet called Víctor Villanueva, and a girl, also Venezuelan, who was rich, depraved and crazy, whom the narrator (Jack Kerouac, in parentheses) called "Venezuela." All very interesting facts, but absolutely not conclusive proof that Villanueva was indeed Teixeira.*

So Víctor Teixeira and Darío Mancini lived together and hung out together and more than one foulmouthed poet began to insinuate other things, things people did not really believe but were happy to repeat or accept with a conspiratorial silence, since they were all taking part in the harassment one way or another.

After the walk through Père Lachaise, Darío and Antonieta became more distanced from each other. Antonieta received only a postcard, like a rubber stamp sealing Darío's intentions, which he had left at the hotel reception. It was a reproduction of *Le Radeau de la Méduse*, with a strange handwritten note that read: *Théodore Géricault: l'orage déchire tout.*

She hadn't been wrong, then. But what did it all mean? Why the sudden acknowledgment, and why the rush to dismantle the dream?

Darío was now living with that strange character Teixeira, and she, well, at least she had met Nicolás. She was surprised to find his rough manners attractive. That and how handsome he was.

They used to call Nicolás Arriechi "Siddhartha Arrecho." He made films, practiced Buddhism, and was always angry. Antonieta thought Nicolás's issue wasn't anger, but that he took

---

* I have recently checked the edition of *On the Road* published by Penguin Books in 2008, subtitled *The Original Scroll*, where all the characters appear with their real names, as Kerouac referred to them in the original manuscript. Víctor Villanueva is indeed Víctor Teixeira. The problem is that Víctor Teixeira, Venezuelan poet, doesn't appear in any civil register, library, anthology or publishers' catalog.

everything too seriously: filmmaking, revolution, Buddhism. Every aspect was absolute, but sometimes these aspects over-lapped. That's why he would explode, why sometimes he would get so drunk that things ended badly, why he was able only to argue and not to discuss.

Despite all that, or because of it, Antonieta liked being close to him. That feeling of having solid ground to stand on but also of an earthquake that she alone could appease, was close to the notion of risk everyone seemed to be searching for, the desire to walk barefoot across the eternal fire.

Antonieta went to Germany with Nicolás in the spring of 1964. They stayed for a few months, while Nicolás tried to get funding to film a documentary on the guerrillas in Venezuela. The deal fell through at the last minute, or at least that was what he told Antonieta, and they had to return to Paris before making the long trip back to Venezuela. The good news was that en route they made a decision: once they were back in Caracas, they would get married.

Some of their comrades were due to return to Venezuela on the same plane as Nicolás and Antonieta. Antón Parra orga-nized a big goodbye party. Like any other attendee, Darío learned only on the day of the party that it would be held at the apartment on Rue Mazarine. Antón just added that he would be arriving a little before eight to bring the food and drinks.

Antón Parra found the apartment spotless. He never knew whether it had been cleaned last minute or it was true that the former chaos really had been Belén's fault. He couldn't complain about Teixeira. He would, however, take Darío to task for living with someone who had spent so many years in the United States and who, now that he was in Paris, was so openly avoiding them.

Everybody arrived en masse at around ten o'clock, and that was the time Víctor Teixeira chose to leave, with a mild goodbye addressed to no one in particular that got lost in the racket made by everyone coming in and getting comfortable. That gesture confirmed Antón's suspicions: he would speak to Darío the next day. That night, however, he was glad Teixeira had gone out. He didn't want any strangers at his party. The only infiltrator in the gathering was Comrade Larralde, who always got drunk and made a scene, but because she didn't live there anymore it wouldn't be a problem.

Darío and Antonieta exchanged only a few words the whole evening. The disaster prompted by Belén would cut their conversation short, leaving it as something resembling a telenovela and a haiku.

"So you're getting married?" said Darío.

"The storm destroys everything," said Antonieta.

Darío didn't understand and wanted to ask Antonieta something, but at that moment Belén started to dance and undress. They went to see her.

When they joined the circle, Antonieta stood next to Nicolás. He took her by the waist. Darío placed himself next to the bedrooms and from there watched Belén, naked from the waist up, dancing in circles. Someone had turned off the living room lights. The third time she went around, he saw the jar in the middle of the room, to which Belén seemed tied by an invisible thread that forced her to orbit around it.

The music, some weird African percussion, had gone from random sounds to a ritual crescendo. Belén, getting carried away with the music, picked up the jar and started spinning. She would hold it closer to the faces of those standing in front, like a luxurious drink she refused to hand over. On one of her circuits, the light filtering from the kitchen allowed Darío to make out its contents. He solved the puzzle in a second, since there were only two pieces to it: Belén must have kept the keys to the room now occupied by Teixeira.

Just then, Darío saw Teixeira opening the door of the apartment. He stood in the doorway for a moment, before passing like a shadow behind the ring of people, looking at him as if asking for an explanation and then entering the circle without waiting for a response.

The comrades noticed Teixeira straight away and also understood that he was somehow connected to the dance. Belén didn't seem to realize and kept spinning a few more times, her eyes fixed on the floor, before bumping into Teixeira. It was then that Belén opened her eyes, or just looked up, screamed in horror and let go of the jar.

Antón Parra was the first to react. He asked for the music to be turned down, but someone switched on the light instead. A new circle had formed around the broken jar, from which a viscous liquid and a small lump had emerged. Víctor Teixeira and Belén were left in the background, her looking at him and him staring at the brain on the floor, which was like an object washed ashore by the waves.

As the party guests started to make sense of the contents, a grimace of distaste and a murmur of disgust and disapproval began to grow among them.

"I need to ask you all to leave," said Antón to everyone, and he turned off the music. "And this shit," he said to Darío, "is your fault."

Darío tried to catch Víctor's eye.

Teixeira just smiled, as if he too were seeing the brain for the first time, or as if his whole life had always been a massive joke that only now, thanks to Belén's inappropriate behavior, was revealing its true scale.

He then made a gesture similar to the one from the start of the party, as if saying hello or goodbye, and disappeared into his room.

The guests started to leave at the crawling pace of cars driving by a road accident. However, Nicolás, Antonieta, Darío, Antón and Belén were present when Edmond came out of the kitchen with a glass jar. They saw him bending down, taking the brain in one of his clean hands and holding it, in a trance, just a few inches from his face, before placing it inside the jar.

Darío would always remember this scene. Edmond playing Hamlet in the living room of his Parisian apartment.

He would also remember the grim happiness he felt when he learned of the union of Víctor Teixeira and Belén Larralde: the monstrous happy life they would share from that night on.

19

Warsaw

After the spilled-brain episode, Darío had to move out of the apartment on Rue Mazarine. He moved in to a hotel in the Latin Quarter, where he stayed for a few weeks until he received Eduardo Gallegos Mancera's letter with some instructions. Gallegos Mancera and Oswaldo Miliani were in Prague, and from there they had secured him a position as a proofreader for the official communications of the Latin American faction of the party.

Darío arrived in Prague in February 1965, arms folded against the chill.

Hence Kafka, he thought, looking at that palette of gray made up of the city, its sky and its citizens.

He wrote to Ramón. The two-month wait distracted him from boredom, but the reply was disheartening: it was still too dangerous to go back to Venezuela. He thought about Paris and imagined the whole city crystallized in its own gestures: it was a museum he no longer wanted to visit.

"Shee-yit."

As the months passed, *shee-yit* went from being an imprecation to the keyword with which to start the day or undertake any action. If the people of Prague were an army of golems that forced him to behave like one too, he was going to do it his way.

In August 1965, he attended some conferences organized by communist writers and intellectuals. Louis Aragon delivered the opening address, after which he wasn't seen at the cultural institute again. The goal was for comrades to meet up and start to draft some working ideas for what would be the Fourth Writers' Congress.

When he was asked to introduce himself and contribute to the discussion at his workshop table, Darío didn't think it was a bad idea to read a poem dedicated to Fidel Castro, in which his death was foreseen. It wasn't clear whether the poem mourned or celebrated that death. In any case, one of the verses was sufficiently problematic to cause a minor scandal. In the verse in question, Darío used some wordplay in which a capital *E* for Engels was added to the word *Slav*, transforming it into *SlavE*.

"Comrade Mancini, is that poem yours?" someone asked.

"No. It's by a countryman of mine."

"And what's his name?"

"Víctor Villanueva."

"Vilanova? Could you repeat it?"

"Vi-lla-nue-va," said Darío, while the comrade wrote it down in a notebook.

On that occasion, Eduardo and Oswaldo had to stop by and scold him. He mustn't forget his situation, the effort they had made to get him out of the country. One must leave aside any individual aspirations and think collectively, about how the individual might help the party.

"Shee-yit," said Darío.

In a sense, Darío's arms remained folded the whole time he was in Prague. He didn't notice the thaw that apparently was appearing between the cracks of the totalitarianism defended by the more orthodox sector. What happened at the Fourth Writers' Congress in June 1967 confirmed his hopes and fears. An important group of writers led the denunciation of the atrocities of Stalinism and appealed for socialism with a human face to be built in Czechoslovakia. That same group, they said, were influential enough that they could make the changes happen.

While that was true, there was also the case of Pavel Kohout. The sanction Kohout received for having read Solzhenitsyn during his address to the congress offered little hope for a brighter future.

Despite the prevailing enthusiasm, especially after Dubček was designated head of the Czechoslovakian Communist Party, Gallegos Mancera knew how to read the storm. In late February 1968, he suggested that Darío go on his way.

"Where to?" asked Darío.

"Where would you like to go?"

"Nowhere."

"I thought you didn't like being here."

"I don't. I hate this shit. It's just that if I could choose where to be, I'd like to be nowhere. Get it?"

"What about Poland?"

"Poland?"

"Well, Warsaw. Things are a little quieter over there."

"Poland, Poland," repeated Darío. "Yeah, why not?"

"Poland it is, then," concluded Gallegos Mancera.

On the way back to his apartment, Darío toyed with the word. Repeating it, like someone tossing a loaded coin: Poland, Poland. When he got home, he poured himself a vodka, downed it and then remembered.

He looked for his copy of *Ubu enchaîné* and stumbled onto that quote by Jarry, in his introduction to *Ubu Roi*, that had always intrigued him: "The scene . . . is set in Poland, which is to say, Nowhere."

What could life have in store for him, who at thirty-six was Nobody and about to live in Nowhere?

"What will I do in Warsaw?" Darío asked Gallegos Mancera the next day.

"You'll be an announcer on Polskie Radio," he said.

Darío felt like a spy.

"I don't speak Polish."

"In Spanish. The international service of Polskie Radio wants all bases covered against Radio Free Europe."

"*NO–DARIO–ON–RADIO*," he said in a robotic whisper.

"What's that?"

"Nothing."

Darío arrived in Warsaw as only a Sergio Pitol character would: on a train, with a fever and without knowing whether he was awake or dreaming. In 1972 he would meet Pitol, who was just back from a three-year stay in Barcelona, nineteen years after what could have been their first encounter, had Darío not been jailed and Pitol not been living the life of a preppy-boy he claimed he'd had during the month he spent in Caracas in 1953.

As he got off the train, the winter cold and the burning heat of his fever tugged him in opposite directions. He hid his face in his coat and scarf while staring at his boots sunk in the dirty snow of the station.

If I don't stop looking at my boots, I'll stay here forever, he thought.

And that may well had been the case had it not been for the strong shove the old woman gave him.

"A good thing it is that tonight at last has your arrival happened."

Hearing that phrase, which he had somehow heard before, or which he would hear afterward, he understood several things at once: that he was in Warsaw, that the old woman hadn't pushed him by accident and that she was in fact pulling him by the arm, encouraging him to follow her, and that, despite it being so bright outside that he almost had to close his eyes, it was nighttime.

He took the piece of paper they had given him with the address out of one of his pockets and held it out it to the old woman.

#15 Marszalkowska Ave. Next to Saski Park. Ask for Joseph.

The old woman stopped for a second and, seeing what it was, made a gesture with her hand and carried on walking. Darío put the paper away, went on following her, trying to hold on to his suitcase and keep up.

"What is now the matter?" said the old woman after a long spell of walking in silence.

Darío had fallen behind. He was looking, motionless, at a construction that blocked out the darkness.

"Who are those men?" asked Darío.

"Soldiers."

"What are they doing?"

"Guarding the tomb of the Unknown Soldier."

"Are they always there?"

"There are two soldiers on guard always, not always the same ones."

"Is that a fire inside?"

"It's the eternal flame. It's always alight."

At last, they arrived at the small building, derelict like the rest of the city, where he would live for the whole time he was in Warsaw.

"*Il est tard,*" said Joseph, after settling him in. "*On parle demain. C'est bien?*"

"*Oui. Pas de problème,*" said Darío.

Overnight, Darío sweated out the fever and got better.

Joseph gave him some general instructions over breakfast. The address of the radio station, how to get to Woronicza Street, the name of the person he needed to talk to, a few things about the city, others about the party and about the bad patch Comrade Gomulka's government was going through.

By midmorning, when Darío was about to leave, the old woman, Mrs. Kazia, showed up; she started to clear the table.

Joseph came to the door and said a few words to her, which she returned to him like someone tossing a ball of wool. In that tangled mess, Darío was able to recognize the Polish language, of which he knew two or three expressions, but he couldn't separate a single thread of the conversation.

How had he spoken to the old woman the previous night? Had they talked in Spanish? Or had a miracle or some demonic possession allowed him to master Polish for an hour? Had it all been a fever dream?

On his way to the radio station, he saw the monument. Two soldiers guarded the eternal flame, now hiding in the dazzle of the morning.

That day he went on air for the first time. He made several mistakes. Sitting in the booth, he realized he had never been in front of a microphone before. He hadn't stopped to think about the sound of his own voice, how to project and modulate it. Also, it was clear that the news translator's Spanish wasn't very good, so he had to improvise on the fly, trying to make sense of it, or making up some message that was more or less coherent.

At first, he didn't pay attention to the content of the news bulletins, focused as he was on finding his own voice as a radio announcer. It wasn't until the first days of March, when the students of the Warsaw University organized a series of protests, that he witnessed firsthand a news story he would broadcast. A couple of days earlier, Gomulka's government had had a couple of students expelled when they'd insisted on staging Adam Mickiewicz's *Forefathers' Eve*, a markedly anti-Russian play. Darío noticed an obvious mistake in the date of the news story he was due to record that morning. It was March 7, and the news bulletin stated that on March 8, the students had charged at the army with sticks, stones and homemade explosives at a rally outside the Warsaw University, and that as a result the authorities had been forced to use their own weapons and make the necessary arrests.

Darío pointed the mistake out to the content coordinator.

"The date is correct," said the coordinator.

Next day, during one of the long breaks between broadcasts, Darío went over to the university. There he saw the throngs of students, their impassioned faces, chants steaming in the morning cold. On the other side of the street were soldiers, lined up and waiting.

The script had been staged perfectly, apart from the detail that the students never attacked the soldiers.

At midday, back at the station, he locked himself in a booth that was rarely used. He ate the meager lunch he had brought in with him and listened to his own voice narrating the events that had just taken place at Warsaw University. He recalled his youth in Catia and saw the news clipping announcing "the arrest of painter and conspirator Darío Mancini," which he had found years later among some papers his mother had given him.

Life felt like a farce written and staged by Alfred Jarry. A performance that could be made to collapse by just adding one letter, a tiny, misplaced piece that could deconstruct, with infinite patience, the mechanism of the universe. That use of pataphysics allowed him to watch the events of those years like a man who goes to the theater to see tragedy, only to burst out laughing.

The protests officially ended on March 28, when Gomulka stopped suppressing the students with a wave of beatings, arrests and summary trials. Then came the purge at all levels of the party. Weirdly enough, Darío was spared from the firings that accompanied the thorough restructure of Polskie Radio and the other apparatuses of the official cultural system.

The enthusiasm generated by the Fourth Czech Writers'

Congress the year before, as well as the election of Dubček, was extinguished with the end of the Prague Spring. In Poland, things cooled off until December 1970, when Gomulka announced price increases in all sectors. Darío recounted with feigned indignation how the Gdansk, Gdynia, Szczecin and Elblag shipyards were attempting to create instability by going on strike. He gave an account of the measures to protect the people, of whom several dozen had been killed by December 18 and a few thousand arrested. With the same impassivity with which he announced these events to the Hispanic listeners of Central Europe, on December 20 Darío read the news of Gomulka's expulsion, backed by Brezhnev in Moscow, and the appointment of Gierek as the new party leader.

Apart from that, he didn't do much. Valerio and María called him the Steppenwolf. Sometimes they would go out to eat and have a drink at the Spatif. María had started at Polskie Radio some months before Gierek's nomination. Until recently she had been married to the Polish cultural attaché in Venezuela, so she knew the country and spoke fluent Spanish. From the start, she felt a special empathy toward Darío, and they would kill time together at work. They mostly talked about classical music. As a result of these conversations, and sensing the mood of modernity Gierek seemed to be promoting, they proposed to the station that they create a classical music program.

In the days before the first broadcast, in the meetings with María to prepare the content of the program, Darío met Valerio Alberti. Valerio was a journalist in Caracas and had left it all behind to follow María here.

They had met in 1966. Valerio worked for *Momento* magazine and wanted to get the Venezuelan distribution rights to the *Poland Illustrated* magazine. At a book launch he met the cultural attaché of the Polish embassy, who, after listening to Valerio, invited him to his house on a Saturday morning.

At ten o'clock, Valerio rang the doorbell at the cultural attaché's house. The most beautiful woman he had ever seen opened the door.

"Nice to meet you, I'm María," she said. "Come on in. My husband will be with you right away."

He instantly understood that he would never distribute *Poland Illustrated*.

"María? Like that, in Spanish?" he said, taking a seat.

"Well, in Polish you add a *j*, but *Marija* sounds funny in Spanish."

The attaché came in and they started talking. María stayed with them, and Valerio was surprised to notice that she wouldn't stop looking at him.

Their affair lasted for a couple of years until the attaché and María returned to Poland. Valerio decided to follow her, but first, he needed to find out how. A friend listened to him and suggested trying the diplomatic route.

"You mean talking to both of them?"

"No, man. Diplomatic channels. How did you meet her? Because her husband was lucky enough, or unlucky enough, to be sent here. If I were you, I'd ask at the ministry. You got nothing to lose. Believe me, I don't think there'd be many candidates among Leoni's people who want to go try the sweet taste of actual socialism."

Sure enough, after a year of paperwork, Valerio Alberti managed to get himself appointed attaché at the Venezuelan embassy in Poland. He arrived in Warsaw in the spring of 1970. When María saw him and learned what he had done to get to her, she dumped her husband and moved in with Valerio. Now María needed to look for a job. She found a position at

Polskie Radio, first as a Polish-to-Spanish translator, and then as an announcer.

The first time both María and Valerio saw Darío was through the glass of the abandoned booth he had made his office. Darío would spend hours in that cage, visible to whoever went down the main corridor of the station, focused on writing in a little notebook. More than writing, Darío seemed to be always doing some kind of calculation or other. Really, he was like a waiter gone mad, trying to write down an impossible order.

When he had gotten to know him better, Valerio dared to ask about his notebook and notes.

"Do you write poetry?"

"I don't know whether what I do is poetry," said Darío. "It's more like a game. Palindromes."

He didn't seem to consider it a big deal. They changed the subject.

The thing with the palindromes had started by chance, even if that chance was the clearest sign of his destiny. One afternoon leaving the Spatif bar after having an aperitif, Darío went into a bookstore that was also on Ujazdowskie Avenue. In the new arrivals section, he found something truly unbelievable: a copy of *Canaima*, by Rómulo Gallegos.

Gallegos had died the previous year. This was a beautiful commemorative edition published by Círculo de Lectores in Spain. He didn't have a clue how the book had ended up there, but he bought it and went back to his apartment without a moment's delay.

Reading that novel was his oracle.

He found the key to his life in one complete sentence, constructed with that deep ingenuity only Rómulo Gallegos's characters have. Marcos Vargas returns to Ciudad Bolívar after his long dull period studying in Trinidad and meets up with his childhood friends. They go *zapoara* fishing, and it's then that he lets out his war cry: "Dammit—I'm mad!"

Darío underlined the sentence. "Dammit—I'm mad." So bold an assertion of agency, the presence of that ferocious *I*, it was all so profound that he felt a stabbing pain in his chest. Was Nobody, in Nowhere, perhaps Someone—was he an *I*, after all? Was he, simply? The novel took him back to his years at the Nueva Cárcel in Ciudad Bolívar, to that city he barely glimpsed when he'd disembarked the steamship *Guayana* with its cargo of prisoners, and which for the five years he was locked up, he could make out from the prison gate during his fleeting dream escapades. Those escapades in which he'd go back to himself, to watch himself sleeping only to then wake up dizzy and repeating "am I, I am," as if returning to himself, threatening to be lost in the wind like his high-flying childhood kite.

For the first time in years, he felt as if he was about to cry. That was when he paused to think, then looked for his notebook. On the first page, he found the little piece of wordplay he had made up the day Gallegos Mancera informed him about his trip to Warsaw. He crossed out the word *no*, and then the *on*, and wrote "Darío Radio," which was gentler and more faithful to his experience in the city until then.

However, the phrase "Darío Radio," considered as a possible frontispiece, would give a misleading impression of his life. The radio was only circumstantial. He tried again—soon "Darío Radio" was "Darío Oirad," but this was meaningless. Dropping the *d* was better—he was left with "*Darío oirá*." Darío will hear. He liked it better still after he'd swapped the terms. "*Oirá Darío*." Though as a statement it sounded weird. It sounded more like a question, a case of concern about his auditory capacity. *Will* Darío hear? But was it about listening? Wasn't it rather about listening to what one writes and writing what one listens to?

He tried this and broke up the first word, and it was like splitting the atom.

"*Oír a Darío.*"

Now it sounded like an order. Hear Darío. He found it funny. He felt like a king in a snowy desert. A fake king. Like Ubu, he thought. Then he tossed the notebook far away, when he realized that name was a palindrome too.

Valerio Alberti spent a long time attempting to decipher the enigma of Darío's personality. It had an inaccessible core that attracted and repelled you at the same time. There were times when he thought he could catch a glimpse of what was hiding behind those deceptively transparent eyes. What he found was even more unsettling: a boy playing and, at the same time, fighting to the death to protect his game.

On one occasion, they stopped speaking to each other for a month. In December 1971, Pablo Neruda's visit to Warsaw was announced, for the staging of his play *Splendor and Death of Joaquín Murieta*. Neruda had just won the Nobel Prize and there was a tremendous sense of expectation. María was given two free tickets, but she had no interest in the play. She gave Darío the tickets for him to go with her husband. Darío said nothing to Valerio and showed up at the Classic Theater of Warsaw with a stunning woman. Valerio had found out about Darío's trick and, without a saying a word, managed to get another free ticket for himself.

He was hardly able to enjoy the performance, so furious was he at Darío's betrayal. He didn't even pay attention when at the end of the play, a frail Neruda came on stage to greet the public. He didn't miss a single movement by Darío or that damn woman, his gorgeous blonde companion. On the way out, in the hall of the Palace of Culture and Science, he pushed

his way over to them. The blonde was talking to Boris Stoicheff, the play's young director, while Darío simply smiled.

When Valerio was about to enter the circle and interrupt the
conversation, a commotion intervened. Neruda and his cohort
had come near to where Stoicheff was standing. The director
did the introductions, including to Darío, and a congregation
surrounded them as if at a press conference.

Even though he was very ill by this time, Neruda, with
his characteristic self-love, couldn't resist seeing an attractive
woman without trying to impress her with his wit or some tired
metaphor. He started to hypnotize her by making connections
between that story set in 1848, in the middle of the Califor-
nian gold rush, and the history of Poland and its struggle for
social justice and proletarian solidarity, by drawing the evident
parallels between his Murieta and Janosik, the legendary Polish
highwayman of the mountains.

Then, so as not to be rude, he addressed Darío and asked his
opinion of the play.

Darío began by saying that the comparison between Murieta
and Che Guevara suggested by the play was not only regret-
table but evidently anachronistic. That reference could almost
be like that verse in which the poet experienced the impact
of Stalin's death as if he had been struck by the ocean. What's
more, he didn't agree with the idea of Murieta being Chilean.
It was a well-known distortion in the translation of the original work, which came from the French, which in turn came
from the English. But all the sources were wrong. According
to a study carried out by a critic and compatriot of his, Joaquín Murieta wasn't Chilean, nor was he Mexican, as was
often claimed, but Venezuelan. And the episode of the rape
of his wife was in fact even more dramatic since the woman
who was raped and murdered was actually Murieta's daughter,

and Murieta himself figured, together with his fellow perpe-trators of the outrage, among the girl's attackers—that is, the rapist of his own daughter. The legend of Murieta as a sort of Latin American Robin Hood was an invention by fantasists in the second half of the nineteenth century, whose aim was to romanticize the riots and tyrannies of the day.

Darío stopped talking, and for a second it seemed the whole palace was holding its breath. Everybody was waiting for the poet's reply.

"What's the name of that critic, your fellow countryman?" asked Neruda when he had recovered.

"Villanueva," said Darío. "Víctor Villanueva."

"That Villanueva has a great imagination."

The public received these words with great enthusiasm.

"No question. Although not as great as yours, my most hon-ored poet," said Darío.

Darío held out his hand and bowed, then he put his arm around the blonde's waist and walked off.

Valerio watched the scene in astonishment. Then he acted offended for several weeks until one night they met at the Spatif and made up. That evening, Darío introduced him to Jola, the blonde from the theater.

In a moment when Jola and María had gone off to the restroom together, Valerio asked Darío:

"Where did you find her?"

"She's a model."

"She's not very nice."

"I know."

"So?"

"Well, you've seen her, haven't you?"

Valerio didn't know if Darío was being serious. It was the sign to back off and not go down that route.

"What's the name of that historian you mentioned the other day?"

"When?"

"With Neruda, when you were talking about Murieta."

Darío started laughing.

"What?" said Valerio.

"I was just kidding around. I told him the plot of *Doña Bárbara*. That's all."

In 1974, Darío decided it was time to visit Caracas.

Even if she didn't show it, Jola was excited by the idea. He was bringing with him the manuscript of his book. He sensed he had constructed something unique, a small verbal mechanism, original and perfect. Simón Alberto had already heard of the book and let him know that the editors at Monte Ávila would be interested in reading it. Publishing it would constitute an irrevocable loss for Darío. He needed, at least, to be on familiar ground when the separation happened.

Jola traveled with two suitcases full of her clothes and shoes. Darío carried the same small suitcase he had brought with him from Prague. He didn't gather up all his belongings or give old Mrs. Kazia any special instructions. He didn't think he'd be staying in Caracas long.

Darío never worried about what happened to the things he left in that apartment. He did, however, regret not having gotten the chance to ask Mrs. Kazia about that mysterious, perhaps impossible, conversation they'd had in the cold of his first night in Warsaw. To discover the place where those words had come from.

20

Caracas

"I can say now, with total conviction," said Oswaldo Barreto, "that we were wrong. That whole revolutionary mess is the proof. Just like some of the decisions I've taken in my life. However, with Antonieta, or for Antonieta, I always made the best decisions. I enrolled her at the Central University so she wouldn't grow old up on the moorland; I stopped her going to India with that crazy guy Arrieti. In fact, it was me who introduced her to Darío."

"What trip to India was that?"

"Your friend doesn't mention that in his text either?"

"No. He talks about some Arriechi, who was married to Antonieta, and a trip to the United States."

"It's Arrieti. Nelson Arrieti. A filmmaker. Nice guy. Intelligent, though deeply troubled. He ended up killing himself at a Buddhist temple in Mérida."

"And the trip?"

"Madness. They spent two years in the United States. In Iowa and New York, I think. Antonieta had graduated from the Central University in 1968 and applied for a studentship at the International Writing Program. He accompanied her. They went together."

"I thought they'd gotten married when they arrived back from Paris."

"No. They married in 1967. After Antonieta got a divorce

from her first husband. While Antonieta was studying on a scholarship, Arrieti toured the United States. It was '69, the same year Kerouac died, and Arrieti was preparing a film about the Beat generation."

"Do you remember the title?"

"I don't. The thing is, they got back to Caracas in '73 with some money. Nelson brought with him the budget he hadn't spent—that is, nearly all of it. Back in Venezuela, what with one thing and another, they managed to save even more.

"Arrieti was a Buddhist. He was obsessed with traveling to India. And in '74, Antonieta would have gone on that crazy trip, if I hadn't stopped her. One day Arrieti bought the flights to New Delhi, one way only. Then, without asking Antonieta, he withdrew their savings from the bank and handed out the cash among the poor in some neighborhood. He said you should be brought to India through an attitude of total open-handedness. Or total poverty. Or some other bullshit of the day.

"I made her come to her senses and Antonieta decided to stay. In the end, Arrieti didn't go either. He was angry, as well as broke. Their relationship was on the rocks by then. As if that weren't enough, Darío returned one or two months later.

"You can't say I was wrong about Darío either. I gave them a room, for him and the Polish girl, at Quinta Flora. Jolanda, that was her name. Beautiful. Insufferable. Once we went to the bullring and she started screaming at the bullfighter: 'Murderer! Murderer.' Can you imagine?

"I told Michaelle, Rafael and Milena, everyone, even Antonieta: We've got to get rid of the Pole.

"The night before they took the ship back to Warsaw (going by ship was another of Jola's great ideas), I explained the plan to Darío and he agreed. It was very simple.

"She was suspicious at first. She found it strange Darío would go on such a long journey with the same skinny suitcase he'd arrived with. Darío explained he had never needed much to be comfortable. The fewer things, the better.

"A group of us accompanied them to the port of La Guaira, apart from Arrieti, of course. Arrieti never hid his hatred for Darío, and he just waved him off from the hammock we had in the living room at Quinta Flora."

"Arrieti and Antonieta also lived at Quinta Flora?"

"Only for a month. Antonieta spent the month shut away. She just had won the Municipal Literary Award. She got overwhelmed by shyness and moved out of the apartment she shared with Arrieti to avoid all contact. She didn't want to answer any telephone calls, not from friends congratulating her or from the press.

"When it was time for them to go to the waiting room before boarding the ship, Darío stayed where he was, with us. Jola asked him what was wrong, and then we left them alone. We went to the car. We'd give him one hour. That way he could decide if he wanted to leave or stay.

"Fifteen minutes later, we saw him heading toward the parking lot, lost, looking for us. We all shouted with delight and I honked the horn. As he was getting closer, I saw how excited Antonieta was. I knew then that the next decision would be about the two of them.

"'What's the matter?' I asked Antonieta.

"'Nothing. I got my wires crossed for a second. I thought it was Teodoro, not Darío, who was coming toward us. And that everything had started again.'

"At the Flora, Arrieti made a big fuss. He was a nice guy, but he was nobody's fool. He shouted at Antonieta but, instead of moving out, he moved in to Darío's room.

"Antonieta complained, but I left things as they were. That night, when we were alone, I suggested to Antonieta that she give Darío the keys to her own apartment. She thought it was a great idea. Darío left and Arrieti calmed down. Even though things cooled down, he and Antonieta didn't sleep together that night. In fact, I don't think they ever did again."

"Where are you going?" asked Nicolás the next morning.
"To Monte Ávila, to sign the contract for the novel," said Antonieta.
As she passed through the kitchen, she picked up the bag Oswaldo had prepared for her, got in the car and drove to her apartment.

That's how Pedro Álamo starts the narration of the last part of this section of the story, which Oswaldo Barreto obviously shouldn't or couldn't tell. It was never clear whether Antonieta and Darío had already loved each other before that day. Whether the dilemmas faced by the female protagonist of *It Is No Time for Red Roses* are autobiographical, or whether the character of Armando is Darío. Or whether Antonieta was witnessing how some of the things she'd imagined had finally become reality.

Nor do I know whether the episode about the postcard, which in that moment of intimacy would go on to decide everything, was real or merely another product of the *Dreamachine*. However, I transcribe it just as I read it in the notebooks, not quoting, but reconstructing it my way, like everything in this file, just for the pleasure of telling the story again.

After their loving and their meeting, Antonieta remembered their walk at Père Lachaise and finally asked Darío something she had never understood:

"What did you want to tell me with that thing about the storm?"

"What storm?"

"The postcard. You wrote that on the postcard."

"What postcard, Antonieta?"

Antonieta got up from the bed. Darío followed her with his eyes, as she passed through the shadows like the lightest cloud. He saw her rummaging inside her bag and bringing him a piece of card. It was a postcard with a detail of *Le Radeau de la Méduse*, by Géricault; and a strange note on the back, in his handwriting.

Théodore Géricault: l'orage déchire tout.

"I'd forgotten about that. What don't you understand?"

"What did you mean about the storm?"

"The shipwreck of *La Méduse*. It's an anagram."

"Huh?"

"Look."

Antonieta looked, then started laughing as she hadn't done since she was a little girl. She checked the sentence several times, comparing the name of the painter and the words Darío had written, playing at matching the letters until the anagram was complete.

Darío thought Antonieta was laughing just for the pure pleasure of playing with words. His delight soared so high upon sensing her delight, it was like a joy that *glideth*, and *gildeth*—a joy that lighted the way to her.

"We could still try one more," said Darío, gleefully.

He notes down the title of the painting, and less than half an hour later, as their bodies cooled, Darío made a second anagram.

Le Radeau de la Méduse: au-delà de la démesure.

At that moment, Antonieta and Darío realized life was nothing but a game. Happy, they were like wild children, and their surrender was beyond measure.

Antonieta was still troubled. Nelson Arrieti (Nicolás Arriechi, according to the notebook) came to the apartment. Luckily, Darío had gone out early so he didn't find him there. What Nelson found, however, was an ashtray full of ash and cigarette butts, piled up and extinguished, as could have been left only by a smoker like Darío.

They had their last fight at Quinta Flora. When Nelson threatened to become violent, Oswaldo intervened and asked him to leave.

"From then on, and until the end, Antonieta and Darío stayed together," said Oswaldo. "They said to hell with everything, traveled the world and were happy. Just like that. They—how can I put it—were a perfect match."

Oír a Darío and *It Is No Time for Red Roses* were both published in 1975. That year, Antonieta listened to the main character and became part of the system herself. The *system*, to her character, was simply love in the most absolute, least tumultuous, safest, most middle-class, most passionate and then re-composed sense of the word. They committed that great betrayal of turning their backs on the world and its wails, in order to indulge their mutual companionship, their constant presence.

Just as Valerio Alberti had done some years earlier, Antonieta pursued a career in diplomacy. She was so attracted to this new life course that she accepted the worst possible destination for that time: General Jorge Videla's Buenos Aires.

They lived in a little apartment by Avenida Coronel Díaz, close to the Venezuelan embassy, until 1977, when they finally got official confirmation of that most platonic relocation: Athens.

But first, they had to return to Caracas for a few days. There they met up with Sergio Pitol, who had just come back from Paris.

"I can't tell you how much we enjoyed your book," Sergio said to Darío.

Then he handed him the letter.

"Don't read it till you're on the plane. Or rather, I think it would be even better if you read it only when you're completely sure you're in Athens."

He had whispered those words in his ear, with the same corrosive conspiratorial demeanor with which he'd joke with his friends in Warsaw. Except this time he seemed to be serious. It was as if Sergio, by insisting, were reminding him of his strange arrival in Warsaw. As if, like Athanasius Pernath, Darío had put on the wrong hat and been inhabiting somebody else's dream ever since.

On the plane, he felt the letter pulsating uncomfortably inside his jacket. Up until then, he had followed Sergio's instructions scrupulously. Antonieta found him tense—he had been acting weird for a few days before the trip. It's normal, thought Antonieta, and she bit her lip.

He had meant to wait until the end. In Paris, where they were to connect to their Athens flight, he couldn't wait any longer.

While Antonieta went to the bathroom, he opened the envelope and read.

Paris, 3/13/77

My dear Darío Lancini, Sergio Pitol has just given me your wonderful OIRADARIO. Thank you, thank you very much for the fascinating hours I've spent with your book, an endless book, because one returns to it over and over, alone and with friends, in the middle of the street, in the middle of a dream.

You have given me a present I won't ever forget. By showing us the two sides of the mirror, you have enriched poetry, you push us deeper into the dizziness of the word.

Thank you,
With a hug,
Your friend,
Julio Cortázar

21

Athens

Nightfall in Greece.

Night for Linger Ease?

The streets kept interrupting one another. Darío hesitated at each crossing, as if by choosing a path he was seeking the most pleasant or wittiest way of saying something. Halfway down the street, any street, he got lost and the word dried on the tip of his tongue.

Darío looked around for Mount Lycabettus and oriented himself.

He reached the fringes of the hill, joined the line for the funicular, boarded and in five minutes was on the Hill of the Wolves. What would it be like to visit at night? At dusk, the cloud of tourists starts to peter out. Perhaps the number of people doesn't vary that much, and it's just down to the mood of that time of the day: the meekness of those who accept being extinguished with the sun.

From above, Darío could make out the labyrinth. Though, since he'd started on his double-texts, everything for him had turned into a frenzy of corners. Previously, palindromes and anagrams had been juggling and roulette, going around the day in eighty worlds just to return to the same place. Now he needed to go deep into the dark, down unmarked paths that take him to places unknown.

What's to be done? You can go back, like Saussure, or choose to go all the way, like Joyce. And then die. A madman is someone who stops halfway, trapped in the crossfire of sense and nonsense.

Take Leañez the Graduate. The eternal exile, always bad-mouthing the country, but some evenings he would go out for a walk with a Venezuelan flag tied around his neck, in his underwear, as if he was Superman.

Or Hannah, who left everything to come and study Heraclitus in his own language. Then she spent two months' salary bringing her library from Caracas, because Hannah couldn't read without feeling as if the gloomy and patient audience of her own books was listening.

People come to Athens thinking they will find a lost beginning. And they find it, but they forget that the beginning is chaos, it's the night. And that's a concept, my dear Siamese twin, we are not ready to understand. We, who brag about Marxism, existentialism and many other similar isms, still have not found a thorough, accurate, deeply artistic expression of death.

As was always the case whenever Darío engaged in rigorous thinking, he had started mentally writing a letter to Arnaldo without realizing he was doing it. He would send it along with some small presents for him, Rafael and Milena. He would sit down to write as soon as he'd gotten back to the apartment. But there was a cocktail party that evening. It had completely slipped his mind. A boring meeting of diplomats. He had promised Antonieta he would go with her, just to keep an eye on Hannah and drag her out by the waist if she made another scene.

"I promise I'll behave," Hannah had told them last time she woke up hungover.

"You spilled a drink on the minister," said Antonieta. "You have no idea what trouble you got me into."

"Was he the minister?" asked Hannah.

"Yes," said Antonieta.

"Don't worry, then. We poets and diplomats are the same breed. We're all crazy."

That evening, Hannah behaved. She only tried to seduce a lord, but he was with his wife, a tall and very attractive woman who knew, discreetly, how to keep her at bay.

Some days later, at the Archaeological Museum of Delphi, sitting in front of the statue of Antinous, Antonieta, Darío and Hannah herself were trying to decipher Hannah's behavior. How was it possible that someone who had translated Rilke, someone who in moments of murky lucidity thought herself an angel, could be so easily dazzled by a title, whether from politics or nobility.

"Let's do something," said Hannah, looking at Antonieta. "I swear I'll marry the first asshole who walks past."

At that moment, Antonio Galo walked right by them.

Darío and Antonieta recognized him and burst out laughing. Antonio turned around, and he also recognized them, but only as a backdrop. Between them, amid the laughter, were Hannah's beautiful eyes, looking at him, hypnotized, hypnotizing him.

Antonieta and Darío made the introductions and left them alone. At the museum gift store, Darío bought a postcard. Then they went.

I'm not sure whether you remember Antonio. He used to hang out with Manuel around the RT days. He's a historian from Lara, just like him. In fact, they're sharing an apartment in London now. They're both doing a PhD at the University of Cambridge. They are Siamese twins, like you and me.

Do you remember our conversations in Warsaw? We always talked about going to Alexandria. You should

come over so we can make that trip. Let me know whether
you're planning on doing this anytime soon, otherwise
I might stab you in the back and go with Antonieta
instead. I'm sending you a postcard. It's the Cecil Hotel
in Alexandria, where Durrell used to stay. When I saw
Antonio and Hannah getting together like that, I thought
about the Quartet. I get the impression that, because
it happened so randomly, they'll stay together forever.
Antonio will be a very happy man, but he will suffer a lot
too. As you know, all angels are terrible. And Hannah is
an angel.
    A big hug,
    Darío

At the end of the summer, Antonio went back to London to resume his investigation into the links between the Catholic Church and the Communist International. Hannah made a few more scenes, said a passionate goodbye to three diplomats she found insufferable and left for London, in the footsteps of Antonio Galo. She left them, as a compensation for her outbursts, a handful of poems from a work in progress that would go by the title *Absence and Light*.

Darío read the poems. It was weird. The texts did nothing to make up for it. If anything, they accentuated the memory of the disaster.

She reminded him of Lucia Joyce. With any luck, Antonio, her husband-father, would see her dancing in their room and spinning around while reading some of the *Sonnets to Orpheus*, with him trying to write some highbrow analysis of the historic memory of a country with amnesia.

Joyce. At last, he had all the time in the world to read him again. As for translating him, perhaps one day. He felt around under his mattress for a copy of *Finnegans Wake*. That book was like a dream machine. He would start reading, but after three or four sentences, he would find himself in the process of deciphering those lines, as if they belonged to some remote language. That book wasn't constructed, as some critics said, with an Anglo-Saxon language at its core, with added fragments or incrustations from other languages. The recognizable foundations, always identical and always diffuse, were connected to the development of the sentence through a syntax that could come only from dreams.

Darío was aware that his own work was comparable only to that of Ramos Sucre and Joyce. That idea would always make him laugh, as well as make him blush slightly, because it was true, and for that reason, it wasn't worth stopping to think about. Like Ramos Sucre, Darío had constructed his body of work without the most often used word in Spanish, *que*, not out of sacerdotal mutilation, as the writer from Cumaná had done, but because of its particular linguistic impossibility. And, like Joyce, he had written something untranslatable. The perfection of a palindrome doesn't allow for transposition. Double-texts allowed for a translation within the same language, a task Darío had done since the beginning, thereby re-ensuring, with the aid of a mirror, the closure of a puzzle that would never be solved.

From Kolonaki, they moved to a beautiful house between Rimini and Kolokotroni. The borough of Filothei was much quieter, away from the commercial area so busy with tourists. In the years they lived in Athens, Darío understood Sartre's decision, which he had previously found so unpleasant, to title his autobiography *Les Mots*. And, especially, his having divided it into those two definite blocks: reading and writing.

While it seemed the height of intellectualism, that existence was the closest he had ever been to his own body: reading, eating, loving, drinking, writing, traveling. Antonieta's earnings at the embassy were enough for them to live comfortably and Darío had enough tranquility for the both of them.

Part of Antonieta's job consisted in mobilizing the constant stream of characters, anywhere between predictable and unhinged, who circulated constantly around the diplomatic corps.

The most exotic were the Venezuelans based in Athens. From those who came over never to return, like Leáñez and his old mother or Isabella, to the *nouveaux riches* who were just passing through, with their wads of US dollars worth 4.30 to 1, which they would change into Greek drachmas that cost them, at an exact exchange rate, one Venezuelan locha.

"Those ones over there are Venezuelan," said Toro Bisbal.

"How do you know?" asked Leáñez.

"That rage with which they're breaking the plates can only be Venezuelan. Shall I show you?"

Energetic as usual, Toro got up from his chair and walked toward the group. He called the waiter over, murmured something in his ear and stayed there talking with the men and women at the table. When the waiter came back with drinks for everyone, they celebrated by clapping and breaking plates.

"I told you, they're Venezuelan. Scholars at the Mariscal de Ayacucho. They're on vacation," said Toro when he came back.

Darío loved those tavernas in Plaka. He was fascinated by that particular misogyny that allowed men to dance only with other men. Those controlled earthquakes that would be livened up by a few drachmas until they were destroying entire sets of dinnerware.

"Venezuela's the same but the other way around. They are breaking the country for a few porcelain plates. But that shit's going to end soon. You'll see."

Darío, Antonieta, Isabella, Montserrat and Leañez the Graduate would listen to Toro Bisbal for a while. Then Darío would light another cigarette and draw his curtain of smoke. Leañez would elaborate his own economic theories and the women, in defiance of the frowning faces of the men, would dance among themselves.

Isabella and Montserrat had escaped, just like them. When they'd arrived, they had discovered that Greece could be an even more chauvinist and retrograde country than Venezuela, but at least they didn't have their family around hassling them.

Isabella had a motor home in which they traveled all over Greece. Darío had been allocated a seat with an ashtray by a window.

"Cigarettes will kill you," said Isabella on one occasion.

"These olive trees would be good to spend the night under. Pull over."

"I said cigarettes will kill you," repeated Isabella.

"I heard you. And I asked you to park the car under those olive trees."

"Can I remind you, I'm the one driving?" answered Isabella.

Darío let the smoke out and smiled.

In Crete, outside the palace of Knossos, he was offered some trinket. A coin from the third century BC, according to the seller. Isabella told him it was quite plausible that the coin was authentic.

"It's the same in Rome. Whenever the council digs up a street, some more coins from the time of the empire pop out."

Darío threw it in the air, let it fall into the palm of his hand and looked at the picture. A labyrinth, explained the peddler. He pointed at the lines on the coin and made the number seven with his fingers.

"Is that the price?" Darío asked Isabella.

"No. He's showing you that the coin is genuine. On one side it has a sphinx, and on the other a labyrinth with seven paths, which is the classical labyrinth."

"Classical, how?"

"Seven is the number of paths you need to get someone lost."

"I'll take it," said Darío finally. And he paid for it.

Some days later, on their way back to Athens, Darío had another look at the engraving on the coin. The Minotaur and the labyrinth. Daedalus. Stephen Dedalus. Logodaedalus.

Logodaedalus? Good title. One of the basic ways of testing an animal's intelligence is to see if the little bug can find its way out of a labyrinth. So yours is a "Machina Labyrinthea," if you'll allow me to use a biologist's denomination. A book that's like a labyrinth, as imagined by that character of Borges's. Pas mal, mon frère.

With love,

Ramón

P.S. When the hell are you guys coming back?

They had asked themselves the same question, give or take the odd word. The first time had been in 1979, with the change of government. Luis Ordaz had come second in the presidential elections, for Democratic Action. However, seeing as the Copei party still had most of the diplomatic corps at the Athens embassy, they felt reassured. From then on, they started planning their trips with more determination. And not only to the Greek islands now. As there were over 1,200 of them, they fantasized about visiting them all and not leaving Greece till then.

During the first two years of Luis Herrera Campins's government, they traveled more than they had ever done before.

Stockholm, Oslo, Cairo, Alexandria, Istanbul, Paris, London and Dublin. It was only then that Darío really became aware of how incredible flying on a plane was. On one of those flights, he remembered the myth of Daedalus and Icarus. From his window, he looked out at the meanderings of the land.

Always on the margins, forgetting about everything that wasn't his wordplay, might he not have tempted the sun himself too?

Darío started to rub his legs.

The passenger on the other side of the aisle, seeing him nervous, tried to calm him down. He was an engineer in materials, but like all engineers, he knew a bit about everything. He insisted there was a much higher likelihood of dying in a car accident than on a plane.

"In any case, if we die, everything will be recorded in the black box. And that would help to perfect these machines, and the probability of them crashing will decrease with time. You know what a black box is, don't you?"

"Yes and no."

"Let me explain."

The engineer spent the rest of the flight explaining to Darío how black boxes work, their role in systems theory, the way a process is analyzed from a blind spot that allows you to see only what comes into and out of its scope, its subsequent use in navigation and flying, the recordings of the cabin and the crew that have enabled the reconstruction of some tragedies.

"You mean this conversation is being recorded in a black box?"

"Oh, no," said the engineer with a smile. "Black boxes record only a part of the flight. Usually the recordings last thirty minutes, for longish itineraries like ours. Once, a friend who works in aviation let me listen to one of those recordings. It's terrible. On the one hand, you have the cold-blooded pilots. On the other, the passengers screaming. Are you feeling OK? Oh, don't be like that. We'll be landing soon. We better change the subject."

After their spell in Athens, whenever they had to travel to other places for work, such as Barbados, China or Spain, Darío never could quite let go of the apprehension, a consequence of that conversation, which would hit him as soon as the plane took off. The image of a black box keeping the words of death within it would obsess him during the flight. Antonieta's clarification, that black boxes were actually bright orange, didn't help matters.

"It's easier to find them that way," said Antonieta.

In early 1982, Antonieta learned she would have to return to Venezuela at some point that year to take on an important position. Isabella and Montserrat, accustomed as they were to goodbyes, behaved as if nothing had happened. Or as if they were sure they'd see one another again very soon, when they knew very well that wasn't the case. Toro Bisbal had already been in the country for a couple of years. He had lately been tipped for Venezuela's Central Bank. Leañez the Graduate, meanwhile, went back to his old ways, going out at night with the Venezuelan flag around his neck, in his underwear. He would take long walks at midnight on some Athens streets nobody but him seemed to know, then return to the patio of his house, where he would set up camp. Sometimes he would listen to his mother's entreaties, but at others he'd refuse to come in until Darío or Antonieta spoke to him.

"What's the matter, Licenciado?" Darío would say as a greeting.

"You're going to freeze," Antonieta would say, covering him with a blanket handed to her by his mother.

"That country is shit. I don't know why you guys would want to go back."

"We've already told you," said Antonieta. "The minister has ordered me to come back."

"The country's about to collapse. Don't say I didn't warn you. You'll come visit at least?"

Darío crouched down and put a hand on his shoulder.

"No, Licenciado. I don't think we will come here again."

Antonieta looked at Darío. That way he had of always telling the truth both attracted and scared her.

Leañez nodded, as if grateful, and stood up. Then the three of them went into the house.

A week before their departure, they received a surprise visit from Galo and Hannah. The apartment had been practically dismantled. The book collection they had acquired during all those years now lay in ordered and numbered boxes. Only a few books remained on a couple of shelves, along with small notebooks and drawing pads. Antonieta had finally managed to persuade Darío to take out everything he had under the bed.

"It's a habit from when he was in prison," Antonieta explained to Galo and Hannah.

Darío shrugged and lit a cigarette.

"I've got nothing to offer you. We should go out somewhere," said Antonieta.

They went to Café Syntagma, on Syntagma Square.

Galo and Hannah had just spent a month in Caracas.

"I don't know. On the one hand, people say life's impossible. On the other hand, the government claims they are going to open lots of new things: the metro, the Teresa Carreño Theater and so many other things," said Galo.

"Toro's been appointed the director of the Central Bank," said Hannah. "Let's see if he has the balls to devalue."

They had dinner and polished off a few bottles of wine. On

the way out, Antonieta raved to Hannah about her latest collection of poems.

"Thanks, lovely. You're the only person who's noticed. I'm working on another now. This time they really are going to have to build me a castle and ask for appointments to see me. I'm the only true poet in that ungrateful country."

Hannah was drunk. Galo had an arm around her waist, but she would escape to start walking a few uneven steps. Darío called a taxi. They bought more booze in a nearby wine store.

Once they were in the apartment, Hannah started to criticize it. From that adorable house in the Filothei area, they had moved to a more modest place, but with better views, on Kanari, in Neo Psychiko.

"This is horrible," said Hannah.

She then tried to steer the conversation back to poetry, but Galo and Antonieta were too busy swapping anecdotes. Galo listened with fascination to the story about Antonieta's grandfather and the horse cemetery. Darío just smoked and pretended to listen to Hannah.

"A house without books is a cemetery. That's what a real cemetery is," said Hannah, looking at Galo and Antonieta angrily.

Then she started opening the boxes of books and scattering them all over the living room.

Galo got up and took hold of her by the arm, but Hannah managed to free herself and dug her nails in his face. A few drops of blood were covering Galo's cheek. Antonieta took him to the bathroom and helped him clean himself up.

In the meantime, Hannah went on taking books out of the boxes and throwing them at the ceiling and floor of the apartment. Suddenly she stopped, exhausted. Darío was looking at her engrossed, calmly smoking his eternal cigarette.

"What are you looking at? Do you like it?" said Hannah. And

as if guided by a hunch, she went over to the shelves and started throwing the books and drawing pads on the floor. When she had cleared them out completely, she started jumping on the books, trampling them. She did this while glancing at Darío now and again and asking him:

"Do you like it? Huh? Do you like it?"

Galo and Antonieta came back from the bathroom. They pinned her arms and forced her to lie down on a sofa on the terrace. They kept her there until she fell asleep. They called a cab. Galo carried her away in his arms. In the shadows of the corridor, they looked like newlyweds.

Darío lit another cigarette, poured himself a glass of wine and downed it, then started to clear up the mess. Antonieta helped him to put the books away in their boxes. Then she went to bed without saying good night.

Darío didn't sleep. He spent the rest of the evening flattening out the pages of his now damaged copy of *Finnegans Wake*, as if the pages were his own extremities trembling on some uncertain flight.

~~~~~~~~~~~~~~~~~~~~~~~~~~

III. The Night

You're the night, Lilah.
A little girl lost in the woods.
You're a folktale. The unexplainable.

—MORPHINE, "THE NIGHT"

22

Paolo and Francesca

People from the provinces send their children to Caracas without realizing they're sending them to the slaughterhouse. If Miguel Ardiles were to come up with statistics on the cases he sees at Forensics, or those he reads about in the press, he would have to admit that the number of deaths wouldn't amount to a significant percentage. However, the young people who do come from the provinces and get killed in Caracas go out with a bang. They die for all the others who remain alive, that majority that would make a perfect example of naturalization were it not for that speck of nostalgia that burns in their throat.

From the first day, Miguel Ardiles could see in Margarita's beautiful lamb eyes that she was damned. In his line of work, it's not good practice having those thoughts: it's up to him to give his patients hope, to make them see that the normality they're after is just one step away. What he can't tell them is, for them, that step is measured in light-years, that it's their own will that makes them into astronauts-in-reverse: what is a small, ridiculous step for humankind becomes a giant, sometimes insurmountable, leap for a man.

Margarita was a depressive. That alone constituted the first motor difficulty for her soul. Depression, for her, was an amber stone that both created misfortune and attracted it. Her family history only reinforced the dark fence that kept her immobilized.

224 ❧ Rodrigo Blanco Calderón

Ardiles sees potential in a clinical case when the patient's narrative generates its own symbols. Images that, rather than merely representing some trauma from the past, orient the reading into the future. Images that are symbols that work as oracles. In Margarita Lambert's story, the symbol in question was a cockroach.

The daughter of a man from the east, of Corsican origins, and a woman from Mérida, Margarita was born in Tabay, a village half an hour from Mérida in the Venezuelan Andes. Who can say how her father ended up on that corner of the plains, a place whose cold climate has nothing in common with the overwhelming heat of his birthplace, El Pilar, in the state of Sucre. In any case, one day he did arrive there; he opened a hardware store and ended up marrying a schoolteacher. The teacher and the store owner planned everything to the last detail: first, lots of hard work and sacrifices, and then having children. But, once they were waist-deep in the daily slog, they forgot all about the main objective of their struggle. It wasn't until she was thirty-eight that the schoolteacher, always surrounded by children, decided to have her own. That explains why Margarita and Fernando, her elder brother, were less than a year apart.

They sent Fernando to Caracas in 2005, as soon as he had finished high school. He was intelligent, but more than anything, he was a very practical person. His parents thought that because Fernando had finished his school studies so easily, he was destined to become an engineer or a doctor. However, the only reason he had done so well was his certainty that life was divided into phases and strategies: if he really wanted to make something of himself, he had to finish school first. Simple as that. Studying, in that sense, was always a means, never an end in itself. In other words, Fernando had all the potential to become a businessman.

Soon after arriving in Caracas, he displayed managerial skills when it came to rigorously and effectively organizing his new home. It was an apartment that had belonged to an aunt who'd never married, which his mother had inherited when the aunt had died. The apartment was, or is, in La Pastora.

"Near where Dr. José Gregorio Hernández died," said Margarita. "Funny, isn't it? How that saint got run over by the only car in Caracas at the time."

"He isn't a saint. As far as I understand, he's only been beatified," said Ardiles. "The other bit isn't true either: there was more than one car back then."

Margarita was somehow disappointed at the clarification. Not only because the psychiatrist had dismantled a legend, but because he failed to understand what faith means: attaining dignity by turning a blind eye.

In any case, whether saint or beatus, run over by the only car or by one car among many back in the day, José Gregorio Hernández represented for Margarita the essence of Caracas: a city where not even the saints were safe from the traffic.

That interest of Margarita's was influenced by the trade in which her brother had ended up working: the buying and selling of used cars. Fernando had enrolled in a technical school to study publicity and marketing. Noticing how good Fernando was at writing, a fellow student got him a job at *Guía Motor*, a Venezuelan racecar magazine. He started writing articles, learned how to edit content for the magazine website and got commissioned to write features on different car races around the country.

With the money he saved during the first two years, and with a little help from his parents, he was able to buy himself an old Malibu. He souped the car up, sold it and got double what he had paid for it. Following this method, it didn't take him long to buy himself a new car. After doing this a few times, he understood the strategy behind it. Unlike studying, buying and selling cars could become an end in itself. That's how he started in business and left his studies.

"Why didn't he do the same with the apartment?" Ardiles asked Margarita.

"Do what?" replied Margarita, as if dazed by the interruption.

"Sell the apartment at La Pastora and buy somewhere else. It's kind of a rough area."

"Because the apartment was under my mother's name. I hadn't yet been in Caracas long, I was starting in psychology, and she wanted to make sure I was in my own place, not just living at my brother's."

"Did you have problems with him?"

"Me?" She seemed offended by the question. "I adored my brother. He had a girlfriend and they had plans to get married. That's all."

It was in December 2008 that they killed him.

"A foolish death," said Margarita, crying. "He was in a bar on Avenida Andrés Bello. Apparently, he had an argument with a man who was hassling Mariela, his girlfriend. The man left, but then, when my brother left the bar, the guy followed him in a car and shot him."

In this way, Margarita was left alone in Caracas. Because of some twisted mechanism of compensation, her mother, too, was left alone in Tabay. A few weeks after Fernando's death, their father died of a heart attack. The alcoholism he had brought with him from his homeland had finally sucked him dry when confronted with the pain of losing his only son. Margarita didn't think about moving back to Tabay, nor did her mother think about moving to Caracas. Each stayed where she was, tied down by her circumstances, mourning the spaces and the customs, as if her memories needed her to stay put so they wouldn't get lost on their way back.

Around that time, Margarita became friends with an Italian man who lived next door. An old man who never used to leave his house and whom she started seeing when, in the early hours, they would happen to meet when both were leaning out of their windows, which overlooked the street that ran down from Amadores to Cardones.

"You can't sleep, huh?" he said the first time he saw her leaning over the balcony, wrapped in a quilt, at four in the morning. "Insomnia's a bitch."

Margarita wanted to answer, but the old man kept talking.

"Francesca is always telling me off, saying my bad mood is due to lack of sleep. Well, that's what she said back when she used to tell me off at all, because she doesn't even do that anymore. I tell her my bad mood is a consequence of what I see *thanks* to my lack of sleep. Francisco de Miranda was right when he complained that this country was a total mess. A country that sleeps so well, that snores its head off, isn't going anywhere. Take the people in the opposite building, the Mary-Ros, if they could see themselves the way I see them, they wouldn't sleep a wink for months. Every night the woman on the seventh floor, apartment on the left, puts her two children to bed, gives them some tea to get them to sleep, and moments later goes out wearing a black dress and high heels. She goes out around ten o'clock, with that look, heading to Avenida Baralt. The fact her children don't know their mother is a whore, excuse my language, is not the worst thing. The worst thing is that they don't wake up all night. I know because I'm watching them, because I spend my night shift waiting for at least one of the two to go to the bathroom or something. But they don't wake up. The mother comes back at six in the morning, she gets changed, washes her face and reappears in her children's room in the same pajamas she'd been wearing to put them to bed. And I think about the tea she prepares for them. About all those teas that add up to a regret. It's dangerous to have tea like that in *any* circumstance, don't you think? Do you understand what I'm saying? You do? Good, because Francesca doesn't."

That night she listened to the old man until six o'clock.

"You see?" said the old man, pointing down.

A woman wearing black stumbled out of a taxi.

"Is that her?" asked Margarita.

"Uh huh," replied the man, triumphantly.

The incipient eagerness of the hour drove each of them back into their nests. Thanks to the old man she was going to be late to her first class. She would go to university without taking a shower. To tell the truth, she was grateful: it had been two hours without thinking about Fernando.

The next night they met again on their respective observation decks.

"They've only just stopped drinking, so they'll probably sleep till midday," said the old man, getting straight to the point.

"Who?" asked Margarita.

"Them. All of them."

"Want some coffee?"

"No, I'm good."

Margarita came back after a few seconds.

"I'm out of coffee," she said.

"They stopped bringing it to me. It was giving me heartburn, so I took it off the list."

"Who does your groceries?"

"The Portuguese guy on the corner. I call him, he takes the order and the kid brings it over. Want the number?"

"That'd be great, thanks."

"A holiday," said the old man. "As if it wasn't enough with all the sleep they're already getting, now February 4th is a holiday! No one can celebrate failures quite like the Venezuelans. And no one forgets about them quite like the Venezuelans either. If something good came out of the '92 coup, it's that a lot of people stayed up all that night. And without drinking, otherwise it wouldn't be an achievement. They were up all night, but they didn't pay attention. They stayed in, watching the same video over and over, the video that was on all the channels when the rebels took over the main transmission station. Zombified, listening in disbelief and incomprehension to a soldier waking them from their sacred sleep to be part of the uprising. And the ones who looked out the window, they only looked southward. Since the Miraflores Palace is less than three blocks away, the neighbors considered themselves front-row witnesses. Which wasn't that wrong either, since then the Internet thing didn't exist, nor did this dumb fashion of having cell phones. So it was true they were listening to the breaking news, the first explosions, the first bursts of gunfire.

"They would watch television and look out to Miraflores, but they wouldn't look down, and so they didn't notice what was going on down in the street in the early hours. And precisely because the coup failed, because half the bombs dropped by the planes never blew up, because the Comandante got scared at the last minute and didn't do what he needed to do, that is precisely why they celebrate. Then when it's carnival time, a lot of children get dressed up like the Comandante. More than one affected intellectual came out and applauded the coup in their Sunday paper column. And in the intervening years, when the applause seemed to have died down, in reality they were just applauding on the inside. And the next government continued with the applause and released them from prison, and in the '98 elections the people applauded publicly again and voted for them, and now you see them on television, out on the street complaining, annoyed because the day's been declared a holiday. Annoyed because the military, after the country's been performing the same self-help farce for more than ten years so they could take power, have ended up believing the applause.

"Late that night, while the future president of the Republic was on TV calling for an uprising against the state, while most people just sat petrified in front of the TV, not fully understanding the message, I saw more than one man heading out to join the coup, I saw them with my own eyes. They came out of the Mary-Ros building, one came from the Dominicans' tenement housing, several from our own building. Do you see? Men who overnight go to answer the call of possible death. Navigating in the darkness of the small hours, with some confused idea about their own lives and the destiny of their homeland, to reach the bright source that had been projected onto their screens. Like little bugs burnt by the light. I will never forget the impression it made on me, seeing those men walking as if they were hypnotized. But nighttime explains a lot. What's really terrifying is that now millions of people keep answering that same death call in broad daylight."

The man stopped talking and, for a time, went on gazing at the lights and shadows of the sloping street. Margarita pictured the old man, with a sudden burst of energy, climbing the balcony railings and jumping into the void.

When she woke up from her brief reverie, the old man wasn't there. Standing on tiptoes and leaning forward, she looked into his apartment, but she couldn't see any movement at all. Had he jumped? The idea was absurd, and for precisely this reason, it was possible. She scanned the asphalt, knowing she wouldn't find anything, but wanting some kind of revelation.

"Here you go," said the old man suddenly.

Margarita gave a start.

It was a piece of paper with a telephone number, written in a trembling hand.

"Tell João you're Señor Paolo's neighbor, from the Lino," said the old man.

All the way through February 2009, Margarita held long late-night conversations with Señor Paolo. That's how she started to learn his story. He and Francesca had come from Italy, arriving in the port of La Guaira in the mid-1950s, in the middle of the Pérez Jiménez dictatorship. As the years went by, he managed to save a small fortune from the many jobs he did in the construction sector, with a good business to cap it all off. He'd never had children.

One day Margarita summoned up the nerve to ask him:

"Señor Paolo, do you ever go out?"

The old man shook his head with all the gentle anger his age allowed him.

"No. I promised Francesca I'd never leave her side. Four years ago she fell over and broke her hip. She hasn't gotten up since."

The next day Señor Paolo didn't show up at the window. Margarita went back into her room at seven in the morning. She shouldn't have asked him that question. Why had she been so indiscreet? She put the TV on. Distracted, she started channel surfing. Every few seconds she'd smell her armpits. There was a special program being broadcast on the state channel, because that day, February 27, was the twentieth anniversary of the Caracazo protests.

February the 27th, thought Margarita.

"Now I can see that the question I asked Señor Paolo was

232 ��� Rodrigo Blanco Calderón

really aimed at myself," said Margarita. "At the time I saw it as a kind of resistance."

"What? Resistance against what?" asked Ardiles.

"I don't know. Against something. I had spent almost a month without going out. It was as if someone had set me that goal. It may sound crazy, but I was glad I'd achieved it."

The mornings passed and Señor Paolo didn't show up. After the third consecutive absence, Margarita hardly ever leaned out over the balcony anymore, and when she did, it was mechanically, just to be sure the bond really had been broken. She would spend the rest of the day in her room, watching TV and smelling her armpits. The marinating of her own smells became the vaporous marker of time. With indeterminate frequency, she would receive increasingly worried calls from her mother. She would reply dryly every time:

"There's nothing going on, mamá. Stop with all the questions. I'm busy."

And she would hang up.

Things really got complicated for Margarita the day they cut off her Intercable service. She was helpless without TV or the Internet. Soon after this, the Portuguese grocer refused to send her a new delivery. She still owned him for the previous one, which she hadn't paid for because she hadn't gone to the bank to ask for new checkbooks or to the cash machine. The afternoon she found out about this new setback, she tried calling again. This time, it was the boy who answered. The Portuguese guy had gone out.

"I can't, Señorita Margarita. Señor João said you need to pay first."

"How about we do this: when you bring the groceries to Señor Paolo, why don't you help me out and bring me a small bag? Some arepa flour, some fruit. Whatever you can."

"That's the problem, Señora Margarita. Señor Paolo hasn't called. And he does a weekly shop. Have you heard from him?"

"No," said Margarita. "I haven't heard anything."

Margarita reckoned she survived for three days eating leftovers scattered around the house. She was like a pigeon eating the crumbs she had thrown to herself. Diarrhea and vomiting became the only distractions. The cramps and nausea were like the murmur that announces a faraway train. From distant territories, she felt the emissions from something that long ago belonged to her: which was just her own body.

One night she dreamed about Fernando. Also about her parents in Tabay. It was a random selection of memories. Its oneiric nature was evident only through its time lapses, in a sort of parodic awareness that stiffened the movements. Margarita remembered being troubled within the dream itself by how conventional those images were. How they fit themselves into past events with no visible modifications.

"The fact my unconscious was so transparent worried me," said Margarita.

Like any good psychology student, Margarita knew that the unconscious is a space that can be inhabited *ad infinitum*. It's the laboratory for the alchemy of images. The only things that get in are those that don't fit anywhere else. That have, in a way, already disappeared.

The most terrible awakenings in literature are those of Kafka's characters. Josef K. and Gregor Samsa open their eyes into a hell that's just beginning and threatens to have no end. Margarita awoke from her madness in all-too-literal Kafkaesque style. She left her utterly normal dreams behind when she felt a sting on her upper lip. Her own screams of fear ended up waking her: a cockroach was biting her lip and refusing to let go.

"It was a small bite, inoffensive, smaller than an ant's. But it's

234 of Rodrigo Blanco Calderón

so small, there's nothing you can do make it any smaller. Now whenever I feel an itch, I get scared. And sometimes it's not even an itch. If I'm worried about something, that's enough for me to imagine the cockroach is still biting my lip. The idea I've let myself get carried away again, and that a giant cockroach will be devouring me when I wake up, terrifies me."

The first thing Margarita did after crying for a long time was to take a shower. She was under the water for more than an hour.

"Recently, on one of my night shifts, I had to see a woman who was sure she'd been raped by a ghost. She was psychotic. But now I totally know how she felt," said Margarita.

After her shower, she started to clean the apartment.

"When you're overwhelmed with idleness, the only things you have to spare are cleaning products," said Margarita. "It makes sense, doesn't it?"

After thoroughly cleaning up the mess, cleaning while her tears cleaned her face, she took another shower. In the following days, she busied herself with settling accounts. She paid overdue bills and settled up for outstanding services. Did the shopping herself. Not a big shop, as she didn't want things to go to waste. She called her mother and said she needed to spend a few weeks with her.

She spent the whole of April recovering in Tabay. They hadn't seen each other since the fleeting visit for her father's funeral. They talked about the possibility of her, her mother, coming to Caracas. That way they could keep each other company. Her mother promised to think about it.

Margarita returned to the La Pastora apartment with a sliver of hope. The first thing she would do that week would be to put her brother's car on the market. She hadn't planned how to spend that money. She just wanted to get rid of the material components of her memories.

When the elevator door slid open, she stood in the corridor for a long time. If someone had seen her, they would have thought she'd forgotten which door was hers. She recalled her conversations with Señor Paolo.

Why not? she said to herself. And rang the bell.

Nobody answered. She gave up and went into her apartment. On the fridge door, held in place by some wax fruits affixed to a magnet, was the note with the grocery store number. She was surprised it had survived the hurricane of idleness and, even more, that of the cleaning spree.

The Portuguese man answered. She surprised him by asking him to speak to the kid. He didn't understand a thing. Margarita really stretched out the preliminary small talk, as if they were old friends, which confused him even more. The Portuguese man must have said something because the kid interrupted the flirtation.

"Are you ordering something, Señora?"

That's what he called her: Señora.

"No. I'm not, really. I wanted to ask you about Señor Paolo, to find out if you've heard anything. If he's called again."

"You haven't heard anything about it?"

"About what?"

"Oh. Right, yeah, when the police were talking to the concierge, she told them you'd gone away."

"The police? Did they go into Paolo's apartment?"

The boy remained silent, as if wondering whether to answer her. In the end, he said:

"No. What happened was even uglier than that."

Margarita heard the Portuguese man in the background, shouting at the kid to hang up in a mixture of Spanish and Portuguese.

"Señora, if you aren't ordering anything, I'm going to have to hang up."

"Yes, I'm ordering something," said Margarita. She listed a few random things. She wanted to speak with this kid in person.

What happened to Paolo and Francesca was inexplicable. The fact that Miguel Ardiles decided to call them that does imply he was looking for an interpretation. However, the core of those lives, the reason why they developed and ended as they did, can't be unraveled.

It was the kid himself who'd alerted the concierge. Señor Paolo hadn't shown any signs of life for a few weeks. They went up to his apartment and listened from outside for a long time. When the silence became unbearable, they just went on in yet more silence, standing outside, like a person who changes position while sitting on an uncomfortable chair. Through the absolute silence, they were now searching for the conclusive smell. But there wasn't any stench to alert them.

They rang the bell a few times. Then they banged noisily on the grille, to see if Señor Paolo would come out angrily to stop the racket. The concierge called a locksmith. They didn't say anything about what it was that they suspected, but the man must have sensed something, because before he was willing to force the door open, after having easily taken out the lock, he asked the concierge whether she owned the apartment.

The concierge had to confess what she was thinking, and the locksmith said he wasn't opening any door without the police present. They called the local station. More than an hour later, two police officers came, they heard all about the situation and gave the locksmith authorization to carry on with his job. When the door was finally opened, they felt shivers down their spines. The police officers were apprehensive, they drew their guns and went into the apartment. They ordered the locksmith, the concierge and the kid to remain in the corridor. They shouted hello and went through the communal areas of the apartment. From the outside, the group could freely see the space that had previously been barred to them. There was the typical decoration of an old couple's home. Everything was impeccable and in order, baroque in its taste and with a musty smell.

"Camacho!" shouted one of the policemen. He was already checking one of the rooms. "Come see this shit."

Camacho turned toward the corridor.

"You stay there. Don't move," he told them.

The bodies were in the main room.

"The poor old couple, are they dead?" the concierge asked the policeman who answered to the name Camacho.

"They are," he said. "But don't come in."

He was pale. He used the radio to communicate with the police station. He explained the situation using some numeric codes. He then started to walk down the stairs.

"Use the elevator," said the concierge.

"I need some fresh air," was the policeman's answer.

The kid was the first to go in. Then the locksmith followed him. The concierge stayed where she was, in the corridor, rubbing her hands together.

When they came into the room, the policeman didn't reprimand them. He seemed grateful for the company. He still had the gun in his hand, not trained on anything, but he didn't dare put it away.

"What's that shiny thing?" whispered the locksmith.

"I don't know," said the policeman.

One of the bodies seemed to be wrapped up in a porous sheet, in a blazing white.

"Shall I switch on the light?"

No one had noticed that they had been in the dark until that point. And that was how they remained.

"It's quicklime," said the locksmith.

"How do you know?" said the policeman.

"I'm also a builder. I work with it. Smell it," he said, touching his nose.

"Is that what quicklime smells like?" asked the boy.

They were about to debate the different smells and properties of lime when they were silenced by a low murmur. The policeman, nervous, aimed his gun at the back of the room. It was then they heard the moan that left them trembling.

"Uhhhhhhh."

The moan of a drowned person, a death rattle of suffocation.

The kid and the locksmith ran out. The policeman, also trying to get away, tripped on the threshold of the room.

"Don't move, or I'll blow your head off," he shouted at the shadows. When he didn't hear anything, he decided to switch on the light.

Señora Francesca looked like a mummy. She had been dead for a few days, and the decay of her thin body was hidden under several shrouds covered with lime. Señor Paolo was an uneven sack of bones with cracked lips. A pitiful conduit for a slow agony.

He was in a coma when he got to the hospital and died two days later.

The hypothesis of a murder was discarded right away. There was no evidence of forced entry into the apartment, nor were there stolen goods or a motive for the crime. There was also the convincing matter of the couple's old age, and the solitude and total isolation in which they'd lived. The police made some half-hearted inquiries about Margarita, who was their neighbor, but they were satisfied with the unusual assistance provided by the concierge, who stated that she had gone away traveling a long time before it happened.

Margarita went back to the balcony in the early hours of the next day. Every now and then, she would see a car disappearing into the tight labyrinth of streets downtown. Two or three lights remained on in the buildings around her. Illuminated windows, which seemed, at first sight, identical but contained beings as disparate as early risers and insomniacs. She tried to imagine the lives of those people, those strangers who may have also been watching her from the other side of the street. She imagined all that and tried to understand what had happened to her, when and how she had gone astray.

Without noticing, she stopped thinking about herself and thought about Paolo and Francesca, about how her neighbor had buried himself alive to honor the eternal vow of fidelity sworn to his wife. A wife, and this is what had stopped her from sleeping that night, who was not.

"They weren't husband and wife," said the concierge, when Margarita stopped by to hear her version of the events. "They were brother and sister."

23

The Strinkis

As if by agreement, Pedro Álamo, Matías Rye and Margarita Lambert all disappeared. In psychiatric jargon, *disappeared* means either that they died or committed suicide, which happens only rarely, or that they got on with their lives.

The short story workshop had ended at the beginning of March, or that's what Ardiles understood from one of Rye's last emails. From then on, their mutual bond seemed to have fallen apart, as if the story that connected them all had been written from out of that workshop.

Pedro Álamo was the one who worried him the least. He could imagine him in his annex in the Santa Inés development, constantly about to go out, or about to be swallowed up forever by that labyrinth he had built himself. Weighing up letters or combinations of words that would open a door to a clearer vision of the past or the future.

Some nights, however, he couldn't sleep for wondering about Margarita Lambert's fate. The first two sessions had been very useful. The last two were alarming. Over the course of Margarita's month in therapy, Ardiles had gotten up to speed on her family history, the trauma caused by her brother's death, the episode with the cockroach. Those events were the preface to the presence that now tormented her, hovering over her like a cloud of anxiety.

After learning what had happened to Señor Paolo, Margarita made the necessary adjustments to start over. She put her brother's car on the market, convinced her mother to come and live in Caracas and enrolled at a sports center where they taught martial arts and self-defense. They had a detailed offering of methodical violence that went from karate, kung fu, judo and tae kwon do, as well as Brazilian jujitsu, boxing and kickboxing, to ornamental alternatives such as capoeira.

Margarita was reminded of *Full Contact*, an old Jean-Claude Van Damme movie. When they were kids, she and Fernando would take turns playing Van Damme and the usual wicked Chinaman who always lost. On that nostalgic whim, which was rather amusing, she signed up for kickboxing.

A few weeks later, the people at the sports center had learned two things: that Margarita was a natural at throwing punches and kicks; and that she and her trainer, Gonzalo Paredes, had fallen in love.

On the street and in bars, they were seen merged into the embrace of the spider, the four legs and four arms tangled up, moving, advancing. Or else apart, talking and gesticulating passionately, outlining their plans for the future.

In their intimacy, they were an adaptation of the novels by Marquis de Sade. Frantic sex, several times a day, with philosophical breaks where they would reconstruct the path that had brought them there.

Gonzalo's story was as seemingly random as that of any loose cannon. A directionless force of nature that could end up pulverized against a wall or blowing the head off a stranger. Orphaned of his mother and raised by a soldier father, Gonzalo had always been trained for life in military ways: the world is a battlefield, anything different from you is the enemy, only cowards back down, borders are there to be conquered, etc.

His anger problems became evident during high school. The alarms went off toward the end of his adolescence: Gonzalo fought back against his father and gave him a beating, as the father had done to him so many times during his childhood. A retinue of psychiatrists and psychologists did manage, with the drone of their words, to numb the boy's irascible nature on occasion. Until one of them, seeing Gonzalo's disposition and body, had the good sense to suggest that he channel all that anger in some professional manner. He recommended him to one of the owners of the sports center, where he would end up working as a trainer. When this man met Gonzalo, he greeted him cheerfully, patting his back and his jaw, sizing him up as if he were acquiring a fighting dog.

During those formative years, Gonzalo learned how to interpret the extensive musical stave of weaknesses that an opponent offers. Martial arts for him were like an instrument for a born musician. It wasn't long before he started participating in national and international championships. It all pointed at an Olympic medal, but Gonzalo saw trophies for what they really are: pieces of junk used as a substitute for money.

He chose the least heroic option: becoming a trainer. Hardening men who wanted to stop being cowards, and giving women, whose most common nightmare was rape, a slim possibility of avoiding it.

Gonzalo wanted to make money. He had imagined creating a sort of gym where people would go to learn to kill and look good. He never put it in those terms. In fact, he probably never thought it through either. But in his head, the experience of power, the possibility of humiliating and inflicting pain on others, of being what they call a monster, was connected to beauty.

He had a few contacts already. People who had promised him a perfect space for what he wanted. Acquaintances who, if he placed a big order on equipment, would give him massive discounts. He just needed a bit of luck and money.

Each time they paused on a landing of love, Gonzalo would tweak the outline of his project. Margarita would listen awestruck, imagining herself beside him, helping him. Gonzalo insisted he just needed a bit of luck, some contacts and a little money to get started. He just needed to find someone who would believe in him and his ideas, who would lend him a small amount, which he'd soon return with added interest.

Margarita's mother never liked Gonzalo. The only time he set foot in the apartment at La Pastora, there was an exchange of glances that was enough to seal a mutual rejection and a marking of the territory. There was no way Gonzalo was going to be coming in and spending time with them. Margarita guessed the reason for this, so when they weren't out together, she would lock herself in her bedroom to think about him.

While she was doing this, in her room, Margarita had a revelation. The idea seemed so evident that she was embarrassed she hadn't thought of it before. It hadn't been long since she had sold Fernando's car for a very good price. Since she'd had no specific plans for spending that money, she had put it away for a four-month fixed term, so as to receive higher interest. She just needed to wait until the end of the fixed term to withdraw the money and lend it to Gonzalo.

"I put the money away mid-March. By mid-July, the fixed term will be unlocked, and then we can use it," Margarita explained to Gonzalo the first time.

Gonzalo was against it. She tried several convincing arguments, but Gonzalo shut the conversation down.

He is too good and proud, thought Margarita.

She backed off for a few days. Then, little by little, she resumed the conversation. This time around she started to use the first-person plural. *We should, if we had, it would be in our interest*—expressions that began to transform the project into

244 ❧ Rodrigo Blanco Calderón

a joint enterprise in which it was unnecessary to stipulate who invested what, or where the other person's benefits would start and end.

As if in sync, Margarita managed to convince Gonzalo in July.

"You've lost your mind," said Margarita's mother when she learned about her plans.

"You've never given Gonzalo a chance, mamá. He's really nice to me. He's a man with great ideas. It's just that no one has ever wanted to help him."

"That man is taking advantage of you. Don't say I didn't warn you."

Gonzalo invested the money in renting a warehouse in the La Urbina industrial area that had stood empty for a while. The owner was renting it out very cheaply on the condition he received six months up front. The man was worried the property would be occupied by those who'd been displaced by the recent heavy rains. Or that the government would expropriate it. Once he had an address for the new gym, Gonzalo could sort the necessary permits, buy the equipment and install it.

Those days were tense but full of solidarity. Gonzalo's excitement would raise her up, as he imagined how things would be next year. Margarita felt she had made the right decisions. Kickboxing was helping her to control her fear of other people, which had started after Fernando's death. With the muscles she had developed and the techniques she had learned, she built an imaginary fence around herself. It's true she had fallen in love, and love is a secret door that opens to irremediable weakness. But luckily, she had fallen in love with Gonzalo, and Gonzalo was, she was certain, the most faithful of guards.

That's why Margarita just couldn't understand what happened next. Both the events themselves and Gonzalo's reaction.

"That shit hole was already occupied. I kicked the crap out of two of those sonsofbitches, but some others came with sticks and I had to run away."

"When did they get in?"

"They were there already."

"And why did you rent it like that? Didn't the guy say he was going to rent it to you so nobody else could occupy it?"

Gonzalo went quiet.

"Don't tell me you rented it without going to see it first. Huh, Gonzalo? Answer me."

"You stay here, I'll sort it out."

"What did the owner say?"

"He's not answering the phone," said Gonzalo, as if holding his breath. "I don't even know if he's the real owner," he said at last.

"We're fucked, Gonzalo. They've robbed us."

"I'll sort it out."

"You'll sort it out? What are you going to sort out? What an asshole, Gonzalo. What an asshole."

Gonzalo exploded.

"Don't call me an asshole. Don't call me an asshole!" said Gonzalo, rising from a whisper to a shout.

Margarita was paralyzed. Perhaps, amid the muteness and the immobility, she managed to glimpse the trap she had fallen into. Gonzalo had taught her many things and might yet teach her more, but he could never teach her how to protect herself from him.

Their idyll had passed the due date on its fixed term, and the problems had begun.

Margarita told her mother about the scam. Her mother said how sorry she was and gave her a hug. She made no comment about Gonzalo. Margarita appreciated that, and began spending more time in the house with her and less inside her room.

Gonzalo started to disappear for two or three days a week. He'd tell Margarita he was working double to make up for the money they'd lost. He had also been given some information: the man who scammed him was still in Caracas. Margarita begged him to leave things as they were, or else go to the police. Gonzalo said no, he told her, calmly now, to trust him, that it wasn't over.

The ambiguity of his schedule, which would transform him by turns into resigned laborer and vengeful mafioso, made them drift apart a little. The life they had built together so fast suddenly became like one of those places in the city where one was very happy once, but which the passing of time, absences or change has made unfamiliar.

Gonzalo had dealings with very strange people during those months. Some were old acquaintances, even friends of his father's, from whom he had for some reason grown apart. But there was another type of character who disturbed Margarita: men or women—sometimes very young, sometimes decrepit old people and sometimes people not too old but who had aged—whom Gonzalo had just met and with whom he would establish a sort of pact.

Out of that crazy cast of characters came the Strinkis.

The Strinkis weren't twins, but they behaved like twins. They liked to say they were brothers and then laugh, whereas in reality they actually were brothers. There was something in the natural way of things, in their interactions with the world, that made them laugh. A something surrounded by a thick cloud of marijuana.

They were street artists. Meaning that they were skaters, graffiti artists, DJs, visual artists, photographers. A simultaneous everything and nothing that was a sign of the times. They had tattoos they'd designed themselves on various parts of their bodies; piercings in noses, or eyebrows, or necks; they wore baseball caps on a scale that seemed to anticipate an attack of hydrocephalus; jeans that were either too wide or too skinny, but always hanging from the equatorial line in the middle of their asses, held up with a shoestring.

Margarita first met them at Isabel's Pizzeria. The came over to say hello to Gonzalo. They did it very respectfully. They hardly looked at her. Without asking permission, they sat at the table and ordered beer and pizza. Five minutes into the conversation, Margarita stopped trying to follow it. And she was sure Gonzalo hadn't understood a thing either. What could Gonzalo and those kids have in common? When they finished their pizza, they downed their beers and moved to the far corner of the place, not before hugging Gonzalo, each in turn.

"Who are those kids?" asked Margarita.

"The Strinkis. They're kids, but they must be like thirty."

"What's that about Strinkis?"

"That's what they're called."

"Why?"

"I don't know."

"How do you know them?"

"I met them here. A couple of drunks wanted to fuck with them the other day and I helped them out."

When they asked for the check, their waiter told them the boys had already paid it. On their way out, Gonzalo held Margarita with one hand. With the other, he gestured goodbye to the Strinkis. They waved their arms, and one of them made a phone gesture as if to say he would call him in the next few days.

The second time Margarita saw the Strinkis was at their house. They lived in a penthouse on cross street eight in Los Palos

Grandes. Gonzalo told her they had invited them to a party, although Margarita didn't know the reason, nor did she ask.

There were a lot of people, but the space was so big that there were only small islands of youngsters, resting on a pouf or some other low piece of furniture, from which crazy girls would burst out desperate to use the bathroom, or to have a drink, or to ask for a cigarette. After walking around for quite a while, going along many corridors and up some stairs, they found the Strinkis at a table on a terrace from where they could see the night over much of the city.

They sat down with them, and once again Margarita tried to follow the conversation. The Strinkis reminded her of a series she'd watched when she was little, the Teletubbies. That association helped her to understand that there wasn't anything to understand. It was all about stimuli, there was no internal structure. One phrase would lead to another, one laugh to the next.

What really exasperated her was her own presence there. Why had Gonzalo accepted the invitation? What could they have in common? Seeing him so solid, so confident in his silence, so detached from whatever the Strinkis might say or not say, she really found the contrast between her boyfriend and his new friends unbearable. Next to them, Gonzalo looked less like a friend, more like a bodyguard. And that, perhaps, was what troubled her the most, since bodyguards are always out of place, sniffing out danger.

Margarita stood up to go to the bathroom. One of the Strinkis pointed the way. She had to go downstairs and walk almost to the entrance of the apartment. When she came out of the bathroom, she saw a long wall covered in books. She walked alongside it lazily, all the way until she found another room, identical to the main room, with more books. In that room, the bookshelves were interrupted only by oases of white walls dotted with small pictures. There she surprised a young man hiding a book inside his jacket.

"Please don't say a word," he said. He was wearing an olive-green jacket, very tight trousers and Converse shoes. "Those assholes don't even know the treasure they've got."

"How come they have this library?"

"It's their parents'."

"And where are they?"

"They left the country soon after April 11th. They left them the apartment, and bye-bye. That and they pad their bank accounts every month."

Margarita took a few steps away from the guy and started to look on one of the shelves. She pulled out a book. It was a collection of letters between Sigmund Freud and Wilhelm Fliess.

"Take it," said the guy.

Margarita hesitated.

"Take it, seriously. It'll be in better hands if you have it. Look at this."

He showed her some sheets, greenish and transparent, piled on top of some books and a video-game controller.

"You see?"

"What is it?"

"A numbered silk-screen printing by Carlos Cruz-Diez. Do you have any idea what this is? How much it's worth?"

Margarita said goodbye with the book still in her hand. It was a paperback and easily covered with her purse. When she got back to the table on the terrace, Gonzalo and the Strinkis didn't notice her. They seemed to be talking about something concrete for the first time.

"It won't be anything permanent," said one of the Strinkis.

"We'll just call you whenever we need you," said the other.

"No problem," said Gonzalo.

Gonzalo didn't talk on the way back to his house. They crept inside, stealthily as usual, even though they knew Gonzalo's father would be asleep by then. The few times she had seen him, he had greeted them with a growl or the briefest glance.

Once they were in his room, half-naked, Margarita asked him about the conversation with the Strinkis.

"It's work," said Gonzalo.

"And?"

"I'm going to do some work for them. Just occasionally."

"Doing what?"

"They need a bodyguard."

24

"Mark Sandman's Funeral"

Miguel Ardiles is one of those people who has a Facebook account in order not to use it. It's an act of private anarchy, like voting blank in the presidential elections. The link between that account and his email address is the anchor that allows him to sound out the requests of a world he likes to despise from the surface.

All of which shows that Miguel Ardiles must have been in an unusual mood the morning of Holy Thursday when he decided to log on to Facebook. He hadn't heard from his friends, the case of Lila Hernández—the victim of the Monster in Los Palos Grandes—was getting postponed every week, and the things he had found in that apartment had infected him with a ferocious bout of insomnia.

He started by declining the accumulated friend requests, to kill off some illusions. He tested himself by looking at the beach photos of some female colleagues who were waiting for his reply, so the slam of his rejection would be truly meaningful. Then he started to turn down event invites.

There was one whose heading made him hesitate and take a look.

EVENT NAME: Mark Sandman's Funeral.
DATE AND TIME: July 3, 2010. From 11 p.m. to 5 a.m.
LOCATION: El Monte
CREATED BY: Night Creatures.
GOING: ___. NOT GOING: ___. MAYBE: ___.

That's some of Matías's crap, thought Ardiles.

He clicked on the group Night Creatures and confirmed that Matías had indeed created it and was its admin. His smile disappeared when he read his own name among the group members:

"Miguel Ardiles: Psychiatrist. *Catcher in the Rye*."

"That fucking asshole," said Ardiles, aloud now.

He checked the profiles of the other members and was horrified at the dismal showcase. Not a group so much as the results of a police raid. There were youngsters, adults and two old people. The youngsters were two girls and a goth boy. Apart from Matías and himself, there were four adults. All four looked like self-confessed killers. The elderly pair, a man and a woman, provoked fear and sorrow in equal measure. They were like those pictures found on city walls, where worried relatives announce the disappearance of old people with Alzheimer's.

"Can you tell me what the fuck you're playing at?" asked a furious Ardiles on the phone.

"You've finally seen the invite?" said Matías, excited.

"Course I've seen it. Get me out of that shit now, or I'm not talking to you again."

"I'll get you out. Stop with the drama. Don't you even want to know what it's about?"

"I don't, to be honest."

"Let's meet up and I'll tell you about it."

Ardiles was silently grateful for Matías's perseverance. He was dying to know what his patient and friend was up to.

"At the Chinese?" asked Miguel.

"No, the temporary prohibition law's in force these days. That's what those assholes are like: communist, conservative and Catholic. Can't it be at yours?"

"You're coming all the way here?"

"If it's not at your place, I'm not telling you anything."

"Shall I pick you up somewhere?"

"I'll get a cab."

If he had known anything about Mark Sandman's life, Miguel Ardiles would have understood Matías Rye's obsession at once.

Ardiles didn't know, for example, that there are two kinds of artists: those who just seem to fall into it, and those for whom it's not a falling, but a calling.

Artists who answer a call tend to be precocious. Those who just stumble and fall are latecomers to the arts, not because of neglect or blindness, but because it's the last hope they have once they've reached a certain point in their lives. Others in similar circumstances find religion. And then there are others still who are saved by neither religion nor science, as Goethe would say, and who die young, or peacefully, at the end of an anonymous existence.

Sandman was an artist who fell into it by accident. He was a musician, a poet, a comic writer, just the same way as he could have been a salmon fisherman on the Atlantic coast of the United States, a graduate in political science or a cab driver.

Mark Sandman was born in Boston on September 24, 1952. The first of four children, to a family of Jewish origins and destiny. Guitelle H. Sandman, despite being a Jew, didn't believe in God. Unfortunately, God did believe in her, and He showed it by tragically appointing her the *chosen one* when He carried off her three sons.

After Mark came Martha, and then Jonny and Roger. Inverting the order of creation, God took away Roger, Jonny and Mark in succession, like a gambler discarding his playing cards.

Born on September 3, 1958, Roger was the last of the lot,

and he faced the greatest obstacles. At four he was diagnosed with cerebral palsy. His short life, which was marked by motor problems and certain learning difficulties, came to an end on November 18, 1978, owing to a cardiac infection. After several surgical operations and vain attempts, his parents, Bob and Guitelle, had to give permission to switch off the life-support machine that had been keeping their youngest son alive.

Jonathan Maynard Sandman was born on April 20, 1956. In the distribution of temperaments, he got to be the nice one, the kidder who pulled funny faces to cheer up the whole family. He liked clowning around, joking, dressing up and performing. As a matter of fact, he stood out playing two different roles in an adaptation of *Zorba the Greek* staged at his school. He had the same adventurous streak as Mark, but without the latter's rebellion or animosity. He traveled to Hawaii, Marseille and Crete, among other exotic destinations. Jonny was a very lively, mobile soul, who sought his path in different corners of the world and at different jobs. But God had other plans for him. On March 5, 1980, one year, four months and fourteen days after Roger's death, God would push Jonny Sandman out of a window during a party. Polytrauma left him with no vital signs. Bob and Guitelle, once again, had to give permission to switch off the machine.

"I guess I'm next." That's how Martha greeted her parents when they arrived at Boston City Hospital after a canceled vacation in Florida. Jonny's body had just been put on medical support and Martha found herself torn between pain for the imminent death of another of her brothers and the fear of what seemed to be divine revenge.

Of the four children, Martha was the only one who was really interested in her Jewish roots. She had spent the summers of 1972 and 1973 in Israel, during a dance tour on which she combined her culture and her artistic aptitudes. The deaths of Roger and

Jonny in such a short period of time made her believe that the family had entered their Year of Mercy, which, according to the prophet Isaiah, in one of the Bible's more controversial passages, is also "the year of the vengeance of our God."

Even if death is the main proof of God's existence, He still needs someone to hear Him. An audience who listens attentively, and fearfully, before being sacrificed and thereby renewing the mystery of His iniquity, and at the same time warranting the continuity of His story.

So God kept Martha alive to repopulate her decimated family with her three children, Alex, Gabe and Amanda. Except that Guitelle wasn't as stupid as Job. God could have given her or her daughter a large offspring to make up for the tragedy. But the math always gave her the same result: "*four minus three.*"

When it seemed as if the sacred wrath had calmed down, Mark thought he had been spared. If that was correct, then this wasn't a case of God's vengeance after all. But if it wasn't God's vengeance, then nothing made sense. On the 1989 album *Tied to the Tracks*, the second by Treat Her Right, Sandman makes reference to two crucial events from his past. It is in "No Reason," a song that stands out not for its virtuosity but for the autobiographical load its lyrics are carrying.

> *There's no reason in this life*
> *Someone lives and someone dies*
> *And it should come as no surprise*
> *'Cause there's no reason in this life*
>
> *Took a knife wound in the chest*
> *They took my money then they left me for dead*
> *Man is killed at a traffic light*
> *I thought that could have been me inside*

You know I went to the beach but I didn't swim
Just watched the waves come breakin' in
Someone try to answer why
Lord, I'm alive and my brothers died

By that point, Sandman's question was understandable. How could he have survived his two innocent, peaceful brothers? From early on, Mark had been the problem boy in his family. He carried the burden of those who see things differently. One of the earliest indications Guitelle had of her firstborn being different was when he was in second grade. He had been able to read easily since the previous Christmas. One day he came home with three school friends. She greeted them as mothers do: kissing them, asking them to sit on the sofa while she brought milk and biscuits.

The kids ate and she left them to play on their own. Half an hour later she noticed with a panic that the house was completely silent. She ran to the living room and found them there, each in a different corner, reading books Mark had given them.

During his childhood, while she was still able to educate him, his mother encouraged the musical streak that had come from her own mother. She would take him to concerts from a very early age, and they would often spend hours listening to records. Before he had learned to play guitar, Mark had formal musical training at the first Troubadours school, where he was part of the boys' choir. The same school where many years later—albeit in its Newton City branch—Martha would end up teaching.

He also showed a special aptitude for languages, which was a premonition of his travels. He learned tortuous German fairly easily, which helped him to impersonate Hitler during class and get himself deported to Siberia, as he called the cold corridor where he had to wait during the hours of solitary punishment.

The real hell for Bob and Guitelle Sandman was Mark's time in high school. Those were the years he started growing his hair, cutting class, smoking cigarettes and marijuana. They took him out of the public school where he'd been studying and sent him to Pembroke Place boarding school, an alternative school better prepared to deal with boys like him. He finished high school there, then was accepted to Windham College in Vermont.

Despite everything, Mark had shown himself to be an intelligent boy in high school. Those subjects he liked, he passed effortlessly, with good grades. His IQ test revealed above-average results. His parents thought college would finally put Mark on track.

At first, things did seem to be going well, but by halfway through the year, the truth was out. Mark's grades were terrible. He was making money writing other people's essays, and forgetting to finish his own.

One day, when Mark went back home, his parents, with the help of a psychologist, gave him a choice: either he could be serious about his studies or start a full-time job, or he'd have to leave home.

Mark picked up his things and left.

No one heard from him for a month. Then he called home and told them he was all right. He was living in a kind of commune with some friends from Vermont. He started reading Jack Kerouac in those months. And also, which was even more dangerous, replicating Kerouac's writings in real life. For example, for a whole winter, he moved in to some abandoned miner's shack near Breckenridge, Colorado, enduring the cold, not washing, like a savage. No one really knows what he lived on, or what he ate. His mother communicated with him by phoning the Gold Nugget, a bar where Mark would stop in for the locals to buy him a drink.

In 1972 he worked as a cook on a fishing boat that moved around the northwest. In 1974 he worked on a fishing trawler that would go down the west coast, from Washington to Oregon, searching for salmon, then from Mexico to Canada, fishing for tuna. While waiting to embark on new fishing expeditions, he worked as a crane operator in a factory close to the Olympic National Park, where he got into the lycanthropic and romantic habit of walking alone in the forest at night.

From Washington, he moved to Alaska. There he worked as a waiter in a restaurant that served only crab, until he realized he was allergic to crab. From Alaska, he went back to Washington to pick up his passport, and from there traveled to Central and South America. He would lose his passport climbing the heights of Machu Picchu. He stopped in Brazil, where he lived for six months, and where for the first time he really devoted himself to his work as a musician.

A serious and rare infection forced him back home, but by then he had found what he'd been looking for: he had the burning heat of experience in his eyes now. Hunger, solitude, hallucinations and wandering paths had been crammed into the backpack that his heart had become. He carried with him the fresh memory of the bands to which he had belonged and then randomly left, like a wolf seeking out the pack only to experience the strange pleasure of leaving it behind. He carried with him the music that was the soundtrack to everything he had lived through. Now, in a few years, he would have to take the opposite journey: he would have to create the life that would go alongside his music.

He rented a small apartment in Cambridge. In his own space, he could focus on listening to music, studying different instruments and composing. His good old, bad old friends reappeared. Mark still wasted some time on the mirage of the night, without ever really entering it. Bob and Guitelle, seeing what their son was spending his money on, refused to give him any more. On one occasion he called them from Texas, where he had been arrested for having a little marijuana in his pocket, asking them to get him out.

At twenty-five, tired of being on the road, he showed up at the Sandman home willing to amend his ways. He would go back to college, applying for a place at the University of Massachusetts. He would support himself by working as a taxi driver.

Since he was studying by day, he had to work the night shift. Although one can imagine him choosing the night anyway. In 1977 Mark Sandman was the real-life version, and an almost simultaneous one, of Robert De Niro in *Taxi Driver*.

One sunny Sunday afternoon, going against his routine, and perhaps trying to make some extra cash, Mark went out for a ride. He picked up a couple of teenagers in Dorchester. Just before pulling over he had a bad feeling about it. Then he thought they were just a couple of kids and that it was such a beautiful Sunday afternoon. Nothing bad could happen.

Soon after he started driving toward the agreed address, one of the teenagers stabbed Mark in the chest. The other took advantage of the moment to steal the eight dollars he had in his shirt pocket. Despite all this, Mark managed to use the radio to call the company's head office and got taken to the hospital. They dealt with him in the intensive-care unit of Carney Hospital. The knife had touched his lungs but narrowly missed his heart.

That day Guitelle couldn't celebrate her birthday, not that she felt like it. She couldn't do it exactly two years later either, since Mark had to undergo another emergency operation. What started as a bad stomachache, after a heavy dinner, gave way to severe complications. The doctors discovered that the stabbing from two years earlier had pierced his diaphragm and that part of the food from that night had gone through that hole.

While Mark was being operated on, Bob and Guitelle surrendered to a tearless whirlwind, to the sterile storm that God, whether invoked or not, had arranged for them. Roger had died eighteen months earlier. Just two months ago, Jonny had died. And now this.

The operation was successful. They fixed the hole in Mark's diaphragm, and he underwent a painful recovery. He then resumed his studies in political sciences and Portuguese. During his studies, he took a summer course at Lisbon University, where he perfected what he ironically, but in strict adherence to his adventures, called "that variation of Brazilian."

Finally, in 1981, at twenty-nine, Mark Sandman graduated with honors. A multinational offered him a very well-paid internship, with the option of a permanent position, but Mark refused.

"I did it for you, Ma," Mark told Guitelle. "Now I'm going to be a rock star."

It's not easy to start the journey toward rock stardom when one is nearly thirty. That's why Mark Sandman entered the music business the only way he could: with all the life baggage, with the distant, murky ways of someone from another era.

Mark had been a die-hard smoker since he was a teenager. Talking to him entailed breaking through the smokescreen that surrounded his words to reach that inner mist that was his voice. His clothing only deepened the mystery. He wouldn't wear trainers, jeans or T-shirts. Always smart shirts and tailored trousers, perfectly cut. He looked like a 1950s detective who'd gotten home and taken his jacket off to have a drink. Gestures, manners, glances, words that would suddenly light up, like a cat's eyes caught by the head lamps of a car driving along a highway in the eternal night.

James Ellroy was one of Mark Sandman's favorite writers, with whom he shared that spiritual synchronicity with the 1950s. Ellroy and Sandman were soulmates in more ways than one. Their histories diverge precisely at key moments, and so the lines of their lives, by growing apart, serve only to complete the features of the same face.

James Ellroy was born in Beverly Hills in 1948. When he was ten, his mother separated from his father, and he and his mother moved to a ten-thousand-person town called El Monte. San Gabriel Valley, according to Ellroy himself, was "the rat's tail of Los Angeles County." And in 1958, El Monte was right in the middle of that valley.

Ellroy, unlike Sandman, had only one traumatic experience in his life: the rape and murder of his mother on June 22, 1958. The culprit was never found. The lost years of homelessness, robbery, jail and drugs were for Ellroy the wake left by that derailed train, which put an end to his childhood. His odyssey was Joycean: losing himself within just a few streets that were connected to the labyrinth of his sick mind.

After overcoming some addiction problems, which led to his doing multiple and fleeting jobs on starvation salaries, Ellroy became a caddy at a golf club. With that basic stability, he started writing what would become the first of his many commercial successes, *Brown's Requiem*, which was published in 1981. He was thirty-three.

Ellroy would publish other novels during the 1980s, but it wasn't until 1987, with the writing of *The Black Dahlia*, that he would start tackling his mother's ghost head on.

Because of her habit of always wearing black, a journalist dubbed Elizabeth Short the Black Dahlia. She was a twenty-

262 ~ Rodrigo Blanco Calderón

two-year-old girl killed in Los Angeles in 1947. Elizabeth Short's body was found cut in half at the waist. The killer, says Ellroy in his memoir, "tortured her for days. He beat her and sliced her with a sharp knife. He stubbed cigarettes out on her breasts and cut the corners of her mouth back to her ears. . . . The killer probed and rearranged her internal organs postmortem."

James Ellroy first learned about this case when he was eleven. At that age, his father (a handsome hustler who in the early 1950s worked for Rita Hayworth, with whom he apparently slept) gifted him a copy of *The Badge*, a book that compiled the most gruesome crimes in the history of Los Angeles. The link that Ellroy, as a boy, could make between this murder and that of his mother was evident, but it wasn't until twenty years after her death that Ellroy dared to give indirect, or fictional, treatment to his foundational trauma.

Starting with that novel—which was dedicated to "Geneva Hilliker Ellroy (1915–1958)"—James Ellroy geared his work toward trying to answer just one question: why do men kill women?

In 1986, a year before *The Black Dahlia* was published, at thirty-one, Mark Sandman was editing an eponymous album by his first important band: Treat Her Right. The name of the band and the record were clearly reminiscent of the name of a Roy Head song from 1965. In it, Head advises every man to "treat her right;" only then, and with a bit of luck, will she "love you tonight now."

Head is a strange singer. With his impeccable tight suit, sporting a quiff more fifties than sixties, less graceful than Elvis Presley and less stiff than Roy Orbison, Roy Head was an unusual blend of Frank Sinatra and Michael Jackson. Today, whether rightly or not, nobody remembers him. The truth is that his song, in the light of everything that was happening then, could have seemed so passé to the point of being naïve. The so-called sexual revolution, that most subtle male invention for subjugating women, was rendering seduction superfluous. The woman who wouldn't open her legs the first time "free love" came calling could be branded a reactionary, an anti-revolutionary, pro-system, and a very long and stupid et cetera.

However, it's possible that Head's song was, unintentionally, a denunciation of the society that emerged after World War II, whose objective was happiness above all else. A decade in which an increasing number of married women dared to divorce and young women consented to casual extramarital sex without guilt or shame. An emerging freedom that overtook the streets of towns and cities all over the US, that came to those bars that kept on climbing till well past midnight, to the cars that received a delivery of Mexican food and a couple of beers through the passenger window, transforming everything, for some lonely hearts, into the perfect forest for hunting.

Mark Sandman's mother wasn't divorced or alcoholic. Nor had she been raped or killed. She lived a long time, a conventional life in spite of the circumstances, and it was she who happened to survive the experience of her three sons' deaths. James Ellroy survived, and Mark Sandman didn't. Guitelle H. Sandman survived, and Geneva Hilliker didn't. The Hilliker curse versus the Sandman curse.

Ellroy was absolutely aware of what he himself calls "the Hilliker curse." A couple of months before June 22, 1958, his mother asked him whom he wanted to live with, her or his father. With his father, James replied. Geneva slapped his face and then James wished her dead. In Ellroy's case, as he has affirmed in his books, interviews and talks, he invoked the curse. His life and literature have been his ambiguous effort to invoke her, afraid she would disappear completely.

In Sandman's case, it was Guitelle who might have invoked the curse. Like artists and dreamers of antiquity, Mark Sandman was to be a medium for confirming or refuting someone else's destiny.

In the crossroads between life and death, Sandman chose dreaming. A choice determined by his own name. During an interview, he got straight to the point: "My surname is like those castles kids make on the beach. It's like I'm living off images that are created and destroyed in a single day. Like the word *morphine*, there's something of the reverie in me."

Although he doesn't mention it in that interview, Mark Sandman was also aware of what the Sandman represents in the Anglo-Saxon imaginary. It's a sort of Charon who carries people from wakefulness to the shore of sleep, and vice versa. Except that instead of receiving an obol, the Sandman places a small heap of sand in the sleepers' eyes. That's the mythical origin of eye rheum.

No more than a secretion, and unpleasant as all secretions are, rheum is, however, a bodily testimony of our return. That's why the Sandman is not only a protective figure but also a fearsome one, since there is always somebody trapped in the sand.

While his pact with life lasted, Sandman venerated women. Guitelle, Martha and the beautiful, sad Sabine, his priestesses. In listening to his music, men might understand that they must treat women right, even if they mistreat you. You must follow them to the end of the world, love them and respect them, even if they don't let you in. You must buy them a drink and run away when their husband comes back. You must drive them crazy with your indifference, if only to justify verses that are the most ardent tribute you can make from afar.

The women in Sandman's music, during the eighties and nineties, lose all corporeality and are shortcuts to the night. A woman's dark hair is like crows that crawl over her shoulders.

The trajectory from Treat Her Right to Morphine is equivalent to that of a man who decides to swap ethics for ideals, a backpack for a torch, as a beacon for his life. Claire, Sheila, Lilah, Candy, Mabel, Justine, Doreen—they are all part of the songs evoking Sandman's evanescent harem. Witches who cast a spell on their cats, dealers who attract good luck around a blackjack table, strange figureheads for an underworld where there is no crying, ghosts in a folk tale whose garments and creases are those of the night over the open fields.

When Matías Rye arrived at Miguel Ardiles's apartment in the hills of Parque Caiza, Ardiles knew nothing of the story I have just told. Nor was he able to understand the things that were about to happen. Leaning on the windowsill next to Matías Rye, he just looked out at the hills around them, a darkness that at that time prevented them from seeing the dense greenery of the area. A darkness that didn't allow Matías to orient himself and to point with any precision at that part of the scrub where now, every Saturday, in the company of the Night Creatures, he would stay overnight.

25

Creatures

On the first Saturday, Matías Rye arrived at El Monte by chance. He had left La Choza bar after drinking a bottle of whiskey and taking just two hours to snort the stash he had planned to last the whole night.

At the bar, he had warmed to a plump lady who accepted his drinks and laughed at his jokes. He could have taken her to a motel if he hadn't spotted, on his way to the bathroom, in the cordoned-off area by the bar, Algimiro Triana. At his table there was another man, also wearing a suit, and three women. At the adjacent table were the bodyguards.

On his way back from the bathroom, after a few fresh lines, he walked into the private area and sat in the only empty chair at Triana's table.

"Tell me, Algimiro, how many rivers are made with our blood?" said Matías.

The bodyguards jumped up and surrounded him.

Triana got the message although he didn't recognize the face. With a glance, he told the head of his security detail to hold back.

"Don't say you don't remember me, kid. Matías Rye! We did the fiction-writing workshop at the Celarg together in '94. Remember?"

"Of course. Matías, I remember you now," said Algimiro, but he went on scanning his face, as if he hadn't yet recognized him.

"So tell me, then, how many rivers have been filled with our blood, huh? You must be happy, Algimiro, you finally achieved your dream, you took the principle of university autonomy and fucked it up the ass."

Triana didn't waste a moment and threw his bodyguards another glance. They picked Rye up and tossed him out of the reserved area. Rye stumbled and fell to the floor, spilling his drink. The woman at the bar saw the scene and went to take refuge at a table in the back.

One of the bodyguards took out a gun and dug it into the middle of his chest.

"Get lost," he told him.

It was time to leave.

He walked a whole block as far as the third avenue of Los Palos Grandes to take one of the cabs that are usually parked outside the Parque Cristal building. The road was empty, the street lighting off. He walked up and down the sidewalk several times, gesticulating. He went back to Avenida Francisco de Miranda and started to walk. After leaving the Parque del Este behind, he realized he was walking in the opposite direction to his house. In any case, he carried on walking down the avenue as far as the corner with the Transport Museum and hailed a cab.

"To Parque Caiza," he said, leaning in through the passenger window.

The cab driver drove off without even answering.

Two more cab drivers came by, and the same happened. From his jacket pocket he took the paper with the remaining white powder and with his little finger spread it over his gums like an ointment. As soon as he felt the tingling in his mouth he started walking. He quickened his pace, laughing as he imagined Miguel's face when he showed up at his door.

He strode all the way down Avenida Francisco de Miranda. He stopped for a moment at the Petare traffic circle and checked the time. It was 12:40 a.m. He looked at the first shanty towns and then glanced over toward the mountains he couldn't see, which come and go like waves spreading out of Caracas, packed with more slums and narrow streets, making Petare one of the biggest and most dangerous boroughs in Latin America.

That'd take balls, thought Matías: walking across Petare at this time of night. Unlike taking a gun to college. Anybody can pull a mean stunt like that.

Matías Rye couldn't forgive Algimiro Triana for having won the *El Nacional* short-story award in 1998. The winning entry, called "Rivers of Blood and Tears," tells the story of a bent plainclothes policeman who wanders around the Central University with a gun in his belt, because by doing so he feels as if he is violating the principle of university autonomy. The story includes a murdered woman found at the banks of the Guaire River, detectives investigating the case while eating greasy empanadas, predictable doses of urban decadence and a bizarre resolution to the conflict.

Algimiro Triana's story was like something from that book about psychiatrists Miguel had recommended to Matías. Son of the political leader Algimiro Triana, who was arrested, tortured and murdered by the political police during Carlos Andrés Pérez's first government, Algimiro grew up in the shadow of his dead father. Having the same name was only the visible part of the symbol. He would never forget a scene from his childhood. The police raiding his house, an officer pointing a gun at his head, and his mother, with a sacrificial demeanor, refusing to reveal her husband's whereabouts. When, soon afterward, they found him dead in one of the cells of the DISIP, the intelligence services, in July 1976, the iridescences of one of his son's billions of dendrites were seized by the idea of destiny.

From then on, Algimiro Triana Jr decided to stand out. So,

like his father, he became the students' representative for the University Council at the Central University of Venezuela. He graduated with honors in medicine and became an illustrious psychiatrist with a promising career ahead.

When Matías Rye met him at the Celarg Fiction Writing Workshop, he couldn't see anything in his character to remind him of the family tragedy. Rather, he seemed like a more sensible Hamlet: someone who had told his father's ghost to go fuck himself.

Some years later, when Algimiro won the *El Nacional* newspaper's short-story award, Rye thought about how unfair life is even when it's trying to make up for things. Triana, someone from whom, in a sense, everything had been taken, was recovering it for himself. Which is why, in the early years of the revolution, when Algimiro Triana started to become a figurehead for the government, Matías rejoiced: his father's ghost had won.

Triana's first mission was the case of Arlindo Falcáo and the Plaza Altamira massacre. Those were hard years of struggle between pro-government forces and the opposition. The words *coup*, *counter-coup* and *self-coup* were like hot-air balloons beginning to wake up. During an anti-government demonstration at Plaza Altamira, a man emptied the magazine of a 9 mm pistol into the crowd. About twenty were injured. Three died. A young woman and two elderly people.

The murderer turned out to be a Portuguese national who had lived in Venezuela for many years called Arlindo Falcáo. His first public statement provided conclusive evidence: Falcáo accused an opposition news channel of having hypnotized him, before kidnapping him at night to prostitute him. Falcáo had spent several months in Portugal. He had gone to escape from the voices he heard and the people pointing at him on the street, the gossip and laughter of people saying he was a homosexual. He wasn't a homosexual. It was the fault of the TV channel, which had hypnotized, kidnapped and prostituted him. In Portugal, nobody knew about it, so they didn't point at him. After a while he returned to Venezuela, confident that the kidnappings and rumors would stop, but they didn't. It was then he decided to dye his hair red and buy a gun. He felt safer with a gun. The hair color also helped, since the journalists from the TV channel would walk by without recognizing him.

That calm continued until December 6, 2002. That night there was a crowd at Plaza Altamira. What were they doing there? He saw the transmission antenna of the TV channel and understood what was going on. They were going to show the crowd the videos they'd recorded when they hypnotized, kidnapped and prostituted him.

Arlindo Falcão wasn't going to allow that to happen. He checked the magazine, removed the safety and walked toward the crowd.

The accusations against the government for having masterminded the massacre started even before some of the injured had been taken to the hospital. A journalist said on TV that the four individuals who had opened fire on the people at a close range and from the four corners of the square had been arrested. The president, in an appearance broadcast by a state channel at nine the next evening, asked the media not to spread untrue accounts of the events, and not to take advantage of the Plaza Altamira tragedy to promote a coup d'état.

"Let's wait for the results of the investigation and see what led poor Arlindo Falcão to commit such a crime," said the president.

By the time of the broadcast, twenty-four hours after the event, the government had already obtained a preliminary diagnosis of Falcão's mental health. It was later learned that the president had requested a psychiatric evaluation at the

DISIP headquarters, where Falcão was being held in custody. The psychiatrist they recommended, who carried out the first evaluation, was a young doctor of proven competence, a government supporter and also the son of a martyr of the hated and misnamed "Fourth Republic." He was, like his father, called Algimiro Triana.

The news spread rapidly around the Caracas College of Psychiatrists, from where it hopped across to the press and television, though without becoming a major scandal. That evaluation was illegal and likely to attract suspicion. The only people authorized to diagnose Arlindo Falcão were the psychiatrists, psychologists and neurologists at Forensic Medicine in the capital. What could have made the president call Algimiro Triana?

"Ultimately that was the last thing that mattered. The action, you might say, was a failure. The president must have thought Falcão could have been just a regular member of the Círculos Bolivarianos who'd gone crazy or acted on his own accord," Miguel Ardiles told Matías Rye the first time they touched upon the subject. "The really fucked-up thing," continued Miguel, "was what Triana did. The guy answered the call from the president of the Republic to commit a crime in no other place than the DISIP headquarters. That is, in the same place his father had been tortured and killed. He returned to the crime scene, not out of revenge, but as a civil servant who needed to question a detainee."

After performing that service, Algimiro Triana started to climb up in the ranks. Congressman, president of the National Electoral Council and then vice-minister of the Interior and Justice. It was said that he was now in charge of the death squads that laid siege to the Central University. Armed bikers who would attack students' gatherings or throw Molotov cocktails at the rector's office.

"I suppose you can guess," said Ardiles to Rye, "who it was that recommended Algimiro Triana. No less than the president's primary physician, his psychiatrist: Dr. Edmond Montesinos."

Amazing he hadn't realized this before. His fixation on Dr. Montesinos went back to the night when he heard that story for the first time.

Instinct, or simply cowardice, forced him to abandon the idea of making an incursion into Petare at that time of night. He had turned left at the traffic circle and then headed toward the main avenue in La Urbina. Near the end of the avenue, he turned right and walked until he reached the highway.

Looking sideways, waiting for the noise of the cars shooting by him to disappear, he ran from island to island until he reached the other side. The slums on that side of Petare looked like an outcrop ready to collapse. Between the slums and the highway, there was a thin barrier made of wire fencing. Matías stopped to urinate under the Jurassic shadow of a tractor. They were building the columns to support a raised train track. Some were covered in concrete, while others still showed their rebar skeletons. Matías Rye decided to follow this line of monumental *Y*-shaped foundations as if he were the last American football player, crazed, on earth.

The coke gave him the impetus he needed to keep walking at a good pace, but it also made him paranoid. Every shadow would turn human and threaten to slit his throat. He hadn't remembered the entrance to Parque Caiza being so far away. I wish I had a joint to calm me down, he thought.

When he was finally able to make out the highway turn-off, the slow descending bend leading to the development where his friend lived, Matías felt a twitch of excitement. The feeling didn't last. When he arrived, he noticed that the police unit wasn't there. He had read in the press that, given the recent trend of throwing bodies around the place, the government had decided to assign a permanent checkpoint to the entrance to Parque Caiza. The measure had had an immediate effect, as no bodies had been found in the area since.

However, when Matías Rye reached the entrance, he found himself alone and in the dark. A few meters away was the first hut of the housing development, abandoned. It was an empty cage, or rather, a scarecrow. A welcome sign for the residents, and a warning to loiterers like him, who didn't know or had forgotten the detail that you can only reach the wild heights of the Parque Caiza development by car.

He walked to the hut and looked through one of the broken windows. Then he walked around the small building until he found the door, which was shut fast with a chain and a padlock. He thought about finishing breaking one of the glass panes and sleeping there, but the idea of being shut inside, not knowing what else could be there, worried him.

He felt a wave of tiredness and whimpered. He checked inside his pockets again, desperate, searching for the cigarette or joint he knew he wouldn't find. All he had were his house keys, his Moleskine notebook and pen, a wallet, a handkerchief and an iPod with the headphones wrapped around the device, the metallic base of which resembled a cigarette case.

He became even more desperate, and for a few endless minutes, he cried. When the snot was blocking up his nose, he started laughing.

I look like a little kid, he told himself. And this is how I'm supposed to write about the night, he thought.

Then, listening to the insects, the animals, the cars skirring past, the rustling sounds of that hour and his own heartbeats, the stones towed along by the dense river of early morning, he understood why people sleep. People sleep because it's the safest way of getting through the night. He also understood that sleepwalkers, insomniacs, prostitutes, taxi drivers, guards, pharmacists and doctors on duty, waiters and poets, and all people who can't sleep when they need to are strange creatures who know what everyone else does not, since they return with their ears full of murmurs, that phrasing of sand that is the language of the night.

But what's happening to me? he said to himself. What would Marcello think of me right now? He imagined Marcello Mastroianni watching him with embarrassment, from his infinite elegance. Rye took out his handkerchief, dried his tears and blew his nose, and then he straightened his suit and smoothed down his hair.

That Antonioni movie, *La Notte*, had made a mark on him. Every time he watched it he would forget he knew the story and suffer all over again about what might happen to Jeanne Moreau's and Marcello Mastroianni's characters. When the story ended, coinciding with the storm passing and the first lights of dawn, he would remember that ultimately, everything that happened at the party had been an effect of the night. That beyond all their problems, the couple had managed to escape the night's traps and stay together. Mastroianni's character is saved because he recovers love and, as a result, the possibility of writing.

Calmer now, he walked around the hut again. On its left, there were the woods that led to the mountain. He looked at his watch: 3:40 a.m. He would be able to hold out, curled up against one of the walls of the hut, until dawn.

He glanced at the woods one more time. It was mad, he thought after a while, but if he didn't do it, nothing that night would have made any sense.

He rearranged his jacket, running his hands over his lapels, and started walking. A snake's hissing accompanied his steps.

He stopped and the hissing stopped. Maybe he would be bitten by a snake. The best thing was to keep going without listening to anything around him. He took out his iPod, searched for Morphine's discography, pressed play and let Sandman's music calm him down.

By the time it was starting to get light, he had listened to the albums *Good* and *Cure for Pain* in full. The opening chords of "Lilah" came on, and he could have listened to that record right through to the end too, but he didn't want to push his luck. The night, he now understood, was a mirage, but one needed to know how to pass through it. He also wanted to go back home soon. He had stumbled across something uncommunicable and for the first time, he felt authorized to write.

Who knows whether Rye did, in fact, have the ability to write his great novel. Let us imagine that for writers like him, the Spirit of Literature confers just one opportunity, just one true revelation, for them to sit down and unravel. Let us imagine Matías Rye received that opportunity, and wasted it.

As he retraced the path he had walked down a couple of hours earlier, he stopped to look at the landscape. There, in a clearing not far up the side of the mountain, he noticed something shudder through the foliage.

A dog, he thought. Or an opossum, he thought, a bit disgusted. Or a man, he told himself and thought it weird he didn't feel fear.

Without thinking, like a sleepwalker, he walked toward the place, determined, making no effort to conceal the noise of his steps on the humidity of the hill. A self-contained quietness, like a magnetic field, made him sense that he was being awaited on the other side of that curtain of grasses. Pushed forward by that strange feeling of warmth amid the cold, he stepped through the curtain and into the clearing he had spotted on the path that would take him back to the highway. In that tamed circular space, he met the Night Creatures.

Matías Rye's explanations of how it had all happened, who they were, how they'd got there and what they did during their meetings were in vain. Miguel Ardiles had already considered all the possibilities: Eleusinian Mysteries, bucolic orgies, the teenage urge to tell horror stories in the dark.

"None of that," said Matías defensively. "You should come yourself one day, then you'll understand."

So far, Matías hadn't witnessed any sex scenes. Antonio and Olga, the goth couple, tended to disappear occasionally, but their absence didn't alter the pulse of the group.

"You'd be surprised to see that there's nothing very different from what people do during the day. Or what happens when friends get together."

"Where's the fun in that, then?" asked Miguel.

"It's not so much about what we do, but the place we've chosen. The woods on El Monte, at night, let you see the quotidian from a different perspective. It's like the negative of a picture."

"And with a little help, right?"

"Actually, no," said Rye, who knew what his friend was getting at. "I'm not going to lie to you. The second time I went, I did take supplies. But I felt so good that I didn't need them."

"I just hope that all this madness will be useful inspiration."

"For the novel, you mean?" said Rye. "What does the novel matter now?"

He seemed calm.

26

Couples Counseling

Gonzalo disappeared in early September. All Margarita got was a phone call to tell her he was going on an important business trip.

"When will you be back?" Margarita had asked.

"Everything's going to be all right. Trust me," was Gonzalo's answer.

Margarita had thought it was something to do with the Strinkis, until she bumped into one of them in the corridors of Engineering at the Central University.

Then, as she mulled things over, she wondered whether there might be another woman involved.

Later she remembered the man who'd swindled them. For a few days she kept a close eye on the papers for some news story that might confirm her suspicions.

When it seemed as though the new situation had become permanent, her mother dared to ask:

"What about Gonzalo?"

Margarita searched around for an answer, then said:

"I don't know."

In October, Margarita began sitting in on some lectures at the Literature Department of the Central University. In December, she enrolled in a creative-writing workshop at a school in Altamira. Between the literature, the psychology and the kickboxing, she would arrive home exhausted. She'd have a brief chat with her mother over dinner and then go straight to bed. Every night she was woken by the purring of the air conditioner that her mother, feeling nostalgic for the plains, had installed in the bedrooms. It was a moment of anxiety followed by one of relief. She felt as if the AC, with its constant roar, was reproaching her for her laziness, while at the same time lulling her, sending her back to sleep.

Her mother had also taken charge of her sadness. She decided to sell the house in Tabay to a neighbor, a cousin of hers. That way she was spared the trouble of managing her plot of land, and at the same time, she'd still have a roof over her head if she ever wanted to go back.

Margarita was excited about the workshop. She'd always liked reading, but she loved the difference it made to read as a writer: finding in books a set of instructions that were invisible to everyone else. Part of that excitement, she admitted from day one, was due to Señor Álamo. That's what she called him in private, even though she would address him as Pedro in class.

After the third or fourth class, she masturbated thinking about Señor Álamo. She enjoyed finishing herself off with that false stimulus. Señor Álamo attracted her in a way that related to the big picture of life, not its crevices or its intimate folds. He came across as a man trying to look older than he really was, quite neurotic, insecure, but with a dark energy she found attractive. It wouldn't matter whether he turned out to have a twelve-inch penis or just a refined sense of humor. Since starting the workshop, she'd begun to see those around her as characters, and herself as the lead protagonist of a story that was already underway.

In January, Gonzalo reappeared at the gym. Margarita was running through boxing combinations with her new coach when Gonzalo entered the ring, dressed to fight. As if on a dance floor, he asked the coach if he could cut in. The coach looked at Margarita. She nodded, like the main character she was, and only then did he step out of the ring. He ducked into her corner, beside the other coaches and the few students present during that dead time of day. They were curious to see how this would all end up.

Gonzalo greeted her with a hook to the ear. Margarita hardly got a chance to react, and the blow landed on her left cheekbone. The coach, seeing her on the canvas, tried to enter the ring. She stopped him with a gesture. Then she got to her feet, bumped her fists and went for Gonzalo.

It was the best she'd ever fought. Gonzalo wasn't able to knock her down again, and she managed to connect with a jab that returned the purple mark he'd left her with during their first exchange.

From that evening on, Gonzalo began to come looking for her. Margarita held out for a week, but the physical reconciliation finally took place one Sunday in a hotel. She tried at first to play the role of an independent woman, but Gonzalo showed up everywhere, following her with a persistence and a zeal she didn't find altogether unappealing. Whatever the reason for his trip, business seemed to have gone well. Gonzalo had a new car, he flashed money around and seemed happy. Gone was the edginess that used to make her feel so uneasy.

Gonzalo didn't offer much of an explanation. He just said he'd been staying with a distant cousin in Colombia, and that everything was fine. She told him about all the classes she was taking, about the sale of the house in Mérida, about her mom moving in for good.

He stared at her for a few seconds, as if mentally classifying the information.

"What?" said Margarita.

"Nothing. You're doing lots of stuff. I'm glad."

Margarita took the opportunity to tell him about her plan to move to Spain.

This time Gonzalo did seem surprised.

"When?"

"I don't know yet. It's still only a plan. I'm interested in a couple of postgraduate degrees at the Autònoma in Barcelona. Still, I want to have it all figured out by the time I graduate."

"Awesome. It all sounds great."

Gonzalo seemed like a different person. He accepted it as only natural that she'd gotten her life together while he'd been away.

The downside of being back with Gonzalo was that the Strinkis were back too.

This time around, they didn't bother her as much. There was something different about Gonzalo's relationship with them. Now they'd show up only when Gonzalo called them. They seemed more grown-up. At least they weren't laughing all the time, and their attitude had become, Margarita thought without really knowing why, somehow "professional."

The change meant that being around them was more tolerable, but that served only to deepen the mystery: why would Gonzalo need guys like these?

Something like love was rekindled. Time seemed to expand as if they could fit more hours into a day, and within three weeks Gonzalo had been included in the planned move to Spain. Her mother noticed the change but didn't say a word: she preferred to speak to her daughter in dreams.

It was a short dream. Just a few flickering images. It was her mother, looking at her with infinite sadness while stroking a cockroach she held in her hand like a baby bird. Margarita tried to speak, to tell her that she understood her sadness, but also that it was temporary. Soon she would speak to Gonzalo and ask him to leave her alone, so things could go back to normal. Because there are no silences in dreams, her mother just shook her head "no" for a long time, continuing to stroke the cockroach's neck.

She let herself go again. This time the process was slow and deliberate. She skipped workshop sessions, stopped attending literature classes, forgot about training and only rarely attended her psychology lectures. She'd go out only to meet up with Gonzalo. She'd come back after two days, looking faded, as if freed from imprisonment. After the third week adrift, her mother came into her room, sat on the bed and gave her a hug. Even though it was only Margarita who'd had the dream, she felt as if her mother had changed her verdict and was giving her a second chance.

They cried in silence and then wiped away their tears. Her mother gave her a piece of paper torn from the yellow pages, a name, an address and a telephone number circled in blue ink: Miguel Ardiles. Psychiatrist. Hospital de Clínicas Caracas. (0212) 577-44-35.

"Did someone recommend him to you?"

Her mother shook her head with a tired laugh.

Margarita started crying again.

"I will get help, mamá. I promise."

Margarita understood that the piece of paper was merely symbolic, but she didn't want to overthink things and so she called the number. No one used the yellow pages anymore and she suspected that the number would no longer exist or that the doctor would have changed his address.

Her connection with the doctor developed almost immediately. Ardiles needed only to look at her and ask a few essential questions to diagnose clinical depression. He would prescribe some pills, but first he wanted to listen to what she had to say.

Margarita seemed relieved by the diagnosis, by the biochemical explanation for her illness and the effect that antidepressants might have on her. She felt hopeful at seeing that some part of her hell could be explained, perhaps disassembled, like a clock.

Although the cockroach anecdote could suggest a psychotic personality, Ardiles kept that opinion to himself. Margarita needed to delve into her own story, so during the first two sessions he listened to her just like a therapist in a TV series.

Hers was a fascinating story. It would switch from moving to terrifying by unpredictable bursts. Sometimes Ardiles would lose himself in the plot and believe he could detect some of Matías Rye's teachings in Margarita's storytelling. At others, he would stop listening midsentence, thinking instead about Pedro Álamo and his useless skill in foreseeing unavoidable tragedies.

Despite the bleakness of her symptoms, Margarita would be able to save herself if she managed to let go of this Gonzalo. But "this Gonzalo" knew it too, and came along to the third session.

"I told Gonzalo I felt better after talking to you, so he wanted to come today."

Margarita spoke in a whisper. She was flushed with embarrassment.

"I'm not sure I understand. Do you want to do couples counseling?"

"No," Gonzalo cut in, "but I've always felt there are some things about myself I have to change. And since me and Margarita are moving to Spain before the end of the year, best to get that fixed soon."

"This year? Margarita, I thought you wanted to move after you'd finished your degree."

"Yes, but now Gonzalo's insisting we go this year."

"And what do you think, Margarita?" asked Ardiles.

"I got this great business opportunity there, but it has to be this year," said Gonzalo. "I told Margarita she can carry on studying in Barcelona and ask them to recognize the subjects she's already done."

Then, as if to make clear to Ardiles that that was none of his business, Gonzalo used the rest of the session to tell his story. He spoke about his difficult relationship with his father and his own anger issues, and even confessed to wetting the bed until he was eleven. It was all delivered in the same repentant, seductive voice.

A psychopath, thought Ardiles. The air conditioner made the hair on the back of his neck and arms stand on end.

"Time's up," said Ardiles at last. "Nice to meet you, Gonzalo."

They all stood up and Ardiles offered his hand to both of them. Then he turned to Margarita:

"I'll see you next week."

Margarita nodded. Meanwhile, from one moment to the next, Gonzalo's expression hardened.

When he closed the door to his office, Miguel Ardiles was trembling.

He had a bad feeling after that session. He was afraid Gonzalo would come back to the consulting room. The prospect of his interview with the Monster of Los Palos Grandes helped him to calm down.

Ramón Camejo Carmona had been set free a month after what happened to Lila Hernández came to light. Apparently, the links between his father, the poet Humberto Camejo Salas, and the revolution had gotten him out. However, the pressure maintained by the media and several women's rights organizations succeeded in getting him put back into detention.

The case seemed trapped between the bureaucratic tangle and the handling of the press, which was trying to transform it into a political scandal. Tired of waiting for the trial, Lila Hernández turned up at the gates of the Supreme Tribunal of Justice and declared herself on hunger strike. Only then was the order given to set the procedure in motion. The police report was processed and the medical, neurological, psychological and psychiatric exams were requested for both perpetrator and victim.

Johnny Campos had come to his office in person to warn him to be ready.

"They could bring him to you anytime this week or next."

To be interviewing Lila Hernández was a given. The Monster, however, was the star.

During that week he forgot about Margarita and Gonzalo. He focused on going over the case.

Nobody was disputing the fact that the young painter Camejo Carmona had taken Lila Hernández to his apartment and that for four months he'd kept her kidnapped and tortured her. He had tied her to a chair, burnt her chest with cigarette butts, hit her until her upper lip was atrophied, raped her, cut off one ear, among even worse abuses, according to the reports in the tabloids.

Camejo Carmona's defense seemed to accept all of this, and then would add a "but" that sought to divert attention toward the nature of the relationship between Ramón and Lila.

From the start, Lila Hernández stated that she had come to her torturer's house only as a model, because Camejo Carmona wanted to paint a picture. That's what he told her to get her into his home. The defense, supporting their client's claims, argued that Lila Hernández was a prostitute.

The press joined the argument, to try to elucidate whether Lila Hernández was, in fact, a prostitute. Her backstory did allow for that suspicion: she came from some forsaken town in the Andes, from a very humble family, and wasn't enrolled in studies or working a steady job in Caracas. And as for her potential as a model, one must admit that, from the pictures taken before the abuses she underwent, she wasn't particularly pretty. The defense made a point of specifying this because if Lila was lying about that, how could they be sure she wasn't lying about everything else?

Lilah (as Miguel Ardiles would refer to her, using the English pronunciation) would point to the murals decorating Ramón Camejo's apartment in Los Palos Grandes as evidence. A photographer from *Últimas Noticias* had managed to get a couple of blurry images before the police sealed the place up. At that point, the argument would move into aesthetic digressions, since Camejo Carmona's murals showed talent and allowed for multiple readings.

It was true that all the characters were women, that many of them were shown dead, murdered, stabbed or in ominous spaces, and that one in particular resembled Lila Hernández. The problem was, as is always the case in relationships between art and life, how to determine that *Lilah* had, through her suffering, inspired one of the tortured characters in the murals by the painter Ramón Camejo Carmona, better known as the Monster of Los Palos Grandes.

The fourth and last session was even stranger than the third. Not only did Margarita come with Gonzalo, but the Strinkis showed up too. Ardiles had to ask them to sit on the sofa, while she and Gonzalo took the two chairs opposite his desk. In the background, they looked like Margarita and Gonzalo's problem children. Or, even worse, the meager audience of a talk show about to be canceled.

Margarita didn't take her eyes off the floor. The two times

Miguel told her he couldn't hear her, she lifted her face and focused on the diplomas hanging behind him. Within a few minutes, Miguel had understood the reason for that visit: they wanted to let him know that the four of them had decided to move to Spain before the end of the year.

Ardiles couldn't understand. Whatever they'd decided, what had that got to do with him?

However, out of basic caution, he decided not to dismiss them just yet. He played the role of the counselor to that circus, their group therapist.

"What are you going to live off? Haven't you heard about the crisis in Spain?"

"I'm so glad you bring that up, doctor. We were just talking about that. My friends have some savings, and so do I."

Gonzalo fell silent for a moment as if waiting for some kind of approval to proceed.

They are fucking with me, thought Ardiles. They are teasing me. Then he nodded.

"With what we're taking with us, we're all good," said Gonzalo. "And that's apart from the business we have planned, which won't fail. However, to be on the safe side completely, we need to take as much cash with us as we can."

They are going to rob me, thought Miguel.

"We know that Margarita could help us out too. She is adamant she doesn't want to travel until she finishes her studies. You already know what I think about that. But I must insist, whatever it takes, because it's what's best for the group. Isn't that right, boys?"

"Sure," said one of the Strinkis, seeming to wake up.

"Of course," said the other Strinki, also seeming to wake up.

Gonzalo stopped talking again, and this time the silence dropped over them like a blanket. Ardiles was no longer afraid. He was just furious. Even with Margarita, who at that point in the conversation was looking for an escape route to China among the patterns on his office floor.

"I think there's been a misunderstanding, guys," said Miguel Ardiles. "I'm a psychiatrist, not a financial adviser."

Then he stood up.

Gonzalo turned toward the Strinkis. They stood up at the same time.

"You're right. I'm very sorry we've wasted your time," said Gonzalo. He made as if to take out his wallet.

"Don't worry about it. I hope everything goes well. Good luck with the trip," said Ardiles, not even looking at Margarita.

On the way out, Gonzalo made an effort to hide his big grin. He hadn't managed to convince Margarita of anything, but it was clear she wouldn't be coming to see Ardiles again.

Miguel Ardiles barely gave Margarita Lambert another thought. He didn't want to hear from her again.

The next day he received a call from Johnny Campos to confirm that the evaluations in the case of the Monster of Los Palos Grandes would be starting the following Monday. Miguel Ardiles waited until the weekend to make his own inquiries.

On Saturday, just before midnight, Ardiles came into Mr. Morrison's. He sat at the bar, ordered a whiskey and waited for Gioconda to show up.

"Twice in a month, doctor? Am I that ill? Tell me the truth."

"You're polymorphously perverse. You're totally fucked."

Gioconda liked diagnoses that sounded like venereal diseases.

"In that case, could you get me a drink?"

"You can order one, but I'm not staying. I just came to talk to you."

"How boring."

The barman set a drink down beside his whiskey. Gioconda took a sip.

"I wanted to ask you about Lila Hernández."

Gioconda straightened her glasses. She pushed her drink back a few inches and put a hand on her hip.

"You too? That's all anybody wants to talk about. Are you playing cop now, doctor?"

"Not exactly."

Ardiles flashed his ID. Gioconda saw the badge of the Police Forensics Department.

"What do you want?"

"No need to be rude. Maybe if I have another drink I won't have to go right away."

"I don't like cops."

"I'm not a cop."

"That's what the badge says."

"No, it doesn't. Read it again."

"I don't like reading. What do you want to know?"

"Nothing serious. Only if Lila Hernández was a prostitute."

"I'm a prostitute. She's just a whore."

"What's the difference?"

"The street, *mijo*. And the *reales*, cause not everyone can afford a body like mine."

"Did she ever work here?"

"In her dreams."

"What's gotten into you?"

"Stupid questions piss me off. If Lila Hernández was a student, a lawyer or a doctor, that animal would be long dead by now."

Gioconda turned around and disappeared through the curtains that separated the stage from the dressing rooms.

Miguel Ardiles left the place feeling like an asshole.

When the concierge at the building saw his ID, she too believed Miguel Ardiles was a policeman. This time he didn't feel like clearing up the misunderstanding, even though he had actually spoken to the superintendent in charge of the case and been given permission.

"Over there," said the concierge, pointing to the apartment, without stepping out of the lift.

"Keys?" said Ardiles.

"Right. Here you are."

The woman crossed herself and the lift doors closed.

Once he was standing at the door, Ardiles hesitated. What was he looking for exactly? How would it help him in his investigation?

As he tried the key, he had an absurd idea: Gonzalo was waiting for him on the other side.

Finally, he opened the Mul-T-Lock grille. He looked through the peephole for a few seconds and then opened the door.

It was dark inside. He waited for the light from the corridor to sketch out some coordinates before closing the door behind him.

Once inside he began to tremble. Those seconds of light had been pointless. Darkness engulfed everything again. He felt like Jodie Foster in the final scene of *Silence of the Lambs*. At that thought, he let out a short dry laugh that reverberated around the hollow space and silenced him again.

You're such a fucking dickhead, Matías, he thought.

He walked for what felt like ages along a tightrope he would later identify as the living room. After this room, there was another smaller one. To the left was the balcony hidden behind some heavy curtains, which, once drawn back, revealed the space he'd just walked through.

He was surprised by this reminder that it was eleven in the morning on a bright Sunday. How had Camejo Carmona achieved such perfect darkness? Seeing some wooden planks bolted to the walls, he realized the windows had been boarded up.

In the second room there was only one piece of furniture, a

small bookcase that he proceeded to examine. On the top shelf, there were three half-full bottles: mescal, pisco and whiskey. On the middle one, paint pots, paintbrushes in different sizes and rags made out of old T-shirts. On the third and last shelf, there were books. *The History of Painting in Italy* by Stendhal, *The Heritage of Apelles* by Gombrich, *Holy Week* by Aragon and *Études pour Le Radeau de la Méduse*, edited by someone whose name he never got to read because at that very moment he felt someone watching him.

There, on the large wall of the main room, was Lilah.

In a matter of seconds he had reached the wall, but he could no longer see her. He pressed the light switch but nothing happened. From up close, and with the help of the flashlight on his cell phone, he could make out Lilah's body dissolving into a chaos of sea, muscle and wood.

He stepped back to get a better look and stumbled over something. A chair. The chair in which Lila Hernández had sat, tied up for four months. There it was, right in the middle of the room, to one side of the tightrope, brushing against him like a bat's wing.

He sat down and wiped the sweat from his forehead. He rubbed his eyes before looking again. When he opened them, there was Lilah. He saw her, this time, in all her glory and in all her horror.

Before leaving, he went over to the bookcase again to make a note of the missing book. It was then that he noticed a sort of tail poking out from behind the bookcase. Carefully, trying not to knock over the bottles, he pulled the shelves a few inches away from the wall. Having confirmed that the painting continued behind the bookcase, he moved it away completely.

It wasn't a tail. It was a rope tied to a woman. Judging by the scene depicted, it could have been any of the women he'd seen at Forensic Medicine. He inspected the rest of the apartment and found more women. Different situations with ailments so specific they could be the result only of an extended captivity or an extended love story.

The main rooms, the study, the kitchen, the utility room, the ceilings and even the skirting board on the balcony were all altered in this way. He needed to urinate, and went into one of the bathrooms.

It was there, as he was about to finish, that he discovered, in the angle between wall and ceiling, the image he'd sensed had been watching him.

In the middle of a greenish weave, a forest, a tall bonfire was swallowing a pair of twins, or one repeated woman, or two very similar women. Their faces were deformed not by the fire itself, but by the pain inflicted by the fire.

Despite the contorted gestures, he was able to recognize, without a shadow of a doubt, the face, the faces, of Margarita Lambert.

It was insomnia time.

27

"Enter Sandman"

Although Matías Rye had abandoned writing for good, he remained faithful to the oral tradition. Sometimes the Creatures would ask him to tell a story. Rye would do cover versions of H. P. Lovecraft and E. T. A. Hoffmann, writers who, like him, were better to listen to than to read.

He would often do it half-heartedly, criticizing himself for using hackneyed tricks and at the same time fascinated by how easily those faces were transformed by fear.

The only story for which he would make an effort, taking care over its effects as if he were perfecting the writing with his voice, was Hoffmann's *Der Sandmann*. This was the story they most frequently requested, and he would always please them, each time introducing new characters, new atmospheres and new descriptions, sieving the same story through different versions until he had revealed the backdrop that is common to all nightmares.

In one of his better versions, if not the best, Nathanael was called Edmond and wasn't born in Königsberg, or some other Prussian city, but in Churuguara, a town in the state of Falcón, western Venezuela, in 1935.

His paternal grandfather, the count of Montesinos, came from Valencia. Nobody understood how a European noble had ended up in that miserable town in a turbulent South American republic, with no other riches but his title and a library of ten books. For the noble count, despite his status, would work the land like any rural peasant.

Among the books he brought with him on that day in 1896 when he arrived in those Falconian lands was *The Count of Monte Cristo*, as he was already a devoted reader of Alexandre Dumas. For that reason, when he came to America, he re-christened himself with the name of Edmond. He didn't need to add the Dantès, since, as luck would have it, his original surname, Montesinos, would serve to make the farce less painful.

His only son and the last of his grandchildren also inherited his name. Dominated by the kingdom of the identical, tired of that life and of forebears who had done nothing but work the land and milk sheep, Edmond Montesinos's son moved away with his wife and children to the city of Barquisimeto. It's not clear what job the deserter son did there, but there is a piece of information about his having moved again with the family to the shores of La Guaira, whose breeze had been recommended by the doctor as a cure for his wife's asthma. Once those health problems had been overcome, the family moved to Caracas.

That is all we need to know about the family of the main character of tonight's *nocturne*.

In 1952, Edmond Montesinos III was seventeen. He was the most intelligent pupil at the Luis Razetti High School, and couldn't wait to make the first of his dreams come true: to study at the Central University of Venezuela. He was still havering between biology and philosophy; such was the breadth of his interests. However, the dream would take some time yet to materialize. The country was under a dictatorship, which had toughened up with particular ferocity that year. Every day there were more people disappeared or murdered, and more political prisoners. The university had been taken over and then shut down.

Even if nobody knew him and he wasn't on any list of suspects, he still took part in the exodus of troublesome students to other Latin American universities. He ended up in Guayaquil, where he started studying medicine. There he fell in love with Flor Lowenstein, daughter of his anatomy lecturer. This man allowed Edmond's visits, recognizing that he was a good student. He was also moved and amazed by his story: his precocious revolutionary awareness, his having been jailed for standing up to the Venezuelan dictator himself during a rally, the torture he endured even though he was still just a boy, the exile.

Flor was a demure young woman. She allowed him only the odd kiss, without opening her mouth, in her living room. Edmond had to settle for seeking release in the slums to which his fellow residents at the boardinghouse had introduced him. He swore in front of his bedroom mirror that before his final exams he would savor that elusive nectar.

Suddenly, his plans changed completely. News had come that the University of Los Andes in Venezuela had reopened its doors. The contingent of exiles met up and decided to return to the struggle.

He didn't say anything to Flor until the last day. When there were only three hours left before he was to embark, he asked her to come to his room in the boardinghouse. She refused, arguing it was not appropriate for a lady to visit her suitor in his home, let alone in that pigsty where the Venezuelan expatriates lived. He confessed he was boarding the midday ship for a long journey back to his country.

"I'm packing my suitcase. It's difficult for me to go out."

"Very well," Flor agreed.

Edmond put down the phone at the reception. He gave the manager a few coins and went back to his room.

The room was clean and tidy. The suitcase, all ready, was

resting on the made bed. Edmond put it on the floor, next to the door, and lay on the bed to wait.

The ships belonged to the Grancolombiana Company. They would leave from Maracaibo, then go to New York, returning from there and passing through the Panama Canal to get to Buenaventura, in Colombia, before finally docking in the Guayas River, in Ecuador. Its return journey was direct from the Guayas River, with another crossing of the Panama Canal, to Maracaibo.

During the journey, he reflected on what had happened. It was all so unexpected. He had never contemplated the possibility of Flor refusing. His own reaction wasn't predictable either, although he would later manage to store that memory in his mind as one of many without distinctiveness or rank. He was surprised, it's true, about the things he'd said. Where had that pure Castilian accent come from? What was he doing reciting Garcilaso de la Vega in the middle of the struggle?

Just before arriving in Maracaibo, the answer came to him. His teacher Marta. How had he missed that? Her accent, her classes on the Spanish Golden Age, her legs and his first feelings of ardor. After joining all the dots, he realized that the answer, the image of Marta, the teacher, had been there all along. On the ship and in the harbors, but also in the boardinghouse room itself, between his moans, between the storm-tossed sheets and Flor's expression of mute terror.

Between biology and philosophy, his feet barely touched the ground. What is in there? The mind, he told himself. Or to be more precise, the brain, he corrected himself. How was he to get there? How was he to understand the relationship? He was ashamed he hadn't thought about these questions before. What had he been until now? An automaton, like any other. An automaton like all people who obey their brain without asking themselves about the laws that govern that mechanism.*

On the night of the day he arrived at Maracaibo, he took a bus to Caracas. He hardly slept during the journey, amazed as he was about his discovery: if one is an automaton of oneself, one could also be somebody else's.

He got off the next morning at Plaza Capuchinos, with a clear future ahead.

He would become a psychiatrist. He would put himself forward for the position of Students' Representative to the University Council. He would be the President of the Medical Association. He would set up the Most Successful Clinic for the treatment of mental illnesses in Latin America. He would be Rector of the Central University of Venezuela. He would be a Famous Writer. He would, naturally, have All The Women He Wanted. And then, why not, to crown all his achievements, he would become President of Venezuela.

Those plans in capital letters could have been seen as madness, or as delusions of grandeur, and in part they were. But it's important to consider the fact that, as we will see, our character was to achieve almost everything he set out to do.

There is one detail we have not yet mentioned, due to a descriptive oversight, but which is crucial for understanding this story: Edmond Montesinos was a very ugly man. Really, ludicrously ugly. He was short, barely five foot two, skinny, and bald, with a big head, crude features and changeable ges-

---

* It is probable that this episode of his youth holds the origin of the biologist's perspective at the core of all Dr. Montesinos's psychiatric work. From his defense of a thesis on the retroviral origin of schizophrenia, through his enthusiasm about Andrei Snezhnevsky's classifications, to what one might consider his personal "metaphysics." All the angles of his thought are contained in the book *Brain, Personality and Destiny*, where he states that "conscience is a multicellular trick. Its existence is what defines the human condition, which consequently is tragic and bothersome."

tures. To cap it off, ever since his youth, he had worn a curly red wig.

His own physique had been the first obstacle he'd had to overcome in life. It was God's will, with His always terrible sense of humor, that he be gifted with the vanity of a Hercules or an Achilles. And when this happens, when the body of a vain man doesn't tally with what historians call "objective circumstances," monsters like these do sometimes appear in the epic, in sports or in politics. Freaks like Bolívar, Messi or Napoleon, reminiscent of William Blake's painting *The Ghost of a Flea*.

These projects in the mind of a future psychiatrist betrayed an absolute contradiction. Was Edmond Montesinos perhaps forgetting the main goal of psychiatry? Hadn't he heard of Georget and his treatise *De la folie*, in which the Frenchman claimed that psychiatry must respond to just one main problem: how to dissuade someone who claims he is a king?

Perhaps to mitigate such a contradiction, there was his enthusiasm for politics, whose main problem is the opposite: how to persuade those who don't believe that I am king? These dialectics of the grotesque provided our character with an ideology.*

Between 1953 and 1958 in Caracas he focused on his medicine studies, the work with his first patients and making a name for himself at the university. In his spare time, he took refuge in the classes of Professor Guillermo Pérez Enciso, whose passion for psychology led him to propose the creation of the School of Psychology at the Central University. Montesinos was the first to enroll.

Oblivious to the country's turbulences, he started working as a volunteer at the Lídice, the notorious madhouse in the

---

* "I am calling grotesque," said Michel Foucault, "the fact that by virtue of their status, [someone] can have effects of power that their intrinsic qualities should disqualify them from having." By extension, he is calling psychiatric power *Ubuesque*.

old part of Caracas. This experience would prove to be crucial, since he would have a head-on encounter with the 1,200 different forms of madness found among the interned patients.

Added to his passion for madness was an even stronger one: his passion for death. At the Vargas Hospital, with the consent of Dr. Blas Bruni Celli, head of pathological anatomy, he would start carrying out his first autopsies. More than merely a precise diagnosis, which no one had asked him for, the young Edmond Montesinos was seeking to contemplate death. To understand it in its circumstances, its humors and its final dispositions.

In the case of patients who were unknown, who were almost always indigent, he took advantage and trepanned the lid of the cranium, spending hours examining the ramifications of the human brain. He followed the crevices with his eyes like a man searching for the way out of a labyrinth.

When the dead did have a family, or even better, when he was lucky enough to have treated them during the last days of their illnesses himself, he liked to scrutinize the color that death, like a fading and unnoticed sun, left on all the faces.

Years went by. The dictatorship had imposed an enforced silence that was an encouragement to study. An atmosphere of rigor mortis that provided the optimal temperature for his reading. The classes and, especially, the company of Dr. Rojas Contreras, head of surgical technique and one of Pérez Jiménez's ministers, became more and more attractive.

The relationship was tense to start with, since Rojas Contreras almost forced him, in this same brief period, to become an anesthesiologist. Rojas Contreras had heard of his student's exile before starting at the Central University, a mysterious exile, since he didn't appear in any National Security records. Nor was he a member of any political party. But the young man's intelligence and skills gradually overcame his mistrust, and the doctor went from being a boss who spied on him, to assuming the distant attentions of a father who was strict, albeit proud of his son.

The monologues he would share with Montesinos revolved around the same subject: anesthesiology. He would talk about the need to form the first generation of true anesthesiologists in the country, since such a delicate, important job couldn't be left in the hands of mere nurses.

"People don't realize it, but anesthesiology has a pivotal role in meeting the New National Ideal."

Every reflection from Rojas Contreras on his job would always end in a vindication of the dictatorship.

"Because what's the job of an anesthesiologist? Send the patient to sleep so that the surgeon can also do their own job. Imagine the pain that would result from the operation if the patient was awake. A horrible thing. Of course, it wouldn't last, as the patient would faint. It's an amazing lesson from the body. There are times when, whether we like it or not, the best thing is just to go to sleep, not to think too much and to let those who know what they're doing, do their job."

Edmond Montesinos thought about *The Anatomy Lesson*. He imagined an impossible version of the painting in which the patient (Rembrandt himself?) watched them probing one of his arms, while, simultaneously, he painted the scene on the canvas with the other.

"National security does the same thing: maintain order so the general can intervene. The general is the country's main surgeon, to whom we owe the extraction of the cancer of *adecos* and communists. And I'm proud to know we've done our bit for the health of the nation."

The comparison was naïve, but Montesinos couldn't hide his emotion.

Toward the end of 1957, on November 21, a cardiology congress was held at the Central University. Rojas Contreras managed to include one of his own papers and another by his pupil that touched tangentially on some subjects related to cardiology.

The Aula Magna was packed with doctors, lecturers and students. It would be Montesinos's first great opportunity to impress this kind of audience. As he was climbing up the wooden steps, nervously pawing at his lecture notes, some students broke into the room, causing mayhem. They shouted slogans against the government and the plebiscite, demanding freedom.

It was like a shot fired in the middle of the concord of those years. The rebels walked out, leaving behind a trail of pamphlets and the tumultuous echo of their slogans.

Despite the interruption, Montesinos intended to go ahead with his lecture. Then he realized that over half the audience had left in the wake of the revolt, with Dr. García, the congress organizer, among them.

Edmond Montesinos climbed down off the platform. He was shaking with anger and humiliation. He wanted to find release by unloading a stream of insults against all those students, together with Rojas Contreras, when he noticed that the other man had gone pale.

"This is not good," said Rojas Contreras. He left without saying goodbye.

One year later, the Junta de Gobierno decreed that from then on, each November 21 would be celebrated as Students' Day. What had happened at the Aula Magna of the Central University, preventing Edmond Montesinos's first public appearance, had simultaneous repercussions right across all the country's main universities.

Impelled by this convulsion and others, such as the January 1 uprising and the general strike, the dictatorship fell, at last, on January 23, 1958.

Many years later, giving an interview about his election as chancellor of the Central University, Montesinos recalled 1958, the year when the country transformed itself at "synaptic speed."

Montesinos knew how to adapt to the new rhythms. He was one of the most ardent agitators in the Schools of Medicine and Humanities, demanding that lecturers complicit with the dictatorial regime stand down. He pointed a finger at Rojas Contreras during a students' assembly, accusing him of harassing and indoctrinating students who hadn't wanted to bow down before the plans of the New National Ideal.

He ended his harangue drenched in sweat, drowned in enthusiastic cries and applause, baptized. Rojas Contreras was even paler than he'd been at the cardiology congress.

Two distinctions crowned his actions during those months. He was elected student delegate to the University Council and, as such, was chosen to speak on the students' behalf in the ceremony to award the *honoris causa* doctorate to the great novelist, Rómulo Gallegos.

Neither the speech by Chancellor De Venanzi nor the one by Mariano Picón Salas managed to make the Master shed a tear the way he did at the words of the young student rep. For Montesinos, however, the emotion he had provoked in Don Rómulo was consigned to the background by the spectacle offered by the first row at the Aula Magna: Jóvito Villalba, Gustavo Machado, Rafael Caldera and Rómulo Betancourt, the four aces in the pack of those days, clapping at his feet.

Come 1959, Edmond Montesinos had graduated from apprentice Jacobin to self-professed revolutionary. After the arrival of the bearded ones in Havana, he began to travel regularly to Cuba. There, using his gift of the gab as a master key, he started opening up doors for himself until he had become a fixture in those long evenings where Fidel Castro and Che were the stars. He also met a Chilean psychiatrist, the author of an interesting study on mental hygiene and delinquency, who already had some experience in fighting elections. His name was Salvador Allende. On one occasion he had to accompany Allende to a neighborhood in Old Havana to examine a group of subversives arrested during a raid. Fortunately, after having carried out the interview, they came to the conclusion that these people were not elements opposed to the regime. It was merely a case of "diverse psychopathological manifestations," so they referred them to the Mazorra psychiatric hospital, run by Major Ordaz.

Montesinos was one of the organizers of Fidel Castro's first official visit to Venezuela and the promoter of the ill-fated meeting between Castro and Betancourt.

On the way back from one of those trips, he was arrested by the government. In jail, he ran into an old acquaintance, Douglas Bravo, who invited him to escape to the mountains of Falcón to help boost the guerrilla movement. Montesinos, because of his nature, declined the invitation, but urged Bravo to fight:

"There's no other way," he encouraged him.

A few days later, Bravo broke out of jail.

Montesinos, for his part, knew that the guerrillas' days were numbered. The shots, if such things were needed, were no longer hitting their marks.

He then started his trip across the nations of the communist bloc: Russia, China, Poland, Czechoslovakia, Romania. In Moscow, he met Andrei Snezhnevsky and became fascinated by his reassessment of the concept of schizophrenia. He found a strategic depth in his widening of the criteria for identifying, and even predicting, underlying forms of schizophrenia.

With the agility of a Fouché, in the space of a year, Montesinos went from communist Russia to imperial England, from Muscovite conductivism to the clinical experimentalism of the Maudsley Hospital, where London University's Psychiatric Institute was then operating.

From the British capital he would make brief incursions into the Burden Neurological Institute in Bristol, where he was a disciple of the legendary doctor William Grey Walter, the author of one of the most important books ever written about the human brain, *The Living Brain*, which ended up playing an unexpected role in the story of the Beat generation.

In 1963 he switched his research center from London to Marseille, to train under the tutelage of Dr. Henri Gastaut, a man of great distinction in the field of electroencephalography. There he successfully presented essays that fed into what would later become the academic version of his book *Brain, Personality and Destiny*.

On weekends he would escape to Paris, where he wandered the bars and cafés in which the Venezuelan exiles, some of them political refugees, used to hang out.

By this time, like the Hydra, his legend was beginning to whip around in all directions. The eminence, the fake, the traitor, the ladies' man, the degenerate— these were some of the nicknames knotted together enigmatically within his short and graceless figure. The hunger for power and an unprecedented intellectual voracity had transformed his ugliness into a mystery in his favor.

The first weekend he went to Paris, no sooner had he gotten out of the taxi at Café Odeon, where Antón Parra was waiting for him, than he secured his first conquest. Antón was with a Venezuelan couple who didn't miss a single detail of his arrival. The man bore some resemblance to Jesus Christ, which women, because of some twisted redemption complex, were unable to resist. Long, straight, brown hair. Long mustache, white skin, and eyes clear as stained-glass windows. Montesinos would later learn that he was a painter, a genius, as all his acquaintances would call him.

Belén was also an artist, or at least that's how she introduced herself that day. She had jumped on him quite brazenly, sitting down right at his table. What impressed him the most wasn't the woman's passionate outburst, since he was already getting used to the magnetic effects of his personality, but the reaction of the painter, if the impassivity with which he let his partner go can be called a reaction at all. Edmond didn't know whether she was his partner, or what degree of commitment there was between them, but, at that moment at least, Belén was the woman who was accompanying Darío, the painter.

That evening, Belén took him to the small apartment Antón had near Boulevard du Montparnasse, on the Rue Daguerre.

That conquest was just a taste of things to come, of the discoveries the city would bring him on each visit. Whether the shape of a corner or of a beautiful woman, a book or some extraordinary piece of information, there wasn't a day in Paris that couldn't bring him a confirmation about Paris: that she, too, just like Caracas, was at his feet.

He would never forget the evenings he spent at France's Bibliothèque Nationale, where at last he was able to gain firsthand access to fundamental psychiatric texts. There he read *Traité médico-philosophique sur l'aliénation mentale ou la manie*, by Pinel. He learned from the original source what until then had been only a legend repeated by psychiatric manuals: about the moment when Pinel, at the Bicêtre Hospital, decides to release some angry madmen from their shackles, only to discover they were neither mad nor angry, on the contrary, they were civilized and grateful for that foundational gesture.*

He was also able to practice his French by reading classics such as Fodéré's *Traité du délire* or Esquirol's *Des maladies mentales, considérées sous les rapports médical, hygiénique et médico-légal.* However, nothing would fascinate him as much as the discovery of a disciple of Esquirol's called Étienne-Jean Georget.

Influenced by German phrenology, so in vogue in Paris at the beginning of the nineteenth century, Georget asserted that mental illnesses had physiological origins, which could be traced through deformities and lesions in the brain and nervous system. Montesinos was captivated by his treatise *De la folie.* Especially its last chapter, entitled "Recherches cadavériques," in which Georget gave an account of everything

---

* There's a fact Matías doesn't know. I tried to tell him about it one night, but he was too obfuscated by Anthony Hopkins to listen. The anecdote, never corroborated, is also mentioned by Alejandro Peralti in the article he wrote about Montesinos when Rosalinda Villegas's death came to light.

It happened during the Caracazo protests, on February 27, 1989. It took place in a ward for the homeless at El Nogal, a nursing facility, where Montesinos was then director. Apparently, on that day, amid the looting and riots that shocked the rest of the city, around twenty schizophrenic patients escaped. A division of the National Guard was waiting for them at the end of the same block and opened fire upon seeing them. Peralti says that the only attempt to investigate what happened was led by a psychologist whose surname was Torres and who worked at the clinic, and who wrote an article in which she stated that the National Guard had been stationed on that corner an hour before the patients escaped. Which was suspicious, since that area wasn't affected by the riots. She also stated that it was almost impossible that those patients could have planned an escape, let alone in those circumstances, given the seriousness of their condition. The hypothesis extracted from the report implied that *someone* had orchestrated the encounter between the National Guard and that group of lunatics. Someone inside the clinic had *set them free* for that purpose. The motive was money: the patients gunned down that day, whose bodies ended up in the mass grave of La Peste, were chronic schizophrenics who either were homeless or had been abandoned by their families some years earlier. The economic measures announced by Pérez's government included cuts in state funding for this institution.

he had learned thanks to the numerous autopsies and cerebral dissections he had performed on the corpses supplied to him by La Salpêtrière.*

Through Georget, Montesinos learned about the case of his most illustrious patient, Théodore Géricault, a pioneering painter of French Romanticism, of whom he had never heard.

First, he looked with scientific curiosity, somewhat detached, at the portraits of madness Géricault had painted for his psychiatrist. Then he obsessed over the history of the wreck of *La Méduse*, and the research Géricault had carried out to produce his most important work: *Le Radeau de la Méduse*. From then on, whenever he could, he would go to that same room in the Louvre and spend hours looking at the painting. He would scrutinize the skin of the dead and the desperate, all with the same deathly hue Géricault had captured on his brief visits to the morgue at the Beaujon Hospital.

While reading catalogs from that era and essays written in the decades following Géricault's death, Montesinos ran into a chilling anecdote about the artist's last days.

Beleaguered by various misfortunes (depression, suicide attempts, being sectioned due to persecutory delusions, bankruptcy, repeated riding accidents), Géricault underwent an operation for a tumor on his lower back. Before the procedure began, he asked not to be sedated: he wanted to examine, with the aid of a mirror, his own operation.

"It must have been extremely painful," said a friend who visited him the following day.

"Not very," replied Géricault. "During the butchery I was thinking about something else."

---

* If Matías had persisted with his novel, he could have capitalized on one aspect of this thing that so fascinated Montesinos: La Salpêtrière, the epicenter of proto-psychiatry, was a women's asylum.

"About what?"

"About my next painting. If I get through this, I will contribute a valuable image to Vesalius's studies. Except that mine would be unique, being the first time an anatomy study has been done with a model who is alive and is himself also the artist."

Géricault died soon after, at thirty-two. He never got to paint that picture.

Montesinos read the last few lines of that story with a racing heart and shaking hands. When he saw whom the anecdote was attributed to, who Géricault's friend was who'd visited him a day after the terrible operation, he felt the blood stop flowing, collecting in furious swirls all around his body. It was Alexandre Dumas.

That weekend he couldn't go back to Marseille. He spent two days in bed with fever, looked after by Antón and Belén at the apartment on Rue Daguerre. When he recovered, Montesinos listened, weakened, to Belén's recollection of his delirium during the illness.

"You told me to save myself."

"Save yourself?"

"Yes. You said: We'll eat you. We'll throw you into the sea."

"How mad. Sorry, baby."

"Don't worry. I know it was the fever talking. But I'm glad you're better. I was scared."

He understood it before he'd arrived back in Marseille. He had stored the disturbing piece of information in some corner of his mind. Among the 147 unfortunate people who boarded the raft, there was just one woman.

Our Edmond returned to Venezuela in 1965. The political wing of the PCV communists and MIR leftists had just signed a peace agreement with Leoni's government, while its radical arm had refused, leading the PCV to split. After that, the collapse of the guerrilla forces was only a matter of time.

For the next twenty years, Montesinos focused on his academic and medical career. He became a resident lecturer at the Central University of Venezuela, and consolidated the most popular psychiatric practice in the country. In the early eighties, he and a colleague founded El Nogal Clinic. By the end of the decade, when he had been a university chancellor and a presidential candidate, he returned to his origins and built the Institute of Neuroscience, which came to be the most important clinic in its field in Latin America.

This last fact was demonstrated by Montesinos himself in the update he presented every two years at Venezuela's National Psychiatric Congress. At the start of the new century, Montesinos was boasting of having cured more than two thousand cases of schizophrenia.

By then, many people knew who Dr. Montesinos really was, but no one would confront him. At most, some psychiatrists showed a little skepticism. The number of schizophrenia cases Montesinos claimed was unbelievable. Percentages like these had been seen only in communist Russia or Fidel Castro's Cuba. But to point to this would be an implied criticism of his method, a timid denunciation. The other big question had to do with the fact that every one of the patients diagnosed and cured by Dr. Montesinos were women.*

On this point, Montesinos would answer, smiling, that his whole life he'd always been surrounded by women.

---

* Peralti devotes a couple of pages to connecting Montesinos's experience in Moscow, under the tutelage of Andrei Snezhnevsky, with his indiscriminate diagnosis of schizophrenia cases. It's well known that Snezhnevsky's softer categories ("moderate schizophrenia," for example) were a tool of repression by the Russian state against Soviet dissidents. In Cuba, however, the hypothesis of a retroviral cause of the illness gained popularity.

Montesinos, according to Peralti's speculations, seemed to have developed an automated version of both perspectives. But what for? That's what the article fails to answer. In his analysis, Peralti omits a fundamental piece of the puzzle. He doesn't seem to spot the connection between two pieces of information that he himself is presenting: the schizophrenia cases presented by Dr. Montesinos and the over two thousand pictures of naked women, Rosalinda Villegas among them, found by the police at his apartment.

"Although the institute was conceived with the aim of attending to both male and female patients, the unanimous preference of women to be treated by me led me to make a decision not long ago: not to admit the few male patients who came to us, once the institute's natural predisposition had become apparent, so as to guarantee the safeguarding of my clientele."

With the exception of the odd troubled friend, Montesinos had only three male patients: Jaime Lusinchi, Rafael Caldera and the Comandante. And he could probably have had Carlos Andrés Pérez if it wasn't for the total and mutual enmity they developed after the 1987 presidential campaign.

More than simply a psychiatrist, Montesinos was fulfilling the courtly role of a personal adviser. He had access to the intimate worlds of those strongmen, he alleviated their feelings of remorse and helped them make decisions.

Work with the Comandante was harder, since at the point when he left the San Carlos barracks, he was almost illiterate. Before Caldera's pardon, and because being jailed forced him to, the Comandante had read a few books. He had read them as a mere distraction, not going beyond an interest in the story or the exoticism of some characters. Montesinos taught him to use books, and culture in general, as what they were: a trap to catch assholes.

Although the task was difficult, he was pleased with himself when he saw the first results at a meeting between the Comandante and some businessmen. He experienced a kind of fatherly feeling, this man who had never had children or wanted them.

In November 1998, when the Comandante won the elections, no one mentioned or recognized his imprint on the self-confident, magnetic ways of the new president. He didn't mind. From the shadows, he was happy to contemplate the turn things were taking, as if he were the invisible creator of a storm.

The Comandante let him choose any embassy or ministry he wanted. Montesinos rejected every offer. He was in his sixties, and he would never forget the words of Dr. Rojas Contreras: always listen to your body. And his body had always asked for the same things: recognition, power and women. Recognition and power, he understood this at last, were ways to get to women. Or the ways through which women would get to him. But after being with dozens, hundreds, thousands of women, attraction and resistance were a leftover rind of a fruit that was now broken and dry.

There was one occasion when the indifference won him over for longer than usual. He was terrified when he realized, by looking at his photos, that he had spent two months without tasting a woman. He was old. He thought about death more and more. Although he had always thought about it, although he had read and written many pages about it, it felt different this time around. Now he was getting closer to death with his body, he was looking into his own hollowness, searching for a reflection at the bottom of the well.

The idea of using the basement came to him one night after writing a poem.

When he had opened the institute many years earlier, he'd thought the basement could be used as a storeroom. He rejected the idea straight away after imagining the constant interruptions in his office from the cleaning staff. Then he toyed with the idea of building a reading room, with the whole of his library, like an air-raid shelter. He didn't do anything in the end, and the basement stood inert, without even a light, like a massive black box holding up the building.

The poem announced itself in the sadness that gripped him

that night, a silence that was unnamed, as if someone else's. His sessions had ended later than usual, and he remained behind, absentmindedly looking over the surface of his desk. He felt as though he had witnessed that scene before, either in a movie or in a dream. A man, who could have been himself or a general, leaned with arms spread over a big desk, staring at it intently. The desk was actually a map, and the man studied it as if wanting to determine the next move for his troops. When he touched the desk with one of his hands, the surface spun with the frenzy of an anthill and turned to sand.

Dr. Montesinos stood up and went down to the basement. He did so with such familiarity that he subsequently thought it odd, as it had been years since he had gone down there. The cleaning staff had been instructed to clean the doctor's office, the courtyard and the basement every weekend, but he had never made sure the order was carried out to the letter.

The door yielded easily. He gripped the handrail of the small staircase, walked down the first steps and closed the door behind him. He reached the bottom step and sat down. The cold ground contrasted with the warm, stale air in the room. Barely a thread of light was filtering under the door, bringing to that well the last twinkle of the desk lamp, which was still on. He remained there, in that night within the night, which was artificial but not impure, for a long while.

He returned to his office, picked up a prescription pad and wrote the lines of his only poem:

OPEN UP SOME CORPSES
Illness, autopsy in the night of the body
dissection on the living.
The corpse becomes the clearest moment
on the faces of truth.

Knowledge follows on where the larva was born.
And death is thus multiple and scattered over time:
it is not this absolute and privileged point,
from which time stops to turn on itself;
little by little, here or there, each of the knots comes here to break.
After death,
trivial and partial death will come too
to dislocate the isles of life that prevail.
The living night dissipates with the brightness of death.

The next morning, with the plans sketched out in his head, he instructed his assistant to start renovation works in the basement as soon as possible. That's how Dr. Montesinos built the Hall of Dreams.

The Hall of Dreams was made up of six doorless cubicles, each equipped with a bed and arranged in the shape of a semicircle. Just one lightbulb in the middle, spilling white light when the patients were still partially awake, and stroboscopic light when they were asleep.

As if intending to reset the history of psychiatry, Dr. Montesinos went back to practices such as hypnotism and sleep therapy. He would hypnotize them with his magnetic power, staring deeply into them and performing the arcane tricks of Franz Anton Mesmer.

The desk would shake with a tremor on its surface, the wood transforming into a map, then a square frame of sand, and the women would start to stumble as if drunk on a chalice of air. Between him and his assistant, they would carry the women from his consulting room to leave them on one of the couches.

Under the white light, the moonlight, the patients would see, or think they saw, Dr. Montesinos taking two little piles of sand from the pockets of his coat, the same sand the desk had turned into, and placing them onto their eyelids. They would feel a sudden heat and then watch (this was the evidence that it was all a nightmare, the effect of some drug, as what eyes could they be watching with?) as Dr. Montesinos would take out their eyes and place them on a tray. With the very same eyes they didn't have, they would see in horrifying detail the empty eye sockets, the stroboscopic light, the dance of the doctor, who had morphed into a Steppenwolf, his claws tearing their dresses apart, the way he pounced on them.

Some of the women, the strongest, wouldn't come back to the consulting room. Others, however, would start to have strange dreams in which Dr. Montesinos appeared, layered between light and darkness, which made them return.

To the latter, he would prescribe one further round of sleep therapy. They would have to open their eyes and accept the truth. They were crazy, and Dr. Montesinos was their salvation. The wolf must first devour them (that's how crazy women think, that's what they'd tell themselves) and then save them.

But that's part of another story, Matías Rye would say, and it will be morning soon.

28

The Monster

"What's your name?"

The woman writhed on her chair. In the light of the small lamp, the man looked more terrifying now than in the other light, that of his car, when he pulled over to the curb a few hours earlier.

"Don't hurt me anymore," she begged. "Please, señor—let me go."

The man slapped her so hard she fell to the floor, chair and all. The woman kicked around on the floor, like a cockroach, for several minutes. Seeing that she couldn't get up, the man grabbed the back of the chair and pulled it back up into place. He tightened the rope, stood in front of her and lit a cigarette. He took a drag and asked again:

"What's your name?"

"I've already told you. Susy."

"Susy's your whore name. What's your name?"

"Lila."

"Liar," said the man and he hit her, this time with his fist. The woman fell over again. The man crouched down and close to the floor he told her: "Your name is María. Got it? María."

His hand was dirty with snot and blood. He went to the bathroom to wash it and came back. He picked her up again with the chair.

"So, what's your name then?"

"María."

"Very good. María what?"

The woman began to cry silently.

"I don't know. You tell me."

"María Zaïde. What's your name?"

"María . . . Saí."

"Zaïde. There's a diaeresis on the *i*. And so you pronounce both the *a* and the *i*. You only need to stress the latter one."

"I don't remember how long he had me repeating that name. If it was just a few hours or the whole night."

"Did he ever tell you who he was?"

"No. And I couldn't ask, as that was the first thing he wanted me to learn: that I was María Zaïde. I repeated it so many times I even learned how to pronounce it."

"It sounds French."

"I don't know, doctor. I didn't want to find out afterward either."

"What are you?"

The man had thrown a bucket of water over her to wake her up. The apartment remained in darkness, with its single lamp on, but a few lines of light were filtering in through some badly covered crack.

Lila felt the moisture cleaning her face and, with disgust and determination, slurped up the traces of blood, snot and tears that had dried out while she was asleep.

"Water," she said.

"What? You are water? Is that what you're saying?"

The woman shook her head.

"I want water."

"You'll drink some water soon. First tell me what you are."

"What he did to me was horrible. But with the help of the surgeon and the other doctors, I'm doing better. What tortures me now is remembering those questions."

"That's the hardest part of the recovery, Lila. We can talk about that later. Now we ought to focus on what happened."

"A whore."

The man smiled.

"That's what you were. Not anymore. Now you're a survivor. But listen carefully. Not just any survivor. You are a survivor who won't survive in the end."

"Like a theater director. He was trying to get you into character, Lila."

"I'm a painter. All painters need models. That was no play. Are you familiar with the term *tête d'étude*, doctor?"

"I don't know. I've never been to the theater, doctor."

"There's nothing worthless about Lila's work. Even Delacroix himself posed during the first *tête d'étude* Géricault made for his masterpiece. Lila, in a sense, has done a service to the nation."

"The breaks were the worst. He would untie me, take me to bed and do all kinds of thing to me. That must have happened during the first month because then for a long time he didn't do anything to me. Well, any of that, if you know what I mean, doctor. But it was only because he was focused on his painting. I realize now that was when he started to give me salty water and less food. That's why I was dehydrated."

"Why would he add salt to the water?"

"I haven't added any salt, María. That's just what water tastes like in the open sea."

"He came up with this idea of saying that we were now on a raft, lost at sea. He gave me less and less food, but that way was better, doctor. So much salty water purged me. And you can imagine the state of the living room."

"Why to the nation? Do you consider yourself a sort of hero?"

"Let me do you a favor, doctor. I'm not a madman, I knew exactly what I was doing."

"And every time he hit me, he'd insist it was a sea surge."

"Do you still hope to escape, María?"

The woman started crying again, lowered her head and nodded a few times in silence.

"Very good. That hope is the Argus, which you're only going to see from a distance, as it's like I told you, you won't be saved."

"Are you going to kill me?"

"Why did you insist on calling her María Zaïde?"

"Not me. The fifteen survivors including Corréard and Savigny."

"From then on, he got madder and madder, doctor. On one of those days, he did that thing to my ear."

"Is it true what the papers say?"

"Yes, doctor. It was a bite."

"I told her it was a *tête d'étude*. Just a rehearsal for my real work. All the things in my apartment are just sketches."

"He tried to treat my wound himself. He also gave me a painkiller, because I couldn't bear it anymore. For a few nights, he even let me sleep in a bed and he was the one who'd come to calm me when the fever made me scream. For a moment I thought he was going to let me go, because I recovered. But as soon as I regained some strength, he tied me to the chair again and that was when he did that thing to my leg."

"Who asked you to sacrifice Lila? The voices? Was it them who asked you to save the fatherland?"

"I'm a painter, a very good painter, that's why the government asked me for the painting. But that's all I am. I'm not a hero."

"He dug a knife into my leg, but this time he didn't treat it afterward. He just went on repeating it'd all be over soon. You'd find it weird, doctor, but by that point, I'd stopped wondering why he was making me suffer like that. And, honestly, I don't know what's worse, thinking that these things just happen, or that they happen because they mean something to someone."

"Did the government ask you to torture Lila Hernández?"

"No. The government commissioned me to do a painting. Maybe the greatest, most important in our history. The thing with Lila was, how can I put it, something that got out of hand. Don't look at me like that, doctor. You must know that these things happen. Especially you."

"Every so often the pain would make me faint. On one of those occasions, when I came to again, I saw him painting. I understood all the hell I was going through was what he needed to paint on the wall. I fainted again. A searing pain in my leg, as if there was someone probing inside my wound, woke me up completely. And it was then I saw him, doctor, doing that wicked, disgusting thing, and I started screaming like crazy and he hit me and from that day on I don't remember anything else."

"What was the painting the government commissioned?"

"That's classified information."

"How do you think you're going to save the nation with a painting?"

"You're the only one here talking about saving the nation, doctor. No one can save this country. I only talked about doing a *service*."

"What service can your painting do?"

"In wartime, anything can help the cause."

"When I woke up he had cleaned everything. From my wound to the living room. He'd even washed and changed his shirt. He wanted to show me what he'd painted. But the house remained in darkness, and the light from the lamp was too dim. I told him so and he said I was right. He drew the curtains and opened the windows."

"Could you at least tell me the painting's motif, its title?"

"Classified."

"For the first few minutes I could barely keep my eyes open. Do the math, doctor. Four months without seeing daylight. When I stopped blinking, I could see the wall for a moment. Then he said that that was enough and he shut everything up again. He tightened the ropes, put a gag on me and went out to celebrate. That's what he said. He had finished his thing. That could only mean he was going to kill me on his return."

"As for this being classified information, you've told me a lot already. How well do you think the news that the Monster of Los Palos Grandes works for the government would go down? Do you think the government will be happy for me to include that in my report?"

"Until then he had always made sure I was unconscious before he went out. I spat out the gag, threw myself on the floor together with the chair and dragged myself toward the balcony. He'd seemed euphoric, I guess because of the wall. He had drawn the curtains, but hadn't shut the windows properly. That's when I started to scream."

"You're right, doctor. At the end of the day, this interview is a mere formality and your report won't matter much. Your own boss is more interested than anyone in ensuring nothing I've said today comes out."

"These months have been terrible, doctor. That man's been supported by the government and I don't know what to do. I won't rest until he gets put behind bars, and killed. You know, he's even gotten into my dreams, like Freddy Krueger. He comes into my dreams and I have terrible nightmares. The worst thing is I can't get the damned painting out of my head,

320 Rodrigo Blanco Calderón

the one that man did on the wall. Whenever I see myself in the mirror, I see that picture again. It's a picture that scares me, because, how can I put it, the picture is beautiful. How can I find beauty in that, doctor? Am I crazy? Say something, doctor, I'm sure you know about these things."

"Johnny Campos? What's this got to do with Dr. Campos?"

"That's classified, *doc.* But if you're still interested, I can tell you the title of the painting, because I like you. And mainly so you're prepared."

"Prepared for what?"

"*The Year of Mercy.*"

29

The Dreamachine

Before he left, Pedro Álamo had arranged for his landlords to give me the trunk containing his notebooks. Señor Armando and Señora Marta, an old couple, welcomed me warmly. They offered me coffee. Having made myself comfortable, I lost all hope. Those hosts in their kindness wanted the same thing I did: to know more about my *friend*.

"I can't really say he was my friend. You'll think it's crazy, but I don't really know why he entrusted me with his things," I said.

"Believe me, I understand. We never felt Señor Álamo was like a real tenant," said Señor Armando.

"Señor Álamo was always very polite, very serious and proper," said Señora Marta. "We have no complaints about his behavior. Never late with his rent. And yet he was so somber and solitary."

"We called him the Steppenwolf," said Señor Armando. "It was Marta who gave him that nickname, really."

The old couple laughed for a while.

"We hoped you'd know something about Señor Álamo. I'm telling you, all this time you were the first person to come visit. Apart from you and the girl who came on Friday night, no one ever came by to see him," said Señora Marta.

"Marta," Señor Armando reproached her.

"What girl?" I asked.

322 ❧ Rodrigo Blanco Calderón

"A beautiful girl, with big eyes. A bit young for him, I thought. In fact, that was the only time we might have had something to complain about. You can't imagine the racket those two made that night. But, I tell you, it reassured me. I was glad to know that the man had some blood in his veins. I always suspected Señor Álamo was, you know, *weird*."

"Marta," said Señor Armando again.

So Pedro Álamo and Margarita Lambert had spent a night together. They made love that Friday night. The tragedy happened on Saturday and by Monday morning Álamo had disappeared, leaving his landlords a brief thank-you note and his instructions about the trunk.

I finished my coffee, said thank you and got ready to leave. Señor Armando helped me carry the trunk to my car.

There are 117 black leather notebooks. Naïvely, Álamo had conceived his obsession as having the same dimensions as Saussure's. I've been going through them over the last few months, reading them, considering them. I'd grab one pile and spend the night digging into those fallen leaves or examining the succession of book spines like somebody watching an impending storm. Afterward, I'd pick them up and drop them back into the trunk, carelessly, as if they were pieces in a faulty Tetris game.

Over half the notebooks are blank. A considerable number of them (twenty-seven) are dedicated to the Monster: "Neercseht," the foundational text that was dictated to him in his youth and the interpretation of all its possible variants.

It was laborious and obsessive work, of no interest whatsoever to anyone but Álamo himself.

I feel as if I've been given the ashes of a stranger. There's no real affection tying me to those remains, but their condition as residues of life, that fine dust left behind by death, forces me to keep them, to return to them with respect.

An inexplicable attitude to be taking, since Álamo hasn't died.

There is another lot of notebooks (eleven in total) that narrate the life of Darío Lancini (or Mancini, according to the text). A fascinating story, albeit incomplete. And so it would remain, if it wasn't for that one time when, because of my insomnia, I stayed up all night watching TV.

There was a classic on, from the nineties, one I hadn't seen before: *The Usual Suspects*, with Kevin Spacey. Spacey's character is called Roger "Verbal" Kint and he's the sole survivor of a massacre on a ship. The plot depends on what Kint tells the police, and his story starts to point toward a mysterious man called Keyser Söze, who becomes the center of the investigation. Of course, it's all a sham on Kint's part, since Kint and Söze are the same person. Or not, maybe Kint never existed.

So the thing is, I watched the movie and decided to follow Kint's example. Make up a more or less credible excuse and start investigating. Hence the psychological autopsy and everything else I came up with.

I've saved the contents of these notebooks, which I have given the title *Dreams* following Álamo's guidelines, in a new folder, together with all the information I had collected in my *The Night* folder. Of course, I didn't tell Álamo about this last detail. I took out the footnotes that I'd written as I read and transcribed the material. I also deleted any trace of my conversations with Oswaldo Barreto. Then I ordered the different parts a bit and, I must confess, tried my hardest to give it some narrative cohesion, something the original texts didn't have and didn't want to have.

More interesting than those notebooks are the ones dedicated to building the Dreamachine. Apart from the notebooks, the trunk contained a stroboscopic lightbulb, a CD with setup drives and two electrodes connected to a USB cable. I didn't pay them much attention until I discovered that, mixed in among the blank notebooks, there were five notebooks full of notes, plans and drawings. That work represents the most lucid part of Pedro Álamo's delirium.

What Álamo calls the Dreamachine is the synthesis of two inventions by the "most brilliant, and least-known, poet of the Beat generation." One Brion Gysin (whose real name was Brian Gysin), believed to be the man who reinvented the cut-up technique, the well-known composition method used by the surrealists and which Gysin revamped with the emerging computing technology of the sixties. With the help of a brilliant, and somewhat tormented, computer engineer called Ian Sommerville—who would die in a car crash the very day he got his driver's license—Gysin developed a program that, based on a few keywords, would select these at random to create written and audible texts.

Gysin is also responsible, this time exclusively, for the creation of the Dreamachine. The device consists of an elongated white-light bulb, surrounded by a cylinder with holes that rotates at variable speed, making the light alternate with an effect very similar to a stroboscopic lamp. "The Dreamachine is the only invention created to be looked at with closed eyes," says Álamo in another note. The goal of the Dreamachine is to produce altered states of consciousness without drugs—that is, by stimulating brainwaves directly.

Gysin was inspired by William Grey Walter's *The Living Brain*, a classic of neurophysiology. It's a book I remember having studied. Especially after a psychiatry congress at which Dr. Montesinos, who had been a disciple of Grey Walter's in Bristol, had mentioned this study as the basis for applying electroconvulsive therapy to schizophrenic patients.

I found some scattered articles online dealing with the application of some of Grey Walter's discoveries in the field of robotics. During my research I spotted that the Spanish edition of *The Living Brain* is published by the Fondo de Cultura Económica. I found the only existing copy, from 1986, at the FCE's bookstore on Avenida Solano.

Reading that book was what made my insomnia less unbearable. The study of the brain, its electrical mechanism, its delta, theta, alpha and beta rhythms, and, especially, what Grey Walter calls *patterns* allowed me to see everything that has happened over the last year from a clinical perspective.

For a while, following what was written in Álamo's notebooks, I tried to experiment with the Dreamachine. I installed the software that was on the CD, set up the stroboscopic light, attached the electrodes to my head and connected the lead to the USB port. Then, after checking everything was in order, I closed my eyes and switched on the stroboscopic light.

Nothing happened.

I never discovered what the Dreamachine was about. When I wrote to Álamo, the only times he'd reply were when I wrote about the Dreamachine. Otherwise, he would just impose on me a silent reading of his emails and his adventures in India, where he had apparently ended up.

The human brain has, to use a Miltonian image, its own universal hiss. A background murmur that is the index of brain activity. That murmur is like an antenna searching for other murmurs, those of external reality. This murmur is so sensitive, so responsive to any stimuli, that often it cannot even be identified in any pure way. Only through brain mapping can a person really come to know their own rhythm. Darío and I, for instance, have the same rhythmic pattern. That's why, thanks to the Machine, I was able to sync myself with his life and dream about it.

My machine works through a feedback-led automated control system. It's not the light that set off the brain rhythms, it's these rhythms that trigger the lamp.

Translating that light, the result of electric impulses of the brain, into syllables and words, was Pedro Álamo's obsession: combining Gysin's Dreamachine and his word-mixing machine into a single invention.

After that one observation, Álamo fell back into the trance of recounting his progress in the study of Sanskrit, or the anecdotes he would pick up from the different communities he had been living with in the last few months, along with passages of the life of Ferdinand de Saussure he would insert as fragments of a hagiography of sorts, which he intended to justify his own steps.

In Maharashtra, for instance, there's quasi-Christian worship of Ferdinand de Saussure. On a cotton farm, inside a very poor little house, I found the portrait of a white man, presumably a European, on a sort of altar. When I asked Ricardo to inquire about it, he was told it was a scientist who had traveled all over the region many years ago. The people in the little house explained that man was a saint, as he had exorcized several men and women.

The portrait, as I was later able to verify, was of Ferdinand de Saussure. That episode must have happened around the year 1875 or 1876. About that time Saussure traveled through several territories in India to prepare his Mémoire sur le système primitif des voyelles dans les langues indo-européennes, *which he would present as his graduate dissertation. The story of the exorcisms must have been known in Saussure's circles, which is the only thing that might explain why Théodore Flournoy asked him for help all those years later.*

Flournoy was an almost unknown writer from the nineteenth century. He was working on a book called From India to the

Planet Mars *and was struggling to interpret the message that Hélène Smith, his medium, wanted to pass on to him. Smith used to incarnate Simandini, a young Indian woman, the wife of Sivrouka, prince of Chandragiri in the sixteenth century. According to Flournoy, Hélène would express herself in writing, through her spirit guide, Léopold, in Sanskrit. Flournoy asked Saussure to analyze the text.*

Saussure concluded it was a sort of poem based in Latin and with fragments in Sanskrit. Hélène Smith, to be clear, did not know these languages when she woke from her trance. The text appears in a biography of Flournoy written by Olivier Flournoy, his grandson. I have produced a humble translation of this—a curious period piece seemingly about Helen of Troy haggling over a pie. I hope you enjoy it as much as I did.

"'You beat a lamb, Da? Why?' said Eleni, 'oh, woe! Oh fie!' 'For a pie for thee, to be eaten at tea, Eleni. Oh, to eat a pie at tea—I envy you!' 'Why, and I envy you, *you square deity! To be a star, to aviate across a sea. . . .' To see a hearty pie for Eleni affects Zeus eventually, and he yields: 'Oh. Well . . . half a pie for a route to sea?' 'For double, you row Medea and me to Euboea too?' (Cutie Eleni won at pie!)"*

Weeks went by and I didn't hear from Álamo. But then I started to receive his emails again with some regularity. In these latest ones he talked more about the sociopolitical situation in India. He detested the "stupid Westerners" in search of their inner peace in those lands decimated by poverty. He dedicated many paragraphs to Ricardo and Raquel, the new friends he had made when he arrived in New Delhi.

He met Ricardo on the street. The man was sitting on the sidewalk, playing horrible Silvio Rodríguez covers that people seemed to like. He had graduated in economics from the Central University of Venezuela, with some research into the impact of economic changes in rural countries such as India. Specifically, in the case of the thousands of workers on cotton farms who would commit suicide each year as a consequence of debt, stress and the lack of competitiveness in the market.

Then, to earn a living, he had joined a big corporation. After a while he went to do a postgraduate degree in Barcelona, where he met Raquel, who was studying at the same university, specializing in human rights.

They fell in love and took advantage of the summer vacation to go traveling. While on a visit to the Greek islands, where they worked as cleaning staff in a hotel, they got married.

When they finished their master's degrees, they set off on a trip to Africa. First to Ghana, and from there they traveled to India. The woman who had been Ricardo's tutor, an expert on poverty, was also in those distant parts and invited them to work with her.

Here in Maharashtra, over five thousand farmers have killed themselves in the last four or five years. The annual average for the whole country is around seventeen thousand. Can you believe it? And that's what Ricardo and Raquel are looking into. Two detectives on the trail of seventeen thousand crimes, committed by the seventeen thousand victims, in one year alone. Or, if you want to put it this way, a single crime with seventeen thousand hypotheses. Do you know of any greater, or more real, enigma than this?

I thought that, deep down, he was referring to the night of July 3. I didn't dare ask anything. The first anniversary of Margarita's death was coming up, and I was sure that if Álamo had something to say, he would say it on his own terms.

Then, around that time, I ran into Matías Rye at the Fondo de Cultura Económica bookstore.

Matías had been avoiding me since that night, but this time I didn't let him go and forced him to tell me everything that had happened. He talked about Pedro Álamo too. I understood that Pedro Álamo was a fucking lunatic. The function of the lunatic is to obfuscate the sane. Lunatics are an excess upon the burden of meaning that the world can bear. They are big fruits that rot from within.

30

The Burning

On Saturday, July 3, Matías Rye had everything ready for Mark Sandman's Funeral. Or Sandmansnight, as he called it, which someday might—and why not—compete with Bloomsday.

In his backpack, he had everything he needed: iPod, speakers, cigarettes, matchbox, flashlight, incense, strap, alcohol and syringe.

Although the Creatures appeared one by one, they were all present by the agreed time. Matías made a small campfire with sticks he had found on his way over. He sprinkled the pile with a bit of kerosene and threw in a match. The hearth summoned them all together. Matías shared out the sticks of incense. When the air around had gotten thick, Matías began to tell Mark Sandman's story.

That evening was his consecration as a *confabulatore nocturni*. When he reached the part about the concert on the outskirts of Rome, on July 3, 1999, he made them feel the lightning bolt that split Sandman's chest in two, just when he was singing his second song, "Super Sex," whose first words, "taxi, taxi," fell upon him like a dagger.

The old couple cried for a while, motionless. Once the old man had recovered, he told the story of his only son, who had been murdered. Another man, who looked like a bank clerk, tried to tell his own story, but one of the girls, Olga, Antonio's girlfriend, stopped him.

"Let's listen to some music," she said.

They all agreed. Matías connected the iPod to the small speakers and made a playlist of all the Morphine albums in order. While *Good* played, and then *Yes*, the Creatures seemed to be scattering. They left the ocher enclosure of the campfire and were swallowed up by the darkness. Then they would come back, with glazed eyes and broad smiles.

Someone had opened a few bottles of wine and the liquid circulated in small plastic cups, which were discarded near the fire and looked like improbable snowflakes.

Matías looked at the sky without thinking about anything.

Suddenly he heard the chords of "Lilah" and reached for his backpack. He took out the syringe and the rest of the paraphernalia. He rolled up his sleeves, cleaned his forearm with alcohol and injected the needle. Before dissolving into the universe, he saw the Creatures around him, watching him. He didn't recognize a thing about them.

From then on, Matías's story becomes distorted. He still struggles to distinguish the truths that were revealed to him that night from what actually happened.

All he remembers is dancing for a long time by the fire with women who were cats or crows. He remembers that wings came out his head and he flew around the world. He remembers an empty box, floating in the middle of the sea, tormenting him.

At one point, he was struck down, and at another, Olga was shaking him by the shoulders.

"She was shouting at me to wake up, but she was doing it in a whisper," said Matías. "And I thought about a beehive and asked her not to sting me."

Someone had put out the fire and switched the music off.

"Be quiet," said Olga in the same tone. "We have to go."

"Where are the others? Where's my backpack?"

"I said be quiet. I've got it here."

"And your boyfriend?"

"Let's go."

"What's going on?" asked Matías, quietly this time.

"I don't know. There're some people around. I heard a woman scream."

"Where?"

"I don't know."

Matías looked up, held his breath and listened. He heard crickets, the rustle of vegetation, the distant roar of the highway. And between the lines of that intricate weave, there they were, still there, the two-string bass, the fading sax, the percussion like hurried footsteps on the street and the unmistakable voice of the man of sand.

"I'll be right back," said Matías.

"Where are you going?"

"I need to go."

"Up to you. I'm leaving."

"And she left," said Matías. "She took my backpack, and I did notice, but at the same time I felt obliged to go back."

He wandered around the hill carelessly, with no clear direction. He didn't know what time it was. It could have been two in the morning, it could have been nearly dawn, he really couldn't have said. But now that he thought about it, it must have been around three or four in the morning, or he wouldn't have seen the fire from so far away.

No sooner had he seen the bonfire than he knew it would be useless to resist. He was a moth and his fate was to embrace the fire. He would burn like a crazy lightbulb, like a butterfly worn out by the weight of its cardboard wings. He would blaze on that stage and on the very same date, the night he had set up and chosen as his ultimate night.

When he reached the last boundary on the hill, before entering the clearing, he stopped. The music had faded and all he could hear now were the crying and pleading of some women.

"I mean, the music had stopped in my head, and my head was telling me to wake up."

There were three men and two women. Of these men, there were two, very close to each other, who stood a step behind, watching what the third was doing. He was massive. Maybe the flames augmented his stature. He had a gun in his hand, and he was waving it like an angry orchestra conductor. He'd talk, point the gun at the head of one of the women, turn right around and keep on talking.

"Not even those who love the night could have loved a night like that," said Matías.

Then the guy with the gun started hitting one of the women. The other woman threw a kick, but the man controlled her as if she were just a little girl. He went back to the first woman, grabbed her by the hair, lifted her from the floor and, when her cries of pain had subsided, threw her into the fire.

"Mamá!" cried the other woman.

The man let her burn, watching her as she writhed, and only then did he fire three shots.

He took the other woman, the daughter, shot her three times in the head and threw her into the fire too.

The other two men, boys to judge by how small they looked, were now crouching, hugging each other, not looking up.

The man with the gun grabbed a barrel Matías hadn't seen and threw it into the bonfire. The flames leaped up so high that the boys bucked up and rolled across the ground, backing away. The man took them by the arms and helped them to stand up. Then they walked off toward the highway.

I was the one who told Matías that Margarita and her mother had been savagely murdered. By Sunday morning the news that the bodies of two women had been found was all over Parque Caiza. The gunshots they had received and the fact they had been burnt was the novelty that had all the neighbors rubbing at their arms and repeating over and over that the country was fucked.

On Monday, at the newsstand on the corner with Medicatura, I bought the paper. Halfway down the page in the crime section there was a beautiful picture of Margarita Lambert. Within twenty-four hours, the news story was already pointing to an ex-boyfriend as the main suspect.

The hypothesis made sense, but there was also that strange call from Pedro Álamo's landlord, telling me that his tenant had left and that there was also something he'd left for me in his annex.

As the week progressed, the investigation confirmed that Gonzalo had managed to leave the country, presumably for Colombia. Both the building's caretaker, who saw how he put the women in his car, and the two boys who were direct witnesses to what had happened, identified Gonzalo. The police believed the story that the Strinkis had also been kidnapped by Gonzalo so he could ask for a ransom. No one wanted to inquire as to why they hadn't met the same fate as Margarita and her mother, or why he had dealt with the women so brutally. Nor did they find out that the victim was depressive, with some psychotic traits, the patient of a psychiatrist who was friends with a minor writer who ran a creative-writing workshop, which was attended by a mysterious copywriter who apparently slept with the victim, who also attended the workshop, on the night before she died and who disappeared the day after, only to reappear a few months later, via email, in India.

"You mean at the India monument, the one here in El Paraíso?" asked Matías.

"No, man. India, as in India."

I ordered two beers. From Solano we'd come all the way to Chef Woo's in Los Palos Grandes.

I told him about the trunk, the emails I'd been receiving, the subtle instructions they contained, Álamo's stories about wandering around cotton farms in India, the new friends he had made, the high rate of suicides among the farming population, Ferdinand de Saussure's skills as an exorcist, the Dreamachine, the hypothesis that by changing one single letter of our Gospel, our whole destiny would be changed completely, and the true life of Darío Lancini.

I talked to Matías Rye about all this, with the detail and passion of a little boy, and he watched me, smiling apologetically.

"What?" I asked him.

"Don't get upset, but I think they're fucking with you."

"With me? Who?"

"Pedro Álamo is in Caracas. I saw him a couple of months ago."

"I don't believe you."

"I promise."

"He must have just come back. Maybe he's over here only for a short while."

"He's in Caracas, Miguel. He's been here all along. I've tracked him down. I can even tell you where he lives."

Matías had seen him under the Armed Forces bridge, checking out the book stalls.

"He's got a beard now and wears a *batola* robe. He hangs out with a woman with long gray hair. She looks like a vagrant, just like him."

I flushed with embarrassment and anger.

"I followed them that day. They live in a little tenement house, just at the bottom of Avenida Maripérez."

"Why were you avoiding me, Matías? For a while, I really thought you had something to do with Margarita's death. Or you'd turned into one of those Soldiers of Christ."

"Where have all those assholes sprung from?"

"I don't know, but it's been more than thirty cases this year. It only takes one lunatic to do a copycat and then you've got all the lunatics doing the same."

"I think we all had something to do with it."

We paid the check and went out onto the street.

"Don't be a stranger," I said.

"You either," he replied.

I knew we wouldn't see each other again. Deep down, we were saying it to ourselves.

Outside, the street was still dark. Like a tunnel, a cave and a labyrinth.

~~~~~~~~~

IV. Tetris

When you play Tetris you have the.
impression that you are building something [. . .]
You have the chaos coming as random pieces, and
your job is to put them in order

—ALEXEY PAJITNOV

31

Epilogue

One afternoon in the early eighties, on an inevitably freezing day, Alexey Pajitnov, a scientist at the Moscow Computing Center, took a break from work and started playing a game of pentominoes.

When he finished his puzzle, in order to extend his procrastination as long as possible, he translated the wooden pieces into a programing language. Some intuition, or perhaps laziness, made him transform the game into a tetromino, a geometric shape composed of four squares, connected at a right angle. Pajitnov called this game Tetris, from the Greek prefix meaning "four."

The BBC documentary ended at two in the morning. I went straight to the computer, signed up to a website and started playing. That's how it began. I played until dawn. Then I showered, had breakfast and went to work like a zombie. I spent the rest of the day fitting pieces in the air, trying, perhaps, to avoid thinking about Matías's last comment:

Did we have something to do with Margarita Lambert's death?

On June 17, 2011, I received an email from Pedro Álamo. It was an electronic invitation to an event at the Chacao Cultural Center, the following evening at seven. It was an event to mark the first anniversary of Darío Lancini's death. Álamo just wrote one line to remind me that Antonieta Madrid would be there.

I didn't reply to the email, nor did I miss the event. It was a lovely evening, but I couldn't help feeling some unease at recognizing, in the various pieces of testimony shared by Lancini's friends and readers, the passages of a life that was now pulsating on the sheets of paper I had in my hands.

That night I received another email from Álamo, asking how it had gone. This time I replied saying I'd seen the invitation too late and hadn't made it to the memorial.

Don't lie. I know you went, and I know that you handed over the manuscript.

At first I was scared. I imagined Pedro Álamo, with his prophet's beard and robe, in the deserted galleries of the cultural center, together with Sara Calcaño, watching from behind the scenes.

Then, when I had thought things through, I got angry. Álamo would toss the pieces out from the darkness, but I was the one who had to carry their load and position them in their place. I didn't write to him again, not even after my encounter with Antonieta Madrid, when I had already gotten rid of everything.

I used the same story with Antonieta Madrid that I'd made up when I saw Oswaldo Barreto. Forensic psychiatrist. Psychological autopsy. Pedro Álamo, a suicide in India. The fictional biography found among his papers.

Antonieta set our date for six thirty the following evening, at the Arábiga café. She gave me precise instructions to go to the tables at the end of the corridor, where it is less busy.

I had spent a lot of that day researching her online. She has her own website, with fragments of her work, interviews and a well-stocked image gallery. I was surprised at how beautiful she had been at various stages of her life, but nothing prepared me for seeing her up close, at leisure. The night at the cultural center I had only had time hurriedly to hand her the manuscript and my card.

She was an incredibly beautiful woman. One of those beauties that hurt you like a dagger to the chest.

We had barely said hello when another woman, identical to Antonieta, but much, much younger came by. And yes, she was even prettier.

"This is my granddaughter," said Antonieta.

"Pleased to meet you," I said.

The girl, being under twenty-five, barely responded.

"Shall I come fetch you in half an hour?"

"Yes. Half an hour's good."

It was clear she would be watching us, and that I had to be quick. I composed myself, adopted my Roger Kint role and told her the story.

"I'm stunned" was the first thing she said.

"I can imagine. Do you know if Darío Lancini ever met Pedro Álamo?"

"I'm almost certain he didn't. There is a mention in there of an encounter at El Buscón some years ago, but I don't remember it."

"Does Álamo's name ring a bell?"

"Of course. He's the guy who won the *El Nacional* competition in '82. I remember it well because it was the year Darío and I came back from Athens. A very strange short story. I never met him. He was never heard of again. I didn't know he'd kept writing."

"And what do you have to say about the manuscript?"

"I'm the one who wants to ask that question. That manuscript, as you call it, is part of my life and Darío's."

"So is it all true?"

"Of course not. A lot of things are made up. Though there

are others I've no clue how that man could have known. Even when he's wrong, he's wrong so precisely that it scares me a bit."

"I understand, but you needn't worry. Like I said, Pedro Álamo killed himself."

"How terrible."

"I know. Do forgive me for having bothered you about such nonsense, but I thought you ought to have the manuscript."

"Thank you."

Antonieta kept leafing through the pages, as if by touching them, some secret and porous writing would blossom.

"It's funny," she said all of a sudden. "The night before Darío died, he had a nightmare. He dreamed about a black box out of which all the words were escaping. He tried keeping them in but couldn't do it. And now you come and return *this* to me."

I said goodbye.

When I got home, I got rid of the trunk and all its contents. I never replied to another one of Pedro Álamo's emails. His latest thing is tracking me down on online game platforms, *El Gaucho Rubio vs. Darío Mancini*, just to remind me that when it comes to Tetris he's still the best.

My revenge has been to recover my sleep and play less. Although I do sometimes wake up in the middle of the night and see the pieces of our recent lives dropping from the ceiling of my room.

Could I have done anything for Margarita?

Can any of us do anything for ourselves?

The Year of Mercy is approaching, according to the graffiti that has sprung up around the city. The link between the graffiti and the charred bodies is clear. The Dream Thieves, the Soldiers of Christ, so proclaim their flyers, are now legion. But for now I haven't yet found the piece that relates to that part of the story.

In my head, I press the shift key and put the images in order, using them—using us—to construct perfect lines that will disappear, like the disappearing bodies that are beloved and destroyed by the night.

June 20, 2010–March 30, 2013

Acknowledgments

This book owes something (a conversation, a timely email, a contact, a valuable piece of information, a correction) to each of the following people: Diego Arroyo, Jacobo Borges, Rafael Cadenas, Minerva Calderón, Simón Alberto Consalvi, Catalina Labarca and Paulina Rematales (in Chile), Ricardo Isea, Matilde Lancini, Abilio Padrón, Teodoro Petkoff, Florencio Quintero, Milagros Socorro, Vasco Szinetar, Alberto Valero, Carlos Wynter Melo and Mario García (in Panama), and Luis Yslas.

To this list, I must add two names that are intimately linked to the writing of this novel. The first is Oswaldo Barreto, with whom I had an initial encounter that lasted over five hours. Only after that conversation did I realize the implications of writing about Darío Lancini, and it was then that I *saw* the novel.

The other name is, of course, Antonieta Madrid. Antonieta was the main source of anecdotes, dates, texts, photos and memories about Darío Lancini, with whom she shared thirty-six years of loving, traveling and writing. I am so very grateful to her, for her support and for permitting me to reimagine, with the freedom that fiction allows, some important passages of her life. This story is also hers.

This novel borrows fragments of works and texts belonging to other authors.

In chapter five, I used several fragments from Roxana Vargas's diary. In mid-2010, when I started writing this novel, her personal blog, where she narrated her hell from beginning to end, was still available online. At the time of writing these words, the blog has been shut down. All that remain are its address (princesasanas.blogspot.com), its title ("Ana and Mia my Queens and Us their Princesses") and one sentence by Roxana as an epitaph ("Everything that feeds me, destroys me").

For the creation of Dr. Montesinos's character, I was greatly helped by the suggestive, dark, disturbing autobiography of Edmundo Chirinos, which can also be found on the personal site of Venezuela's most famous psychiatrist.

In chapter thirteen, the line I attribute to Arnaldo Acosta Bello actually belongs to Rafael Cadenas: "A sleepless landscape that talks to him," from the poem "Henchman."

The anagrams "*Théodore Géricault: l'orage déchire tout*" and "*Le Radeau de la Méduse: au-delà de la démesure*" belong to the beautiful book *Anagrammes renversantes: ou Le sens caché du monde*, by Étienne Klein and Jacques Perry-Salkow.

The explication of anagram theory was taken from the book *Semiótica del anagrama: La hipótesis anagramática de Ferdinand de Saussure*, by Raúl Rodríguez Ferrándiz.

There are more appropriations and intertextual games throughout the novel. The keys to finding their sources are there too. Explaining these things is as funny as explaining a joke, but the current age's blind faith in "originality," in a sense more Kodamic than Borgesian, compels me to make these clarifications, and one more:

Although inspired by painful events that have occurred in Venezuela in recent years, this is a work of fiction.

R. B. C.

Translators' Note

Rodrigo Blanco Calderón's *The Night* contains a lot of intricate wordplay that can't be directly "translated" as such. Most of this wordplay has been newly created in English to suit specific character names and particular situations—with only a few exceptions. We have kept the title of Darío Lancini's book, *Oír a Darío*, in its original Spanish; and two French anagrams (*l'orage déchire tout,* and *au-delà de la démesure*) have been retained in French, just as they appear in the original novel, on pages 181 and 205. For those palindromes attributed to Lancini that appear on pages 37, 58-63 and 196, we have selected pre-existing English palindromes to take their place. (Some of our selections are better known than others. A few favorites were found in Jon Agee's delightful collections of illustrated palindromes—highly recommended if you don't know them already.) Everything else—anagrams, gramograms, palindromes, and acrostics—is new for this translation. However, for any readers with some knowledge of Spanish who might enjoy seeing the ingenuity of Lancini's original palindromes, these are the examples of his work that appear in the equivalent places in Rodrigo's original novel:

Yo hago yoga hoy

Yo sonoro no soy.
Yo corro, morrocoy.
Leí, puta, tu piel.

¿Son ruidos acaso diurnos?
Son robos, no solo son sobornos.
No te comas la salsa, mocetón.

Ácida saeta. Al abad anonadaba la atea sádica.

Luz azul
Ojo rojo
Negra margen
La ruta natural
Solapa a palos
La farra garrafal
Asó al rey ayer la osa

N. H. G. and D. H.